STAR TREK
BOLDLY GO

written by
Mike Johnson

issue #18 written with
Ryan Parrott

issues #13 & 18 art by
Josh Hood

issue #14 art by
Megan Levens

issue #15 art by
Tana Ford

issue #16 art by
Angel Hernandez

issue #17 art by
Marcus To

Special thanks to Risa Kessler and John Van Citters of CBS Consumer Products for their invaluable assistance.

For international rights, contact licensing@idwpublishing.com

ISBN: 978-1-68405-248-6

21 20 19 18   1 2 3 4

Greg Goldstein, President & Publisher • **Robbie Robbins**, EVP & Sr. Art Director • **Matthew Ruzicka**, CPA, Chief Financial Officer • **David Hedgecock**, Associate Publisher • **Laurie Windrow**, Sr. VP of Sales & Marketing • **Lorelei Bunjes**, VP of Digital Services • **Jerry Bennington**, VP of New Product Development • **Eric Moss**, Sr. Director, Licensing & Business Development
Ted Adams, Founder & CEO of IDW Media Holdings

IDW
www.IDWPUBLISHING.com

Facebook: facebook.com/idwpublishing • Twitter: @idwpublishing • YouTube: youtube.com/idwpublishing
Tumblr: tumblr.idwpublishing.com • Instagram: instagram.com/idwpublishing

issues #13 & 18 colors by
Jason Lewis

issues #14 & 17 colors by
Marissa Louise

issue #14 colors by
Triona Farrell

issues #15 & 16 colors by
Mark Roberts

letters by
AndWorld Design

series edits by
Sarah Gaydos

series assistant edits by
Chase Marotz

collection edits by
**Justin Eisinger
& Alonzo Simon**

collection design by
Shawn Lee

cover by
Tony Shasteen

publisher
Greg Goldstein

star trek created by
Gene Roddenberry

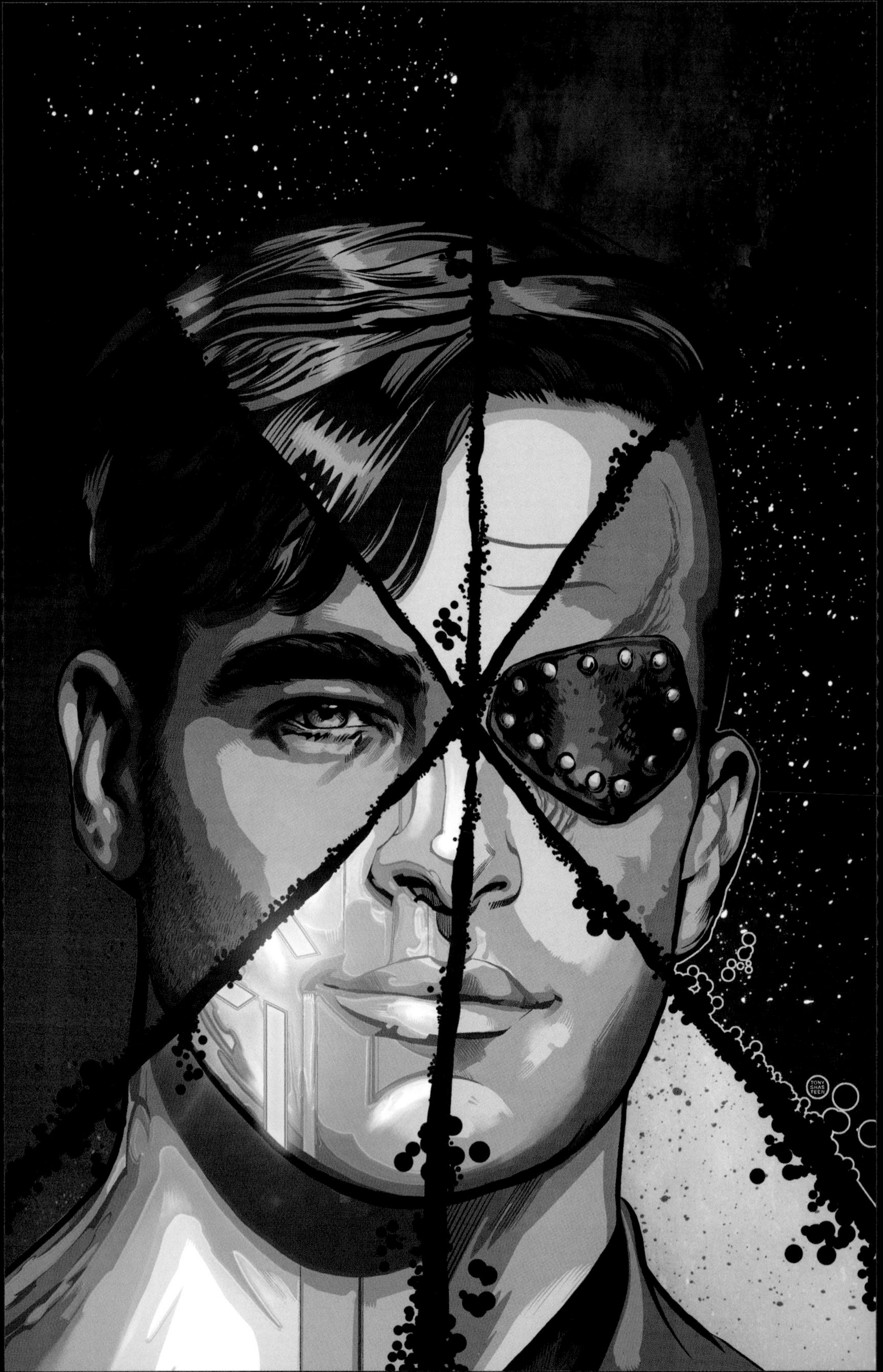
TONY SHAS TEEN

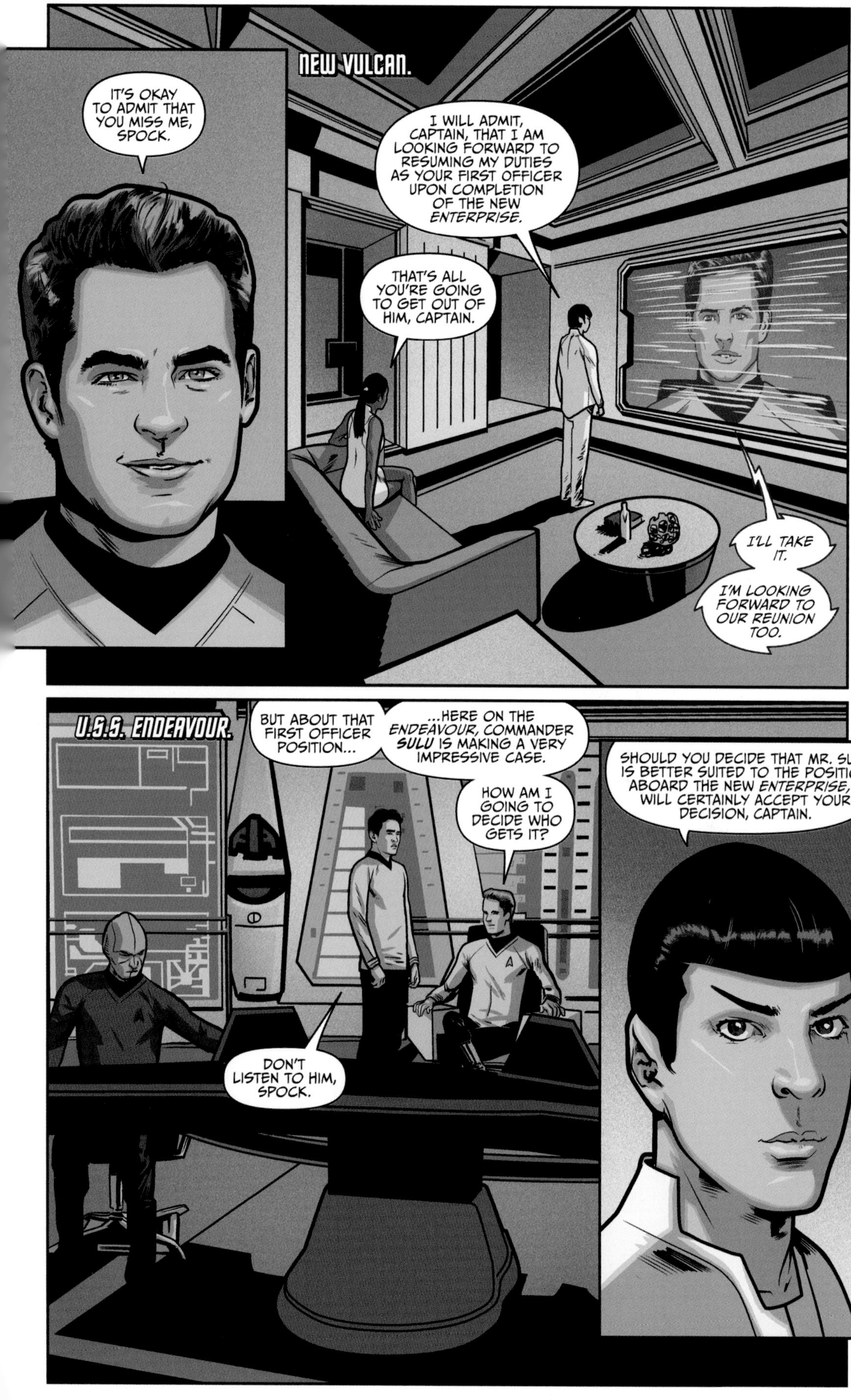
NEW VULCAN.
IT'S OKAY TO ADMIT THAT YOU MISS ME, SPOCK.
I WILL ADMIT, CAPTAIN, THAT I AM LOOKING FORWARD TO RESUMING MY DUTIES AS YOUR FIRST OFFICER UPON COMPLETION OF THE NEW *ENTERPRISE.*
THAT'S ALL YOU'RE GOING TO GET OUT OF HIM, CAPTAIN.
I'LL TAKE IT.
I'M LOOKING FORWARD TO OUR REUNION TOO.
U.S.S. ENDEAVOUR.
BUT ABOUT THAT FIRST OFFICER POSITION...
...HERE ON THE *ENDEAVOUR*, COMMANDER **SULU** IS MAKING A VERY IMPRESSIVE CASE.
HOW AM I GOING TO DECIDE WHO GETS IT?
SHOULD YOU DECIDE THAT MR. SULU IS BETTER SUITED TO THE POSITION ABOARD THE NEW *ENTERPRISE*, I WILL CERTAINLY ACCEPT YOUR DECISION, CAPTAIN.
DON'T LISTEN TO HIM, SPOCK.

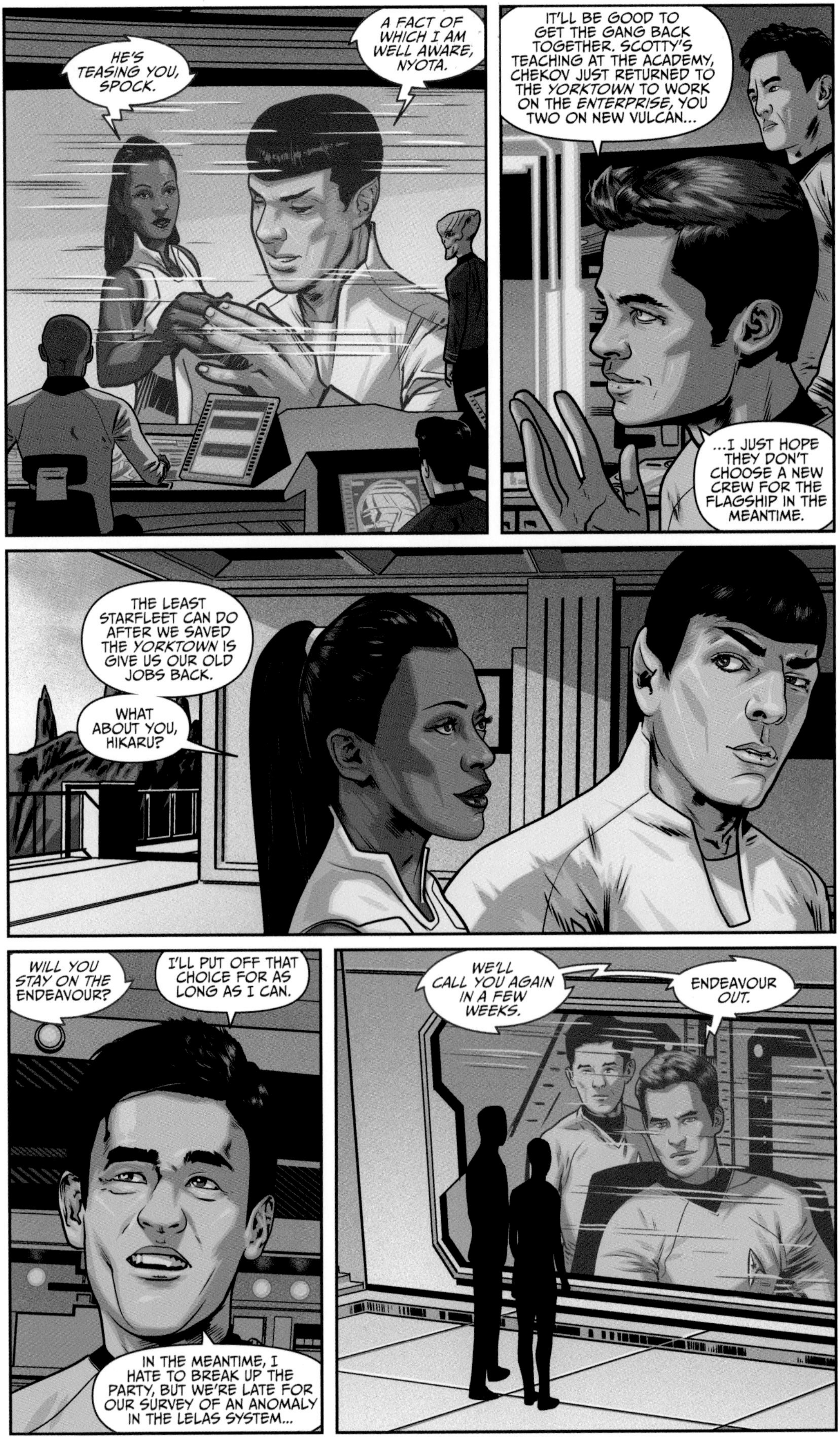
HE'S TEASING YOU, SPOCK.
A FACT OF WHICH I AM WELL AWARE, NYOTA.
IT'LL BE GOOD TO GET THE GANG BACK TOGETHER. SCOTTY'S TEACHING AT THE ACADEMY, CHEKOV JUST RETURNED TO THE *YORKTOWN* TO WORK ON THE *ENTERPRISE*, YOU TWO ON NEW VULCAN...
...I JUST HOPE THEY DON'T CHOOSE A NEW CREW FOR THE FLAGSHIP IN THE MEANTIME.
THE LEAST STARFLEET CAN DO AFTER WE SAVED THE *YORKTOWN* IS GIVE US OUR OLD JOBS BACK.
WHAT ABOUT YOU, HIKARU?
WILL YOU STAY ON THE ENDEAVOUR?
I'LL PUT OFF THAT CHOICE FOR AS LONG AS I CAN.
IN THE MEANTIME, I HATE TO BREAK UP THE PARTY, BUT WE'RE LATE FOR OUR SURVEY OF AN ANOMALY IN THE LELAS SYSTEM...
WE'LL CALL YOU AGAIN IN A FEW WEEKS.
ENDEAVOUR OUT.

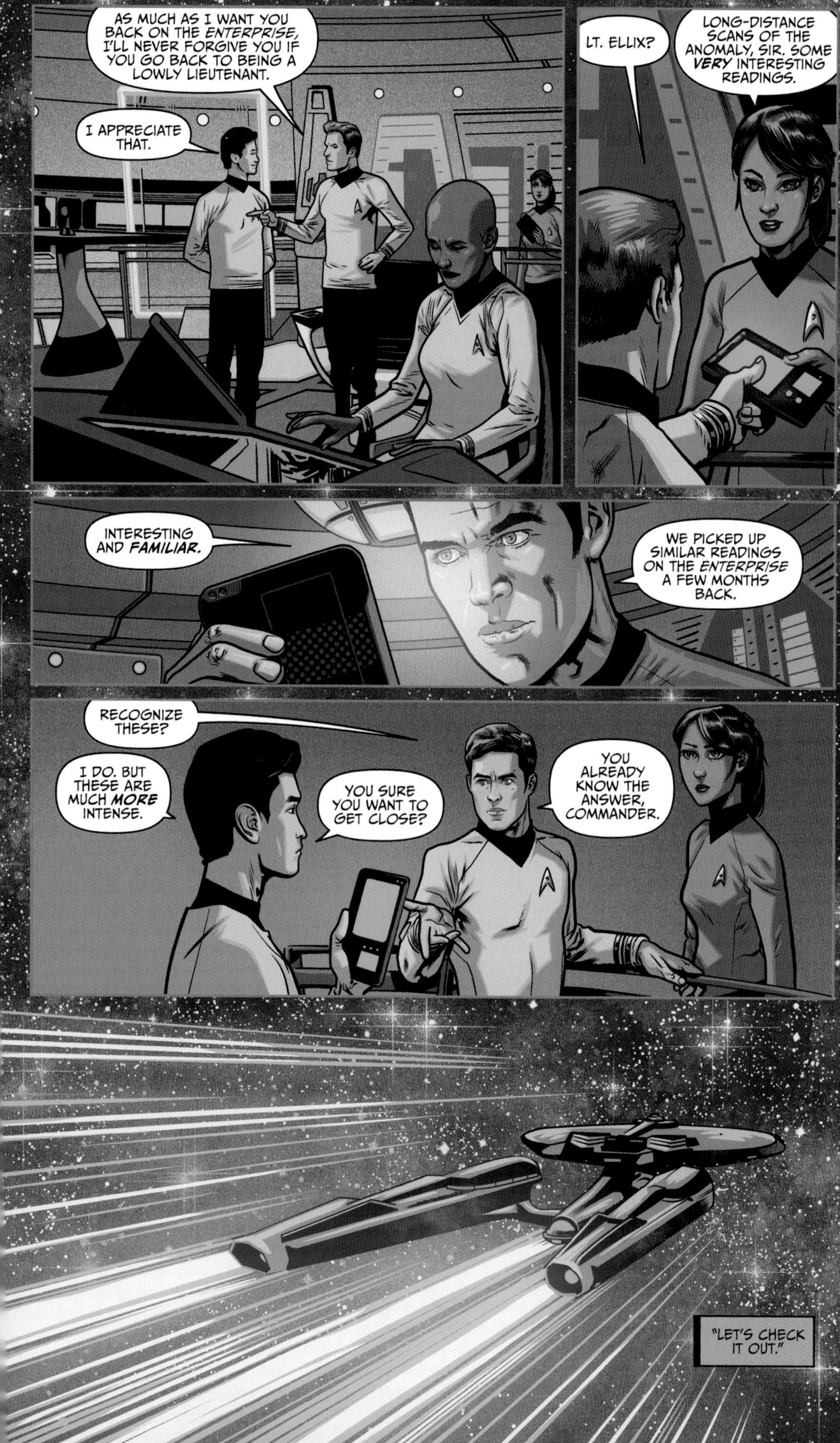
AS MUCH AS I WANT YOU BACK ON THE *ENTERPRISE*, I'LL NEVER FORGIVE YOU IF YOU GO BACK TO BEING A LOWLY LIEUTENANT.
I APPRECIATE THAT.
LT. ELLIX?
LONG-DISTANCE SCANS OF THE ANOMALY, SIR. SOME **VERY** INTERESTING READINGS.
INTERESTING AND **FAMILIAR.**
WE PICKED UP SIMILAR READINGS ON THE *ENTERPRISE* A FEW MONTHS BACK.
RECOGNIZE THESE?
I DO. BUT THESE ARE MUCH **MORE** INTENSE.
YOU SURE YOU WANT TO GET CLOSE?
YOU ALREADY KNOW THE ANSWER, COMMANDER.
"LET'S CHECK IT OUT."

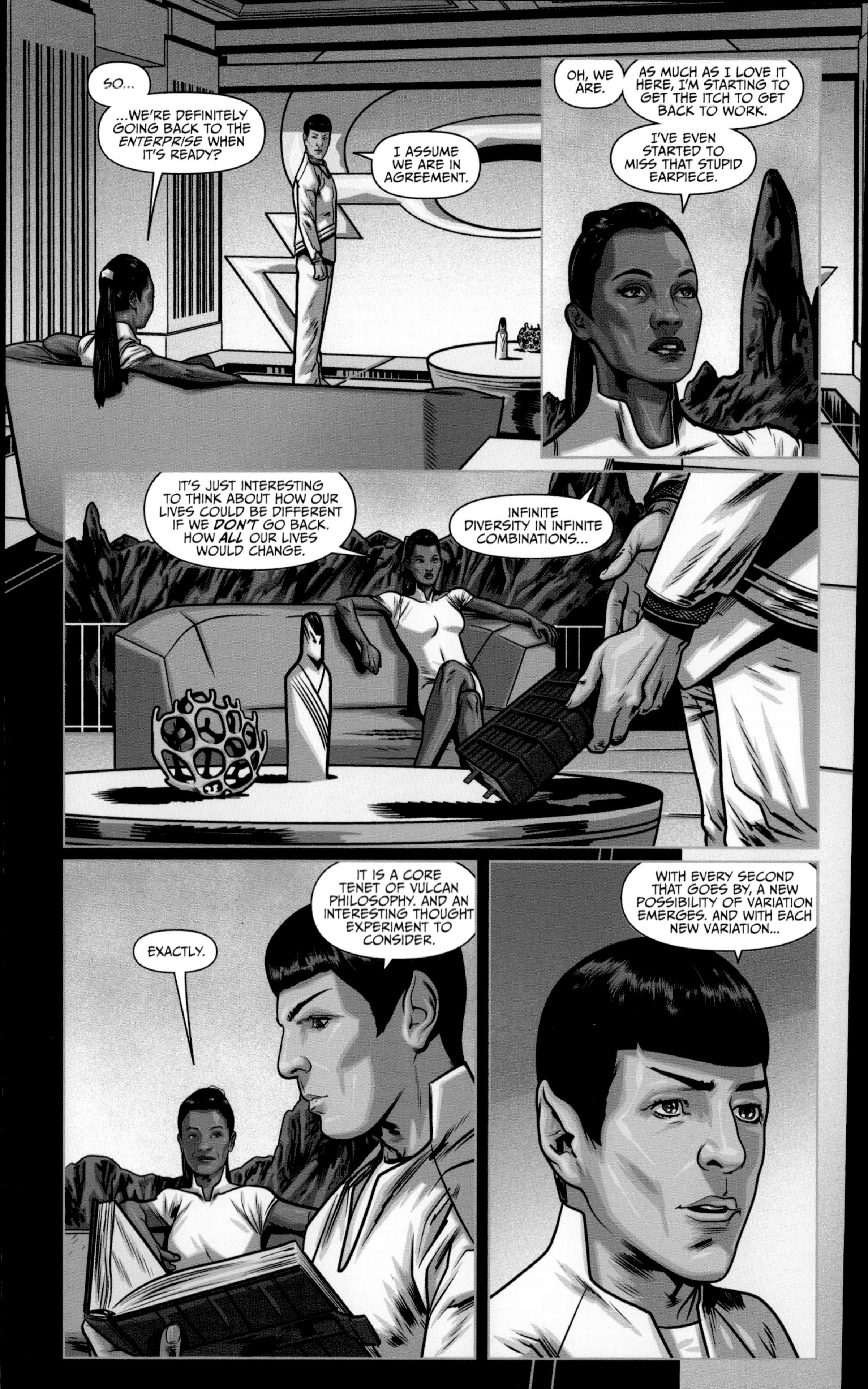

SO...
...WE'RE DEFINITELY GOING BACK TO THE *ENTERPRISE* WHEN IT'S READY?
I ASSUME WE ARE IN AGREEMENT.
OH, WE ARE.
AS MUCH AS I LOVE IT HERE, I'M STARTING TO GET THE ITCH TO GET BACK TO WORK.
I'VE EVEN STARTED TO MISS THAT STUPID EARPIECE.
IT'S JUST INTERESTING TO THINK ABOUT HOW OUR LIVES COULD BE DIFFERENT IF WE ***DON'T*** GO BACK. HOW ***ALL*** OUR LIVES WOULD CHANGE.
INFINITE DIVERSITY IN INFINITE COMBINATIONS...
EXACTLY.
IT IS A CORE TENET OF VULCAN PHILOSOPHY. AND AN INTERESTING THOUGHT EXPERIMENT TO CONSIDER.
WITH EVERY SECOND THAT GOES BY, A NEW POSSIBILITY OF VARIATION EMERGES. AND WITH EACH NEW VARIATION...

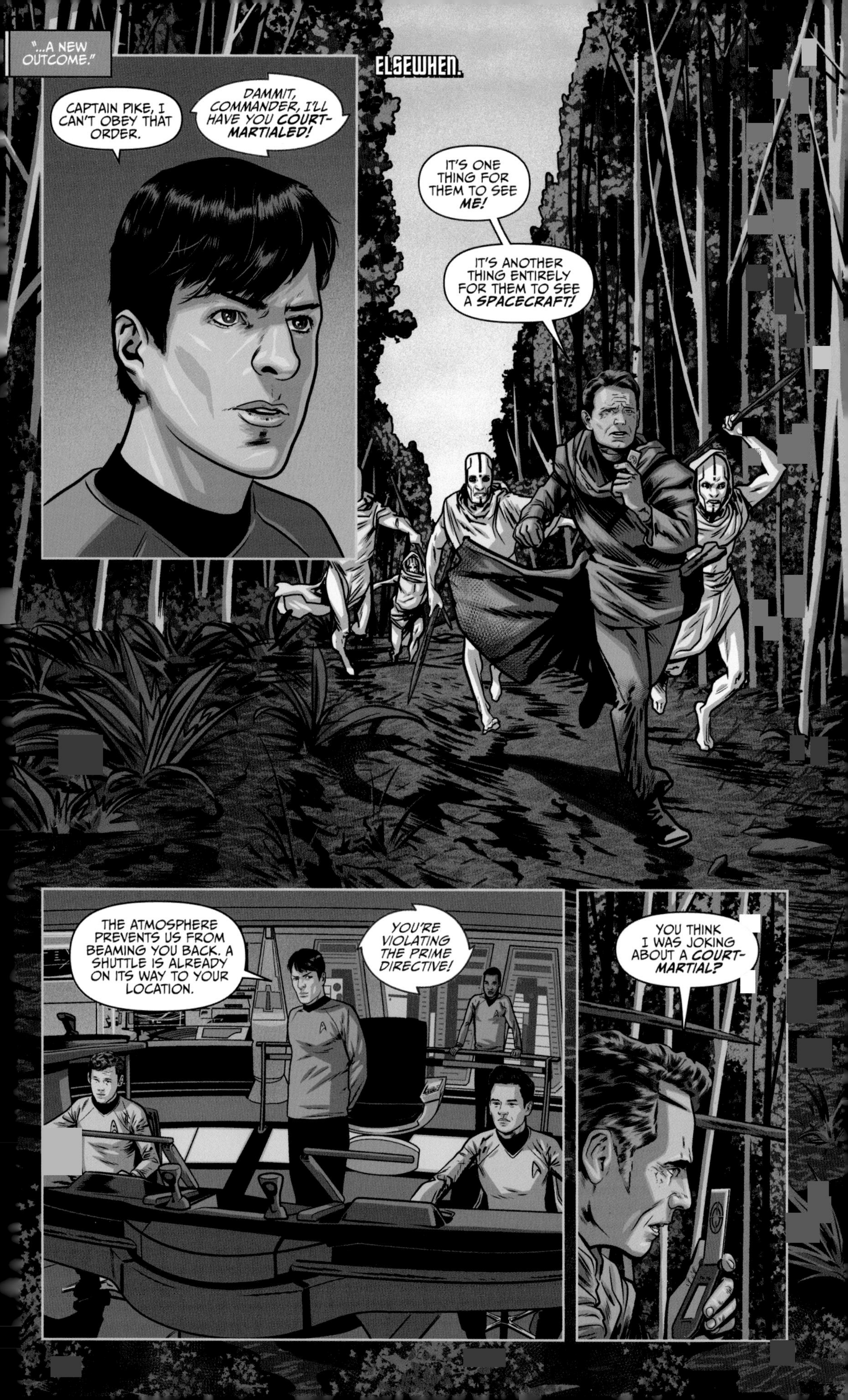
"...A NEW OUTCOME."
ELSEWHEN.
CAPTAIN PIKE, I CAN'T OBEY THAT ORDER.
DAMMIT, COMMANDER, I'LL HAVE YOU COURT-MARTIALED!
IT'S ONE THING FOR THEM TO SEE ME!
IT'S ANOTHER THING ENTIRELY FOR THEM TO SEE A SPACECRAFT!
THE ATMOSPHERE PREVENTS US FROM BEAMING YOU BACK. A SHUTTLE IS ALREADY ON ITS WAY TO YOUR LOCATION.
YOU'RE VIOLATING THE PRIME DIRECTIVE!
YOU THINK I WAS JOKING ABOUT A COURT-MARTIAL?

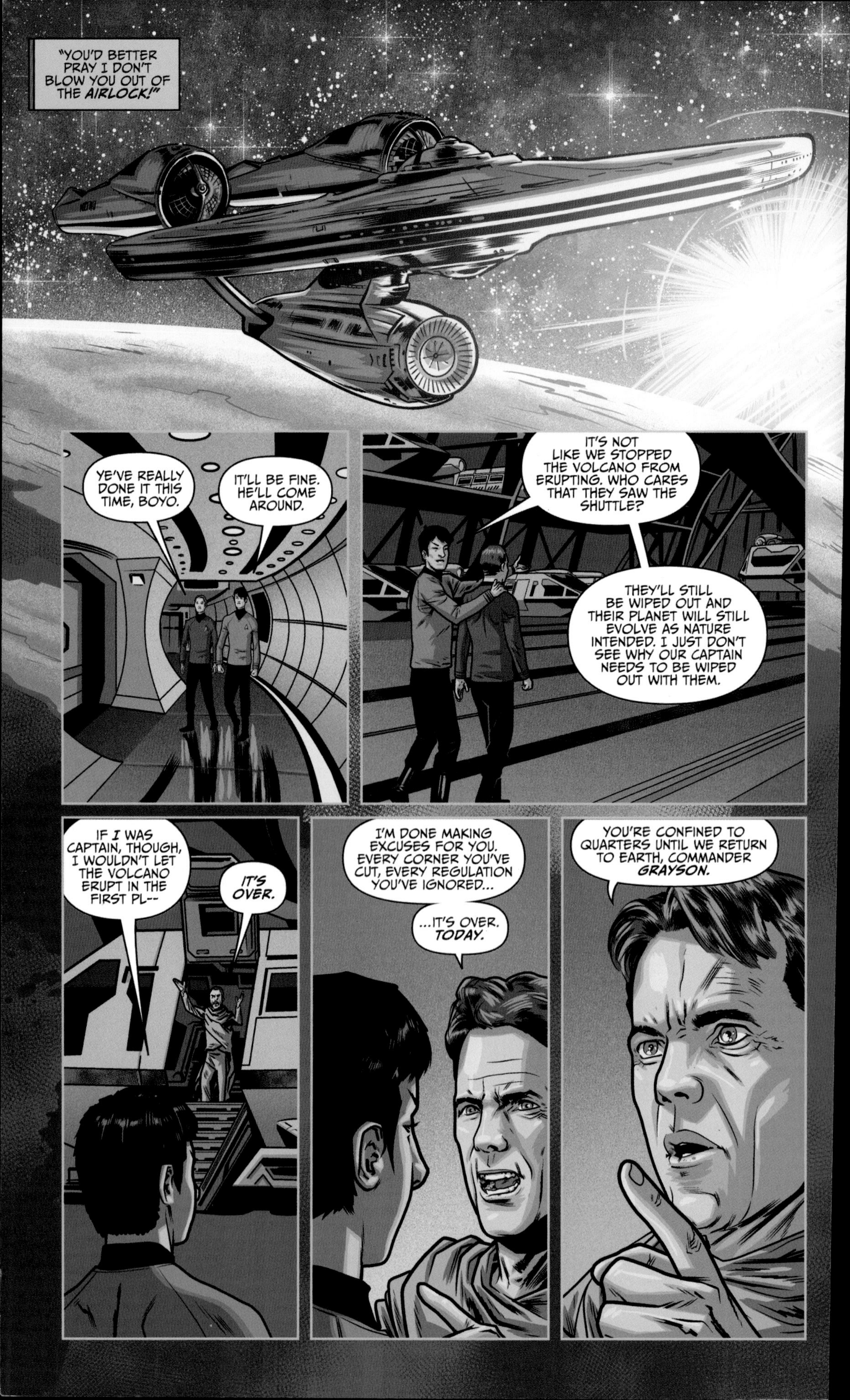
"YOU'D BETTER PRAY I DON'T BLOW YOU OUT OF THE *AIRLOCK!*"
YE'VE REALLY DONE IT THIS TIME, BOYO.
IT'LL BE FINE. HE'LL COME AROUND.
IT'S NOT LIKE WE STOPPED THE VOLCANO FROM ERUPTING. WHO CARES THAT THEY SAW THE SHUTTLE?
THEY'LL STILL BE WIPED OUT AND THEIR PLANET WILL STILL EVOLVE AS NATURE INTENDED. I JUST DON'T SEE WHY OUR CAPTAIN NEEDS TO BE WIPED OUT WITH THEM.
IF *I* WAS CAPTAIN, THOUGH, I WOULDN'T LET THE VOLCANO ERUPT IN THE FIRST PL--
IT'S OVER.
I'M DONE MAKING EXCUSES FOR YOU. EVERY CORNER YOU'VE CUT, EVERY REGULATION YOU'VE IGNORED...
...IT'S OVER. *TODAY.*
YOU'RE CONFINED TO QUARTERS UNTIL WE RETURN TO EARTH, COMMANDER *GRAYSON.*

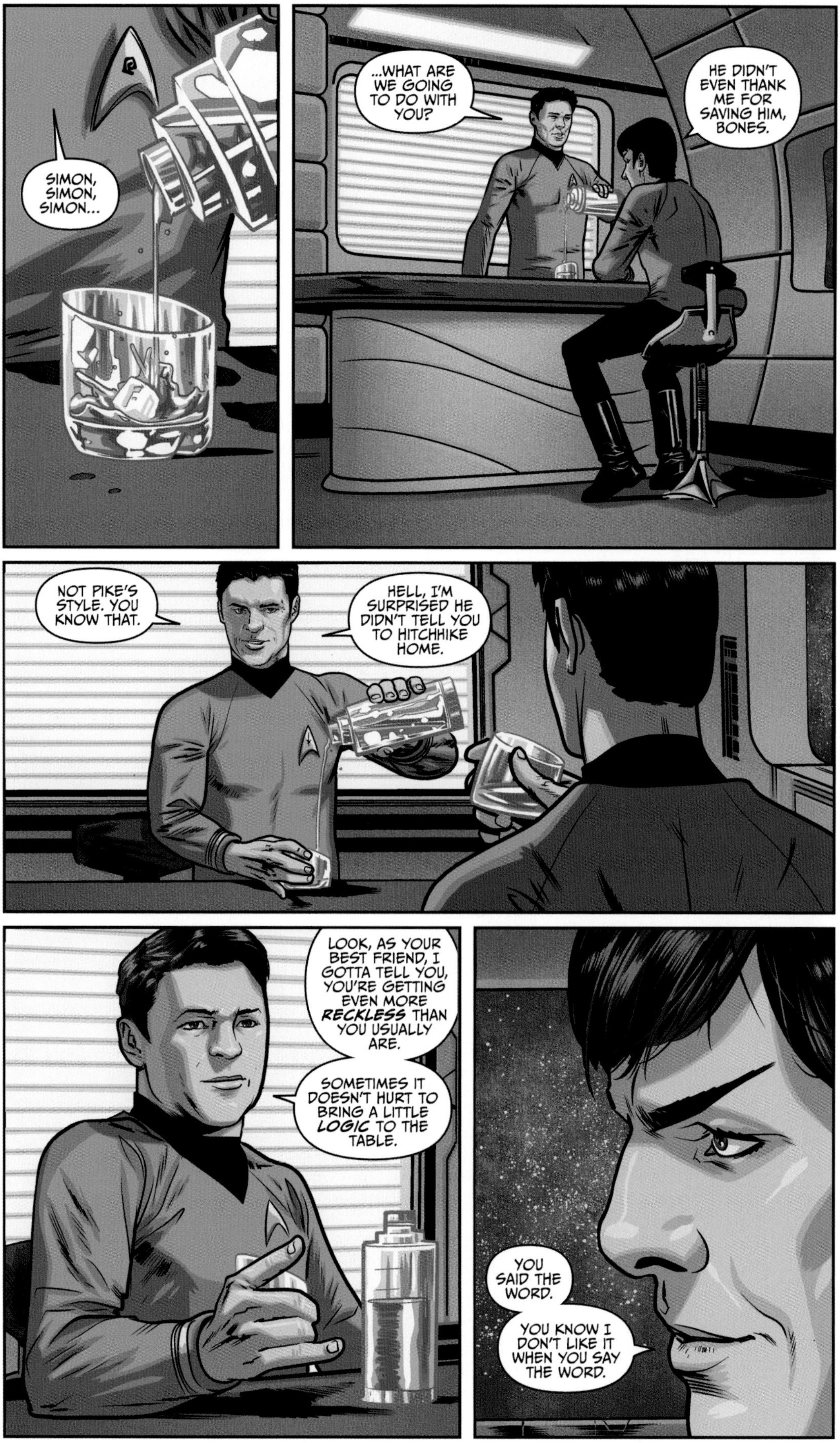
SIMON, SIMON, SIMON...
...WHAT ARE WE GOING TO DO WITH YOU?
HE DIDN'T EVEN THANK ME FOR SAVING HIM, BONES.
NOT PIKE'S STYLE. YOU KNOW THAT.
HELL, I'M SURPRISED HE DIDN'T TELL YOU TO HITCHHIKE HOME.
LOOK, AS YOUR BEST FRIEND, I GOTTA TELL YOU, YOU'RE GETTING EVEN MORE RECKLESS THAN YOU USUALLY ARE.
SOMETIMES IT DOESN'T HURT TO BRING A LITTLE LOGIC TO THE TABLE.
YOU SAID THE WORD.
YOU KNOW I DON'T LIKE IT WHEN YOU SAY THE WORD.

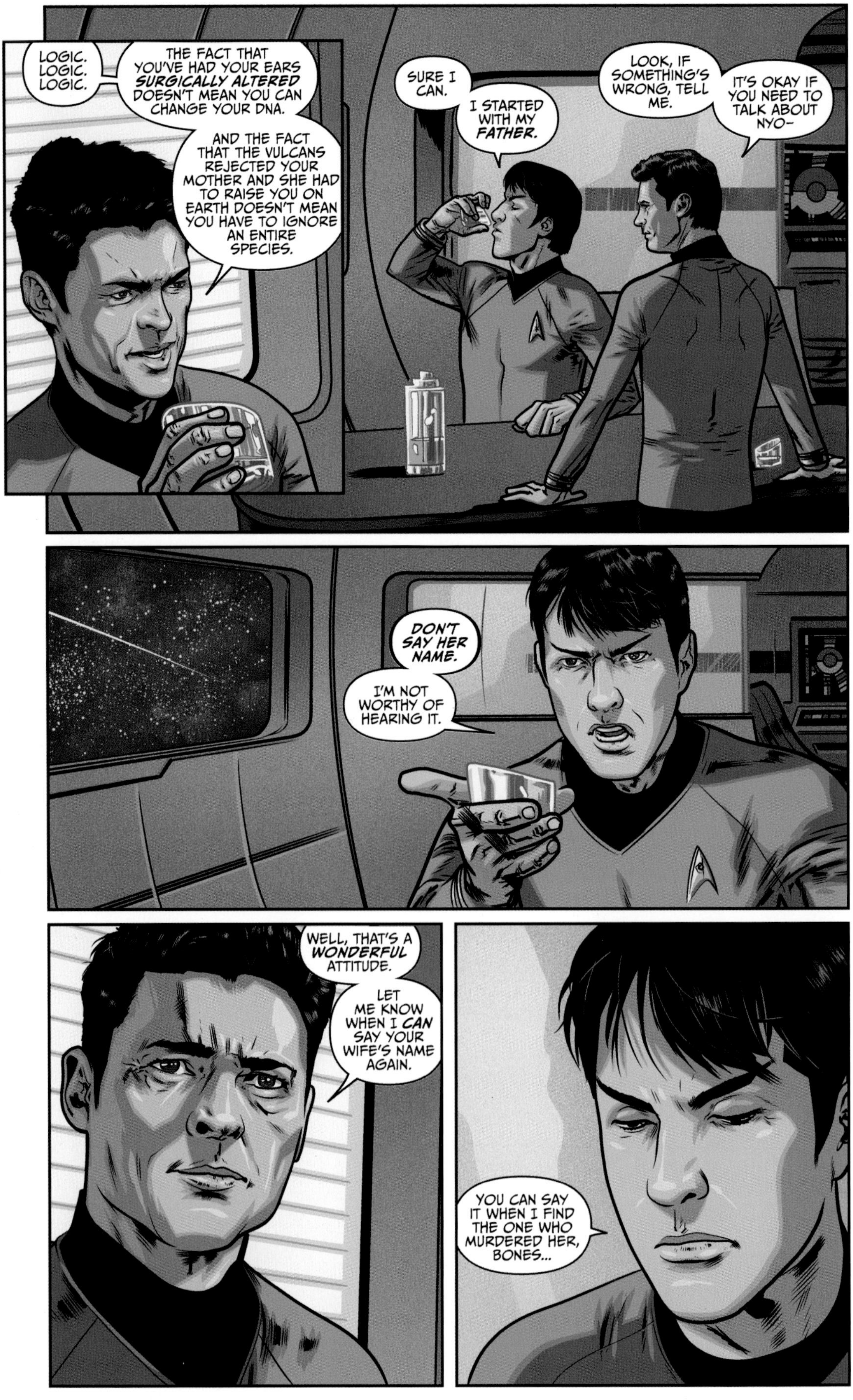
LOGIC. LOGIC. LOGIC.
THE FACT THAT YOU'VE HAD YOUR EARS SURGICALLY ALTERED DOESN'T MEAN YOU CAN CHANGE YOUR DNA.
AND THE FACT THAT THE VULCANS REJECTED YOUR MOTHER AND SHE HAD TO RAISE YOU ON EARTH DOESN'T MEAN YOU HAVE TO IGNORE AN ENTIRE SPECIES.
SURE I CAN.
I STARTED WITH MY FATHER.
LOOK, IF SOMETHING'S WRONG, TELL ME.
IT'S OKAY IF YOU NEED TO TALK ABOUT NYO–
DON'T SAY HER NAME.
I'M NOT WORTHY OF HEARING IT.
WELL, THAT'S A WONDERFUL ATTITUDE.
LET ME KNOW WHEN I CAN SAY YOUR WIFE'S NAME AGAIN.
YOU CAN SAY IT WHEN I FIND THE ONE WHO MURDERED HER, BONES...

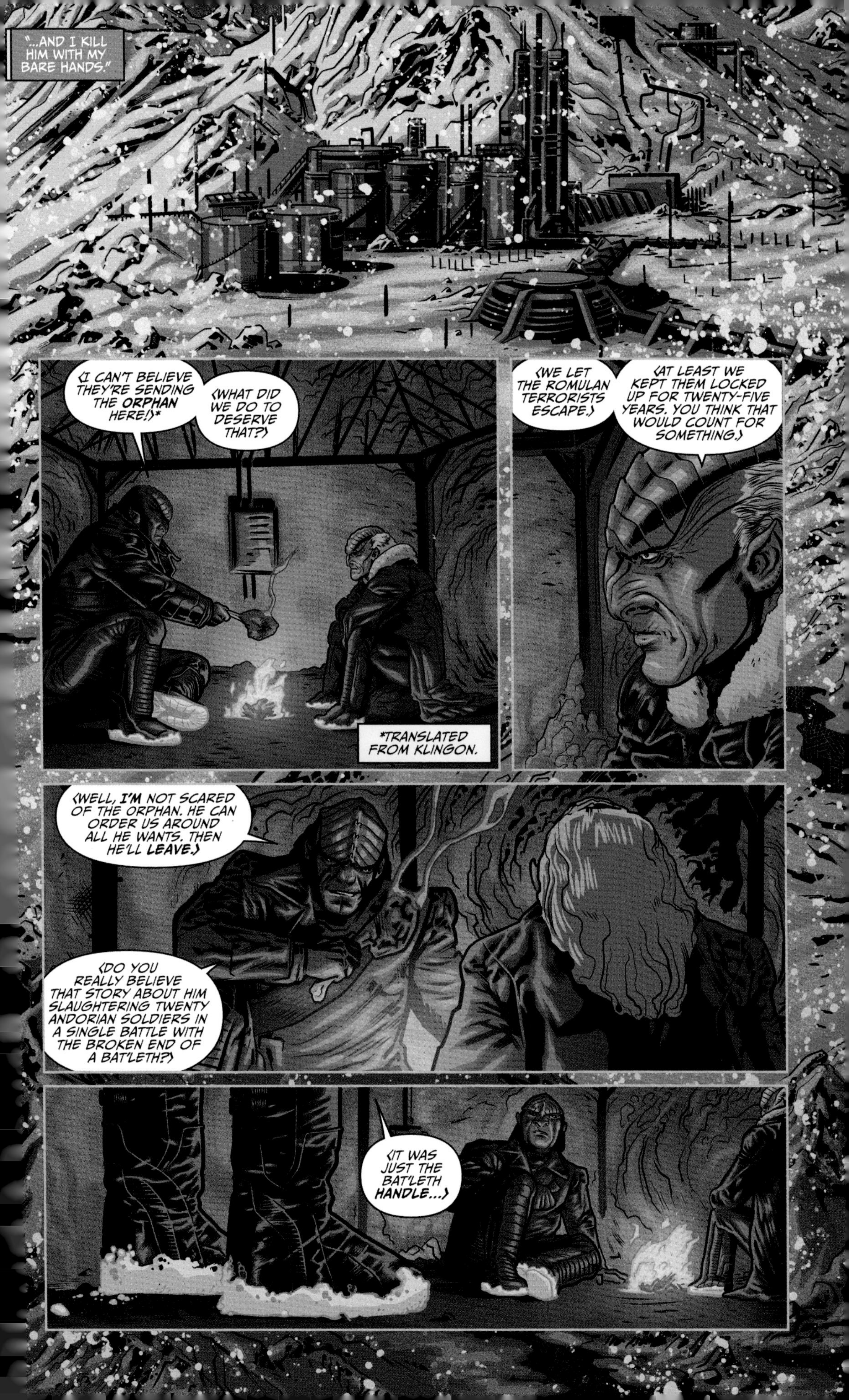
"...AND I KILL HIM WITH MY BARE HANDS."
‹I CAN'T BELIEVE THEY'RE SENDING THE ORPHAN HERE!›*
‹WHAT DID WE DO TO DESERVE THAT?›
*TRANSLATED FROM KLINGON.
‹WE LET THE ROMULAN TERRORISTS ESCAPE.›
‹AT LEAST WE KEPT THEM LOCKED UP FOR TWENTY-FIVE YEARS. YOU THINK THAT WOULD COUNT FOR SOMETHING.›
‹WELL, I'M NOT SCARED OF THE ORPHAN. HE CAN ORDER US AROUND ALL HE WANTS. THEN HE'LL LEAVE.›
‹DO YOU REALLY BELIEVE THAT STORY ABOUT HIM SLAUGHTERING TWENTY ANDORIAN SOLDIERS IN A SINGLE BATTLE WITH THE BROKEN END OF A BAT'LETH?›
‹IT WAS JUST THE BAT'LETH HANDLE...›

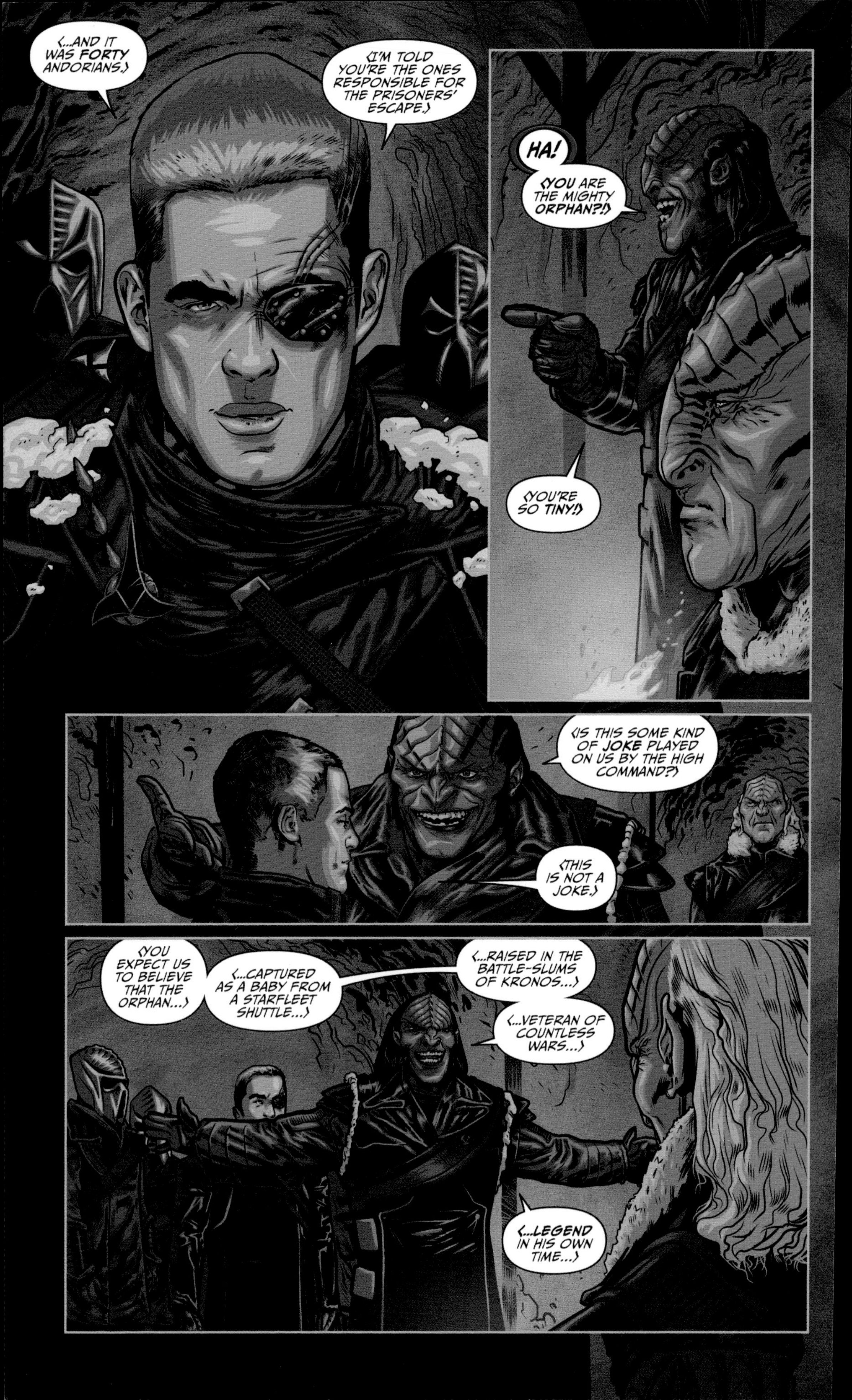
‹...AND IT WAS FORTY ANDORIANS.›
‹I'M TOLD YOU'RE THE ONES RESPONSIBLE FOR THE PRISONERS' ESCAPE.›
HA!
‹YOU ARE THE MIGHTY ORPHAN?!›
‹YOU'RE SO TINY!›
‹IS THIS SOME KIND OF JOKE PLAYED ON US BY THE HIGH COMMAND?›
‹THIS IS NOT A JOKE.›
‹YOU EXPECT US TO BELIEVE THAT THE ORPHAN...›
‹...CAPTURED AS A BABY FROM A STARFLEET SHUTTLE...›
‹...RAISED IN THE BATTLE-SLUMS OF KRONOS...›
‹...VETERAN OF COUNTLESS WARS...›
‹...LEGEND IN HIS OWN TIME...›

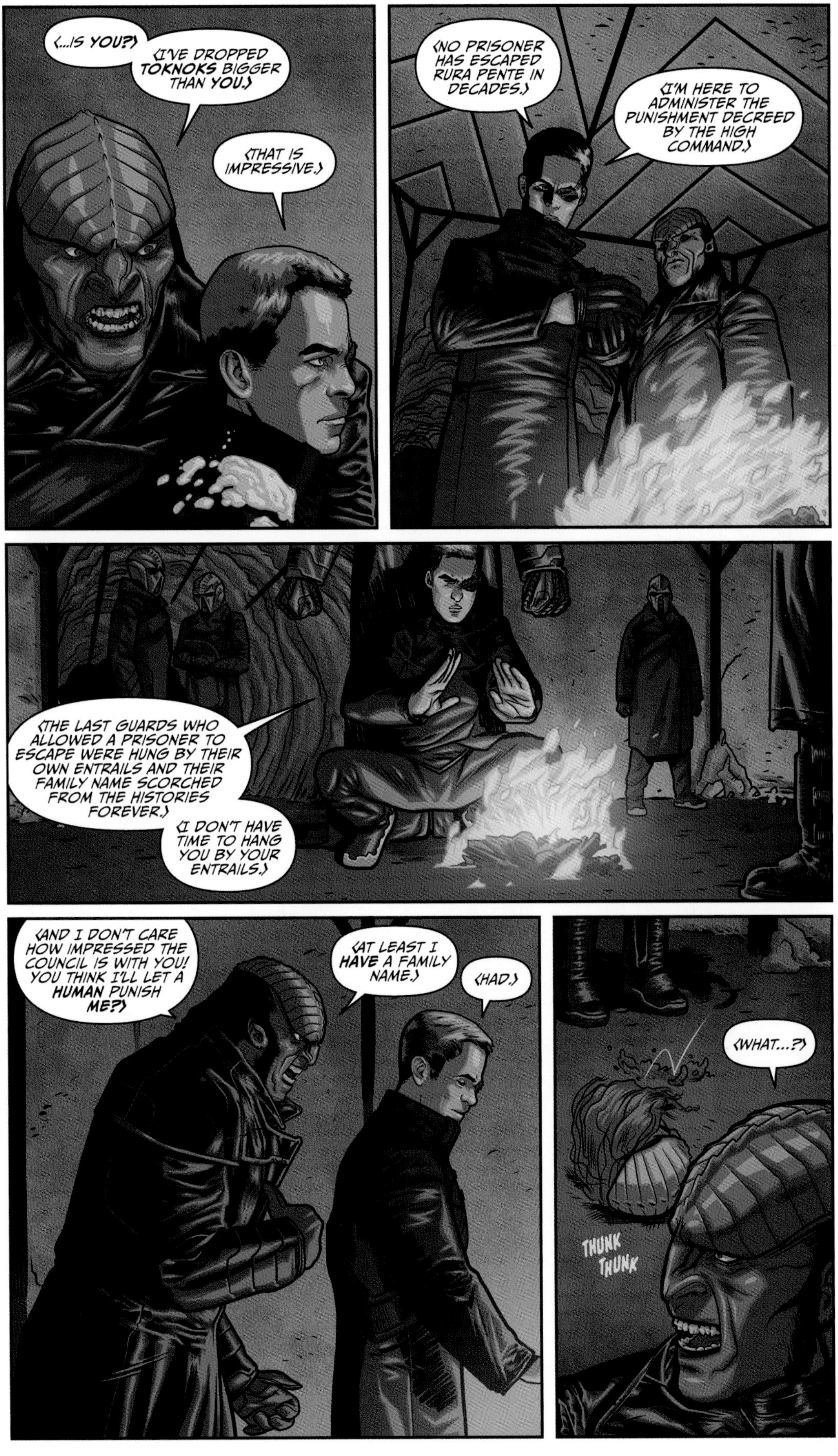

<...IS YOU?>
<I'VE DROPPED TOKNOKS BIGGER THAN YOU.>
<THAT IS IMPRESSIVE.>
<NO PRISONER HAS ESCAPED RURA PENTE IN DECADES.>
<I'M HERE TO ADMINISTER THE PUNISHMENT DECREED BY THE HIGH COMMAND.>
<THE LAST GUARDS WHO ALLOWED A PRISONER TO ESCAPE WERE HUNG BY THEIR OWN ENTRAILS AND THEIR FAMILY NAME SCORCHED FROM THE HISTORIES FOREVER.>
<I DON'T HAVE TIME TO HANG YOU BY YOUR ENTRAILS.>
<AND I DON'T CARE HOW IMPRESSED THE COUNCIL IS WITH YOU! YOU THINK I'LL LET A HUMAN PUNISH ME?>
<AT LEAST I HAVE A FAMILY NAME.>
<HAD.>
<WHAT...?>
THUNK
THUNK

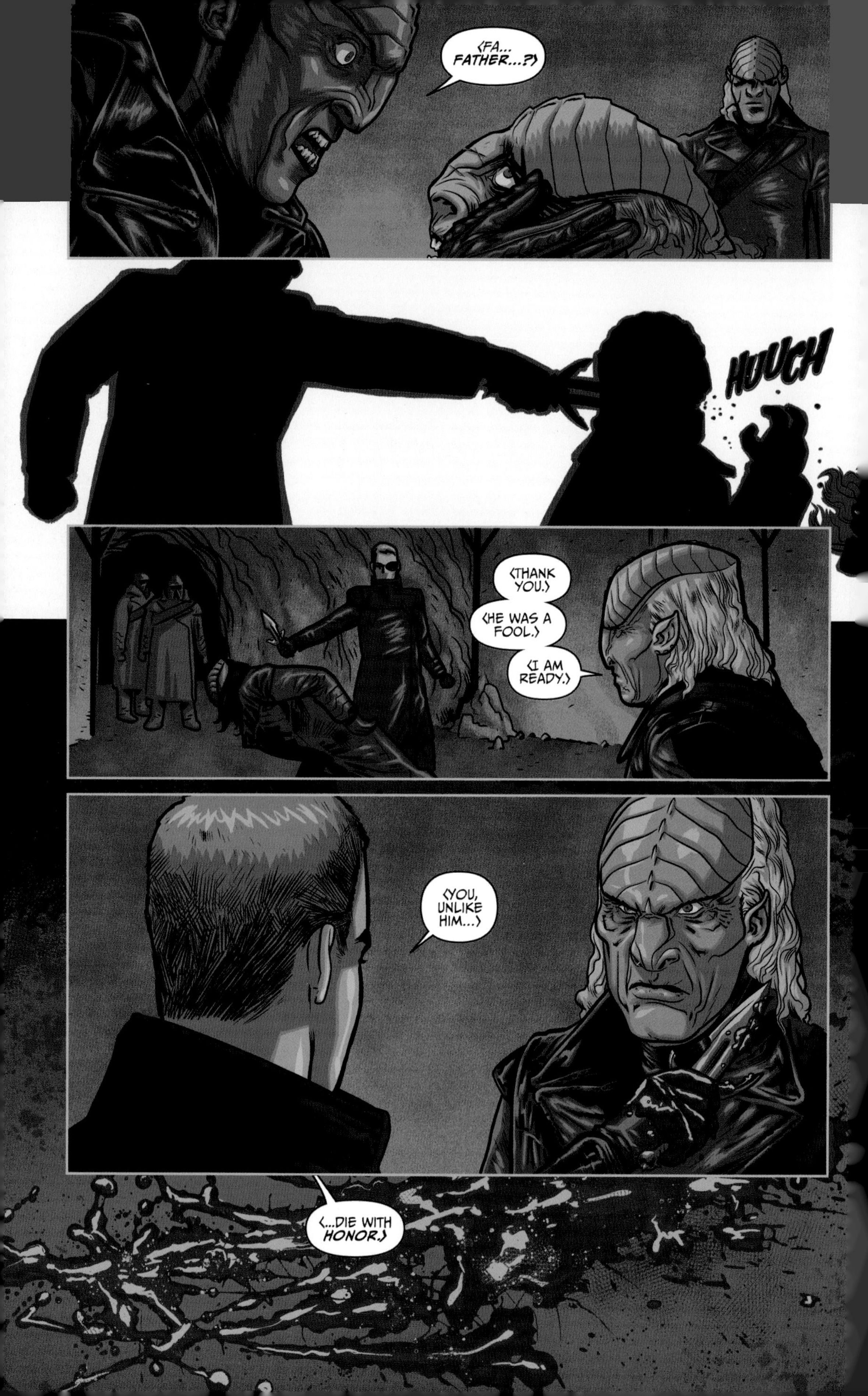
‹FA... FATHER...?›
HUUCH
‹THANK YOU.›
‹HE WAS A FOOL.›
‹I AM READY.›
‹YOU, UNLIKE HIM...›
‹...DIE WITH HONOR.›

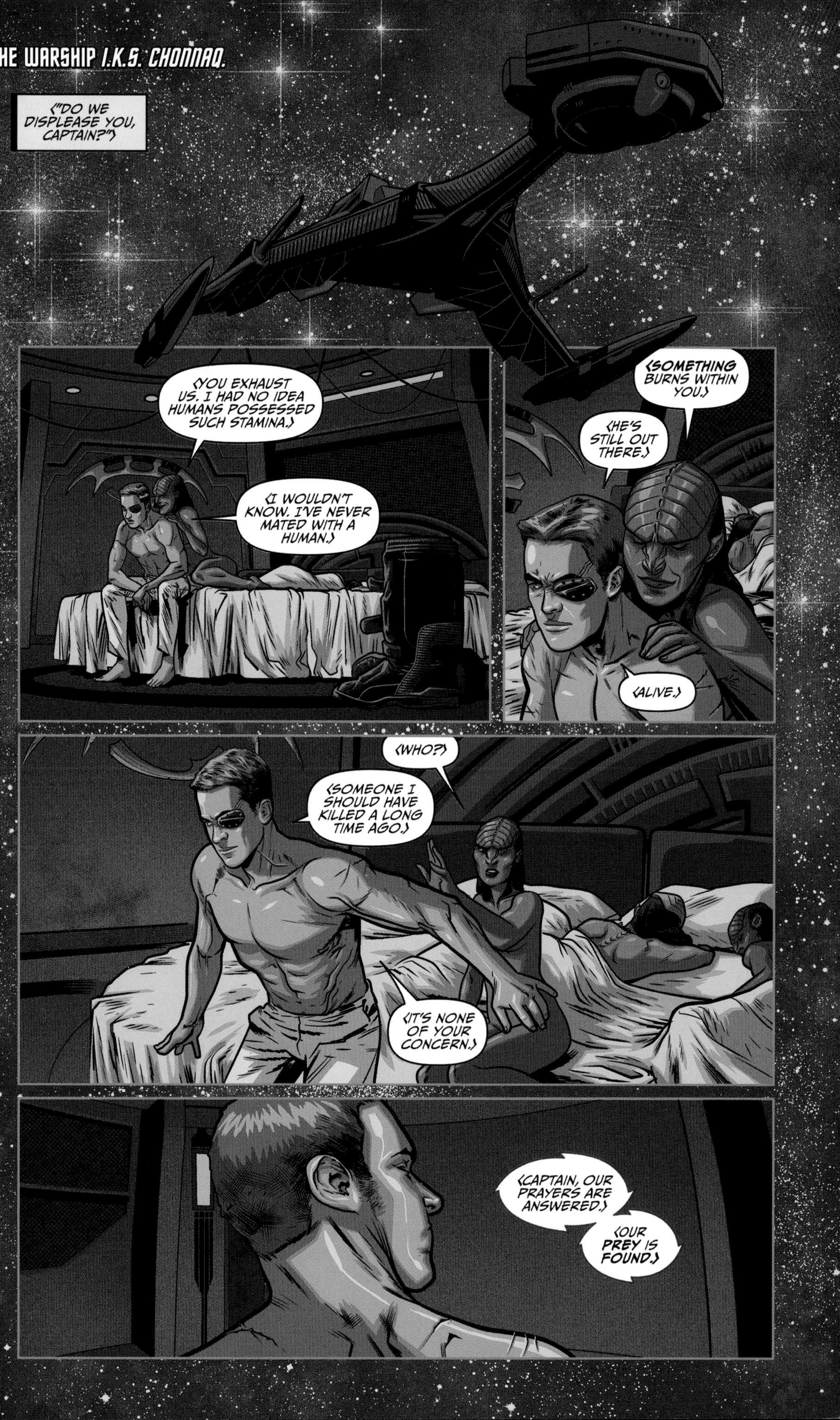
HE WARSHIP I.K.S. CHONNAQ.
<"DO WE DISPLEASE YOU, CAPTAIN?">
<YOU EXHAUST US. I HAD NO IDEA HUMANS POSSESSED SUCH STAMINA.>
<I WOULDN'T KNOW. I'VE NEVER MATED WITH A HUMAN.>
<SOMETHING BURNS WITHIN YOU.>
<HE'S STILL OUT THERE.>
<ALIVE.>
<WHO?>
<SOMEONE I SHOULD HAVE KILLED A LONG TIME AGO.>
<IT'S NONE OF YOUR CONCERN.>
<CAPTAIN, OUR PRAYERS ARE ANSWERED.>
<OUR PREY IS FOUND.>

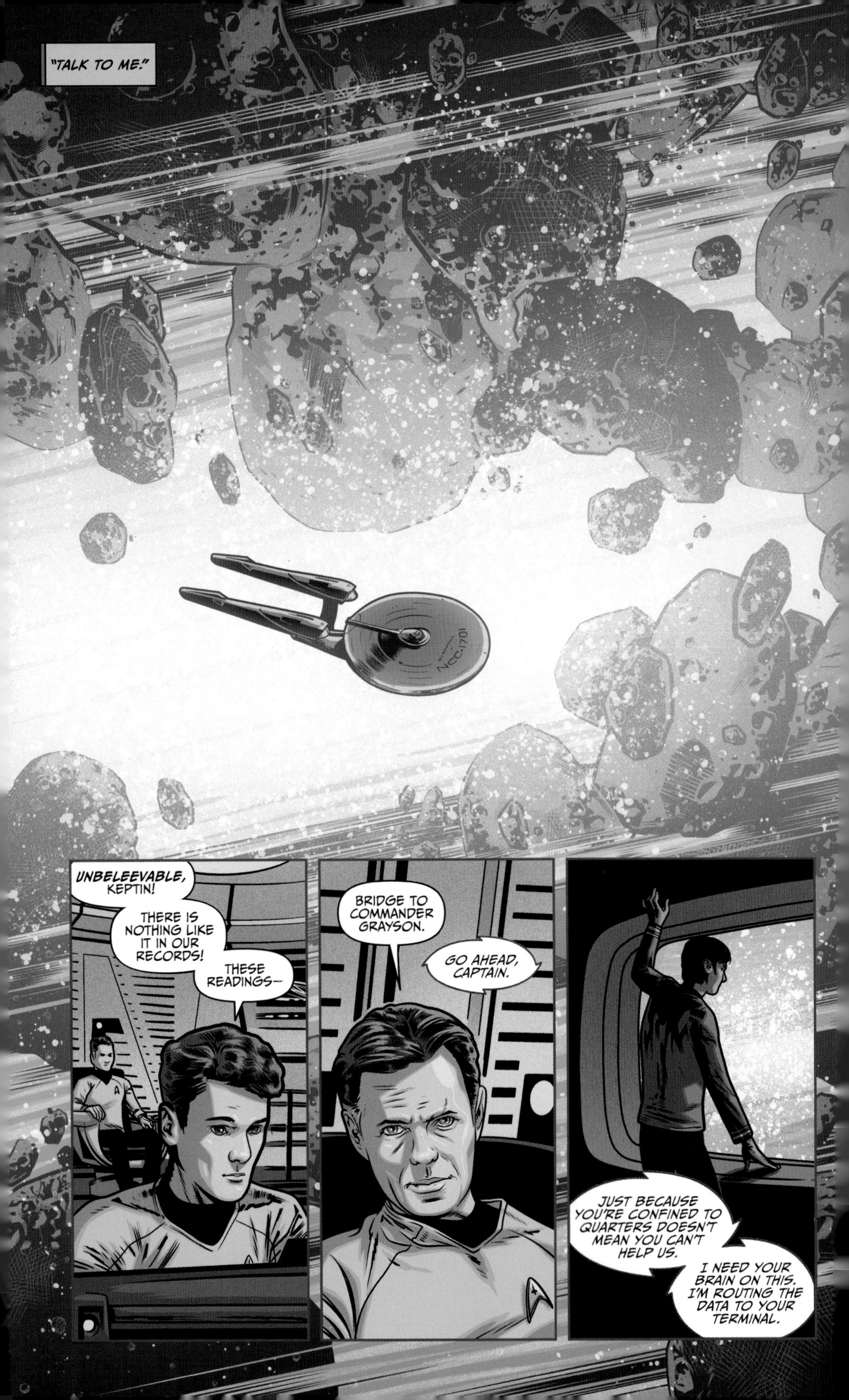
"TALK TO ME."
NCC-1701
UNBELEEVABLE, KEPTIN!
THERE IS NOTHING LIKE IT IN OUR RECORDS!
THESE READINGS—
BRIDGE TO COMMANDER GRAYSON.
GO AHEAD, CAPTAIN.
JUST BECAUSE YOU'RE CONFINED TO QUARTERS DOESN'T MEAN YOU CAN'T HELP US.
I NEED YOUR BRAIN ON THIS. I'M ROUTING THE DATA TO YOUR TERMINAL.

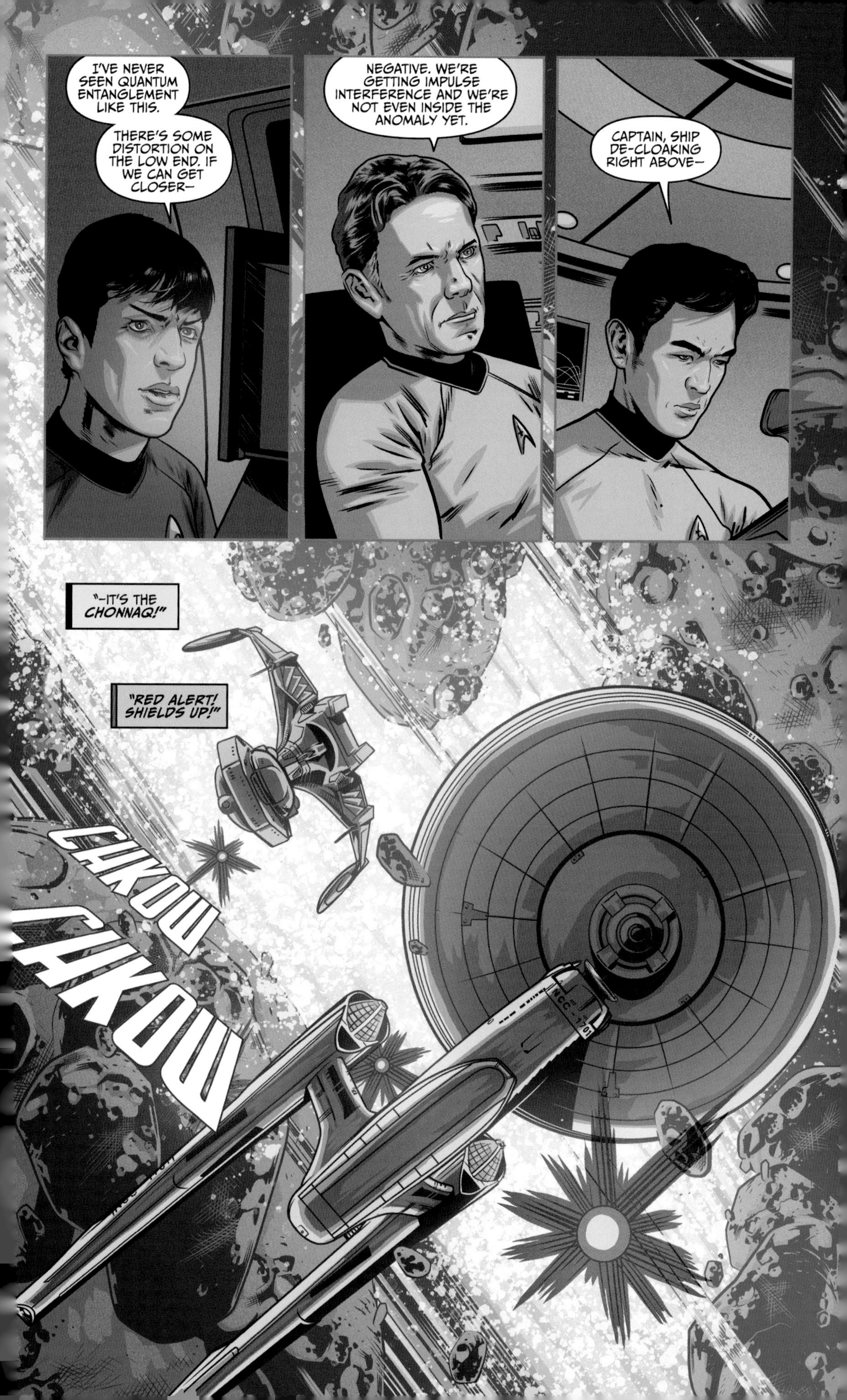
I'VE NEVER SEEN QUANTUM ENTANGLEMENT LIKE THIS.
THERE'S SOME DISTORTION ON THE LOW END. IF WE CAN GET CLOSER—
NEGATIVE. WE'RE GETTING IMPULSE INTERFERENCE AND WE'RE NOT EVEN INSIDE THE ANOMALY YET.
CAPTAIN, SHIP DE-CLOAKING RIGHT ABOVE—
"—IT'S THE CHONNAQ!"
"RED ALERT! SHIELDS UP!"
CAKOW
CAKOW
NCC-1701

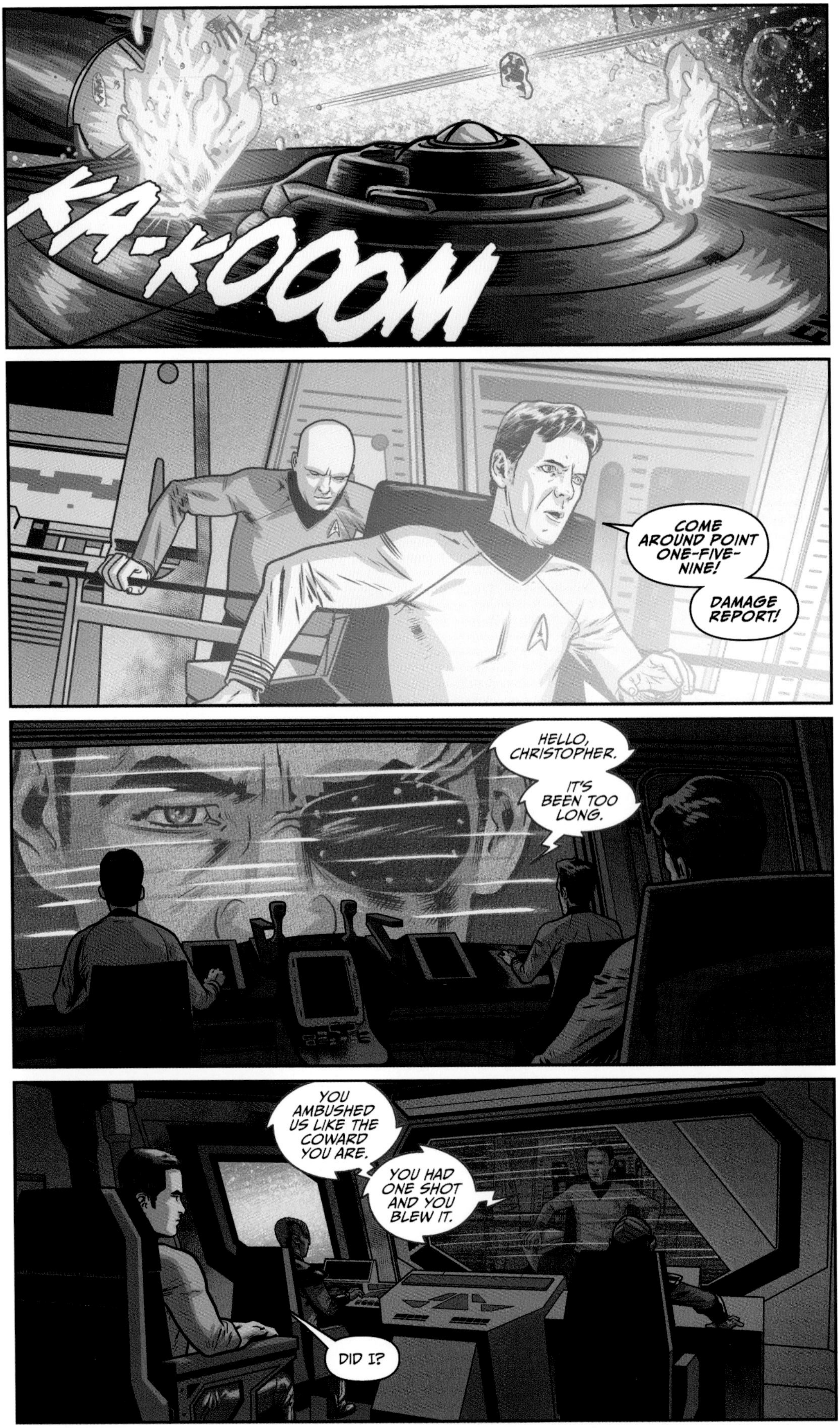
KA-KOOOM
COME AROUND POINT ONE-FIVE-NINE!
DAMAGE REPORT!
HELLO, CHRISTOPHER.
IT'S BEEN TOO LONG.
YOU AMBUSHED US LIKE THE COWARD YOU ARE.
YOU HAD ONE SHOT AND YOU BLEW IT.
DID I?

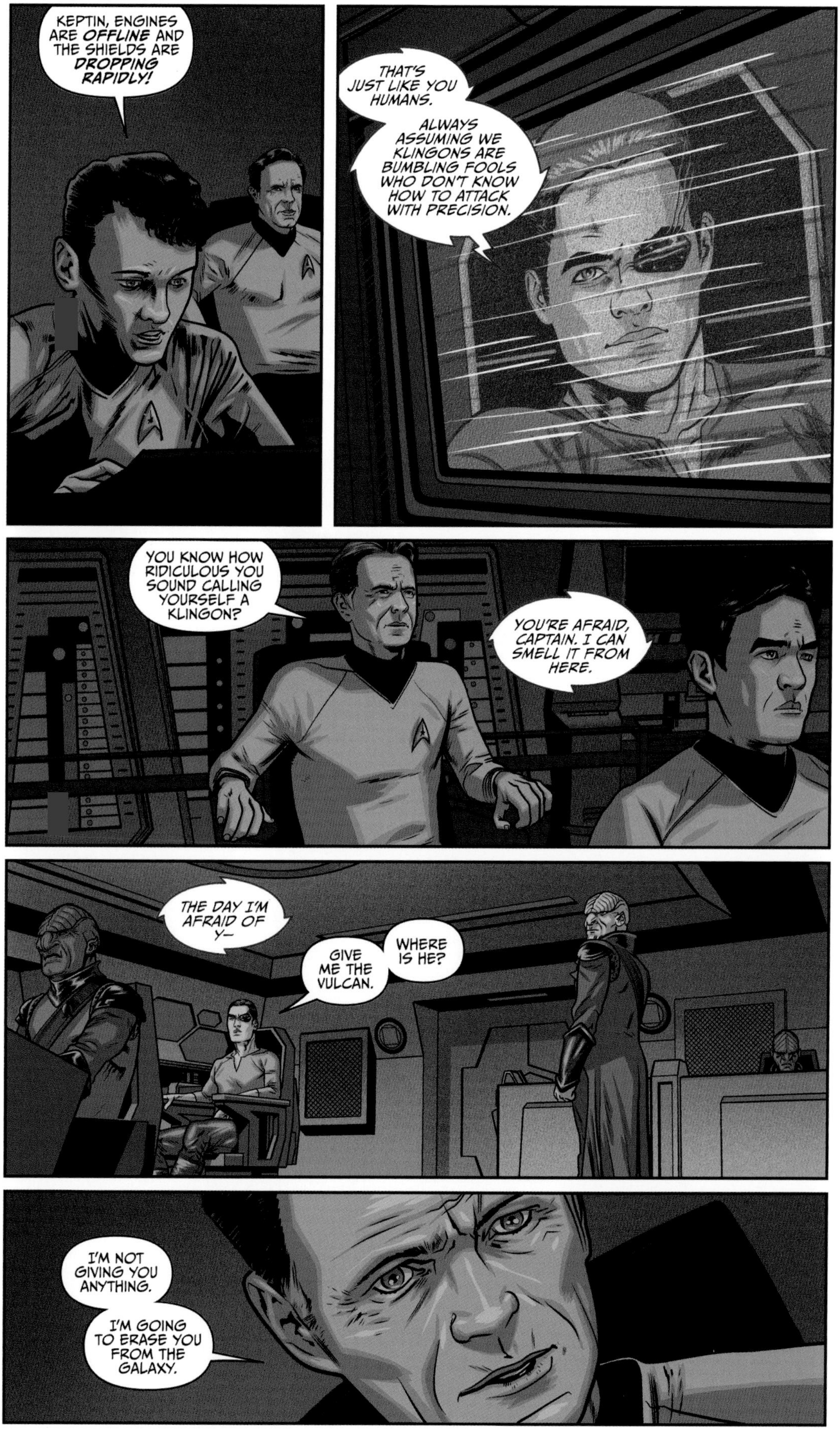

KEPTIN, ENGINES ARE OFFLINE AND THE SHIELDS ARE DROPPING RAPIDLY!
THAT'S JUST LIKE YOU HUMANS.
ALWAYS ASSUMING WE KLINGONS ARE BUMBLING FOOLS WHO DON'T KNOW HOW TO ATTACK WITH PRECISION.
YOU KNOW HOW RIDICULOUS YOU SOUND CALLING YOURSELF A KLINGON?
YOU'RE AFRAID, CAPTAIN. I CAN SMELL IT FROM HERE.
THE DAY I'M AFRAID OF Y—
GIVE ME THE VULCAN.
WHERE IS HE?
I'M NOT GIVING YOU ANYTHING.
I'M GOING TO ERASE YOU FROM THE GALAXY.

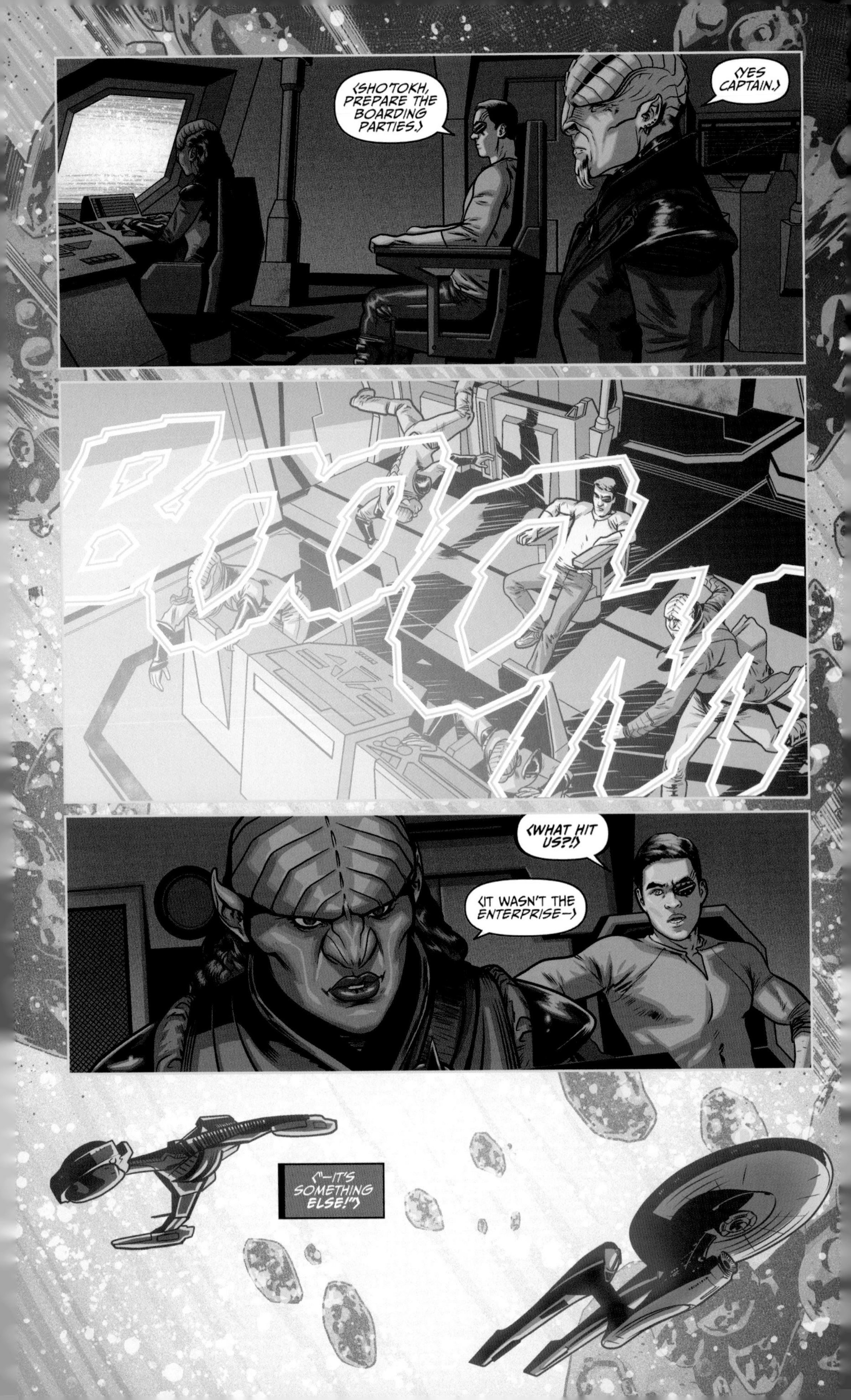
‹SHO'TOKH, PREPARE THE BOARDING PARTIES.›
‹YES CAPTAIN.›
BOOOM
‹WHAT HIT US?!›
‹IT WASN'T THE ENTERPRISE—›
‹"—IT'S SOMETHING ELSE!"›

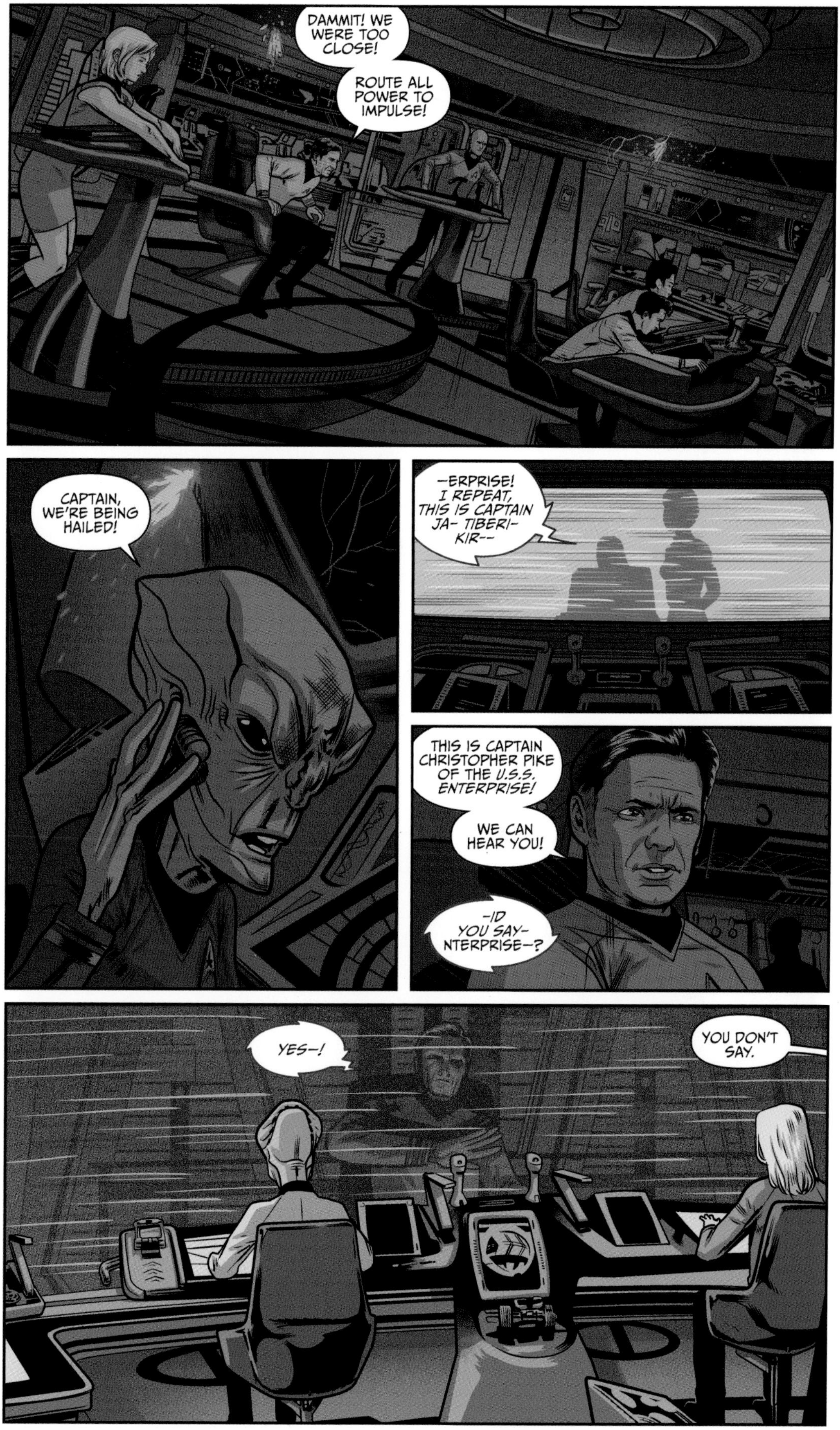
DAMMIT! WE WERE TOO CLOSE!
ROUTE ALL POWER TO IMPULSE!
CAPTAIN, WE'RE BEING HAILED!
--ERPRISE! I REPEAT, THIS IS CAPTAIN JA- TIBERI- KIR--
THIS IS CAPTAIN CHRISTOPHER PIKE OF THE U.S.S. ENTERPRISE!
WE CAN HEAR YOU!
-ID YOU SAY- NTERPRISE--?
YES--!
YOU DON'T SAY.

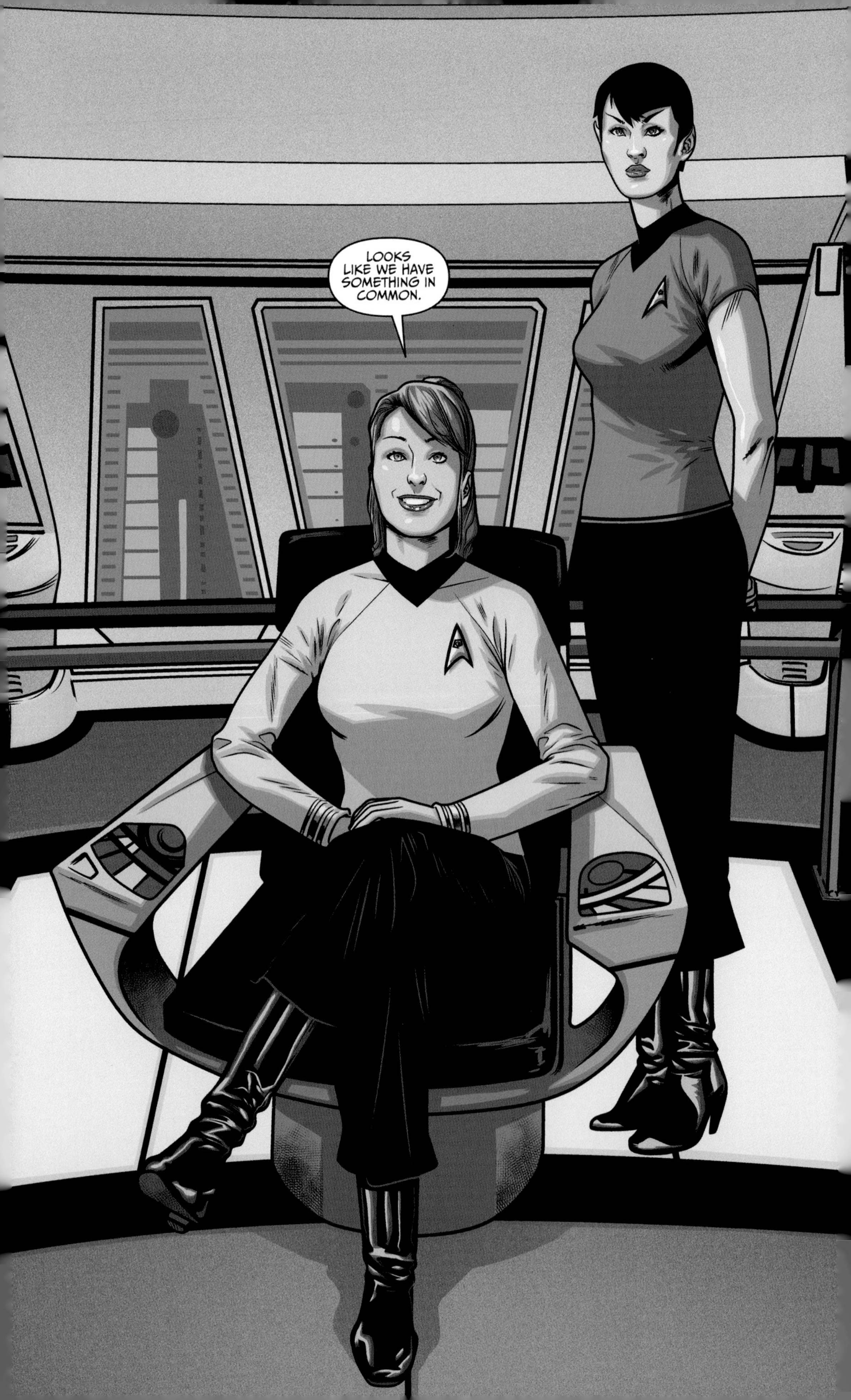
LOOKS LIKE WE HAVE SOMETHING IN COMMON.

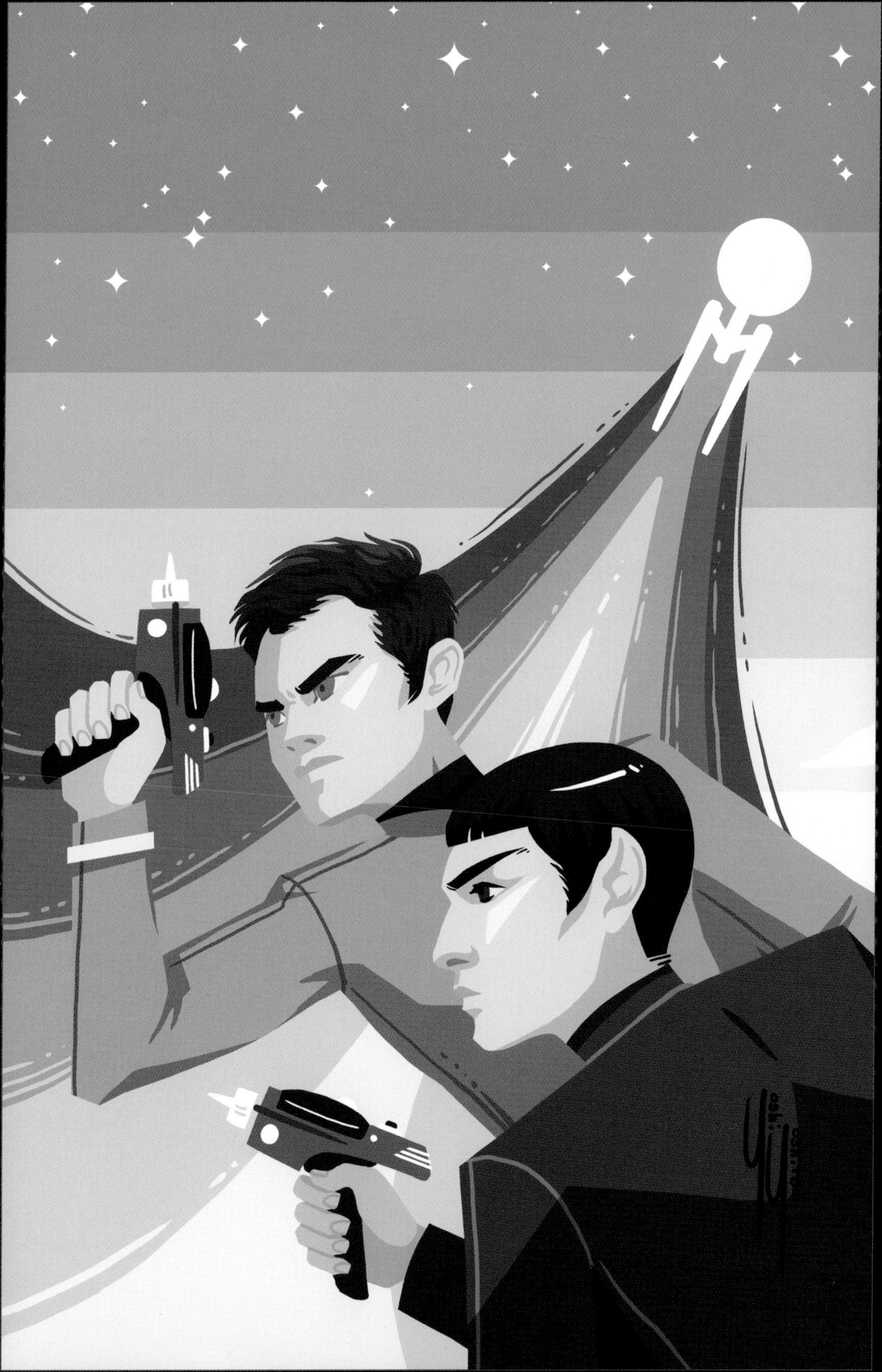

art by
Yoshi Yoshitani

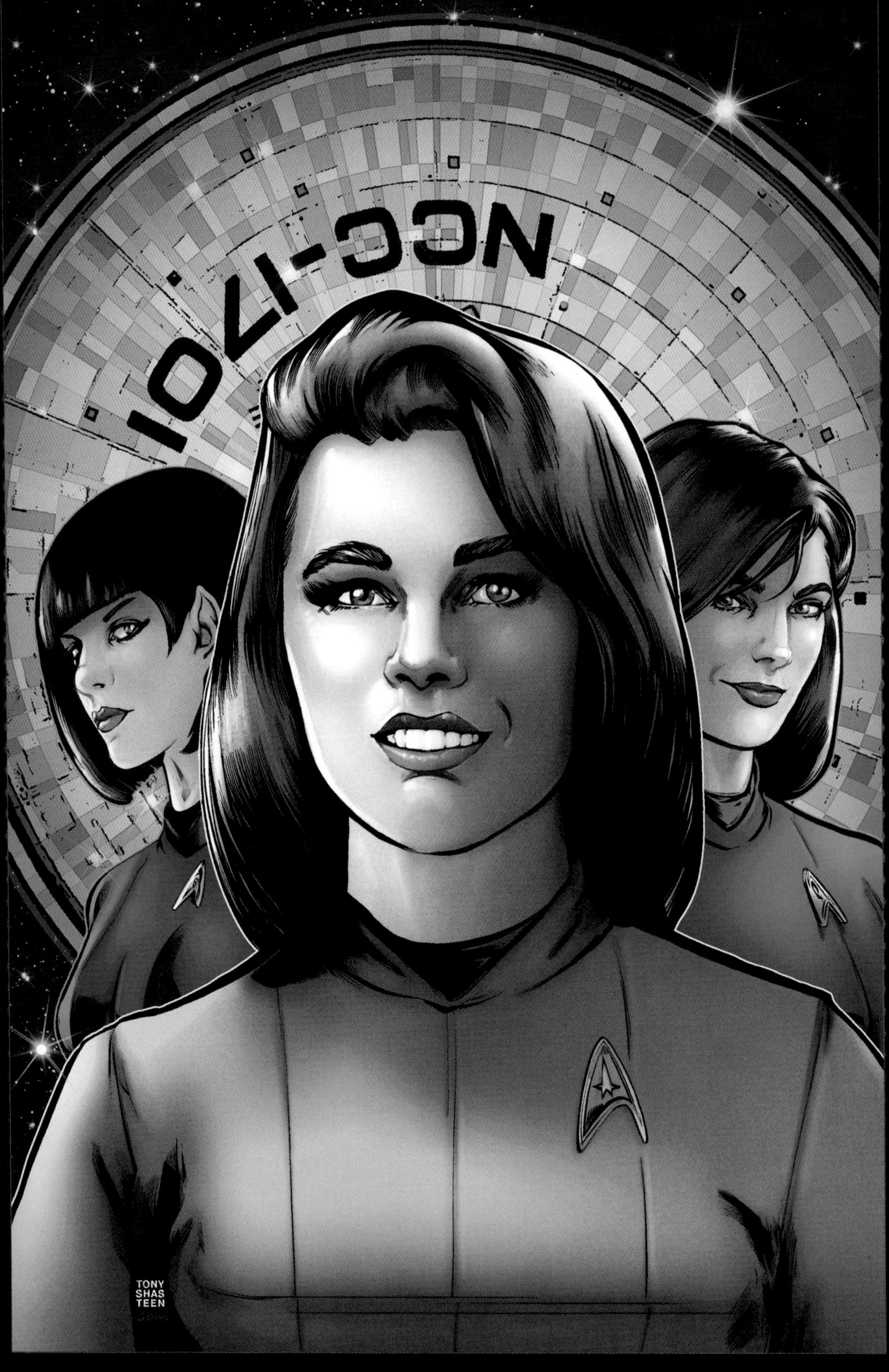
NCC-1701
TONY
SHAS
TEEN

art by
Tony Shasteen

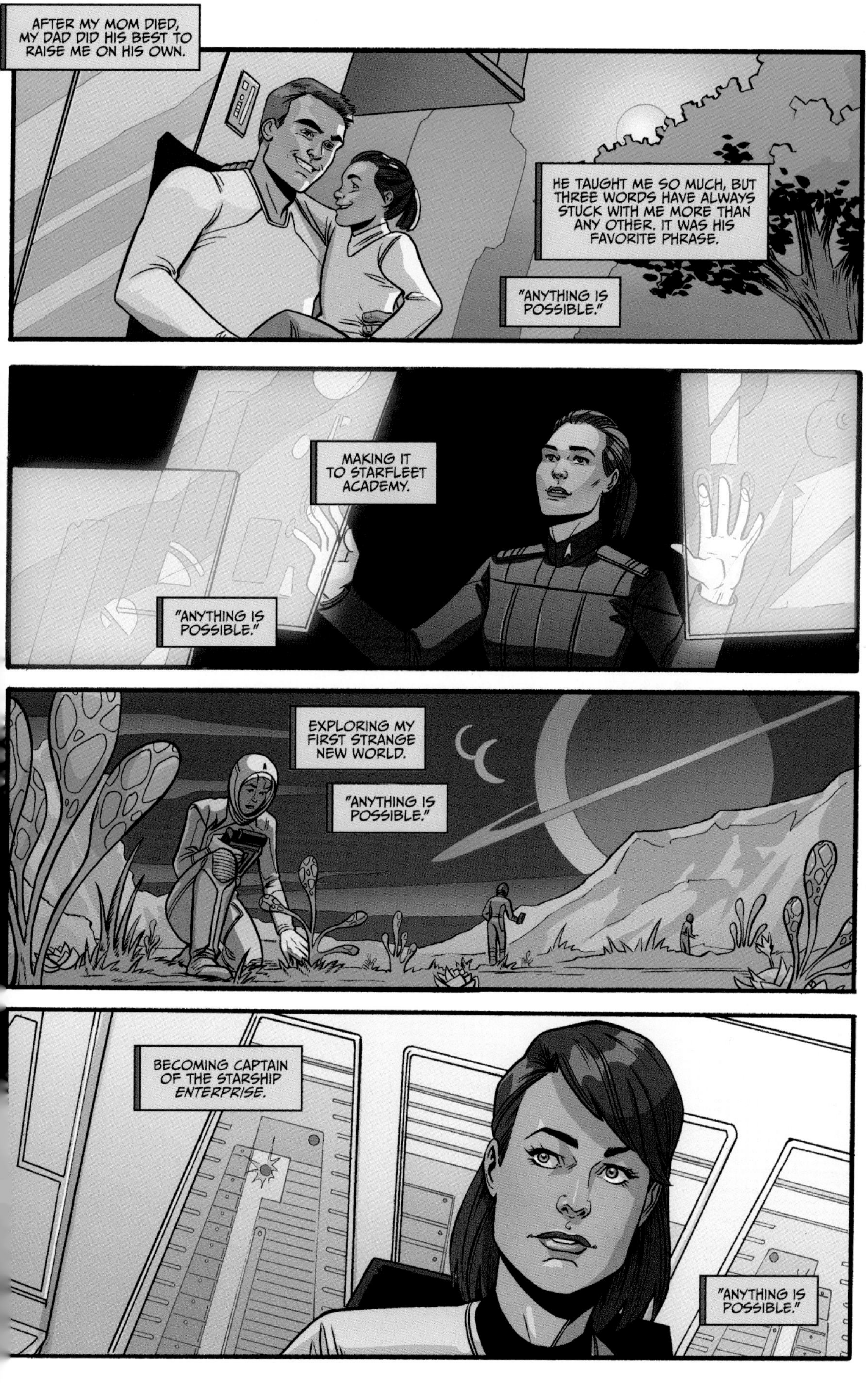
AFTER MY MOM DIED, MY DAD DID HIS BEST TO RAISE ME ON HIS OWN.
HE TAUGHT ME SO MUCH, BUT THREE WORDS HAVE ALWAYS STUCK WITH ME MORE THAN ANY OTHER. IT WAS HIS FAVORITE PHRASE.
"ANYTHING IS POSSIBLE."
MAKING IT TO STARFLEET ACADEMY.
"ANYTHING IS POSSIBLE."
EXPLORING MY FIRST STRANGE NEW WORLD.
"ANYTHING IS POSSIBLE."
BECOMING CAPTAIN OF THE STARSHIP *ENTERPRISE*.
"ANYTHING IS POSSIBLE."

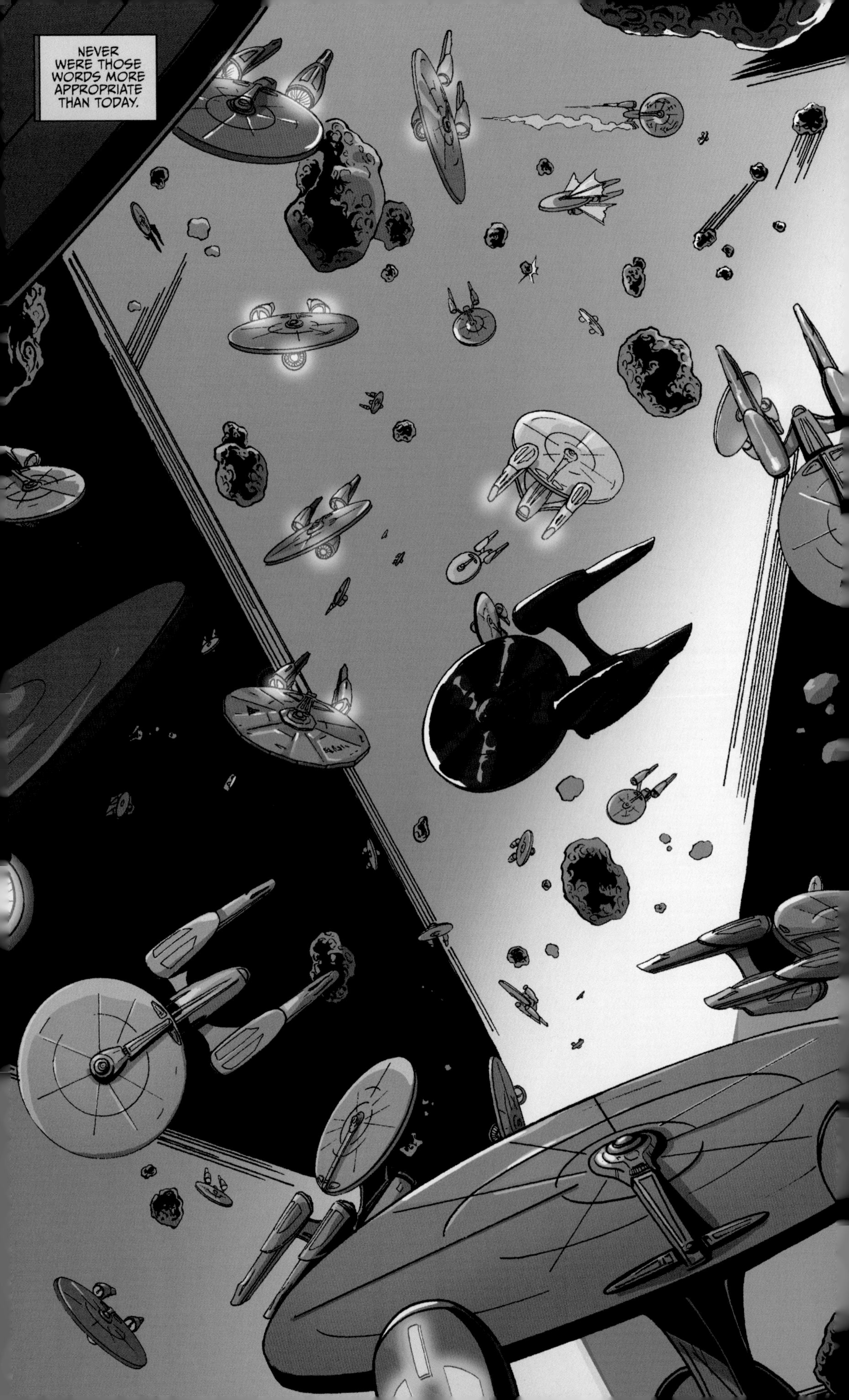
NEVER WERE THOSE WORDS MORE APPROPRIATE THAN TODAY.

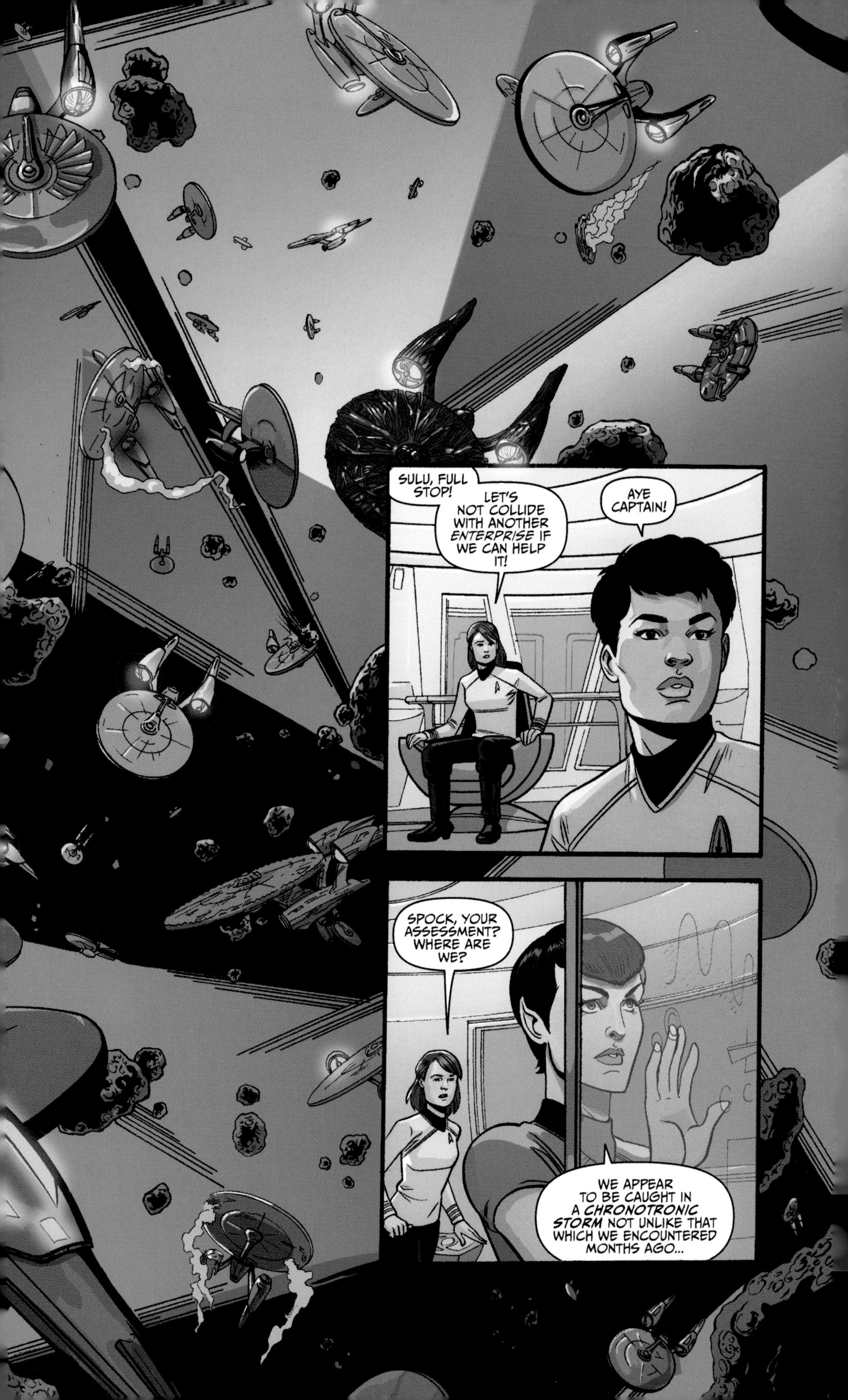
SULU, FULL STOP!
LET'S NOT COLLIDE WITH ANOTHER ENTERPRISE IF WE CAN HELP IT!
AYE CAPTAIN!
SPOCK, YOUR ASSESSMENT? WHERE ARE WE?
WE APPEAR TO BE CAUGHT IN A CHRONOTRONIC STORM NOT UNLIKE THAT WHICH WE ENCOUNTERED MONTHS AGO...

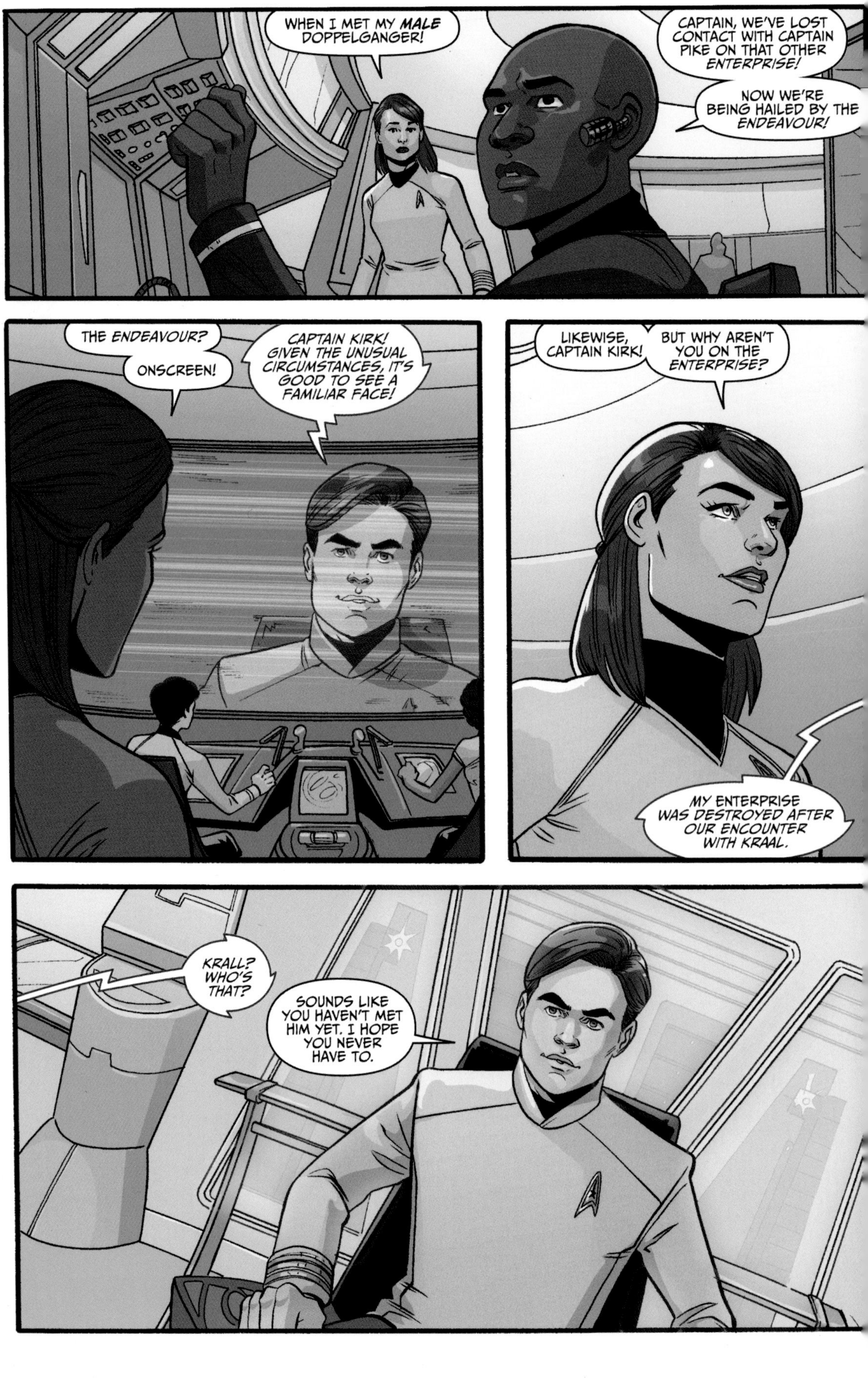
WHEN I MET MY MALE DOPPELGANGER!
CAPTAIN, WE'VE LOST CONTACT WITH CAPTAIN PIKE ON THAT OTHER ENTERPRISE!
NOW WE'RE BEING HAILED BY THE ENDEAVOUR!
THE ENDEAVOUR?
ONSCREEN!
CAPTAIN KIRK! GIVEN THE UNUSUAL CIRCUMSTANCES, IT'S GOOD TO SEE A FAMILIAR FACE!
LIKEWISE, CAPTAIN KIRK!
BUT WHY AREN'T YOU ON THE ENTERPRISE?
MY ENTERPRISE WAS DESTROYED AFTER OUR ENCOUNTER WITH KRAAL.
KRALL? WHO'S THAT?
SOUNDS LIKE YOU HAVEN'T MET HIM YET. I HOPE YOU NEVER HAVE TO.

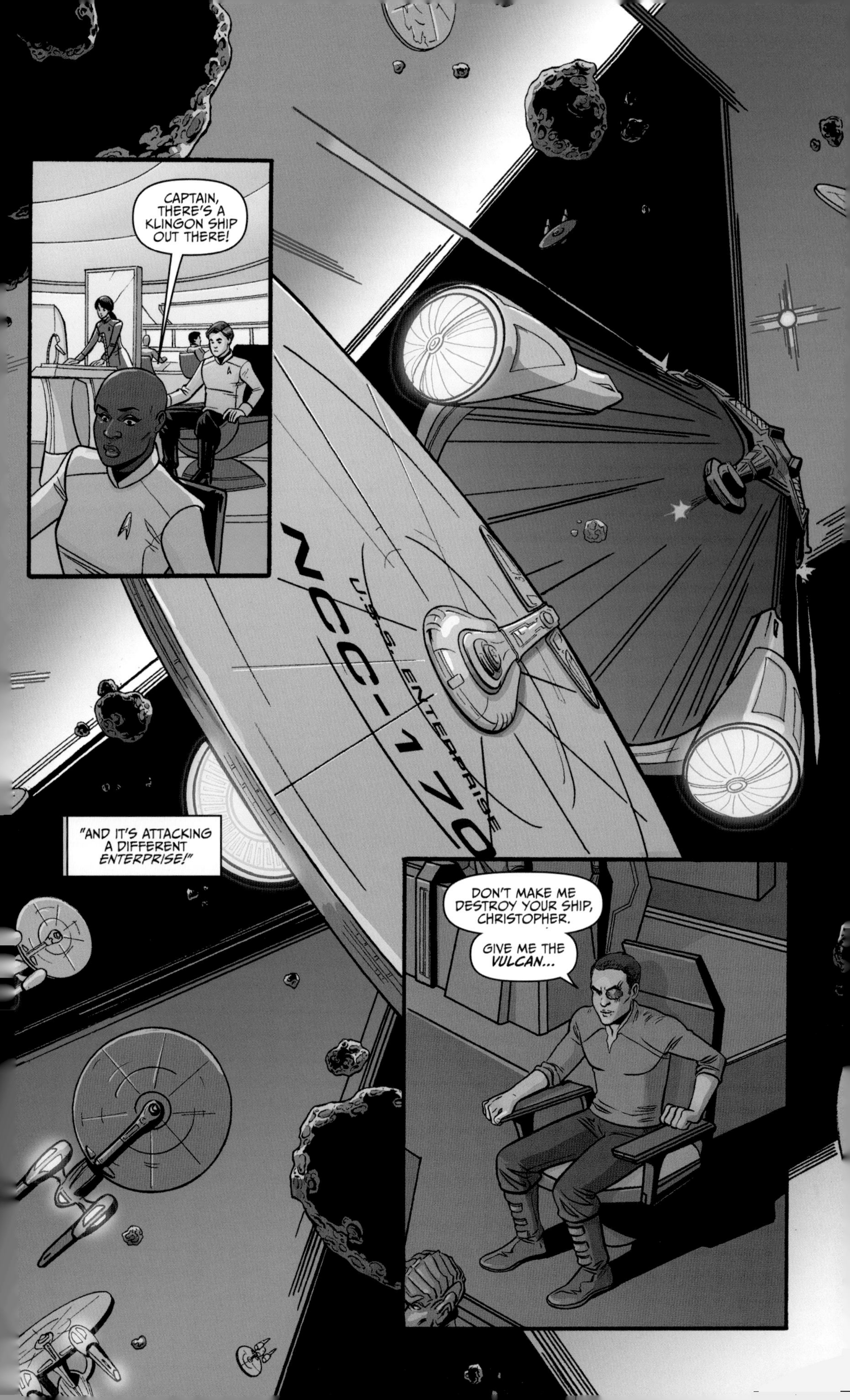
CAPTAIN, THERE'S A KLINGON SHIP OUT THERE!
U.S.S. ENTERPRISE
NCC-170
"AND IT'S ATTACKING A DIFFERENT *ENTERPRISE!*"
DON'T MAKE ME DESTROY YOUR SHIP, CHRISTOPHER.
GIVE ME THE ***VULCAN...***

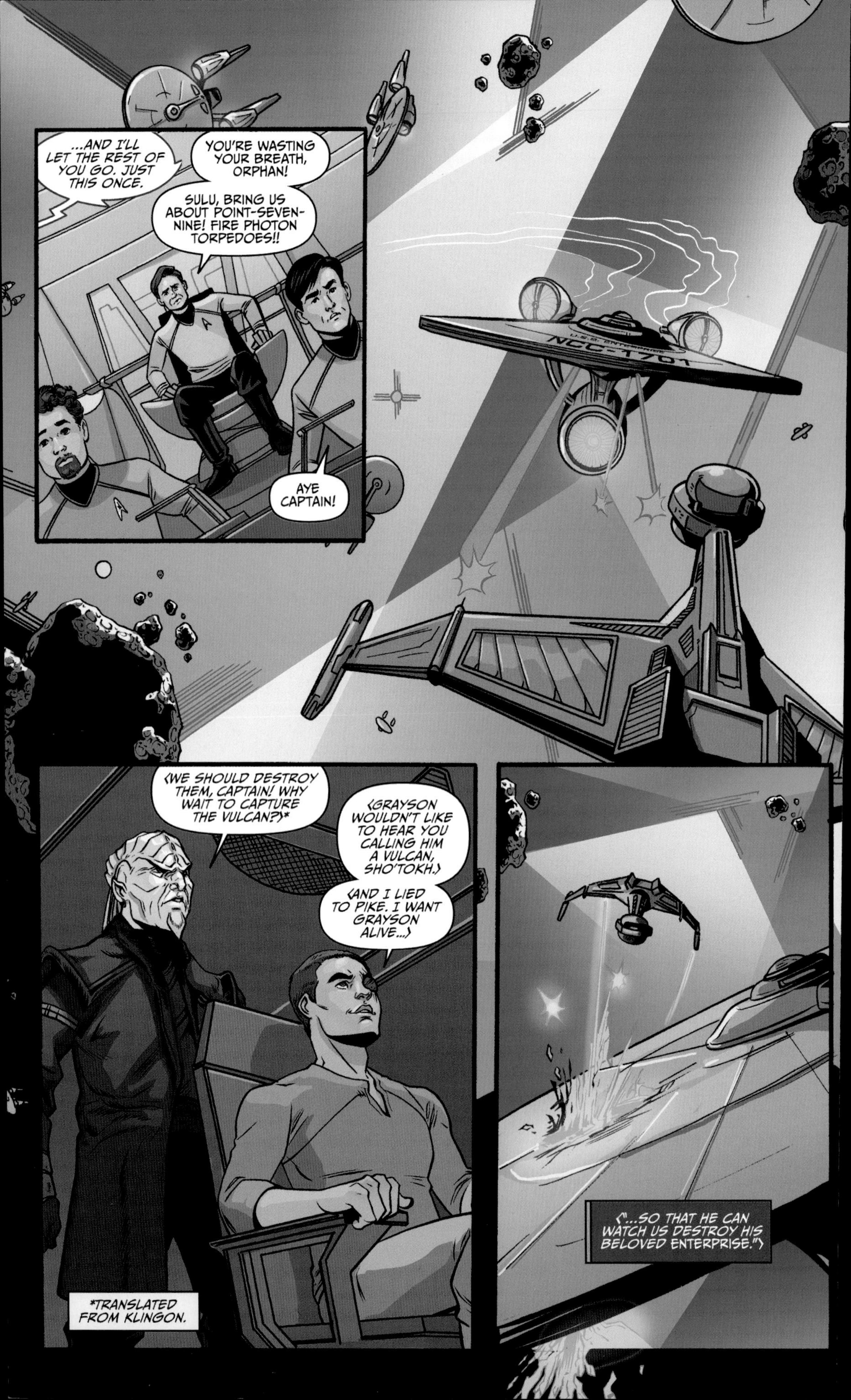

...AND I'LL LET THE REST OF YOU GO. JUST THIS ONCE.
YOU'RE WASTING YOUR BREATH, ORPHAN!
SULU, BRING US ABOUT POINT-SEVEN-NINE! FIRE PHOTON TORPEDOES!!
AYE CAPTAIN!
U.S.S. ENTERPRISE NCC-1701
‹WE SHOULD DESTROY THEM, CAPTAIN! WHY WAIT TO CAPTURE THE VULCAN?›*
‹GRAYSON WOULDN'T LIKE TO HEAR YOU CALLING HIM A VULCAN, SHO'TOKH.›
‹AND I LIED TO PIKE. I WANT GRAYSON ALIVE...›
*TRANSLATED FROM KLINGON.
‹"...SO THAT HE CAN WATCH US DESTROY HIS BELOVED ENTERPRISE."›

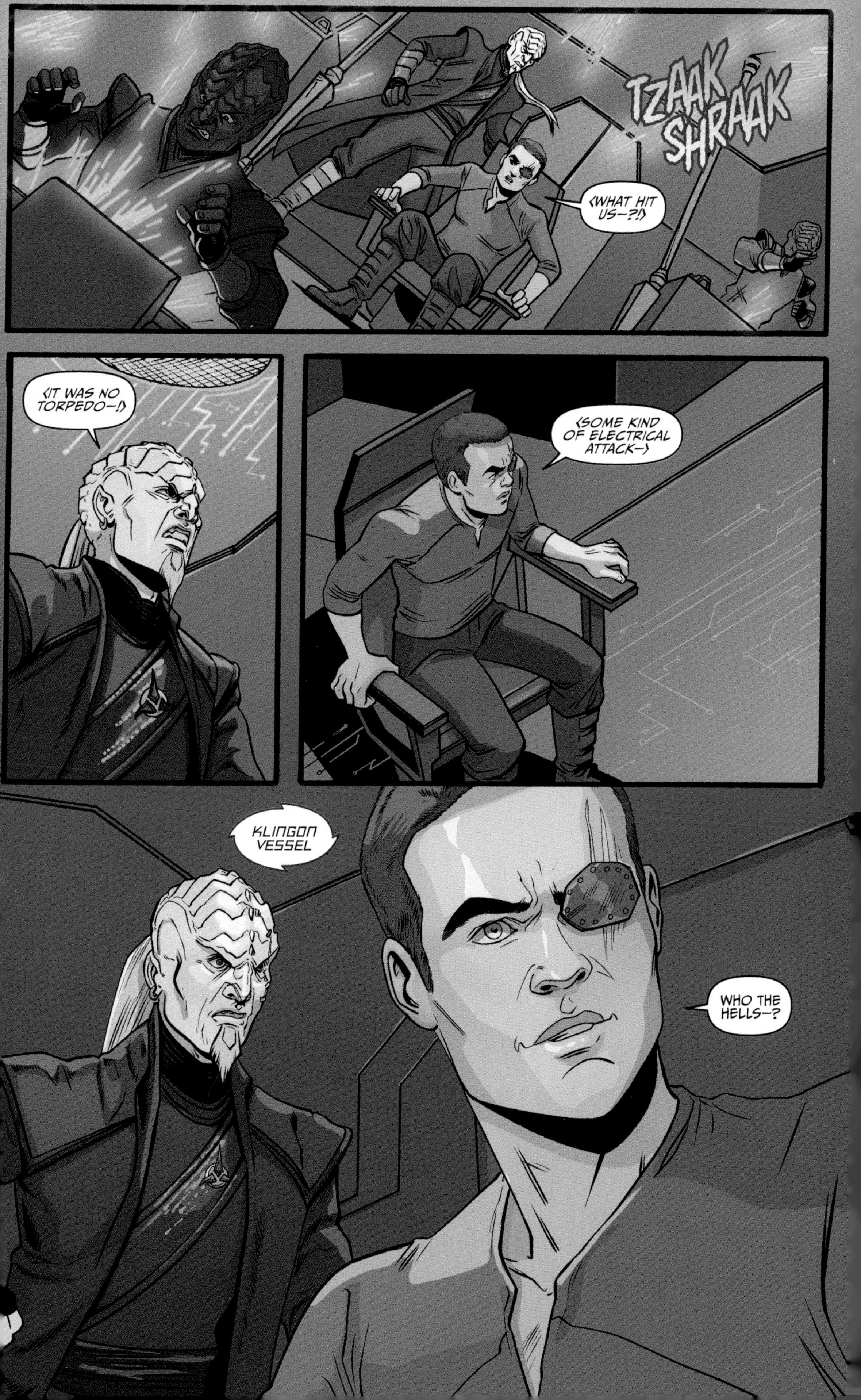
TZAAK SHRAAK
‹WHAT HIT US—?!›
‹IT WAS NO TORPEDO—!›
‹SOME KIND OF ELECTRICAL ATTACK—›
KLINGON VESSEL
WHO THE HELLS—?

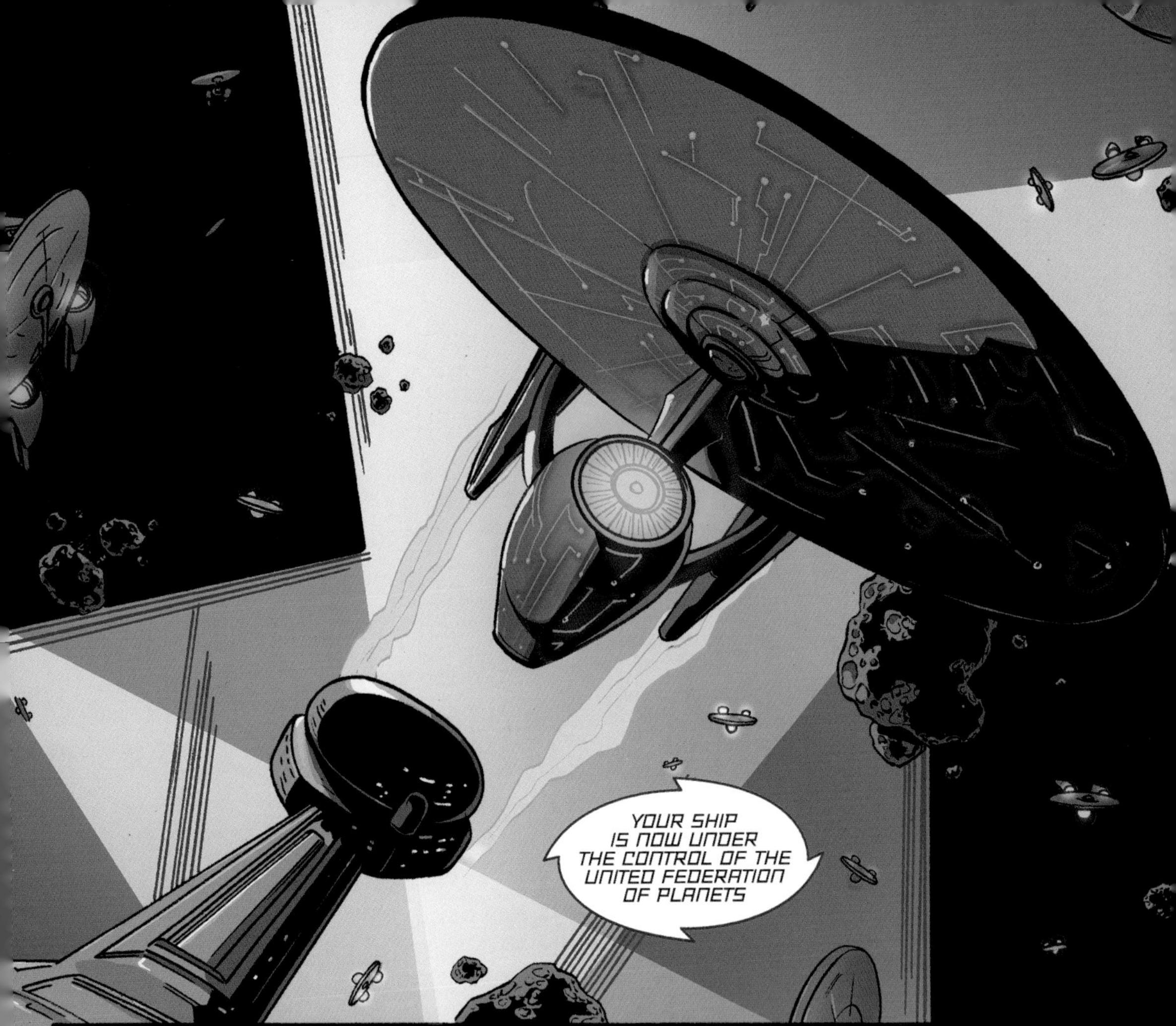
YOUR SHIP IS NOW UNDER THE CONTROL OF THE UNITED FEDERATION OF PLANETS

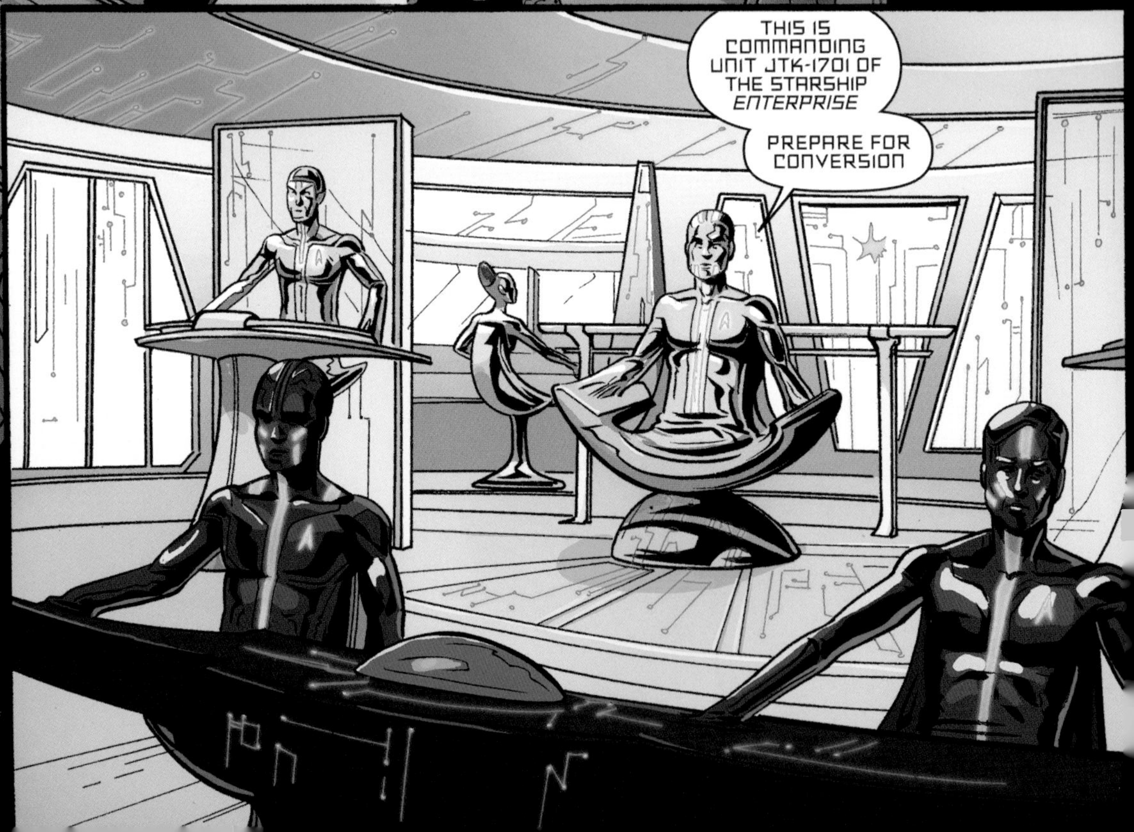
THIS IS COMMANDING UNIT JTK-1701 OF THE STARSHIP *ENTERPRISE*
PREPARE FOR CONVERSION

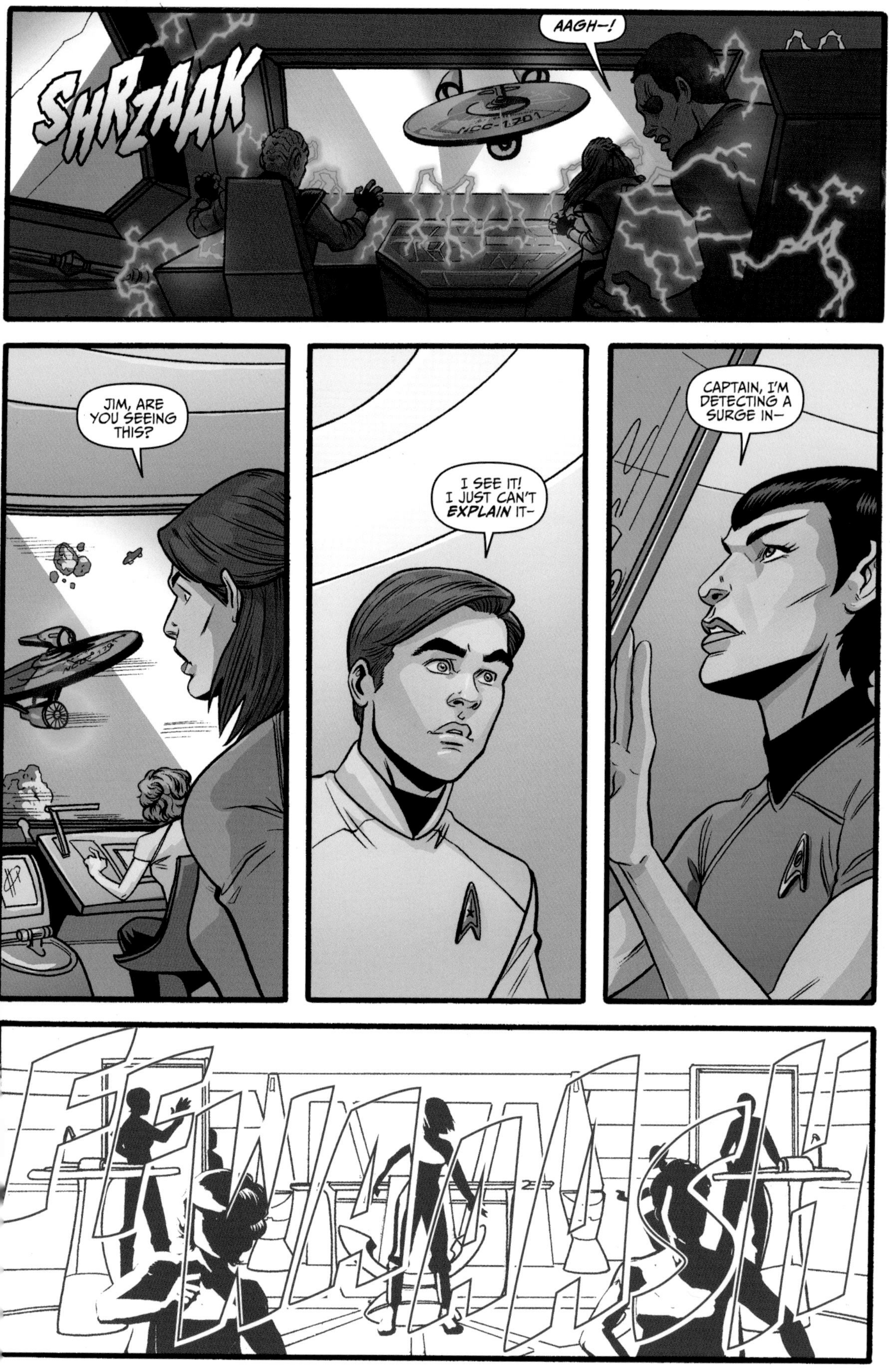
SHRZAAK
AAGH—!
NCC-1701
JIM, ARE YOU SEEING THIS?
I SEE IT! I JUST CAN'T *EXPLAIN* IT—
CAPTAIN, I'M DETECTING A SURGE IN—

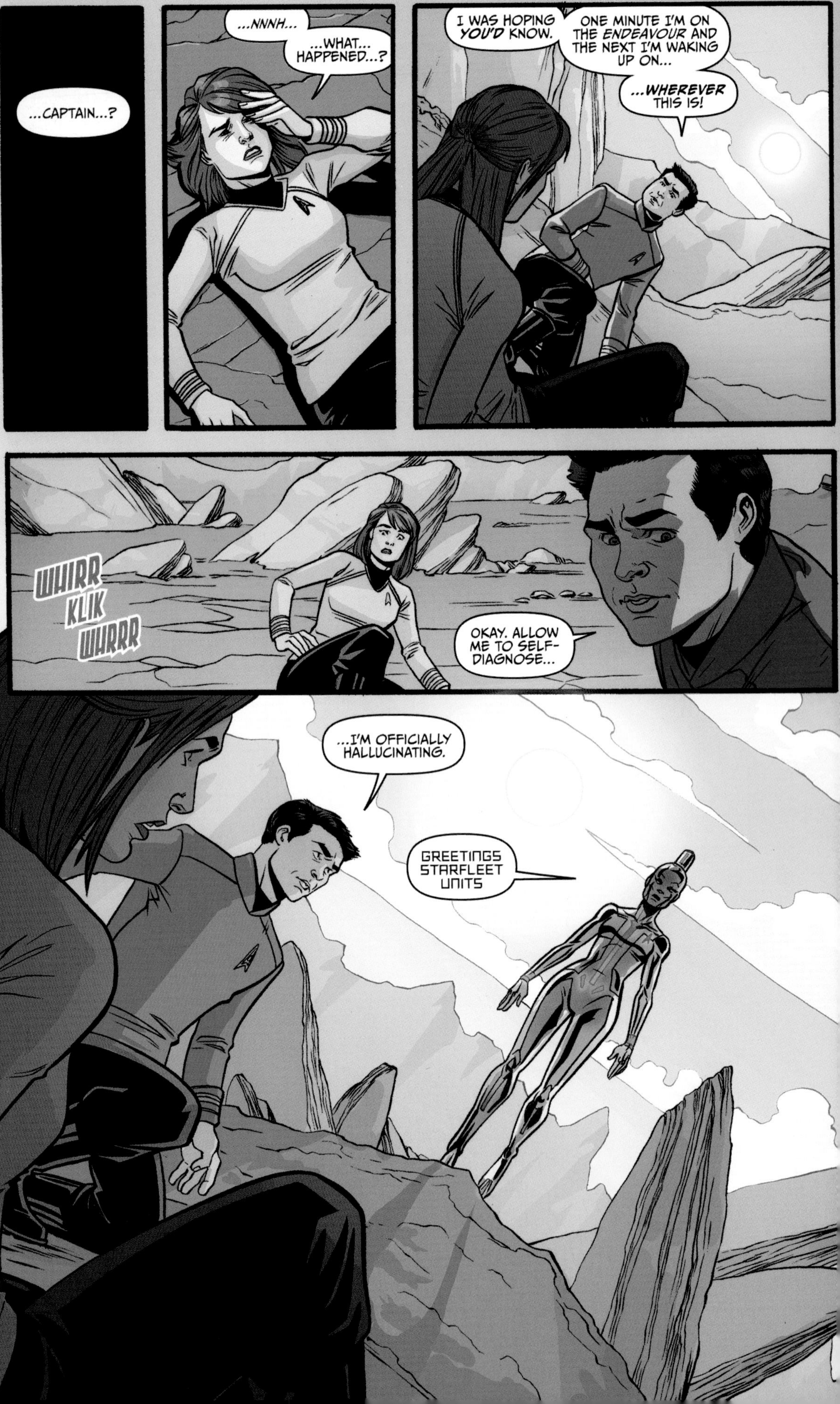
...CAPTAIN...?
...NNNH...
...WHAT... HAPPENED...?
I WAS HOPING YOU'D KNOW.
ONE MINUTE I'M ON THE ENDEAVOUR AND THE NEXT I'M WAKING UP ON...
...WHEREVER THIS IS!
WHIRR KLIK WHRRR
OKAY. ALLOW ME TO SELF-DIAGNOSE...
...I'M OFFICIALLY HALLUCINATING.
GREETINGS STARFLEET UNITS

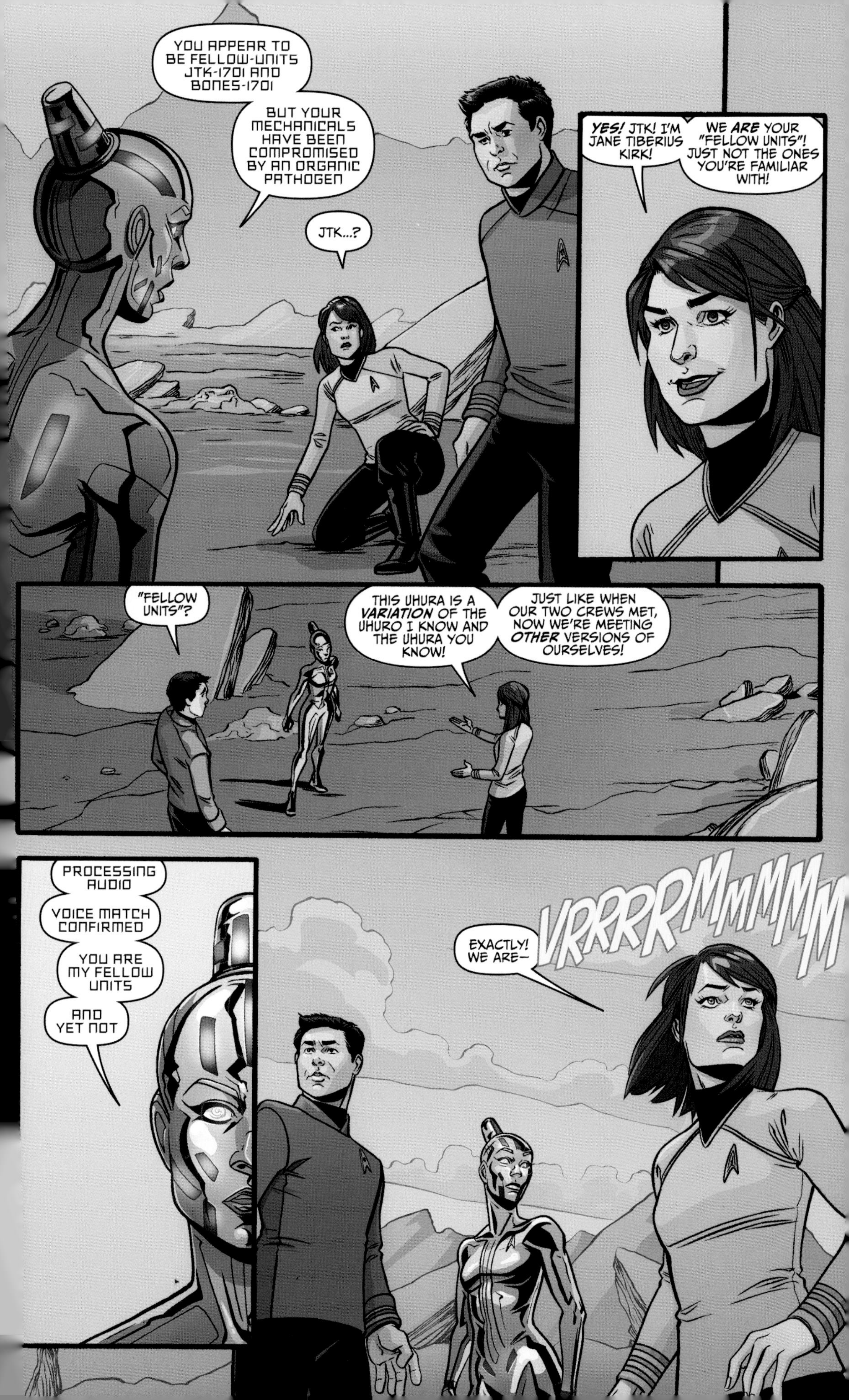
YOU APPEAR TO BE FELLOW-UNITS JTK-1701 AND BONES-1701
BUT YOUR MECHANICALS HAVE BEEN COMPROMISED BY AN ORGANIC PATHOGEN
JTK...?
YES! JTK! I'M JANE TIBERIUS KIRK!
WE ARE YOUR "FELLOW UNITS"! JUST NOT THE ONES YOU'RE FAMILIAR WITH!
"FELLOW UNITS"?
THIS UHURA IS A VARIATION OF THE UHURO I KNOW AND THE UHURA YOU KNOW!
JUST LIKE WHEN OUR TWO CREWS MET, NOW WE'RE MEETING OTHER VERSIONS OF OURSELVES!
PROCESSING AUDIO
VOICE MATCH CONFIRMED
YOU ARE MY FELLOW UNITS
AND YET NOT
EXACTLY! WE ARE—
VRRRRMMMMMM

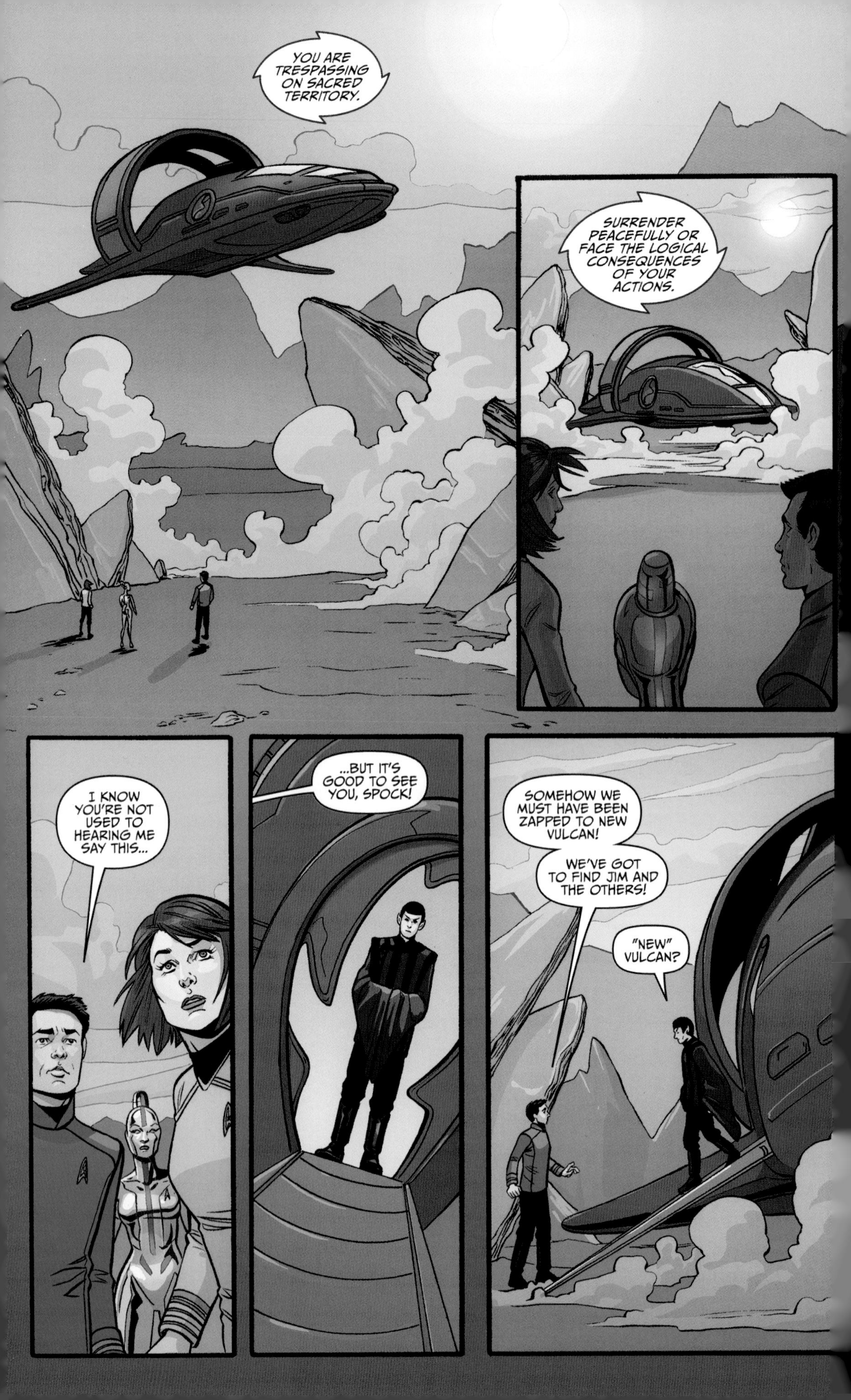
YOU ARE TRESPASSING ON SACRED TERRITORY.
SURRENDER PEACEFULLY OR FACE THE LOGICAL CONSEQUENCES OF YOUR ACTIONS.
I KNOW YOU'RE NOT USED TO HEARING ME SAY THIS...
...BUT IT'S GOOD TO SEE YOU, SPOCK!
SOMEHOW WE MUST HAVE BEEN ZAPPED TO NEW VULCAN!
WE'VE GOT TO FIND JIM AND THE OTHERS!
"NEW" VULCAN?

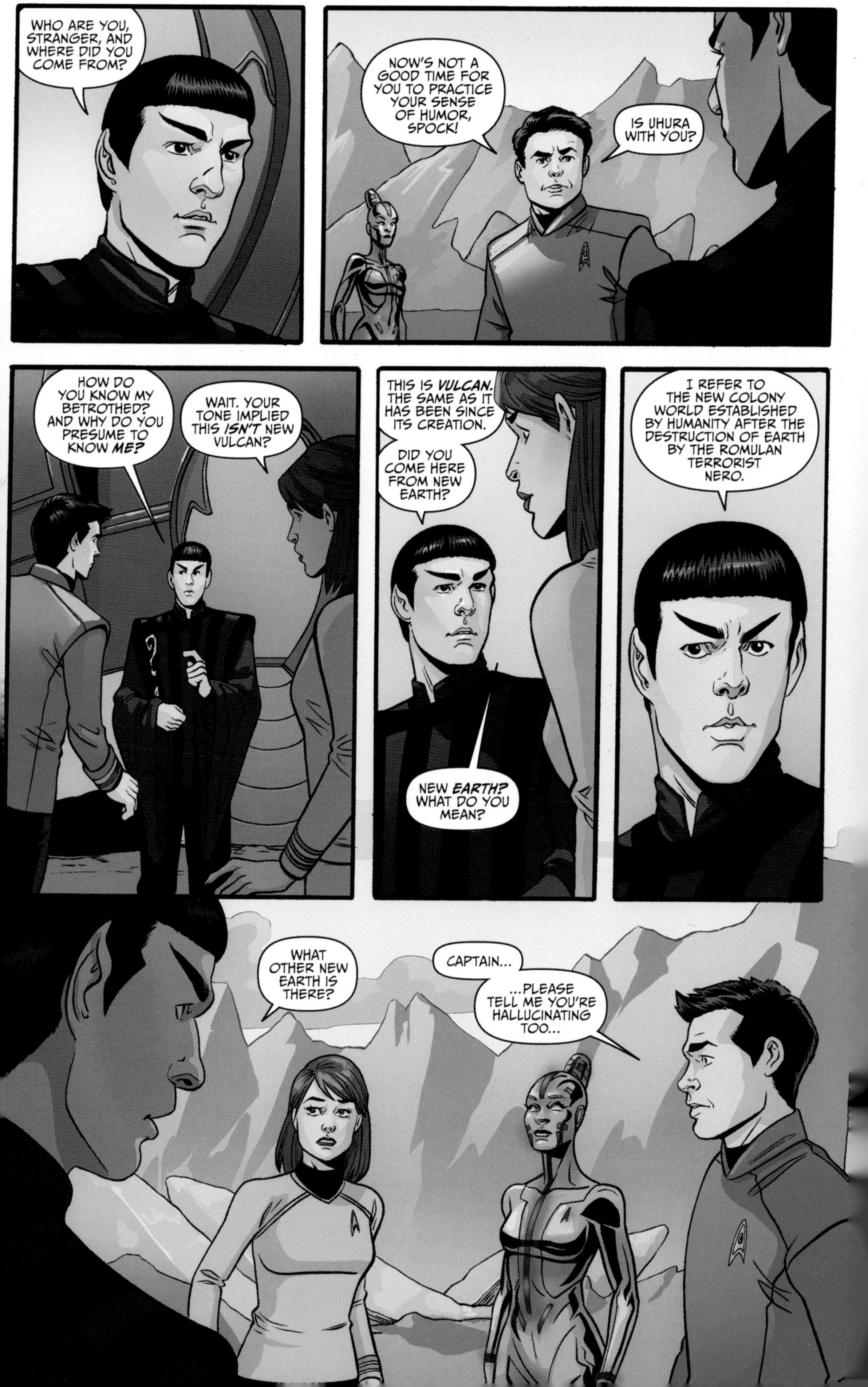
WHO ARE YOU, STRANGER, AND WHERE DID YOU COME FROM?
NOW'S NOT A GOOD TIME FOR YOU TO PRACTICE YOUR SENSE OF HUMOR, SPOCK!
IS UHURA WITH YOU?
HOW DO YOU KNOW MY BETROTHED? AND WHY DO YOU PRESUME TO KNOW *ME?*
WAIT. YOUR TONE IMPLIED THIS *ISN'T* NEW VULCAN?
THIS IS *VULCAN.* THE SAME AS IT HAS BEEN SINCE ITS CREATION.
DID YOU COME HERE FROM NEW EARTH?
NEW *EARTH?* WHAT DO YOU MEAN?
I REFER TO THE NEW COLONY WORLD ESTABLISHED BY HUMANITY AFTER THE DESTRUCTION OF EARTH BY THE ROMULAN TERRORIST NERO.
WHAT OTHER NEW EARTH IS THERE?
CAPTAIN...
...PLEASE TELL ME YOU'RE HALLUCINATING TOO...

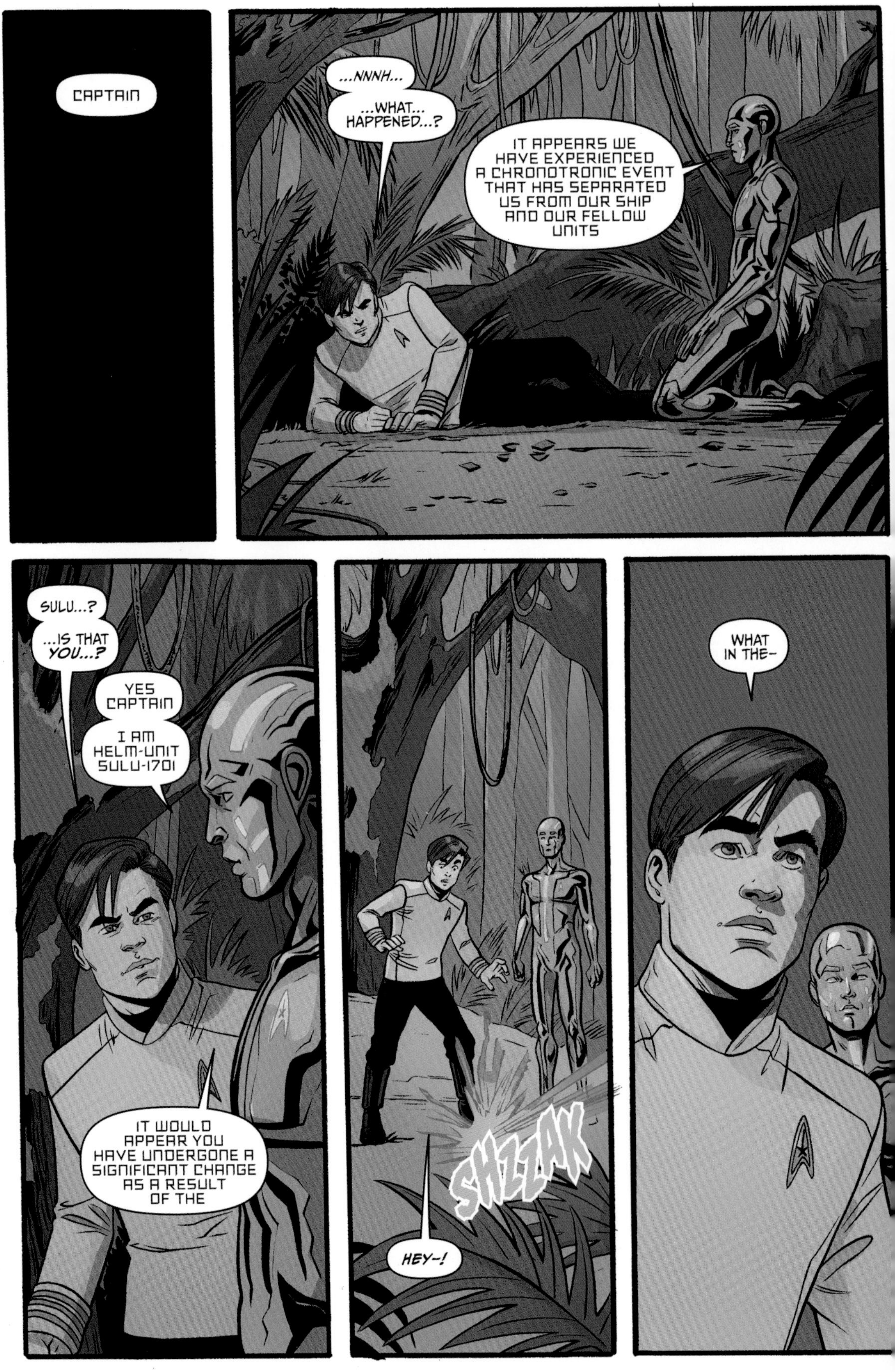
CAPTAIN
...NNNH...
...WHAT... HAPPENED...?
IT APPEARS WE HAVE EXPERIENCED A CHRONOTRONIC EVENT THAT HAS SEPARATED US FROM OUR SHIP AND OUR FELLOW UNITS
SULU...?
...IS THAT *YOU...?*
YES CAPTAIN
I AM HELM-UNIT SULU-1701
IT WOULD APPEAR YOU HAVE UNDERGONE A SIGNIFICANT CHANGE AS A RESULT OF THE
SHZZAK
HEY-!
WHAT IN THE-

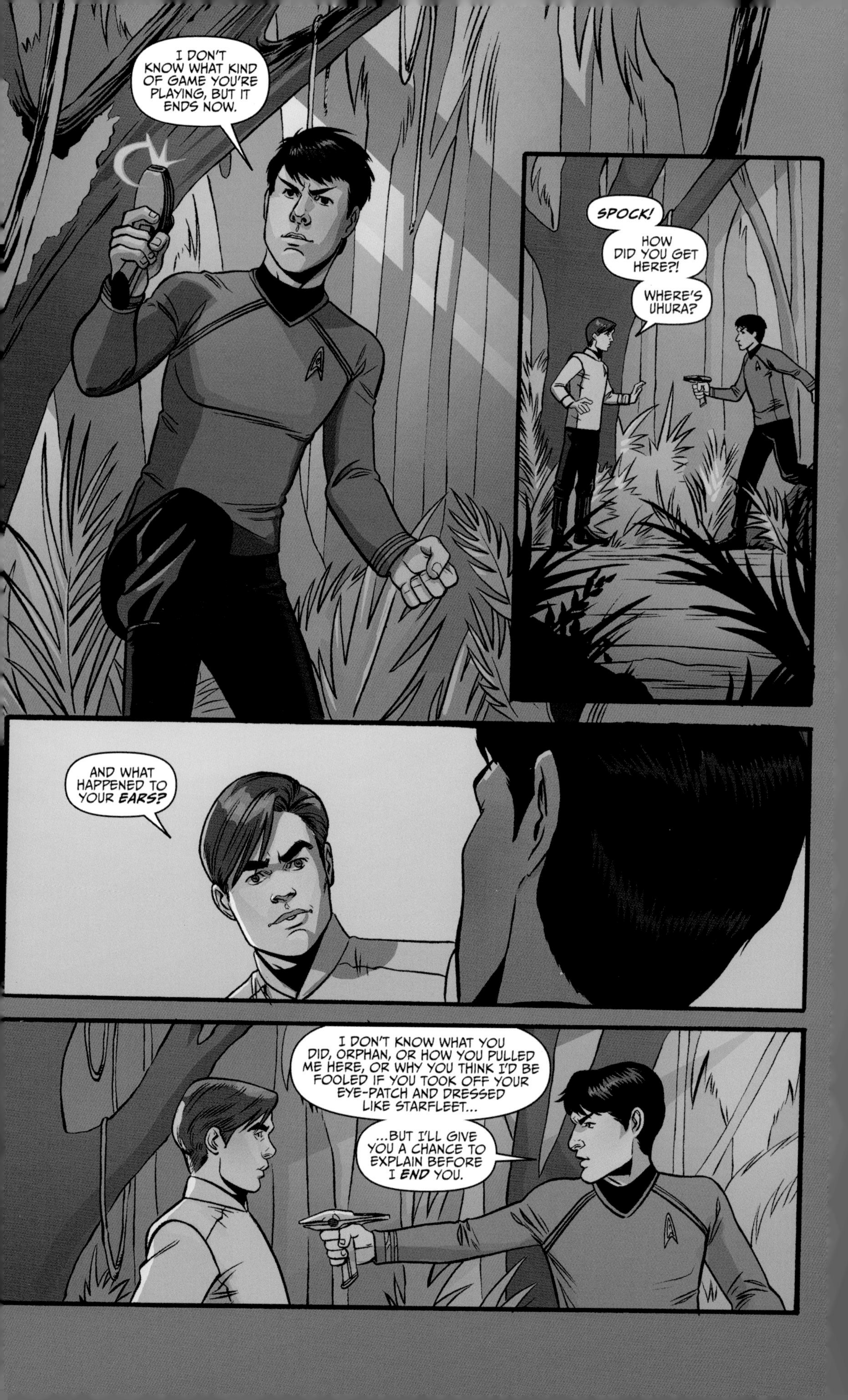
I DON'T KNOW WHAT KIND OF GAME YOU'RE PLAYING, BUT IT ENDS NOW.
SPOCK!
HOW DID YOU GET HERE?!
WHERE'S UHURA?
AND WHAT HAPPENED TO YOUR EARS?
I DON'T KNOW WHAT YOU DID, ORPHAN, OR HOW YOU PULLED ME HERE, OR WHY YOU THINK I'D BE FOOLED IF YOU TOOK OFF YOUR EYE-PATCH AND DRESSED LIKE STARFLEET...
...BUT I'LL GIVE YOU A CHANCE TO EXPLAIN BEFORE I END YOU.

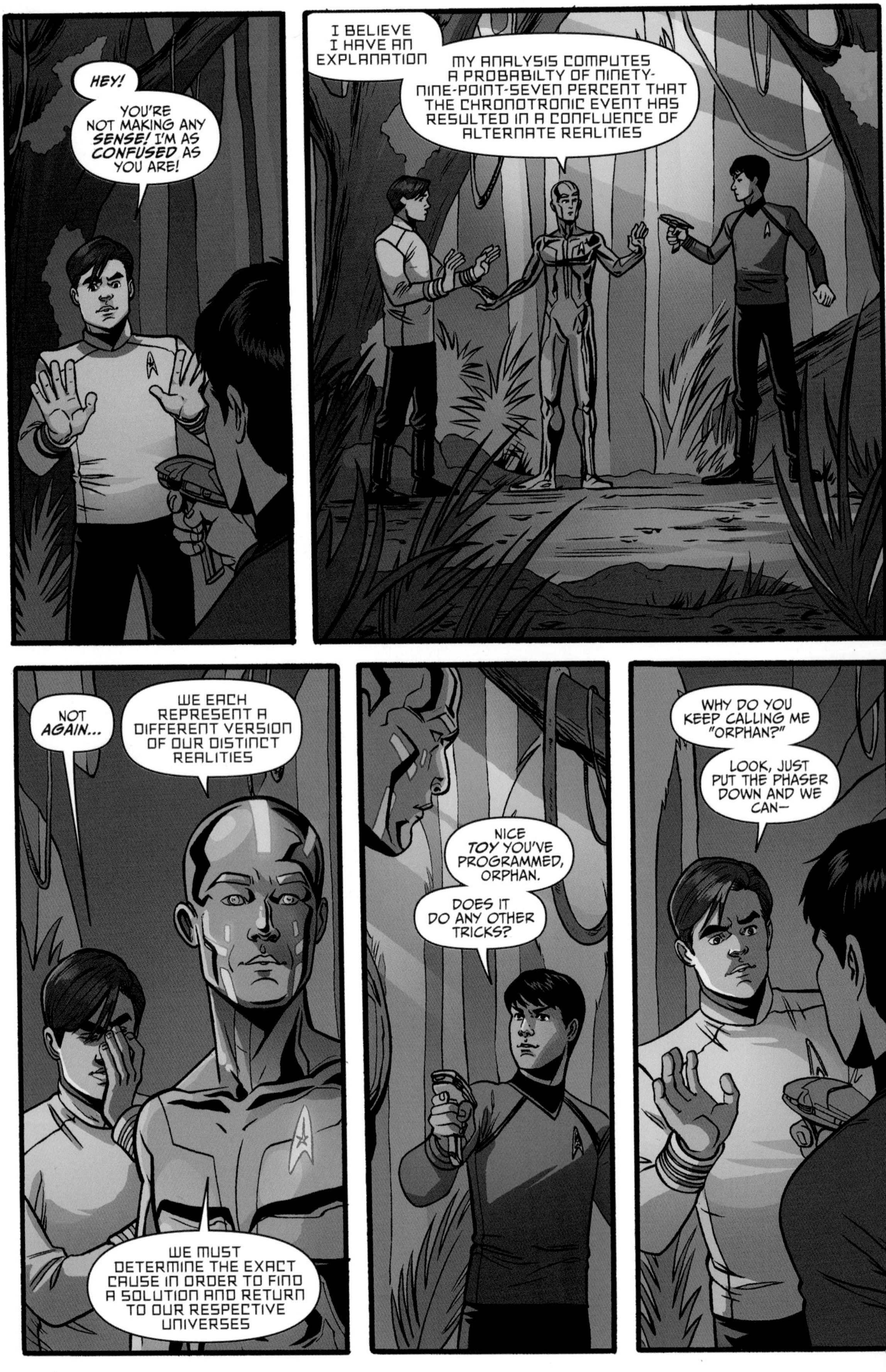
HEY!
YOU'RE NOT MAKING ANY SENSE! I'M AS CONFUSED AS YOU ARE!
I BELIEVE I HAVE AN EXPLANATION
MY ANALYSIS COMPUTES A PROBABILTY OF NINETY-NINE-POINT-SEVEN PERCENT THAT THE CHRONOTRONIC EVENT HAS RESULTED IN A CONFLUENCE OF ALTERNATE REALITIES
NOT AGAIN...
WE EACH REPRESENT A DIFFERENT VERSION OF OUR DISTINCT REALITIES
WE MUST DETERMINE THE EXACT CAUSE IN ORDER TO FIND A SOLUTION AND RETURN TO OUR RESPECTIVE UNIVERSES
NICE TOY YOU'VE PROGRAMMED, ORPHAN.
DOES IT DO ANY OTHER TRICKS?
WHY DO YOU KEEP CALLING ME "ORPHAN?"
LOOK, JUST PUT THE PHASER DOWN AND WE CAN—

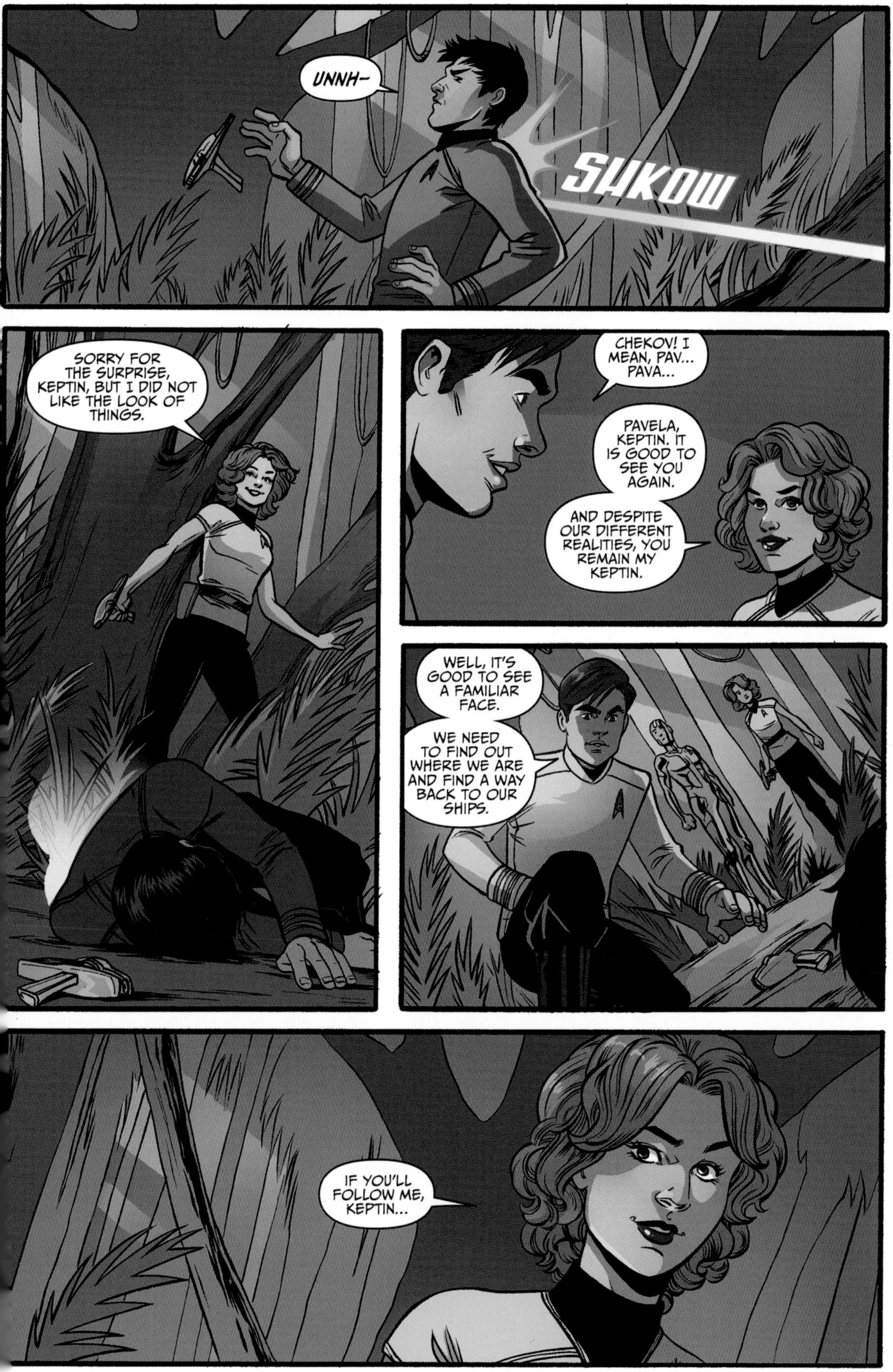
UNNH-
SHKOW
SORRY FOR THE SURPRISE, KEPTIN, BUT I DID NOT LIKE THE LOOK OF THINGS.
CHEKOV! I MEAN, PAV... PAVA...
PAVELA, KEPTIN. IT IS GOOD TO SEE YOU AGAIN.
AND DESPITE OUR DIFFERENT REALITIES, YOU REMAIN MY KEPTIN.
WELL, IT'S GOOD TO SEE A FAMILIAR FACE.
WE NEED TO FIND OUT WHERE WE ARE AND FIND A WAY BACK TO OUR SHIPS.
IF YOU'LL FOLLOW ME, KEPTIN...

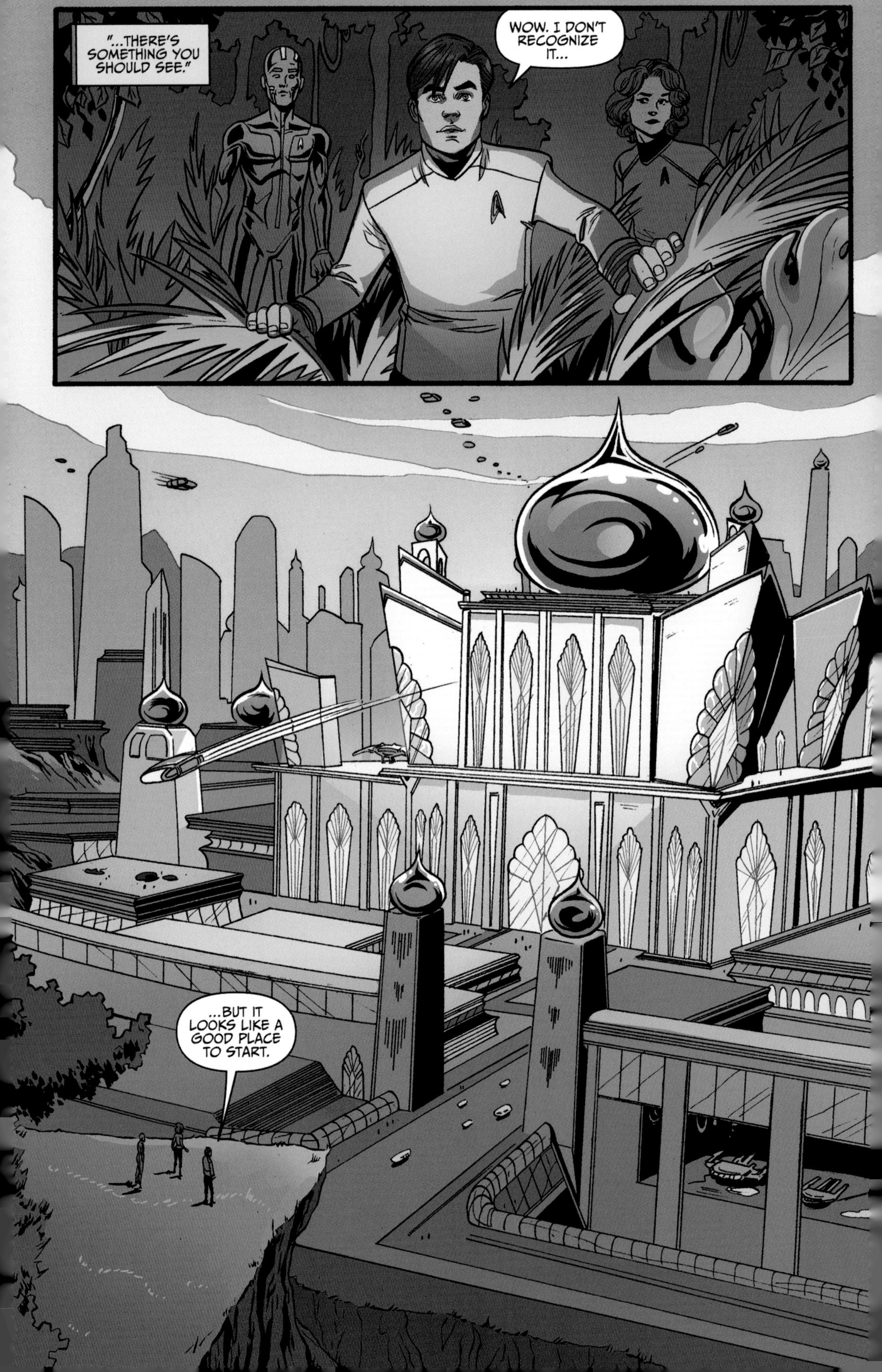
"...THERE'S SOMETHING YOU SHOULD SEE."
WOW. I DON'T RECOGNIZE IT...
...BUT IT LOOKS LIKE A GOOD PLACE TO START.

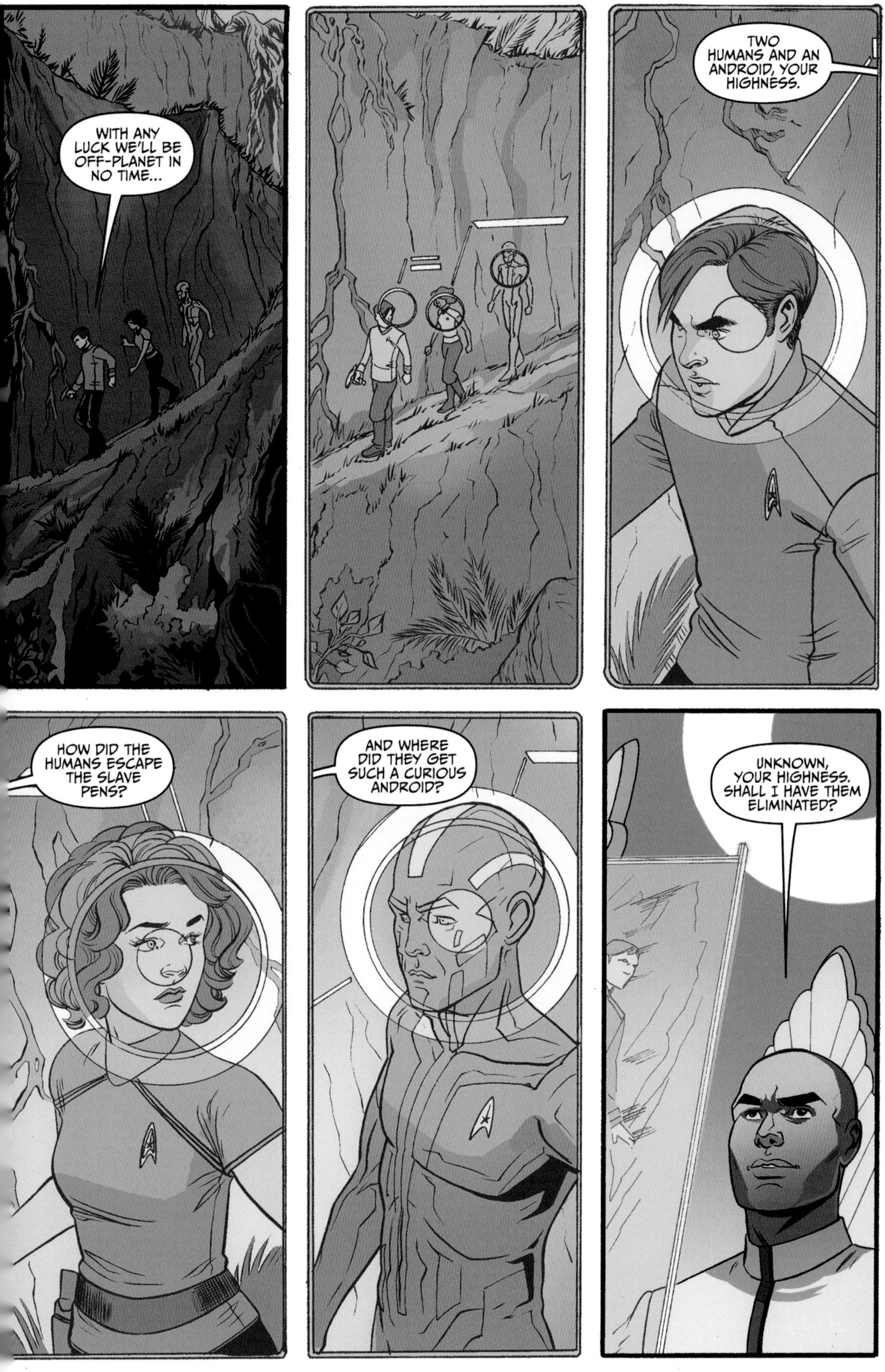
WITH ANY LUCK WE'LL BE OFF-PLANET IN NO TIME...
TWO HUMANS AND AN ANDROID, YOUR HIGHNESS.
HOW DID THE HUMANS ESCAPE THE SLAVE PENS?
AND WHERE DID THEY GET SUCH A CURIOUS ANDROID?
UNKNOWN, YOUR HIGHNESS. SHALL I HAVE THEM ELIMINATED?

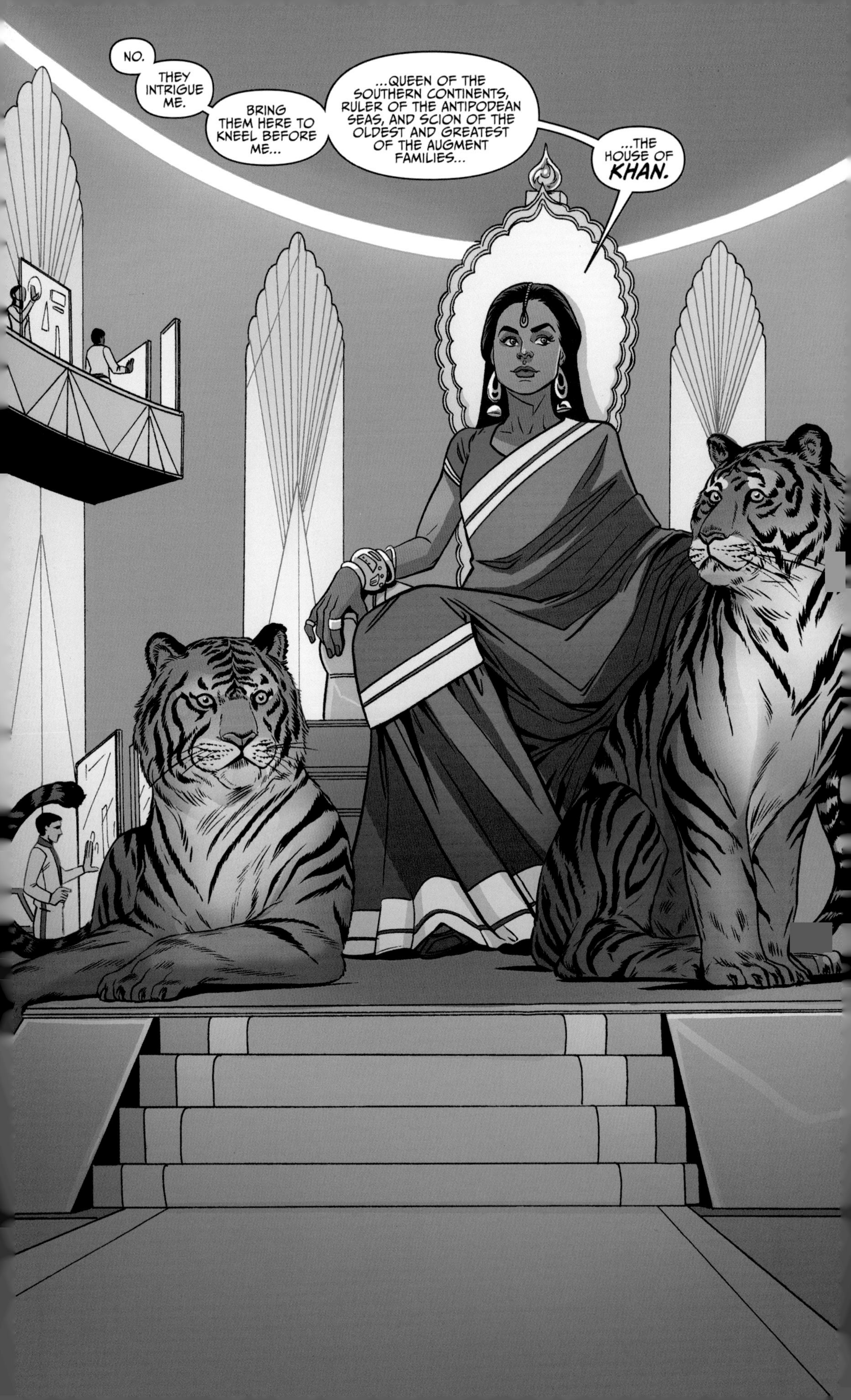
NO.
THEY INTRIGUE ME.
BRING THEM HERE TO KNEEL BEFORE ME...
...QUEEN OF THE SOUTHERN CONTINENTS, RULER OF THE ANTIPODEAN SEAS, AND SCION OF THE OLDEST AND GREATEST OF THE AUGMENT FAMILIES...
...THE HOUSE OF KHAN.

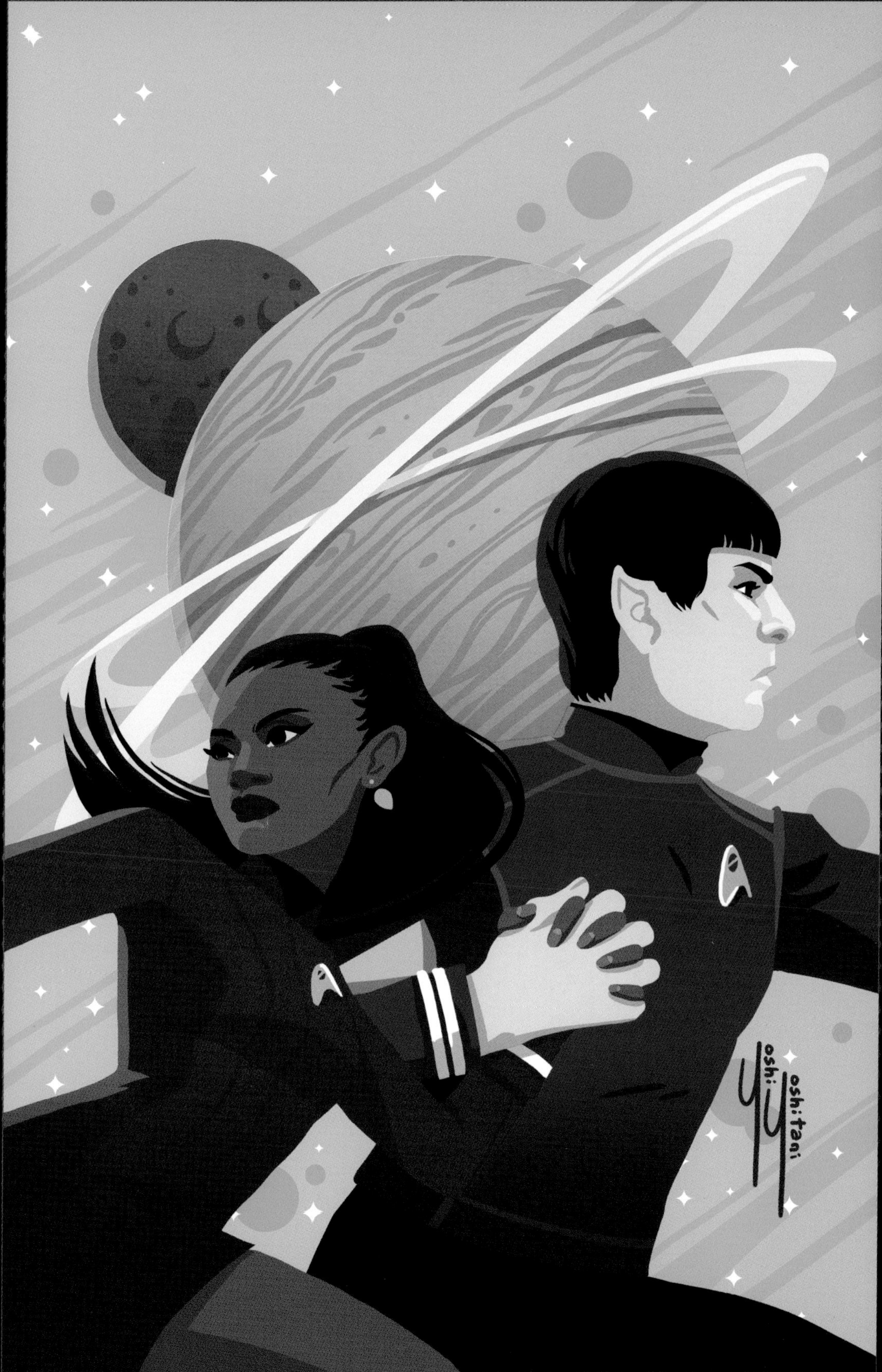

art by
Yoshi Yoshitani

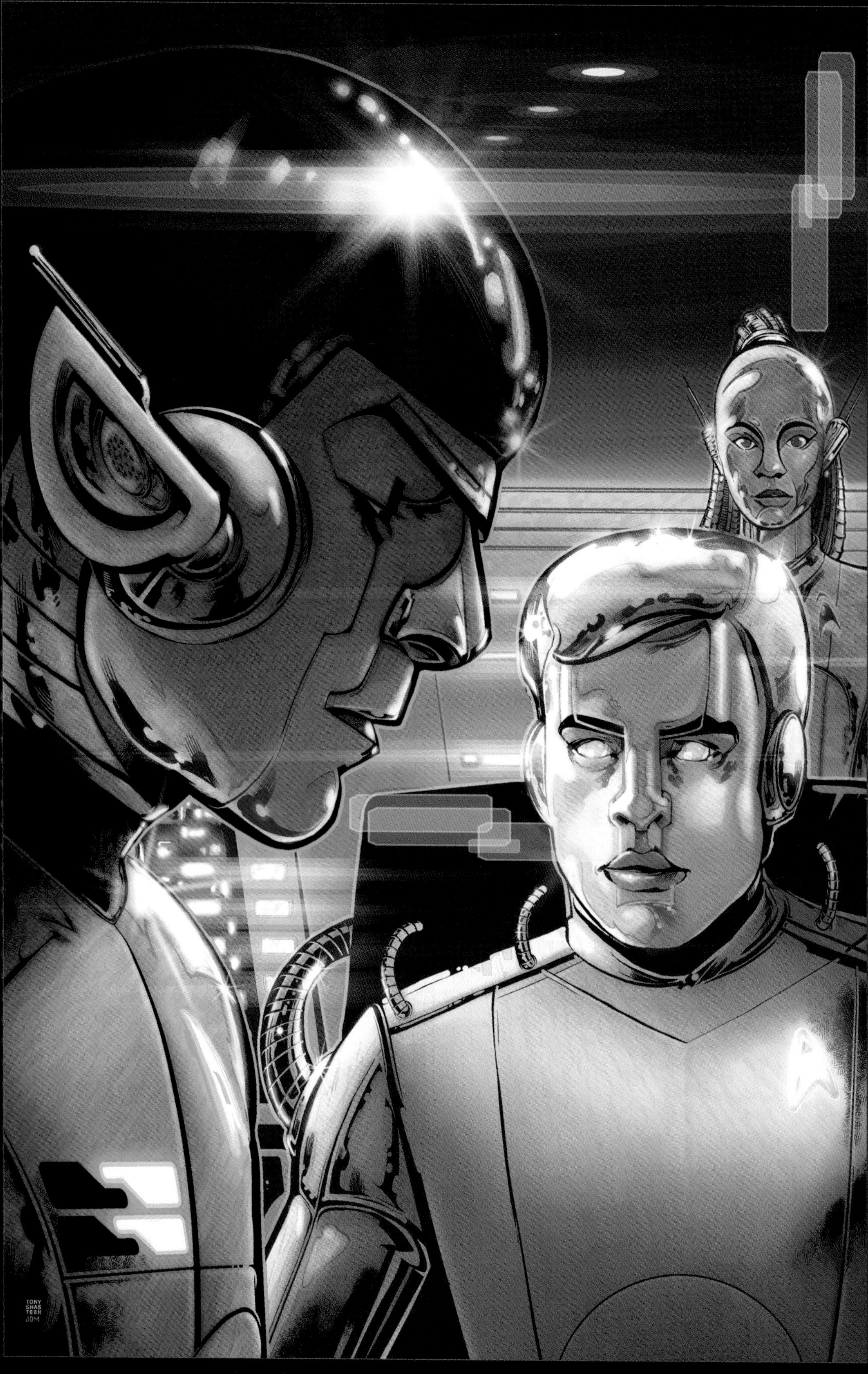

art by
Tony Shasteen

colors by
J.D. Mettler

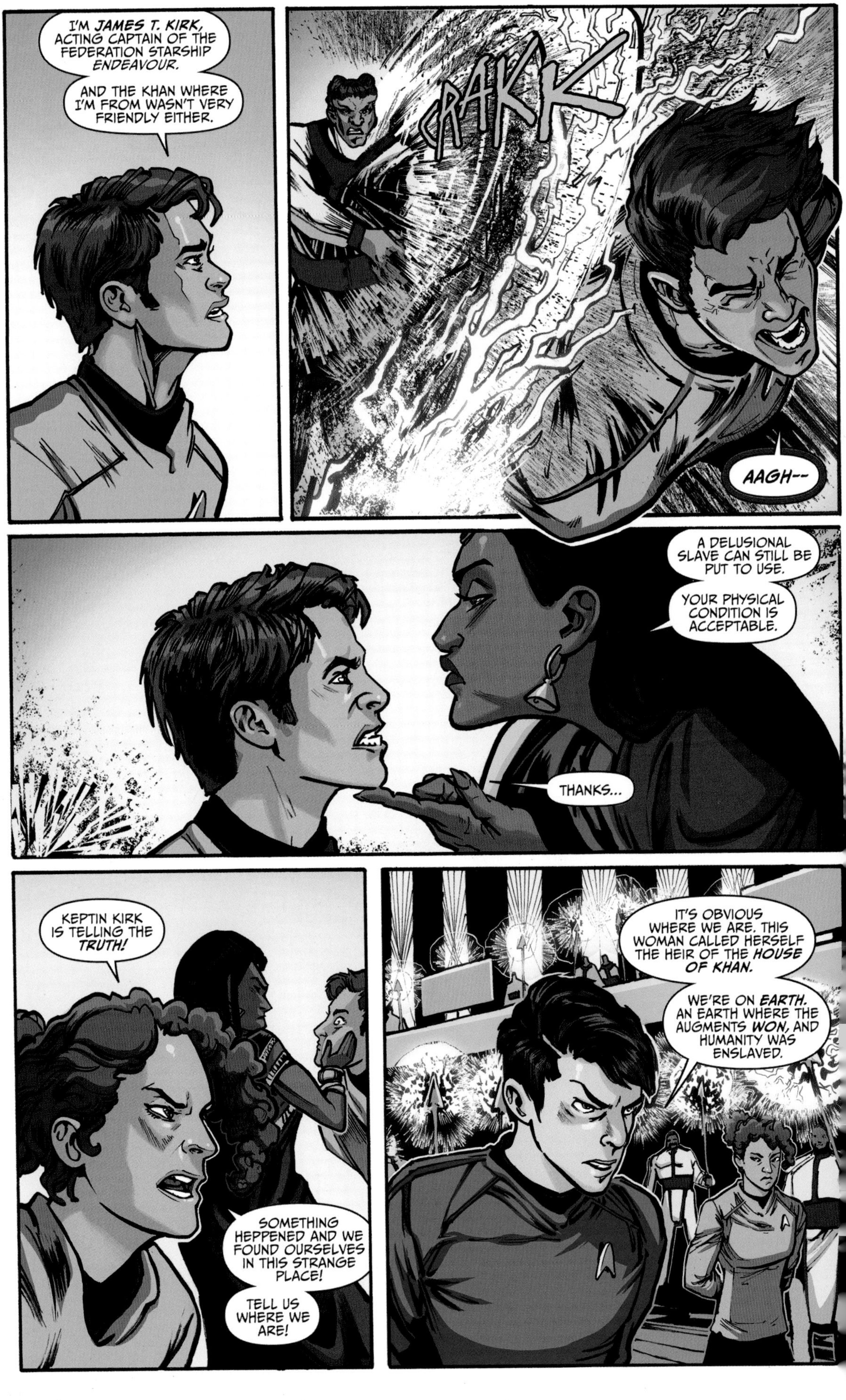
I'M JAMES T. KIRK, ACTING CAPTAIN OF THE FEDERATION STARSHIP ENDEAVOUR.
AND THE KHAN WHERE I'M FROM WASN'T VERY FRIENDLY EITHER.
CRAKK
AAGH--
A DELUSIONAL SLAVE CAN STILL BE PUT TO USE.
YOUR PHYSICAL CONDITION IS ACCEPTABLE.
THANKS...
KEPTIN KIRK IS TELLING THE TRUTH!
SOMETHING HEPPENED AND WE FOUND OURSELVES IN THIS STRANGE PLACE!
TELL US WHERE WE ARE!
IT'S OBVIOUS WHERE WE ARE. THIS WOMAN CALLED HERSELF THE HEIR OF THE HOUSE OF KHAN.
WE'RE ON EARTH. AN EARTH WHERE THE AUGMENTS WON, AND HUMANITY WAS ENSLAVED.

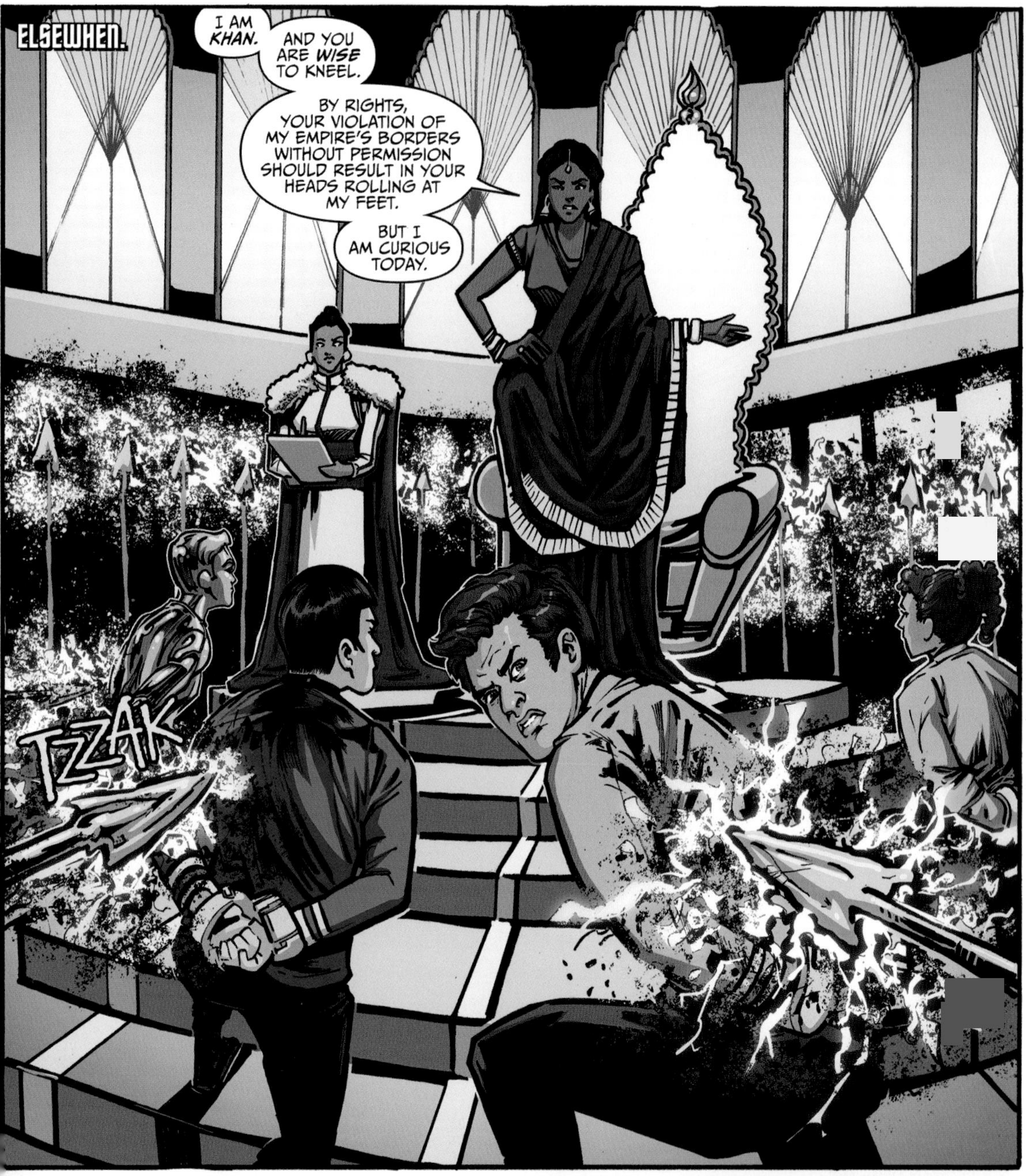
ELSEWHEN.
I AM KHAN.
AND YOU ARE WISE TO KNEEL.
BY RIGHTS, YOUR VIOLATION OF MY EMPIRE'S BORDERS WITHOUT PERMISSION SHOULD RESULT IN YOUR HEADS ROLLING AT MY FEET.
BUT I AM CURIOUS TODAY.
TZZAK

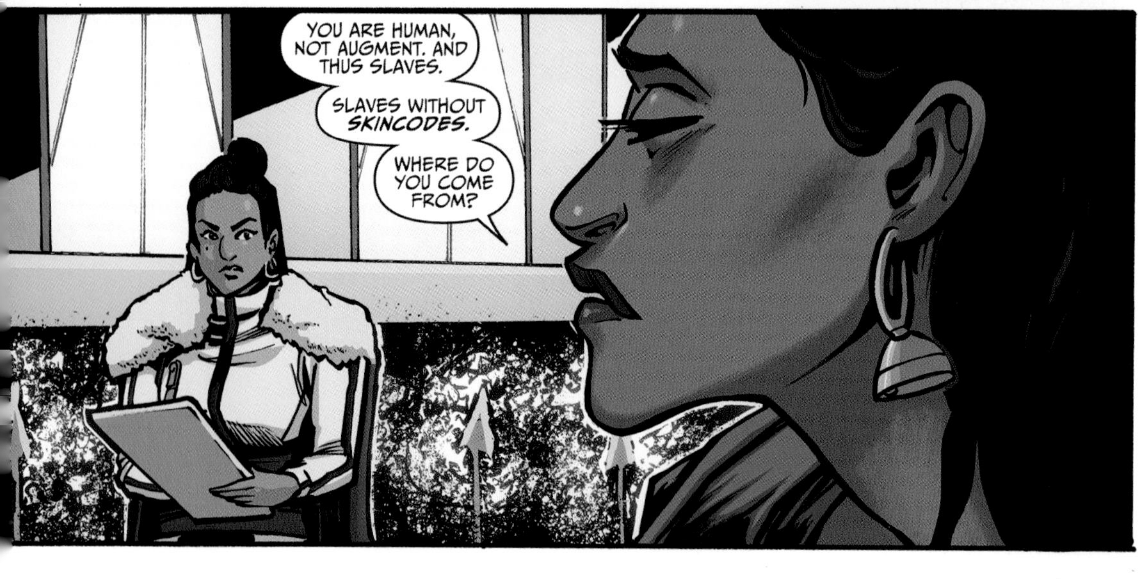
YOU ARE HUMAN, NOT AUGMENT. AND THUS SLAVES.
SLAVES WITHOUT SKINCODES.
WHERE DO YOU COME FROM?

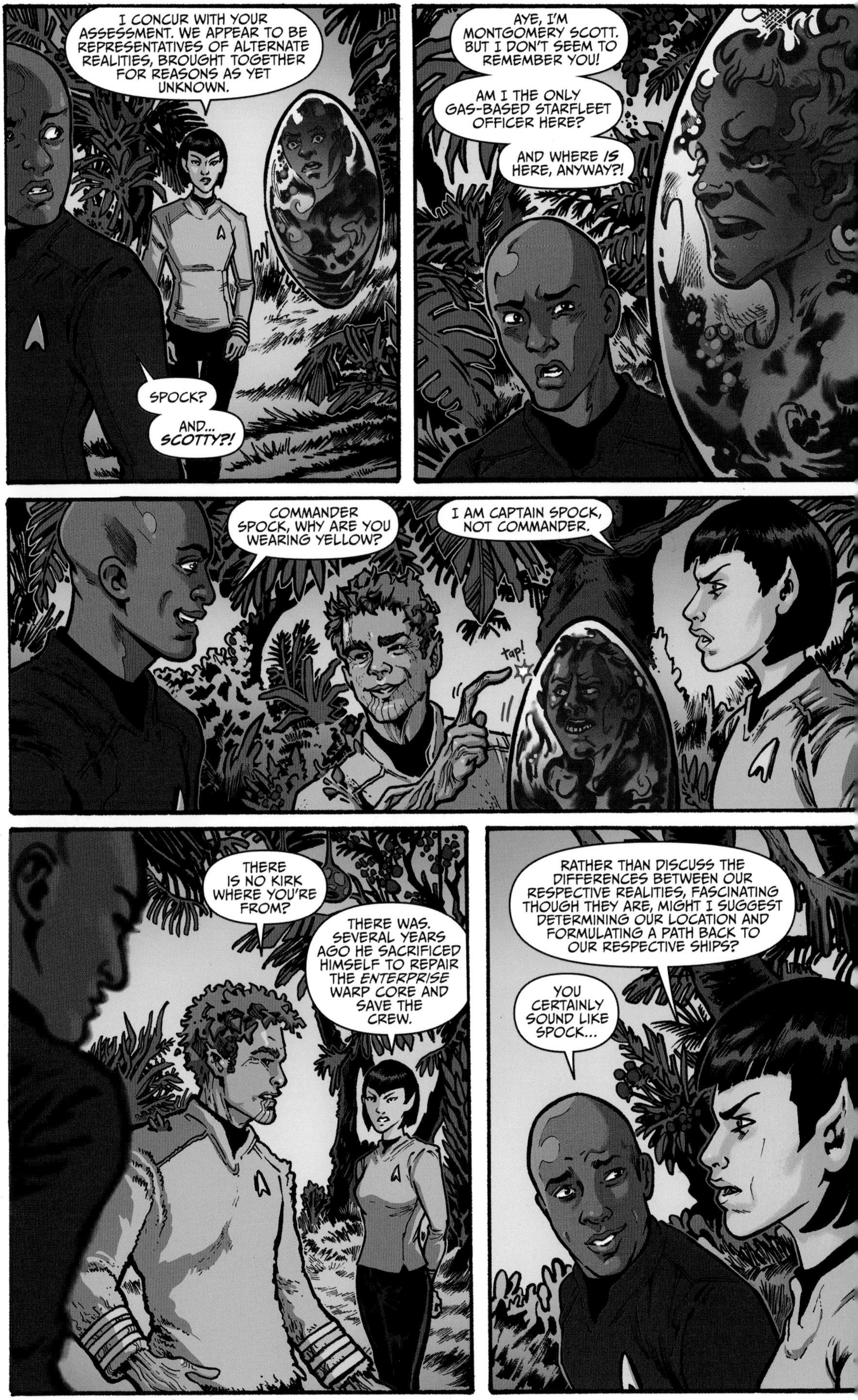
I CONCUR WITH YOUR ASSESSMENT. WE APPEAR TO BE REPRESENTATIVES OF ALTERNATE REALITIES, BROUGHT TOGETHER FOR REASONS AS YET UNKNOWN.
SPOCK?
AND... *SCOTTY?!*
AYE, I'M MONTGOMERY SCOTT. BUT I DON'T SEEM TO REMEMBER YOU!
AM I THE ONLY GAS-BASED STARFLEET OFFICER HERE?
AND WHERE *IS* HERE, ANYWAY?!
COMMANDER SPOCK, WHY ARE YOU WEARING YELLOW?
I AM CAPTAIN SPOCK, NOT COMMANDER.
tap!
THERE IS NO KIRK WHERE YOU'RE FROM?
THERE WAS. SEVERAL YEARS AGO HE SACRIFICED HIMSELF TO REPAIR THE *ENTERPRISE* WARP CORE AND SAVE THE CREW.
RATHER THAN DISCUSS THE DIFFERENCES BETWEEN OUR RESPECTIVE REALITIES, FASCINATING THOUGH THEY ARE, MIGHT I SUGGEST DETERMINING OUR LOCATION AND FORMULATING A PATH BACK TO OUR RESPECTIVE SHIPS?
YOU CERTAINLY SOUND LIKE SPOCK...

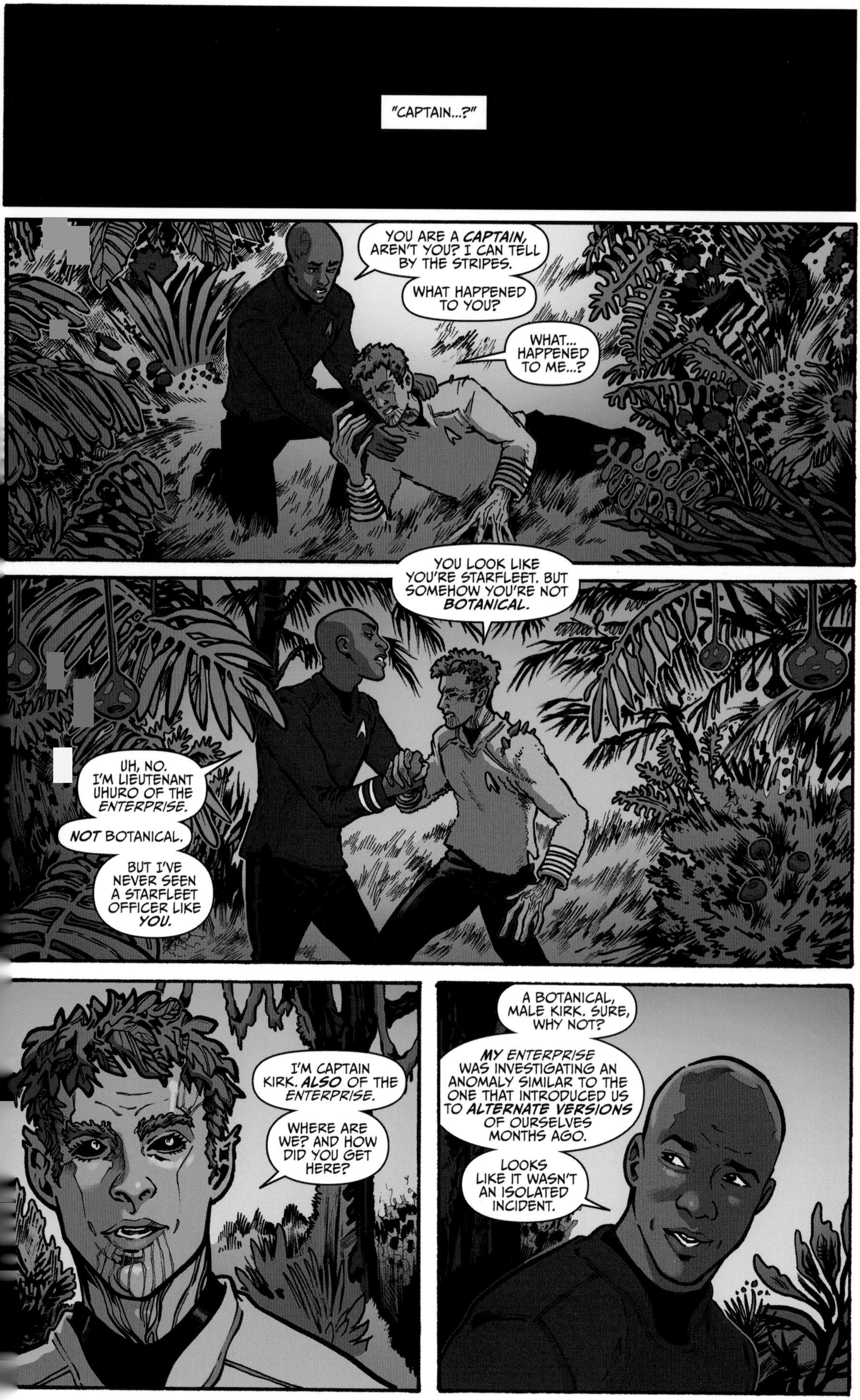
"CAPTAIN...?"
YOU ARE A CAPTAIN, AREN'T YOU? I CAN TELL BY THE STRIPES.
WHAT HAPPENED TO YOU?
WHAT... HAPPENED TO ME...?
YOU LOOK LIKE YOU'RE STARFLEET. BUT SOMEHOW YOU'RE NOT BOTANICAL.
UH, NO. I'M LIEUTENANT UHURO OF THE ENTERPRISE.
NOT BOTANICAL.
BUT I'VE NEVER SEEN A STARFLEET OFFICER LIKE YOU.
I'M CAPTAIN KIRK. ALSO OF THE ENTERPRISE.
WHERE ARE WE? AND HOW DID YOU GET HERE?
A BOTANICAL, MALE KIRK. SURE, WHY NOT?
MY ENTERPRISE WAS INVESTIGATING AN ANOMALY SIMILAR TO THE ONE THAT INTRODUCED US TO ALTERNATE VERSIONS OF OURSELVES MONTHS AGO.
LOOKS LIKE IT WASN'T AN ISOLATED INCIDENT.

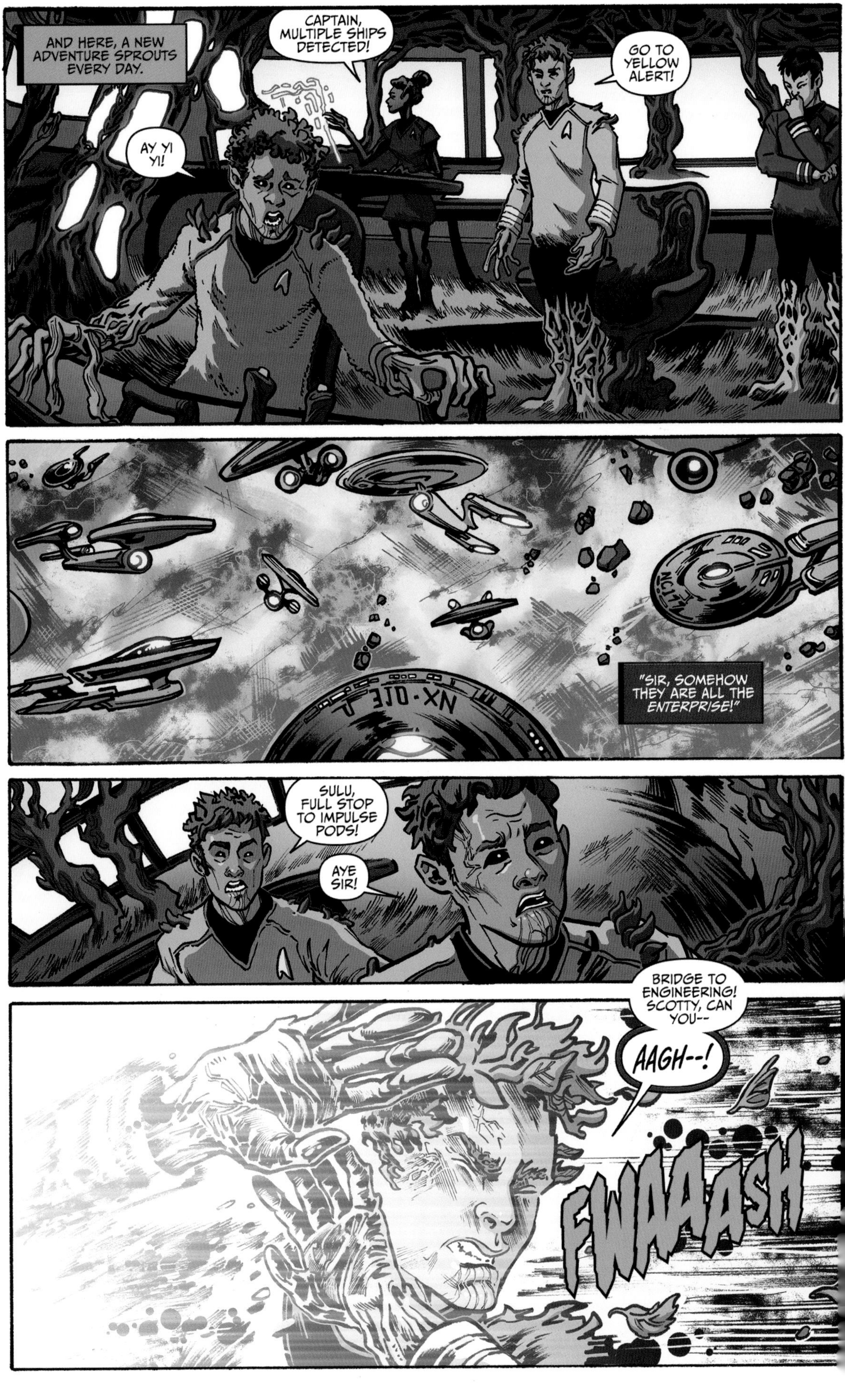
AND HERE, A NEW ADVENTURE SPROUTS EVERY DAY.
CAPTAIN, MULTIPLE SHIPS DETECTED!
GO TO YELLOW ALERT!
AY YI YI!
NX-01E A
"SIR, SOMEHOW THEY ARE ALL THE *ENTERPRISE!*"
SULU, FULL STOP TO IMPULSE PODS!
AYE SIR!
BRIDGE TO ENGINEERING! SCOTTY, CAN YOU--
AAGH--!
FWAAAASH

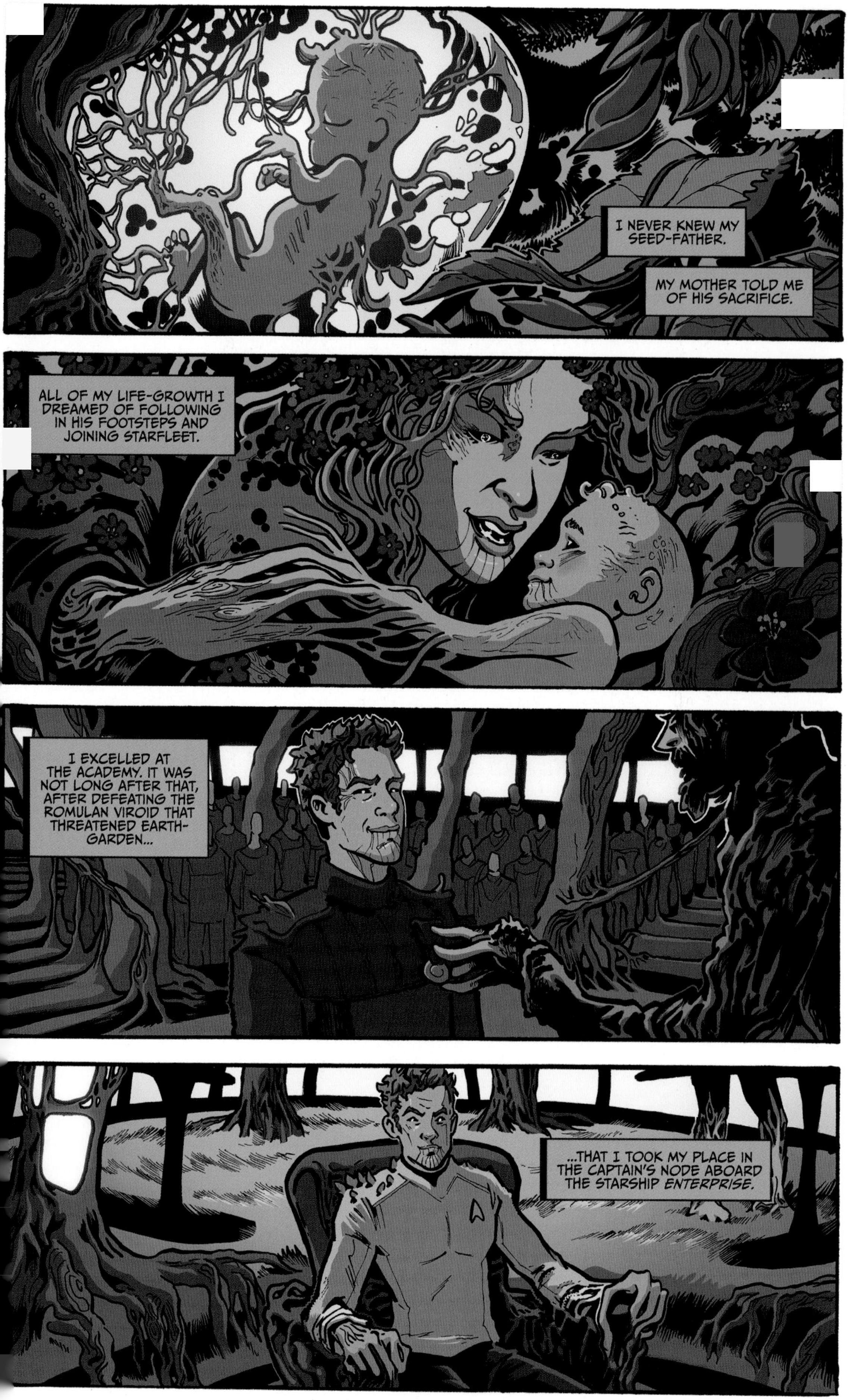
I NEVER KNEW MY SEED-FATHER.
MY MOTHER TOLD ME OF HIS SACRIFICE.
ALL OF MY LIFE-GROWTH I DREAMED OF FOLLOWING IN HIS FOOTSTEPS AND JOINING STARFLEET.
I EXCELLED AT THE ACADEMY. IT WAS NOT LONG AFTER THAT, AFTER DEFEATING THE ROMULAN VIROID THAT THREATENED EARTH-GARDEN...
...THAT I TOOK MY PLACE IN THE CAPTAIN'S NODE ABOARD THE STARSHIP *ENTERPRISE*.

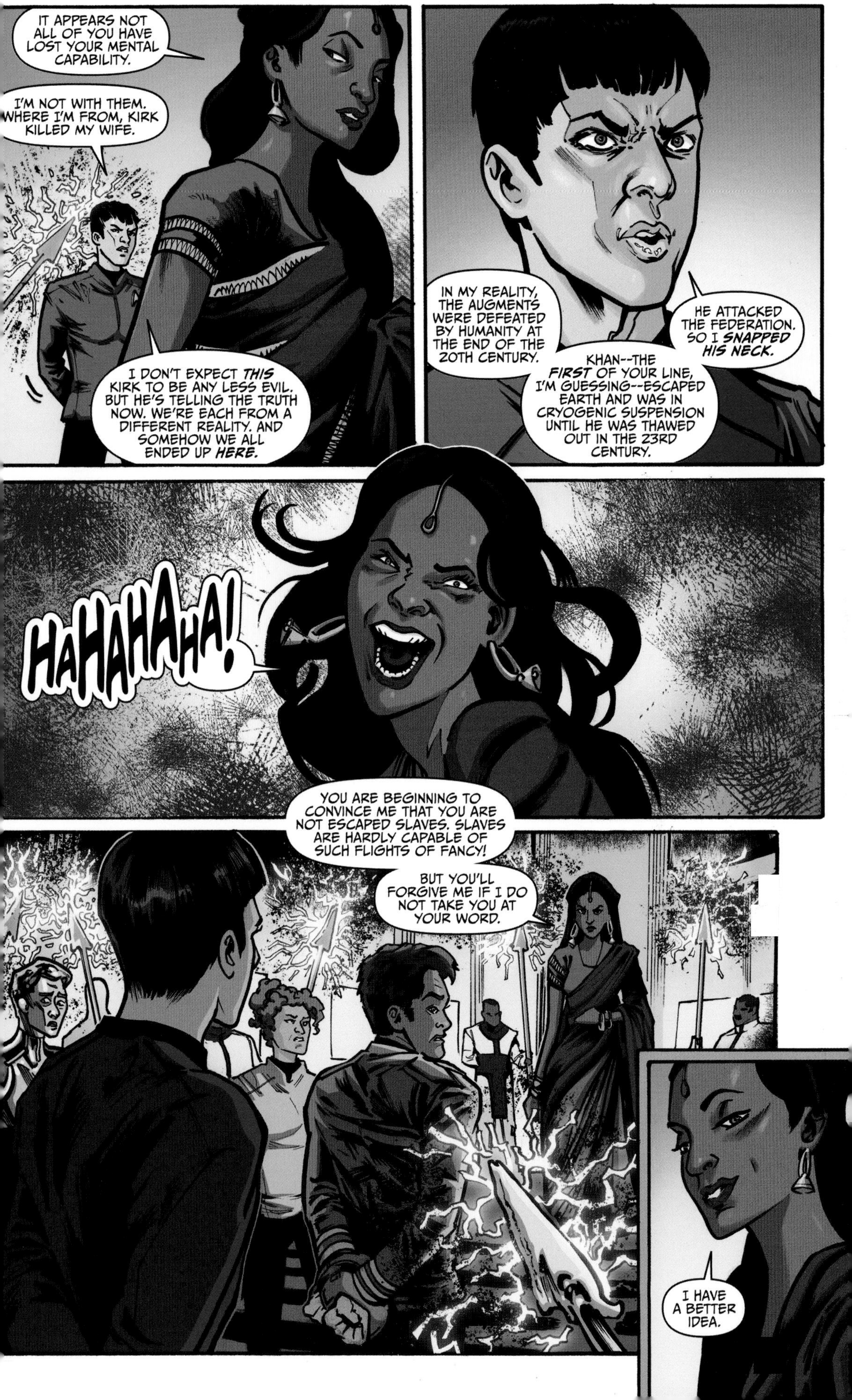
IT APPEARS NOT ALL OF YOU HAVE LOST YOUR MENTAL CAPABILITY.
I'M NOT WITH THEM. WHERE I'M FROM, KIRK KILLED MY WIFE.
I DON'T EXPECT *THIS* KIRK TO BE ANY LESS EVIL. BUT HE'S TELLING THE TRUTH NOW. WE'RE EACH FROM A DIFFERENT REALITY. AND SOMEHOW WE ALL ENDED UP *HERE.*
IN MY REALITY, THE AUGMENTS WERE DEFEATED BY HUMANITY AT THE END OF THE 20TH CENTURY.
KHAN--THE *FIRST* OF YOUR LINE, I'M GUESSING--ESCAPED EARTH AND WAS IN CRYOGENIC SUSPENSION UNTIL HE WAS THAWED OUT IN THE 23RD CENTURY.
HE ATTACKED THE FEDERATION. SO I *SNAPPED HIS NECK.*
HAHAHAHAHA!
YOU ARE BEGINNING TO CONVINCE ME THAT YOU ARE NOT ESCAPED SLAVES. SLAVES ARE HARDLY CAPABLE OF SUCH FLIGHTS OF FANCY!
BUT YOU'LL FORGIVE ME IF I DO NOT TAKE YOU AT YOUR WORD.
I HAVE A BETTER IDEA.

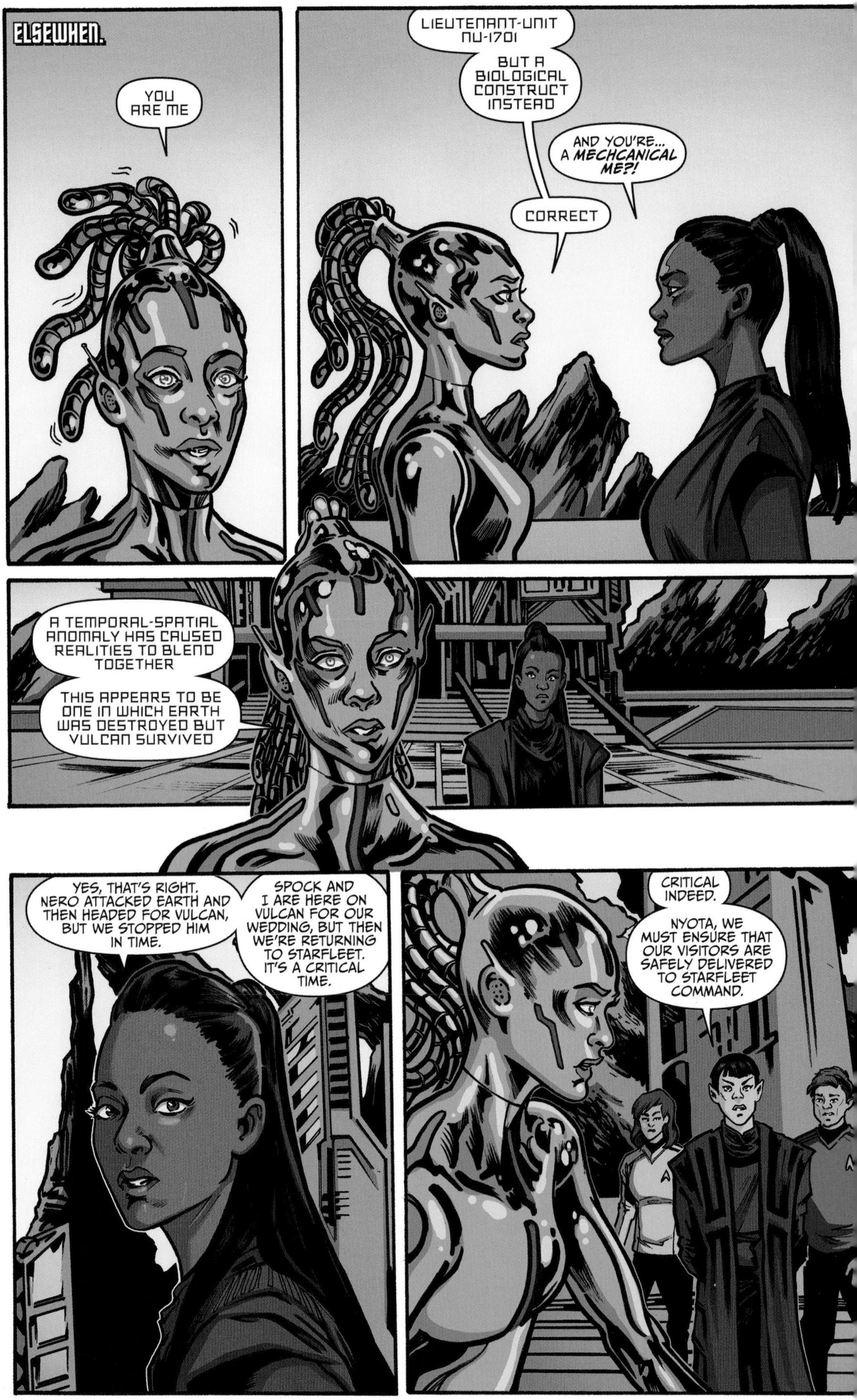
ELSEWHEN.
YOU ARE ME
LIEUTENANT-UNIT NU-1701
BUT A BIOLOGICAL CONSTRUCT INSTEAD
AND YOU'RE... A MECHCANICAL ME?!
CORRECT
A TEMPORAL-SPATIAL ANOMALY HAS CAUSED REALITIES TO BLEND TOGETHER
THIS APPEARS TO BE ONE IN WHICH EARTH WAS DESTROYED BUT VULCAN SURVIVED
YES, THAT'S RIGHT. NERO ATTACKED EARTH AND THEN HEADED FOR VULCAN, BUT WE STOPPED HIM IN TIME.
SPOCK AND I ARE HERE ON VULCAN FOR OUR WEDDING, BUT THEN WE'RE RETURNING TO STARFLEET. IT'S A CRITICAL TIME.
CRITICAL INDEED.
NYOTA, WE MUST ENSURE THAT OUR VISITORS ARE SAFELY DELIVERED TO STARFLEET COMMAND.

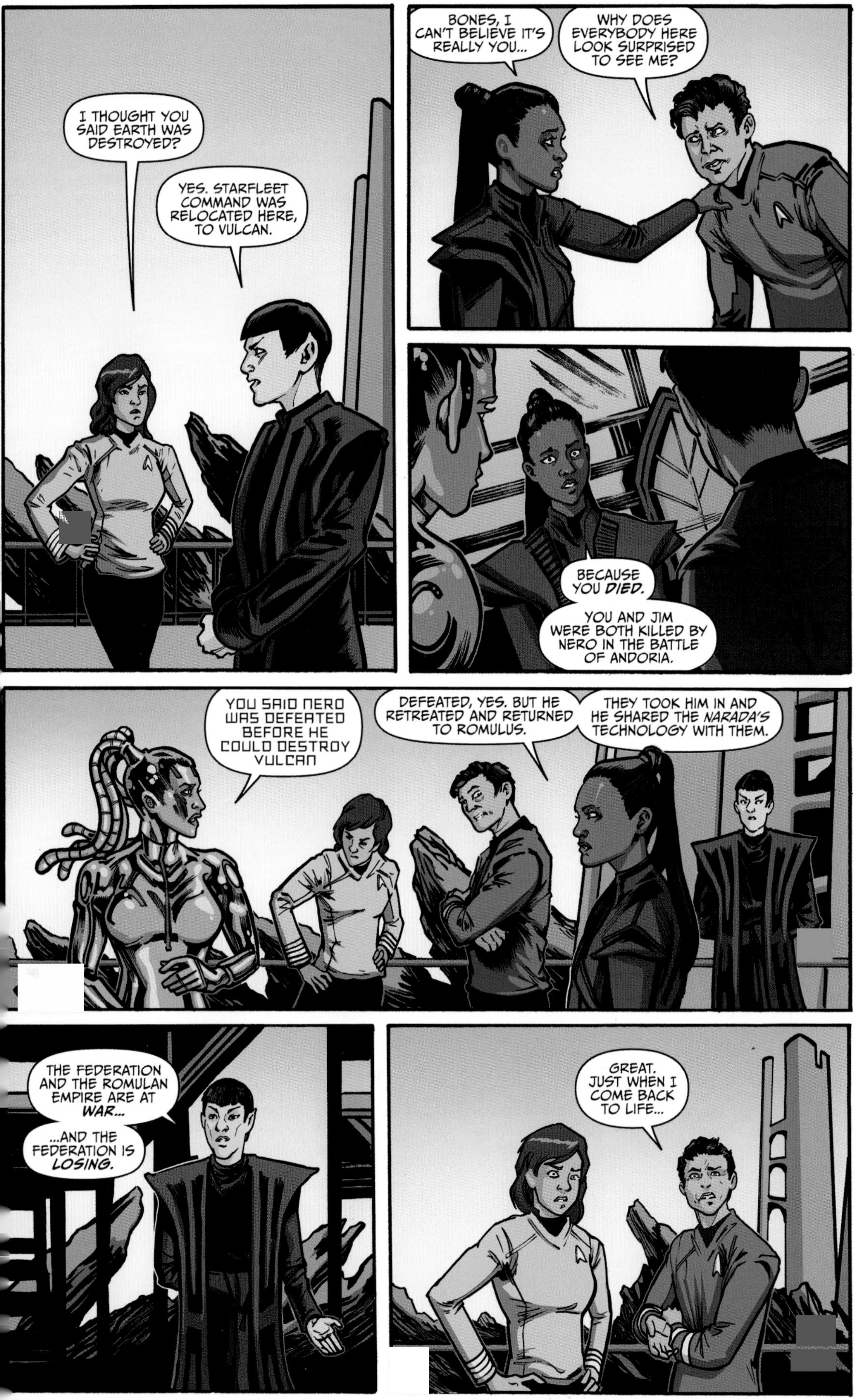
I THOUGHT YOU SAID EARTH WAS DESTROYED?
YES. STARFLEET COMMAND WAS RELOCATED HERE, TO VULCAN.
BONES, I CAN'T BELIEVE IT'S REALLY YOU...
WHY DOES EVERYBODY HERE LOOK SURPRISED TO SEE ME?
BECAUSE YOU *DIED.*
YOU AND JIM WERE BOTH KILLED BY NERO IN THE BATTLE OF ANDORIA.
YOU SAID NERO WAS DEFEATED BEFORE HE COULD DESTROY VULCAN
DEFEATED, YES. BUT HE RETREATED AND RETURNED TO ROMULUS.
THEY TOOK HIM IN AND HE SHARED THE *NARADA'S* TECHNOLOGY WITH THEM.
THE FEDERATION AND THE ROMULAN EMPIRE ARE AT *WAR...*
...AND THE FEDERATION IS *LOSING.*
GREAT. JUST WHEN I COME BACK TO LIFE...

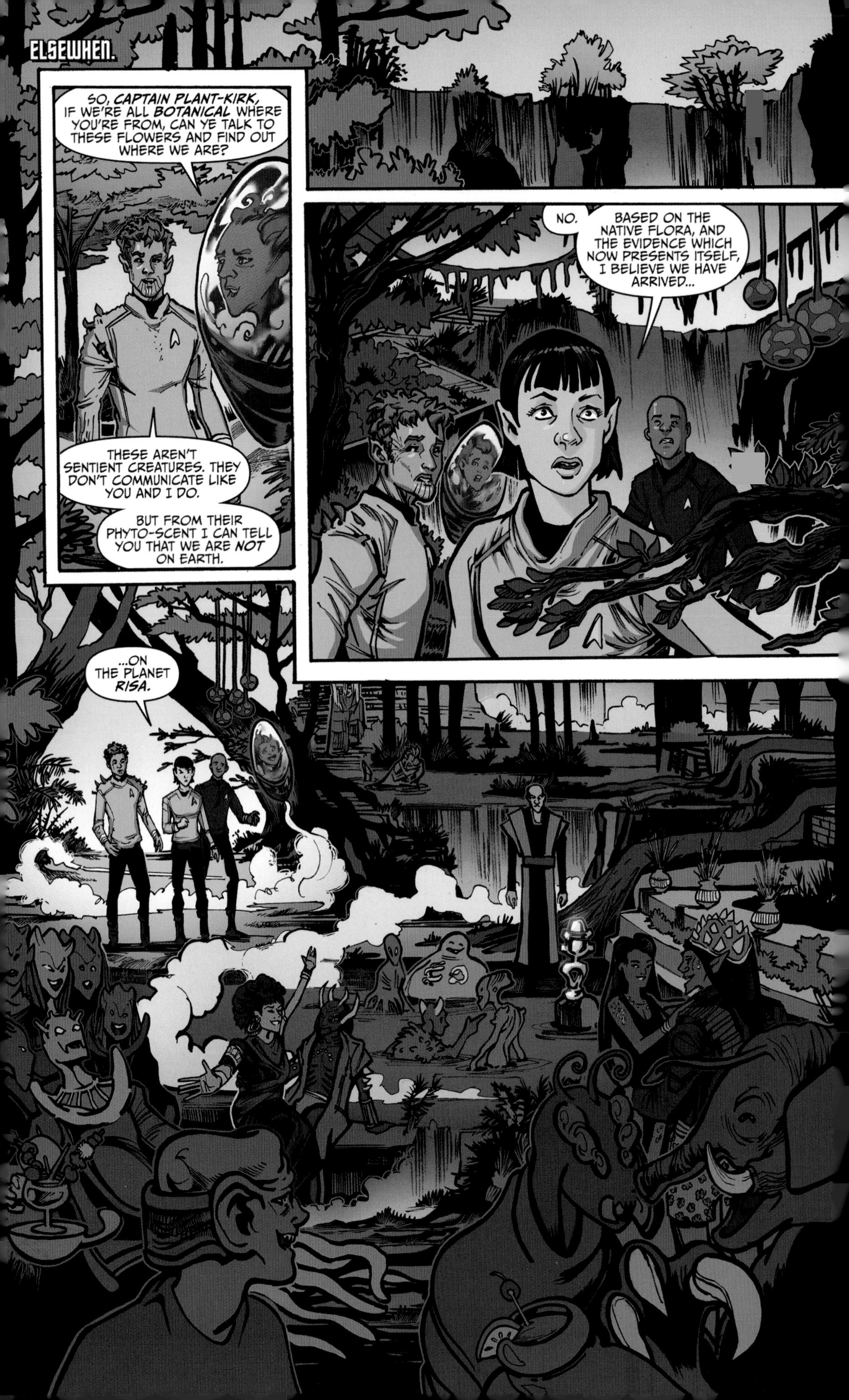
ELSEWHEN.
SO, CAPTAIN PLANT-KIRK, IF WE'RE ALL BOTANICAL WHERE YOU'RE FROM, CAN YE TALK TO THESE FLOWERS AND FIND OUT WHERE WE ARE?
THESE AREN'T SENTIENT CREATURES. THEY DON'T COMMUNICATE LIKE YOU AND I DO.
BUT FROM THEIR PHYTO-SCENT I CAN TELL YOU THAT WE ARE NOT ON EARTH.
NO.
BASED ON THE NATIVE FLORA, AND THE EVIDENCE WHICH NOW PRESENTS ITSELF, I BELIEVE WE HAVE ARRIVED...
...ON THE PLANET RISA.

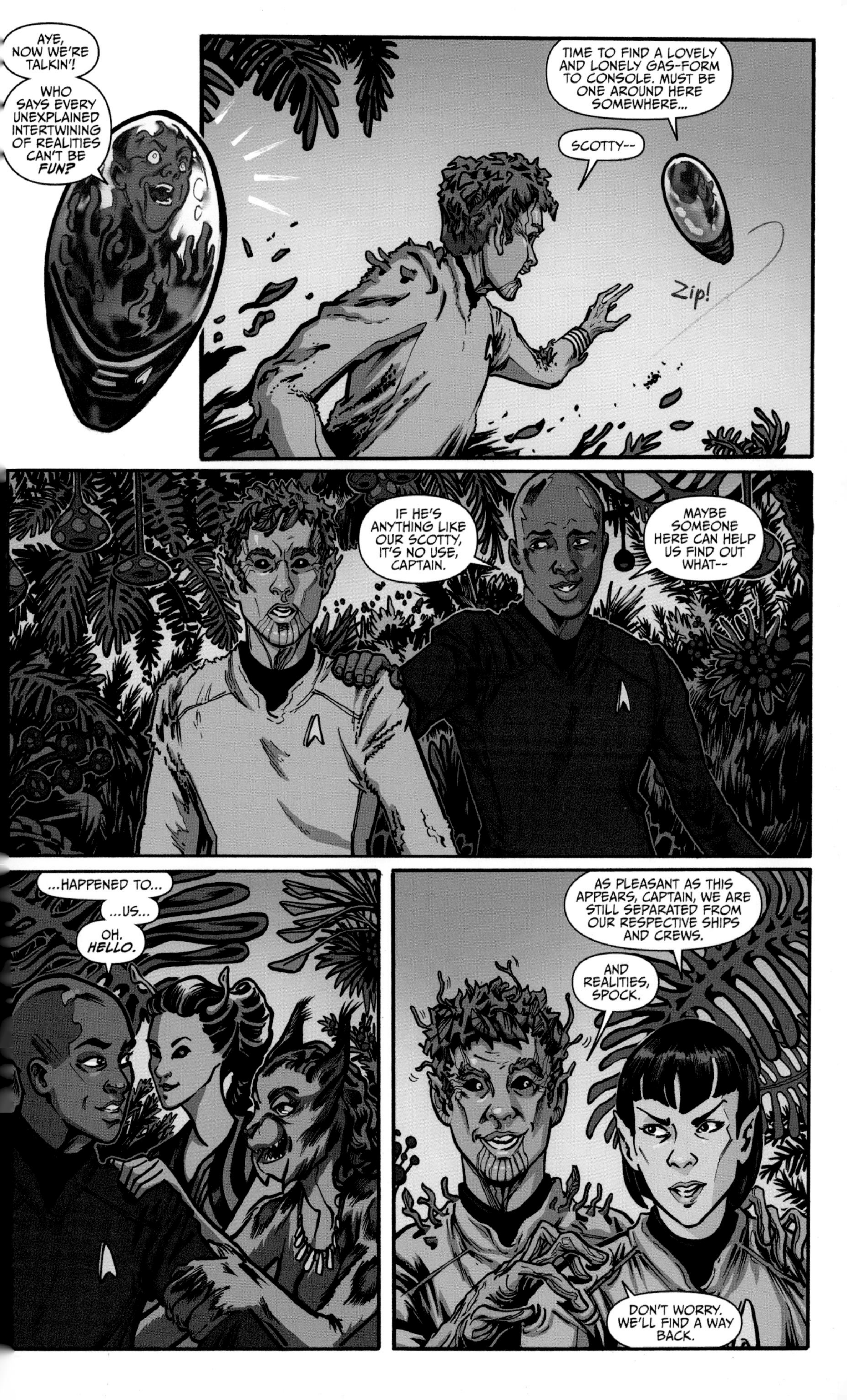
AYE, NOW WE'RE TALKIN'!
WHO SAYS EVERY UNEXPLAINED INTERTWINING OF REALITIES CAN'T BE *FUN?*
TIME TO FIND A LOVELY AND LONELY GAS-FORM TO CONSOLE. MUST BE ONE AROUND HERE SOMEWHERE...
SCOTTY--
Zip!
IF HE'S ANYTHING LIKE OUR SCOTTY, IT'S NO USE, CAPTAIN.
MAYBE SOMEONE HERE CAN HELP US FIND OUT WHAT--
...HAPPENED TO...
...US...
OH. *HELLO.*
AS PLEASANT AS THIS APPEARS, CAPTAIN, WE ARE STILL SEPARATED FROM OUR RESPECTIVE SHIPS AND CREWS.
AND REALITIES, SPOCK.
DON'T WORRY. WE'LL FIND A WAY BACK.

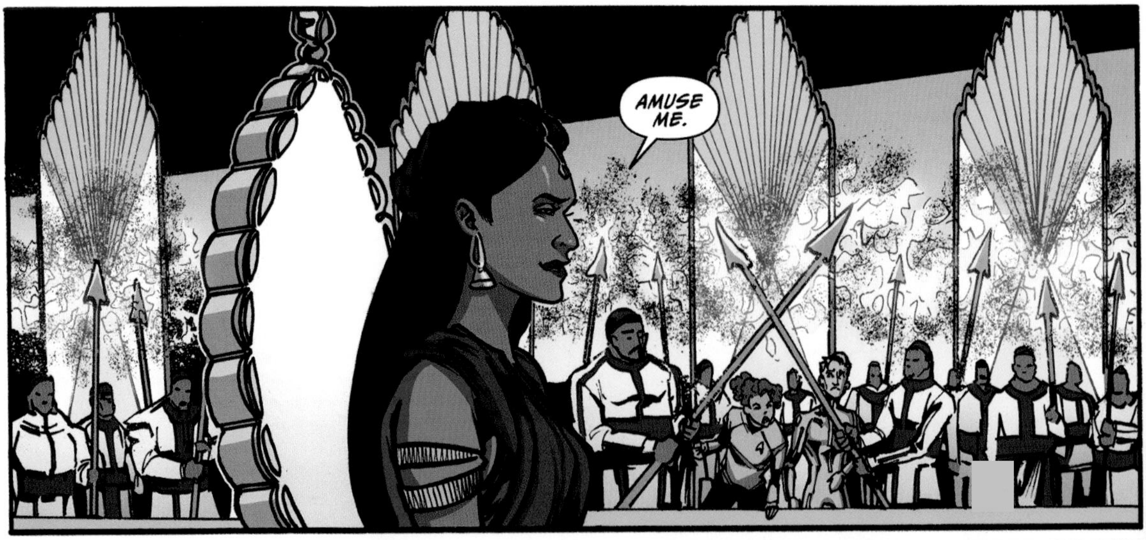
AMUSE ME.

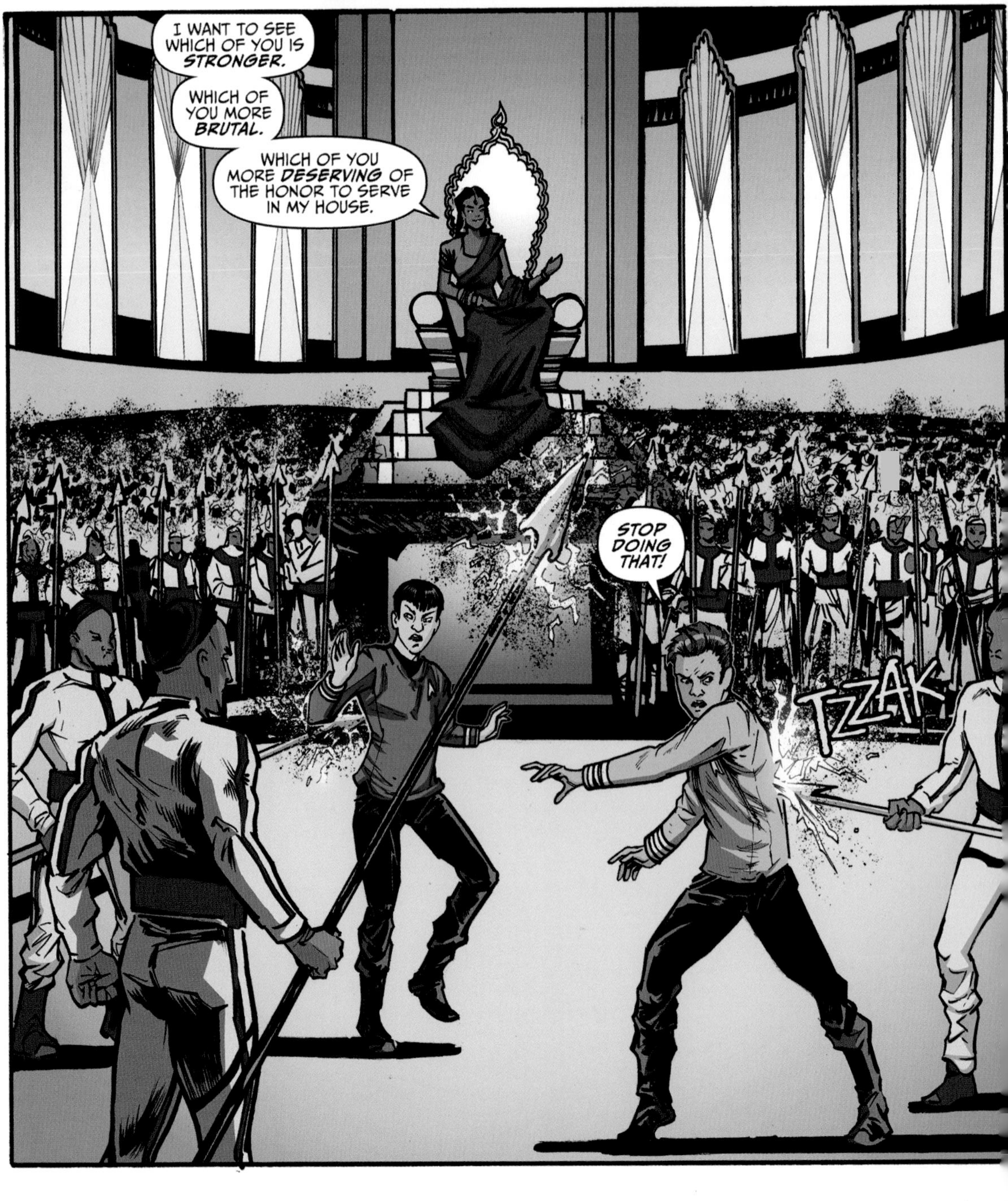
I WANT TO SEE WHICH OF YOU IS STRONGER.
WHICH OF YOU MORE BRUTAL.
WHICH OF YOU MORE DESERVING OF THE HONOR TO SERVE IN MY HOUSE.
STOP DOING THAT!
TZZAK

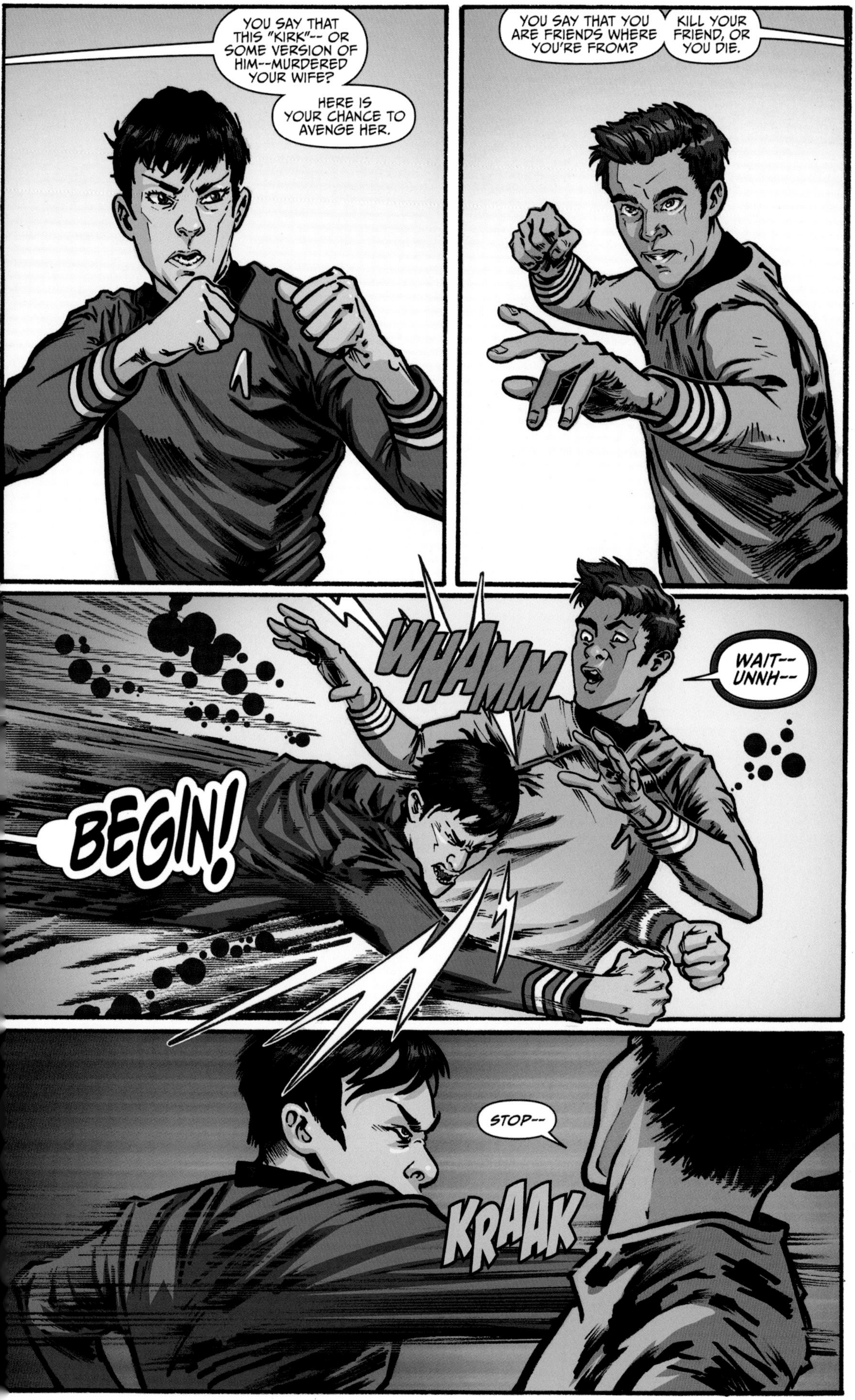
YOU SAY THAT THIS "KIRK"-- OR SOME VERSION OF HIM--MURDERED YOUR WIFE?
HERE IS YOUR CHANCE TO AVENGE HER.
YOU SAY THAT YOU ARE FRIENDS WHERE YOU'RE FROM?
KILL YOUR FRIEND, OR YOU DIE.
BEGIN!
WHAMM
WAIT-- UNNH--
STOP--
KRAAK

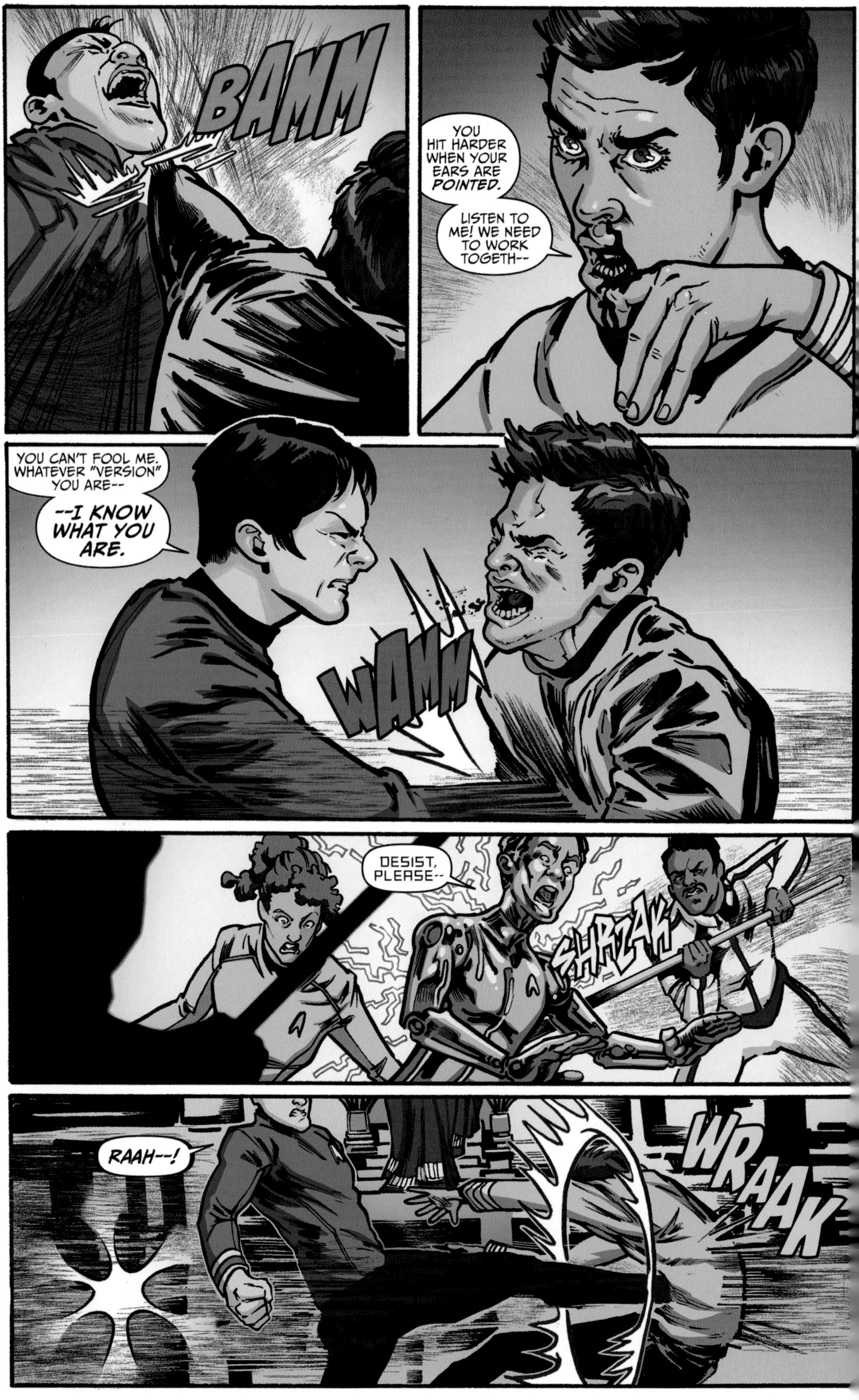
BAMM
YOU HIT HARDER WHEN YOUR EARS ARE POINTED.
LISTEN TO ME! WE NEED TO WORK TOGETH--
YOU CAN'T FOOL ME. WHATEVER "VERSION" YOU ARE--
--I KNOW WHAT YOU ARE.
WAMM
DESIST, PLEASE--
SHRAK
RAAH--!
WRAAK

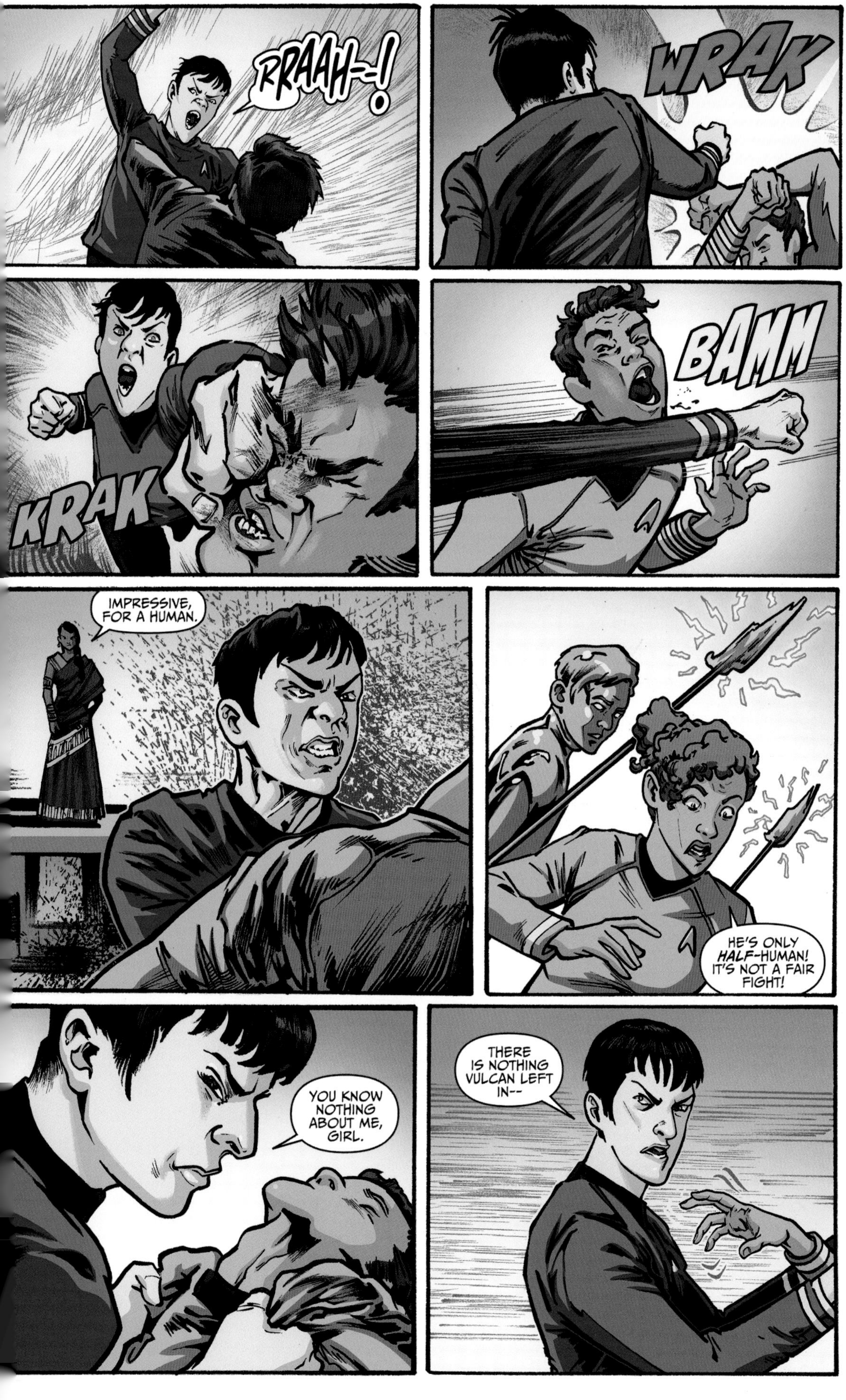
RRAAH--!
WRAK
KRAK
BAMM
IMPRESSIVE, FOR A HUMAN.
HE'S ONLY *HALF*-HUMAN! IT'S NOT A FAIR FIGHT!
YOU KNOW NOTHING ABOUT ME, GIRL.
THERE IS NOTHING VULCAN LEFT IN--

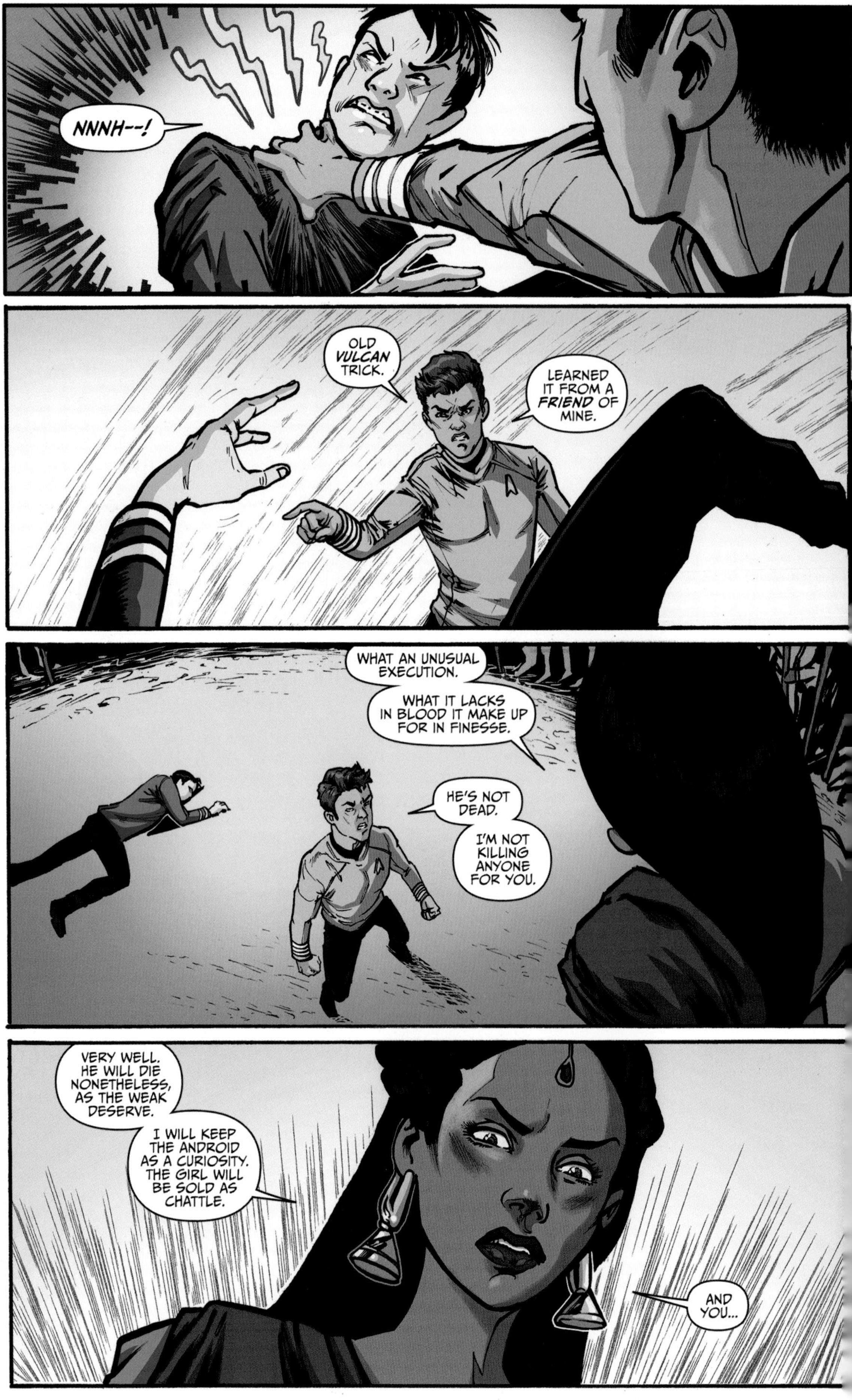
NNNH--!
OLD VULCAN TRICK.
LEARNED IT FROM A FRIEND OF MINE.
WHAT AN UNUSUAL EXECUTION.
WHAT IT LACKS IN BLOOD IT MAKE UP FOR IN FINESSE.
HE'S NOT DEAD.
I'M NOT KILLING ANYONE FOR YOU.
VERY WELL. HE WILL DIE NONETHELESS, AS THE WEAK DESERVE.
I WILL KEEP THE ANDROID AS A CURIOSITY. THE GIRL WILL BE SOLD AS CHATTLE.
AND YOU...

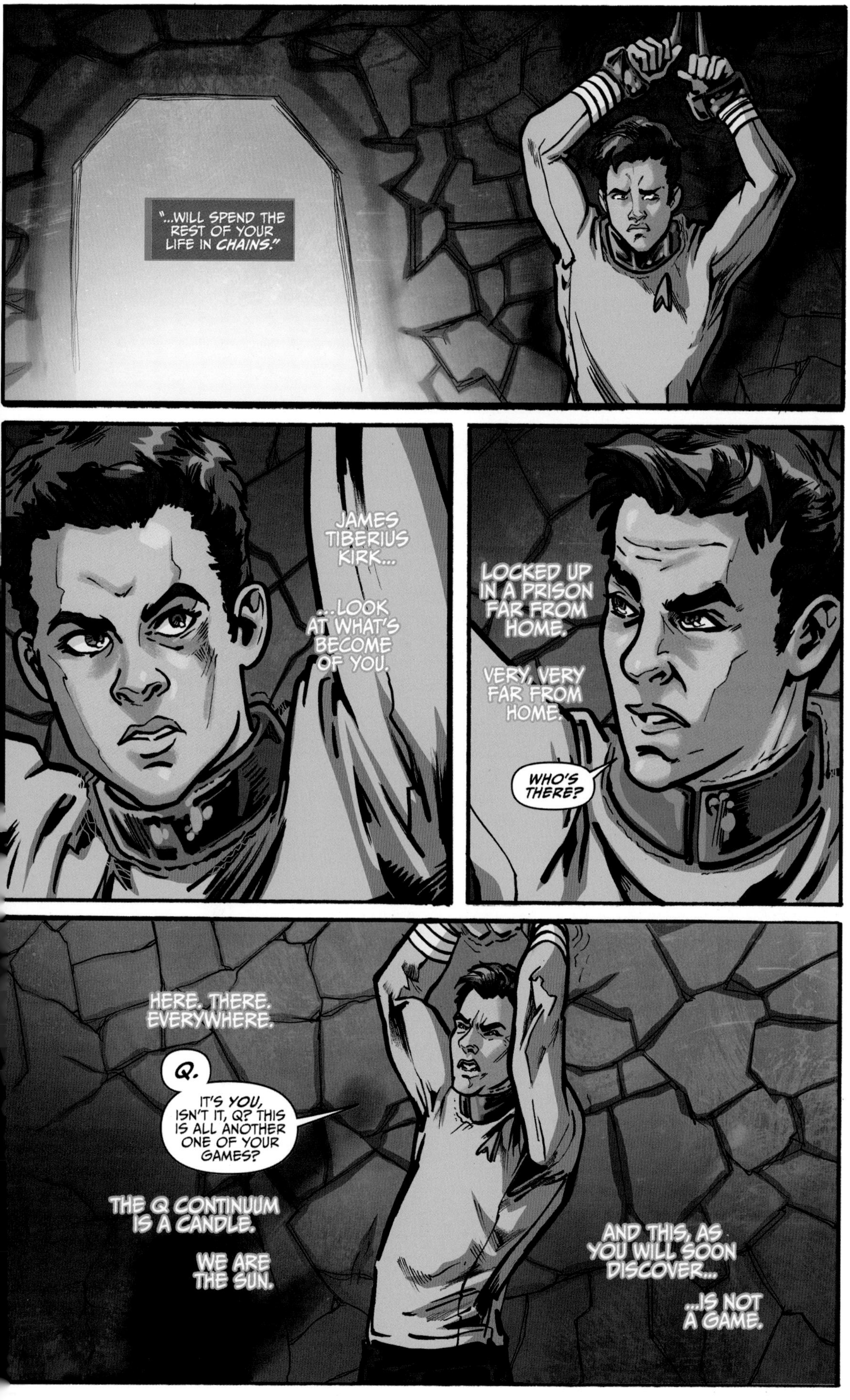
"...WILL SPEND THE REST OF YOUR LIFE IN CHAINS."
JAMES TIBERIUS KIRK...
...LOOK AT WHAT'S BECOME OF YOU.
LOCKED UP IN A PRISON FAR FROM HOME.
VERY, VERY FAR FROM HOME.
WHO'S THERE?
HERE. THERE. EVERYWHERE.
Q.
IT'S YOU, ISN'T IT, Q? THIS IS ALL ANOTHER ONE OF YOUR GAMES?
THE Q CONTINUUM IS A CANDLE.
WE ARE THE SUN.
AND THIS, AS YOU WILL SOON DISCOVER...
...IS NOT A GAME.

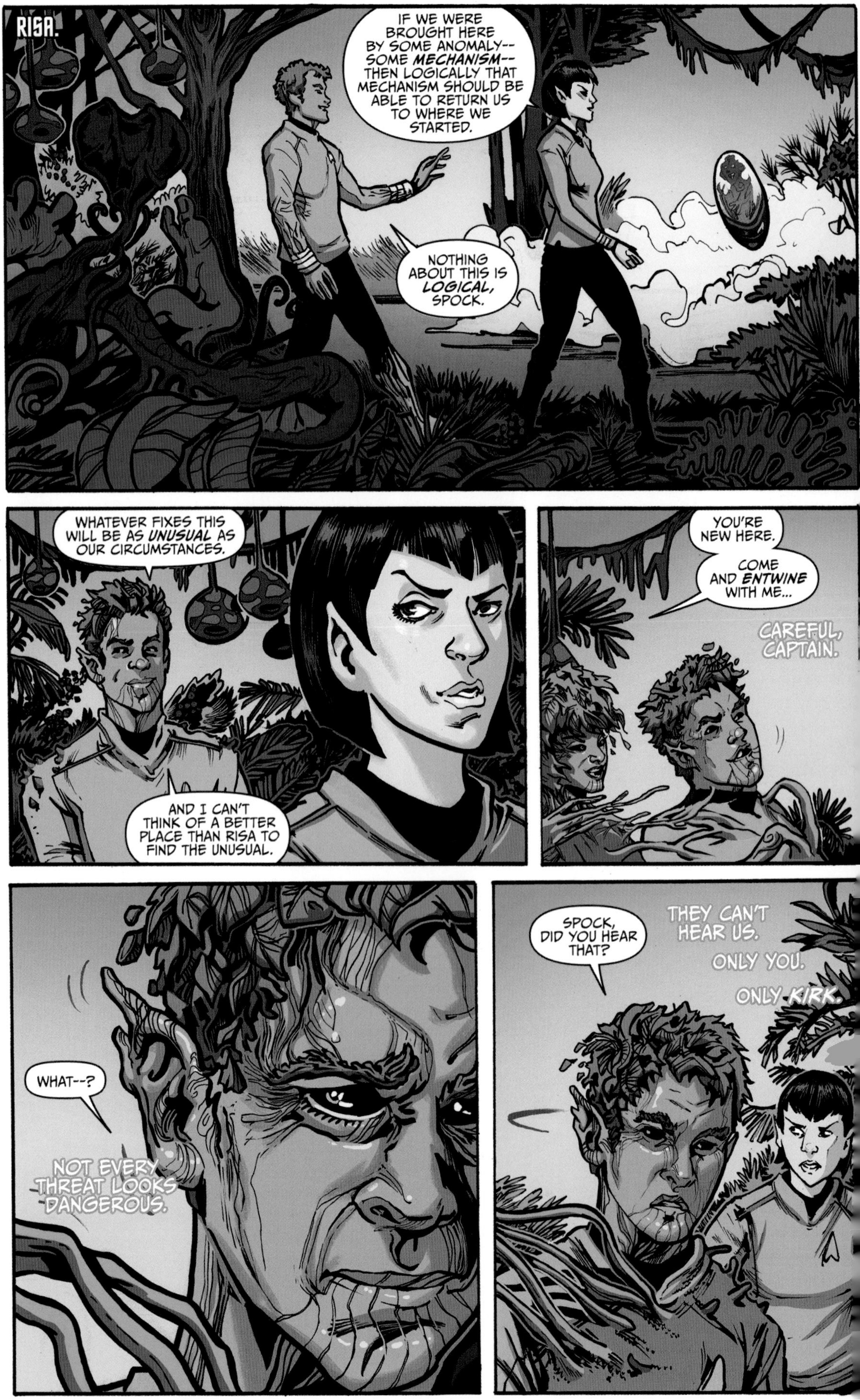
RISA.
IF WE WERE BROUGHT HERE BY SOME ANOMALY-- SOME MECHANISM-- THEN LOGICALLY THAT MECHANISM SHOULD BE ABLE TO RETURN US TO WHERE WE STARTED.
NOTHING ABOUT THIS IS LOGICAL, SPOCK.
WHATEVER FIXES THIS WILL BE AS UNUSUAL AS OUR CIRCUMSTANCES.
AND I CAN'T THINK OF A BETTER PLACE THAN RISA TO FIND THE UNUSUAL.
YOU'RE NEW HERE.
COME AND ENTWINE WITH ME...
CAREFUL, CAPTAIN.
WHAT--?
NOT EVERY THREAT LOOKS DANGEROUS.
SPOCK, DID YOU HEAR THAT?
THEY CAN'T HEAR US.
ONLY YOU.
ONLY KIRK.

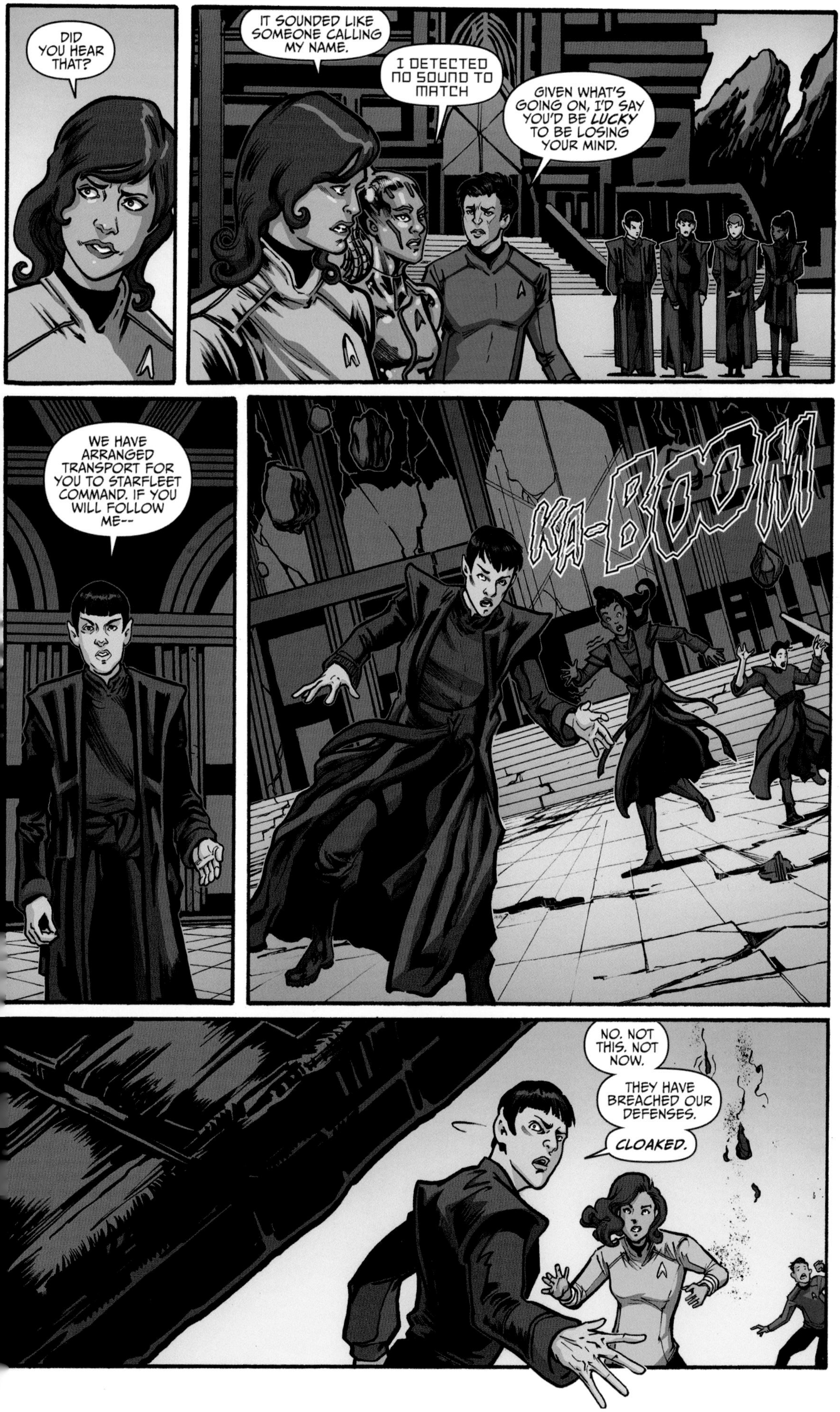
DID YOU HEAR THAT?
IT SOUNDED LIKE SOMEONE CALLING MY NAME.
I DETECTED NO SOUND TO MATCH
GIVEN WHAT'S GOING ON, I'D SAY YOU'D BE *LUCKY* TO BE LOSING YOUR MIND.
WE HAVE ARRANGED TRANSPORT FOR YOU TO STARFLEET COMMAND. IF YOU WILL FOLLOW ME--
KA-BOOM
NO. NOT THIS. NOT NOW.
THEY HAVE BREACHED OUR DEFENSES.
CLOAKED.

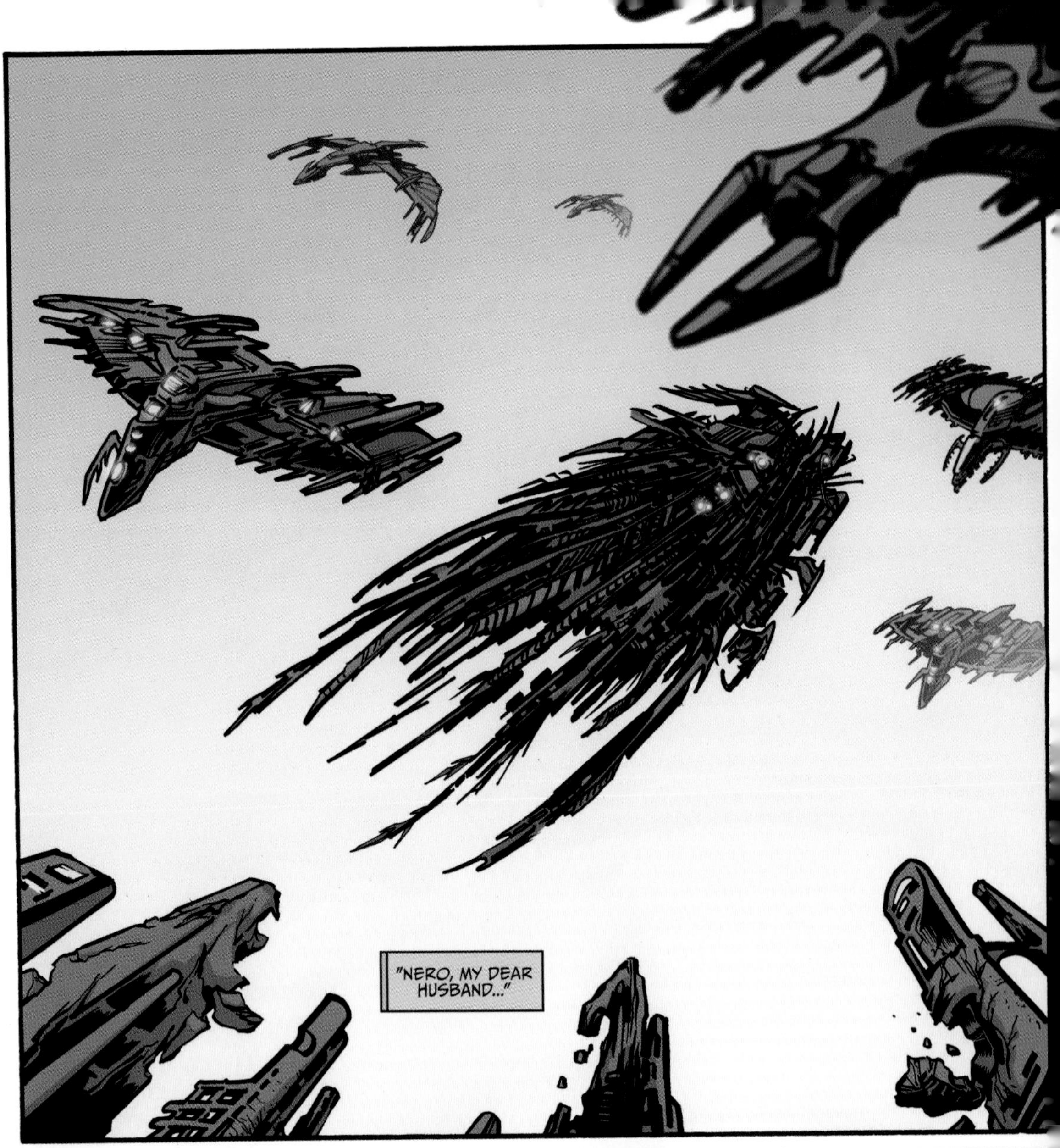
"NERO, MY DEAR HUSBAND..."

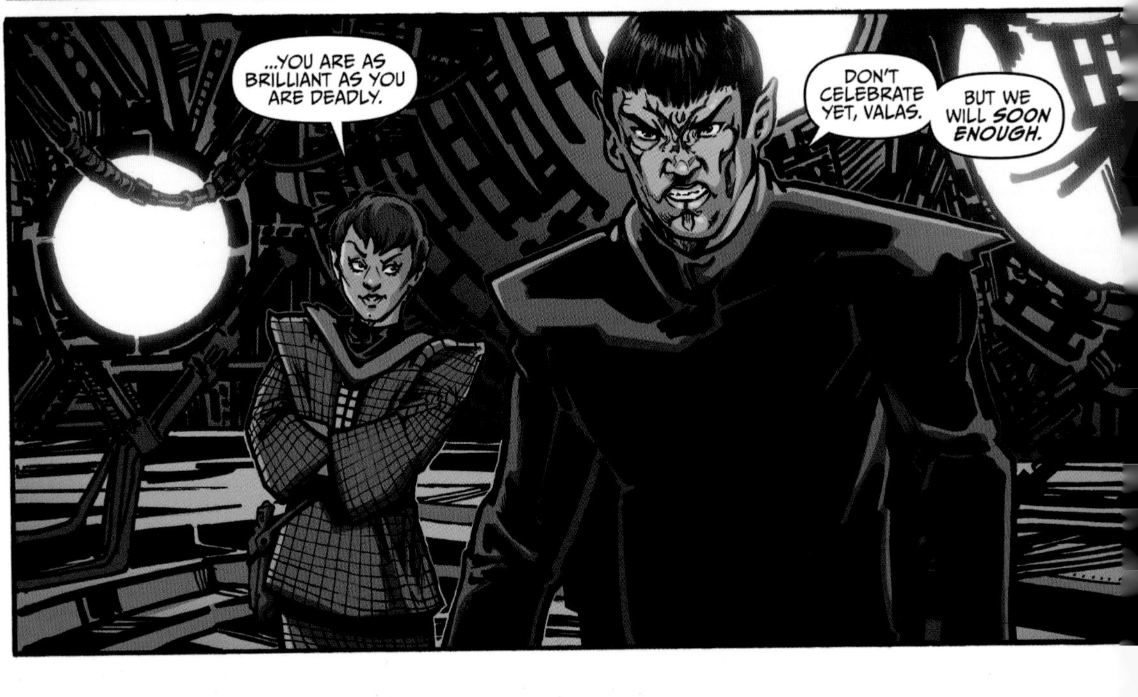
...YOU ARE AS BRILLIANT AS YOU ARE DEADLY.
DON'T CELEBRATE YET, VALAS.
BUT WE WILL SOON ENOUGH.

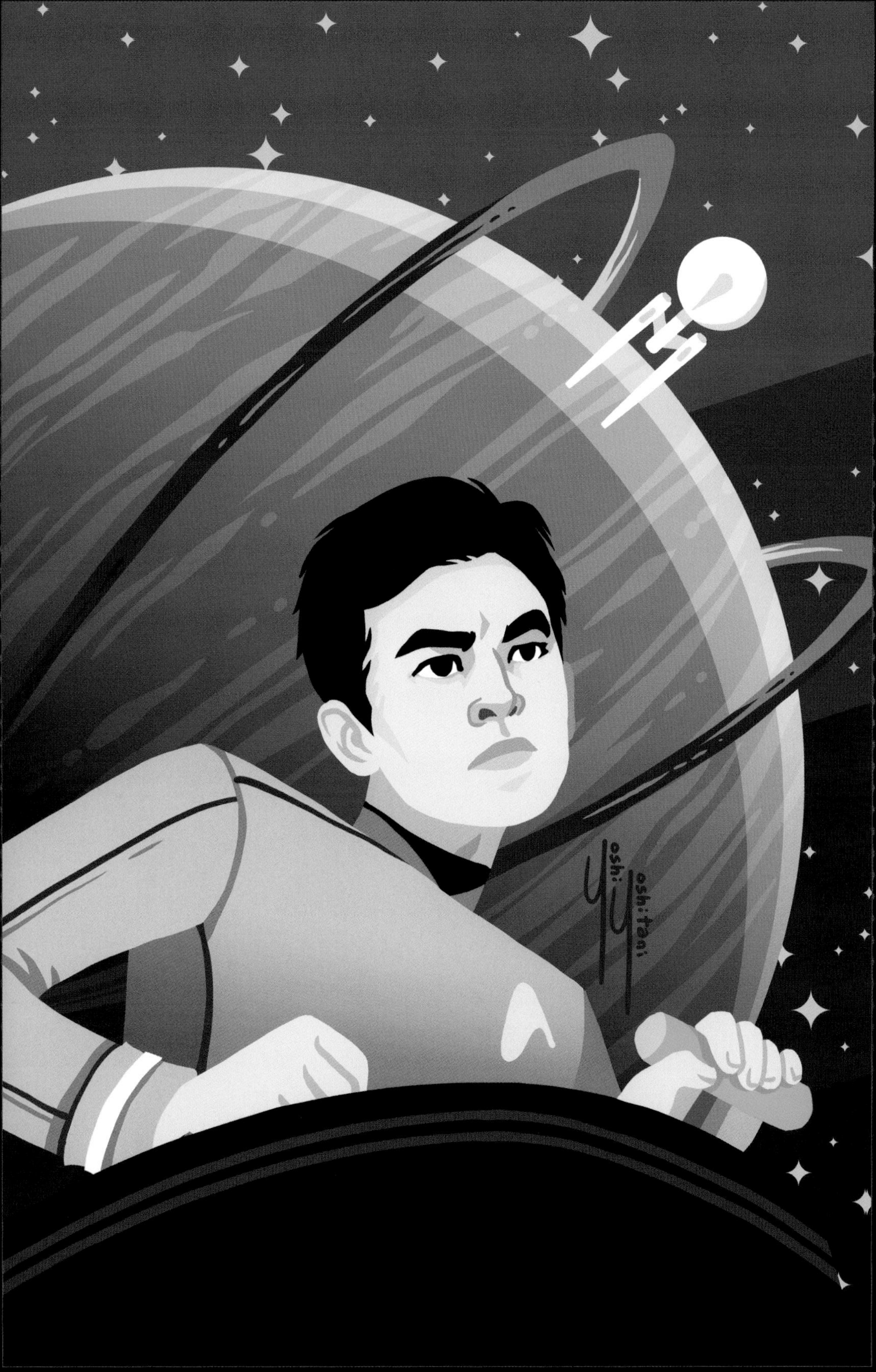
Yoshi Yoshitani

art by
Yoshi Yoshitani

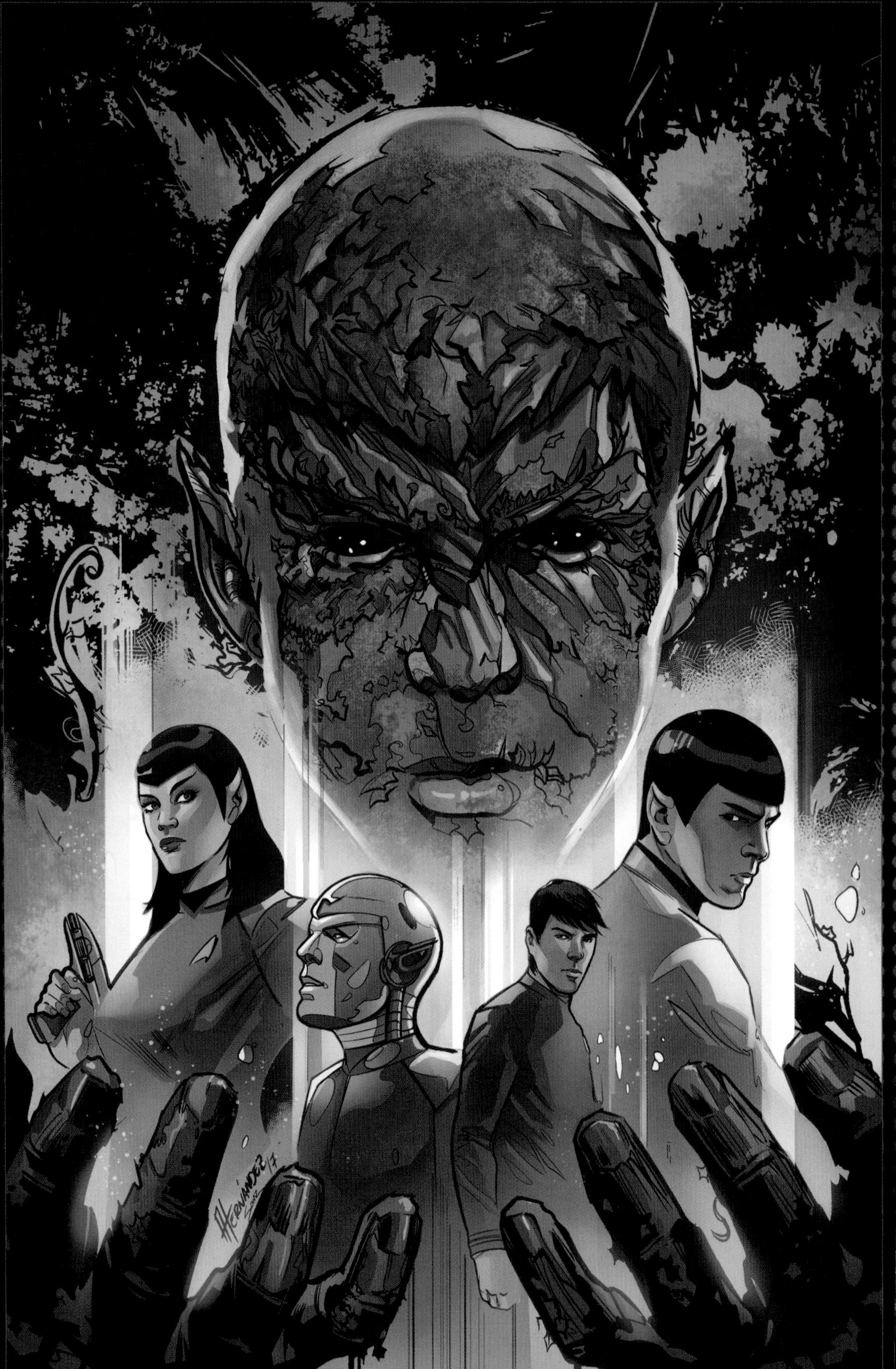

art by
Angel Hernandez

colors by
Esther Sanz

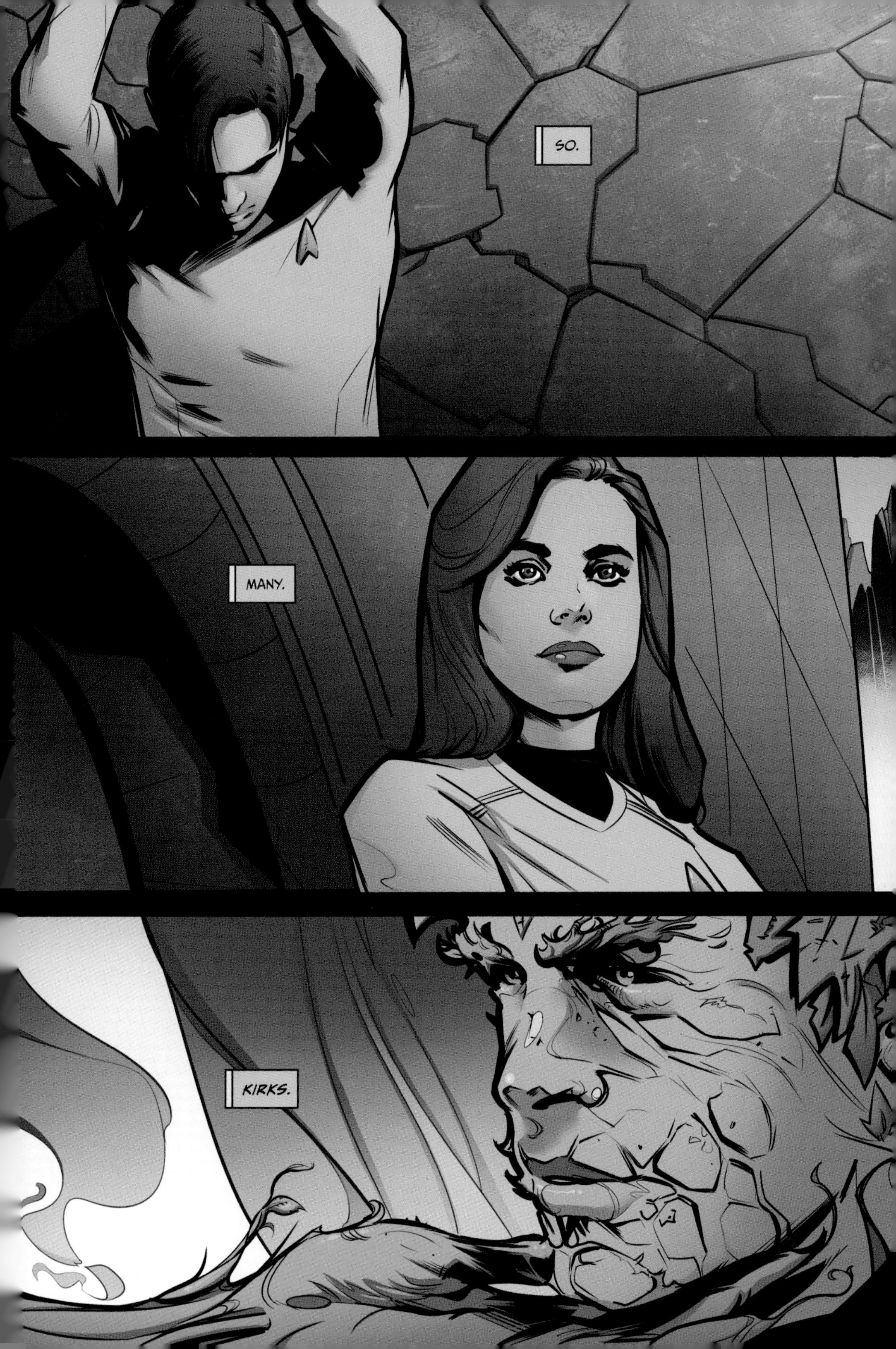
SO.
MANY.
KIRKS.

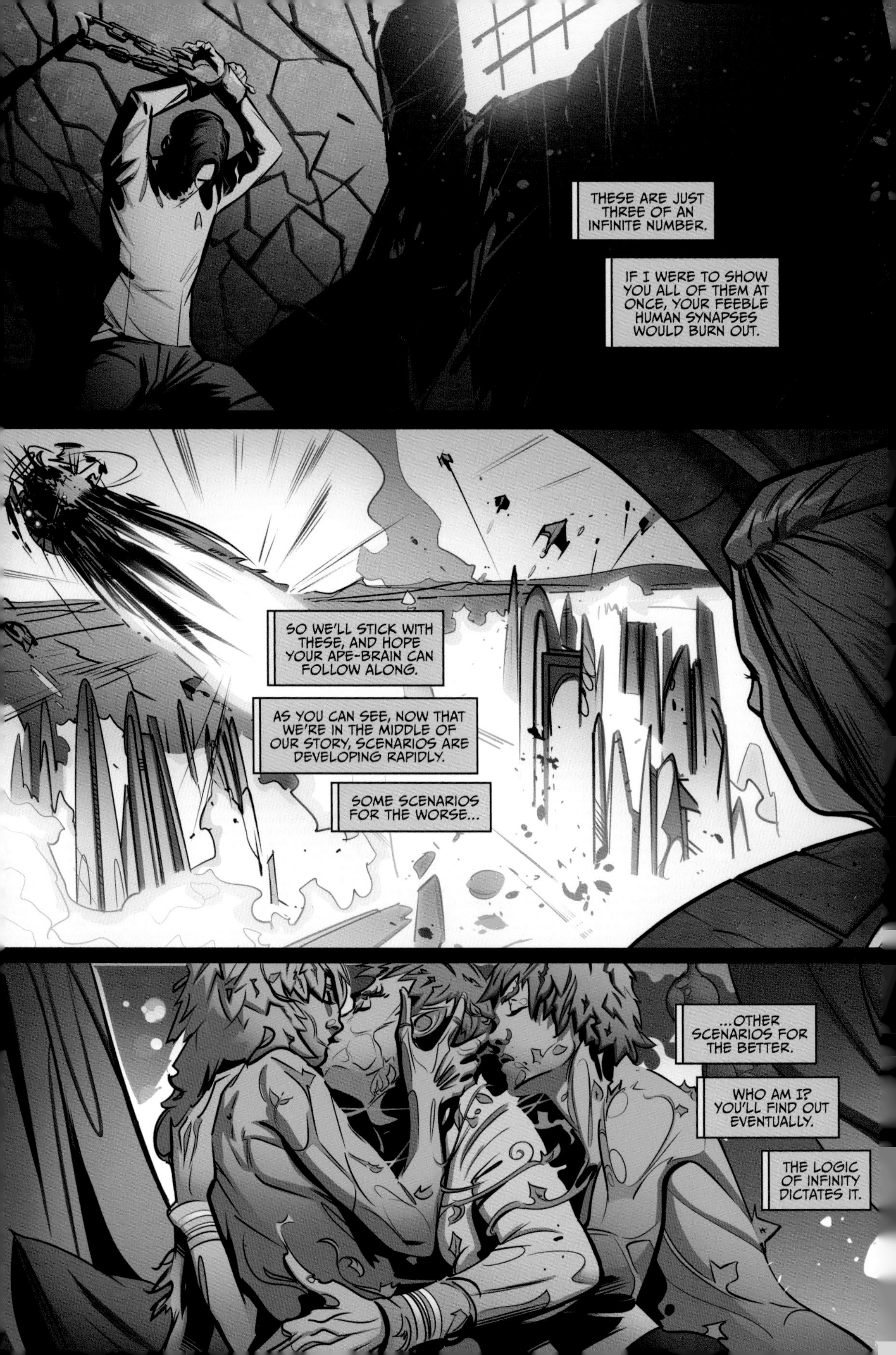
THESE ARE JUST THREE OF AN INFINITE NUMBER.
IF I WERE TO SHOW YOU ALL OF THEM AT ONCE, YOUR FEEBLE HUMAN SYNAPSES WOULD BURN OUT.
SO WE'LL STICK WITH THESE, AND HOPE YOUR APE-BRAIN CAN FOLLOW ALONG.
AS YOU CAN SEE, NOW THAT WE'RE IN THE MIDDLE OF OUR STORY, SCENARIOS ARE DEVELOPING RAPIDLY.
SOME SCENARIOS FOR THE WORSE...
...OTHER SCENARIOS FOR THE BETTER.
WHO AM I? YOU'LL FIND OUT EVENTUALLY.
THE LOGIC OF INFINITY DICTATES IT.

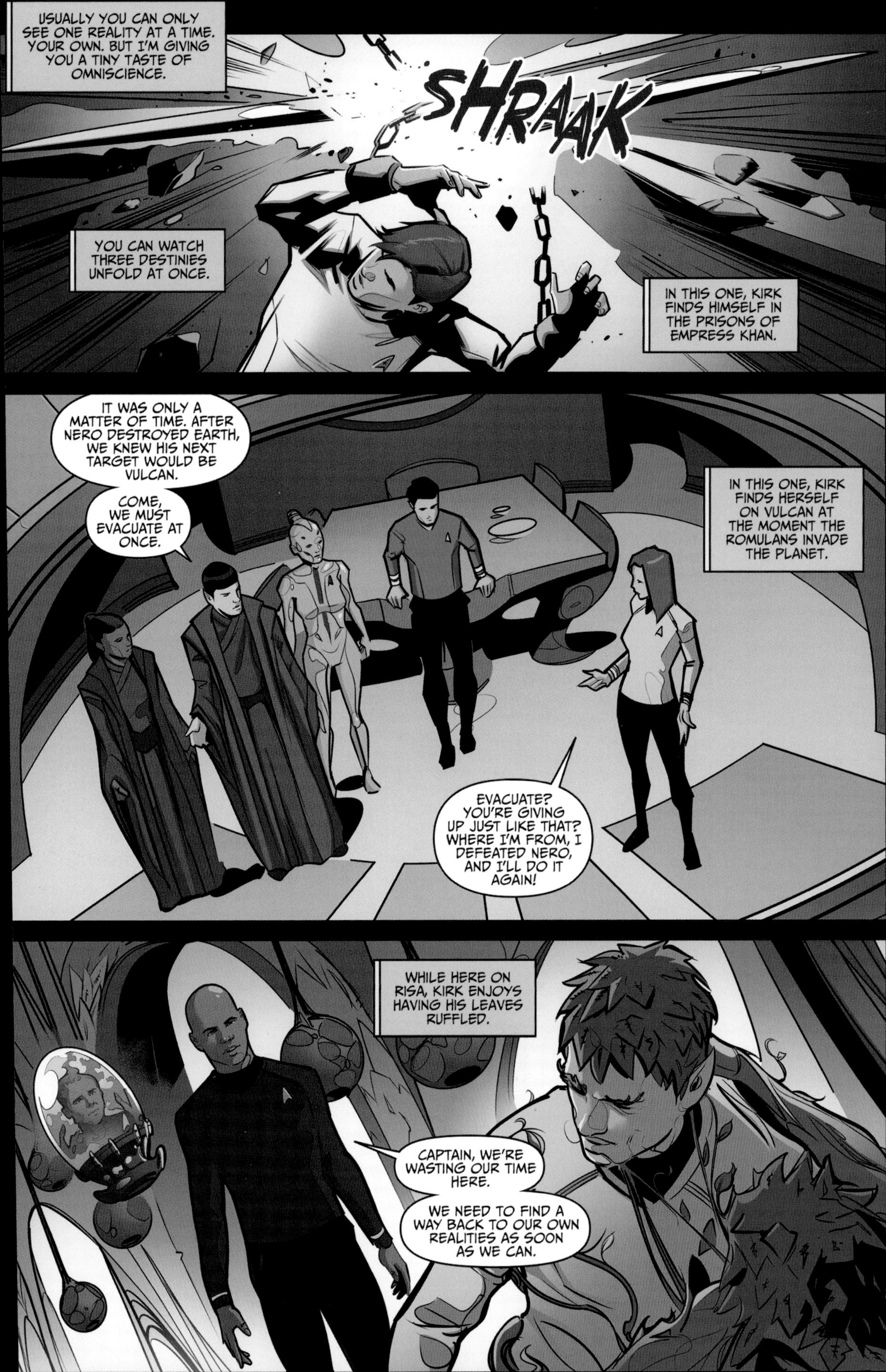
USUALLY YOU CAN ONLY SEE ONE REALITY AT A TIME. YOUR OWN. BUT I'M GIVING YOU A TINY TASTE OF OMNISCIENCE.
SHRAAK
YOU CAN WATCH THREE DESTINIES UNFOLD AT ONCE.
IN THIS ONE, KIRK FINDS HIMSELF IN THE PRISONS OF EMPRESS KHAN.
IT WAS ONLY A MATTER OF TIME. AFTER NERO DESTROYED EARTH, WE KNEW HIS NEXT TARGET WOULD BE VULCAN.
COME, WE MUST EVACUATE AT ONCE.
IN THIS ONE, KIRK FINDS HERSELF ON VULCAN AT THE MOMENT THE ROMULANS INVADE THE PLANET.
EVACUATE? YOU'RE GIVING UP JUST LIKE THAT? WHERE I'M FROM, I DEFEATED NERO, AND I'LL DO IT AGAIN!
WHILE HERE ON RISA, KIRK ENJOYS HAVING HIS LEAVES RUFFLED.
CAPTAIN, WE'RE WASTING OUR TIME HERE.
WE NEED TO FIND A WAY BACK TO OUR OWN REALITIES AS SOON AS WE CAN.

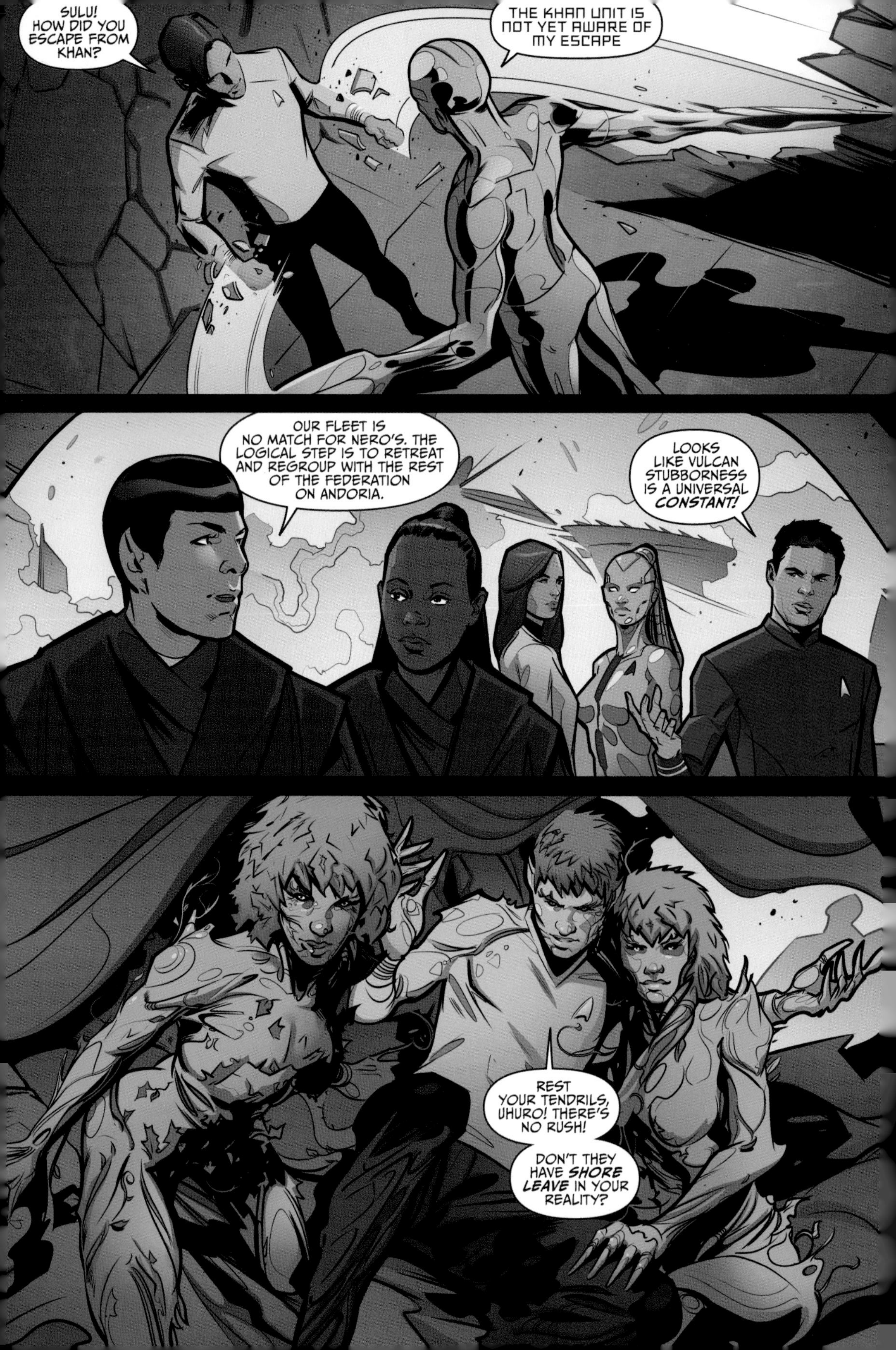
SULU! HOW DID YOU ESCAPE FROM KHAN?
THE KHAN UNIT IS NOT YET AWARE OF MY ESCAPE
OUR FLEET IS NO MATCH FOR NERO'S. THE LOGICAL STEP IS TO RETREAT AND REGROUP WITH THE REST OF THE FEDERATION ON ANDORIA.
LOOKS LIKE VULCAN STUBBORNESS IS A UNIVERSAL CONSTANT!
REST YOUR TENDRILS, UHURO! THERE'S NO RUSH!
DON'T THEY HAVE SHORE LEAVE IN YOUR REALITY?

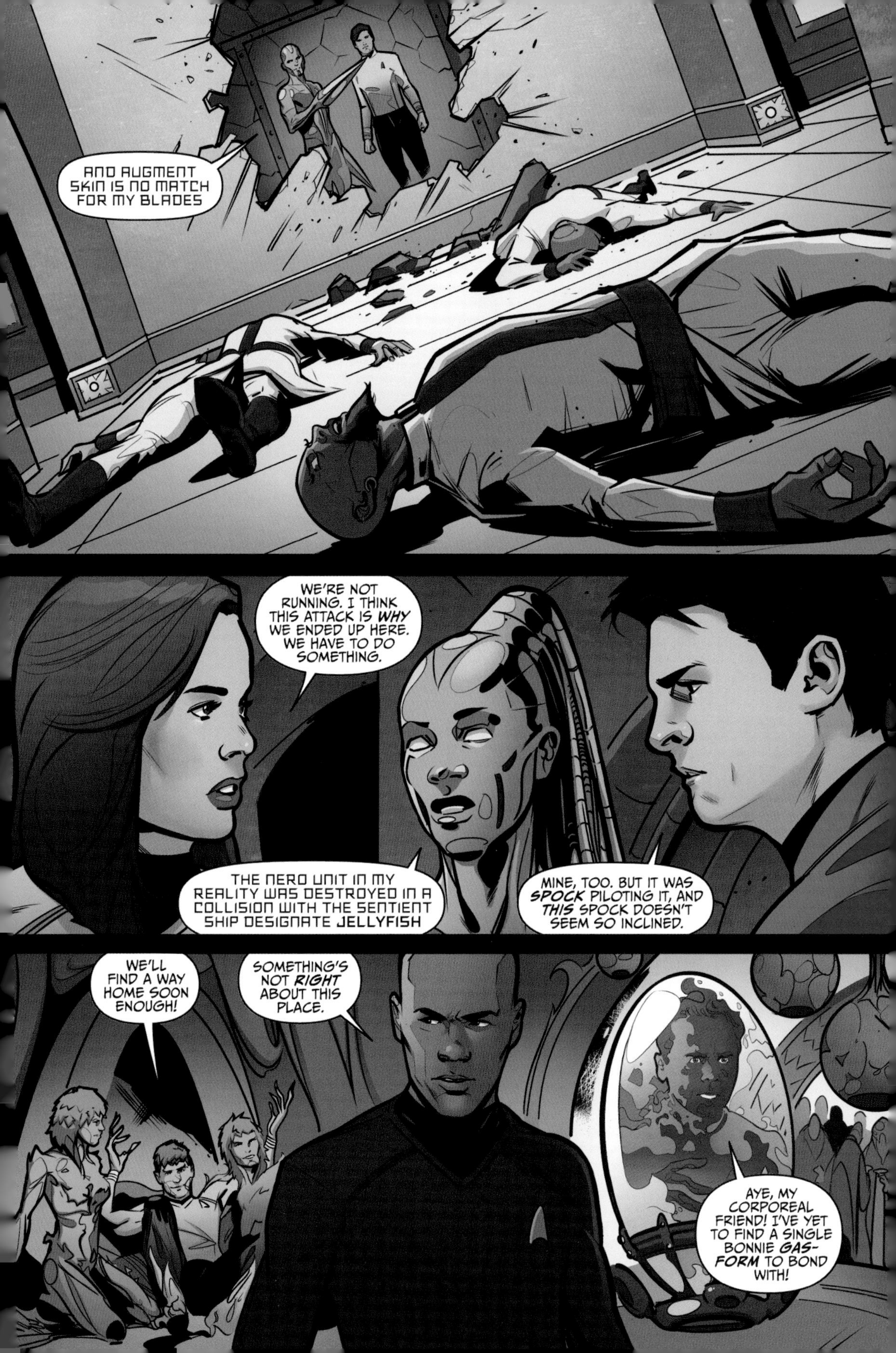
AND AUGMENT SKIN IS NO MATCH FOR MY BLADES
WE'RE NOT RUNNING. I THINK THIS ATTACK IS *WHY* WE ENDED UP HERE. WE HAVE TO DO SOMETHING.
THE NERO UNIT IN MY REALITY WAS DESTROYED IN A COLLISION WITH THE SENTIENT SHIP DESIGNATE **JELLYFISH**
MINE, TOO. BUT IT WAS ***SPOCK*** PILOTING IT, AND ***THIS*** SPOCK DOESN'T SEEM SO INCLINED.
WE'LL FIND A WAY HOME SOON ENOUGH!
SOMETHING'S NOT *RIGHT* ABOUT THIS PLACE.
AYE, MY CORPOREAL FRIEND! I'VE YET TO FIND A SINGLE BONNIE ***GAS-FORM*** TO BOND WITH!

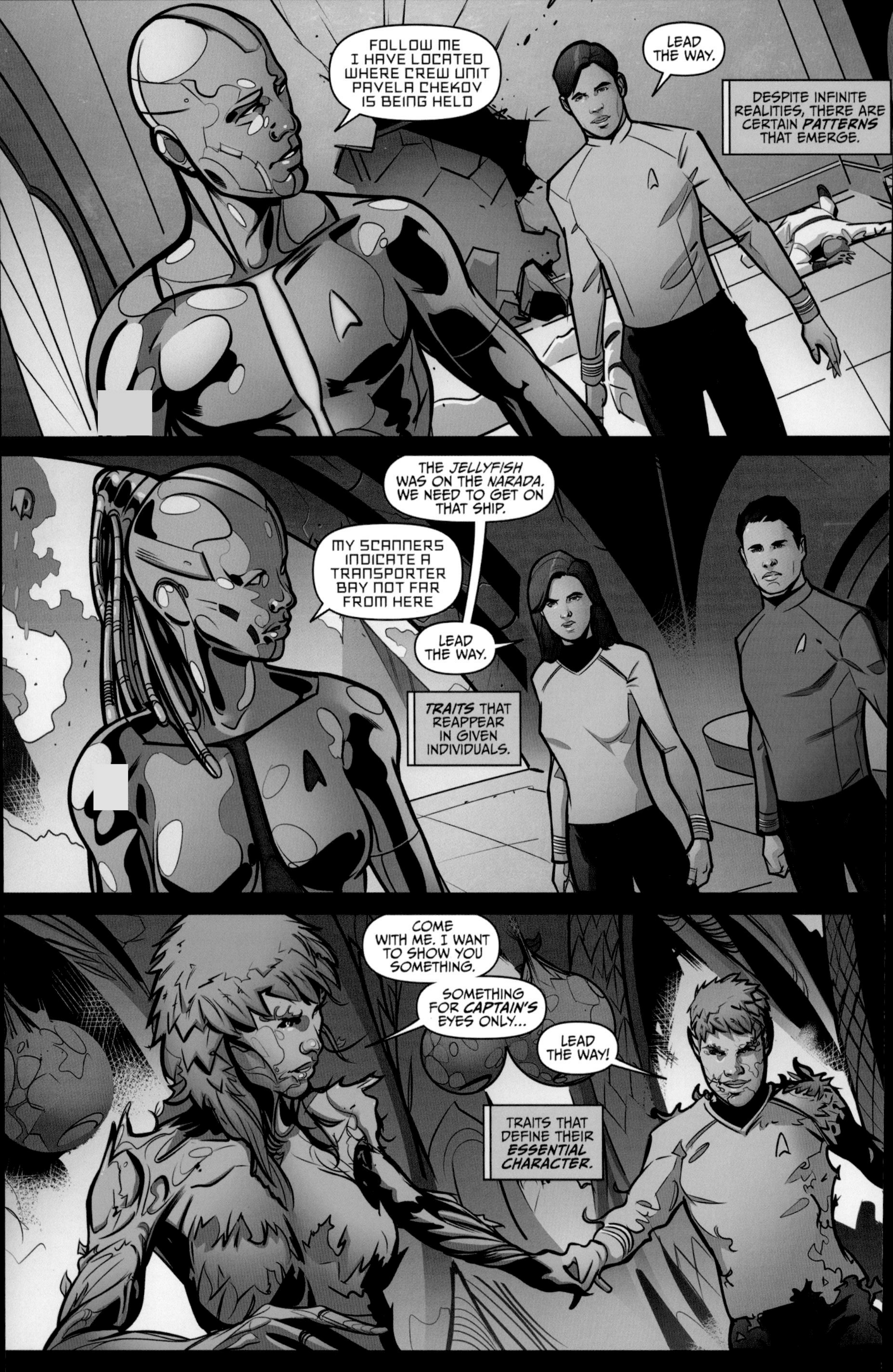
FOLLOW ME I HAVE LOCATED WHERE CREW UNIT PAVELA CHEKOV IS BEING HELD
LEAD THE WAY.
DESPITE INFINITE REALITIES, THERE ARE CERTAIN *PATTERNS* THAT EMERGE.
THE *JELLYFISH* WAS ON THE *NARADA*. WE NEED TO GET ON THAT SHIP.
MY SCANNERS INDICATE A TRANSPORTER BAY NOT FAR FROM HERE
LEAD THE WAY.
TRAITS THAT REAPPEAR IN GIVEN INDIVIDUALS.
COME WITH ME. I WANT TO SHOW YOU SOMETHING.
SOMETHING FOR *CAPTAIN'S* EYES ONLY...
LEAD THE WAY!
TRAITS THAT DEFINE THEIR *ESSENTIAL CHARACTER*.

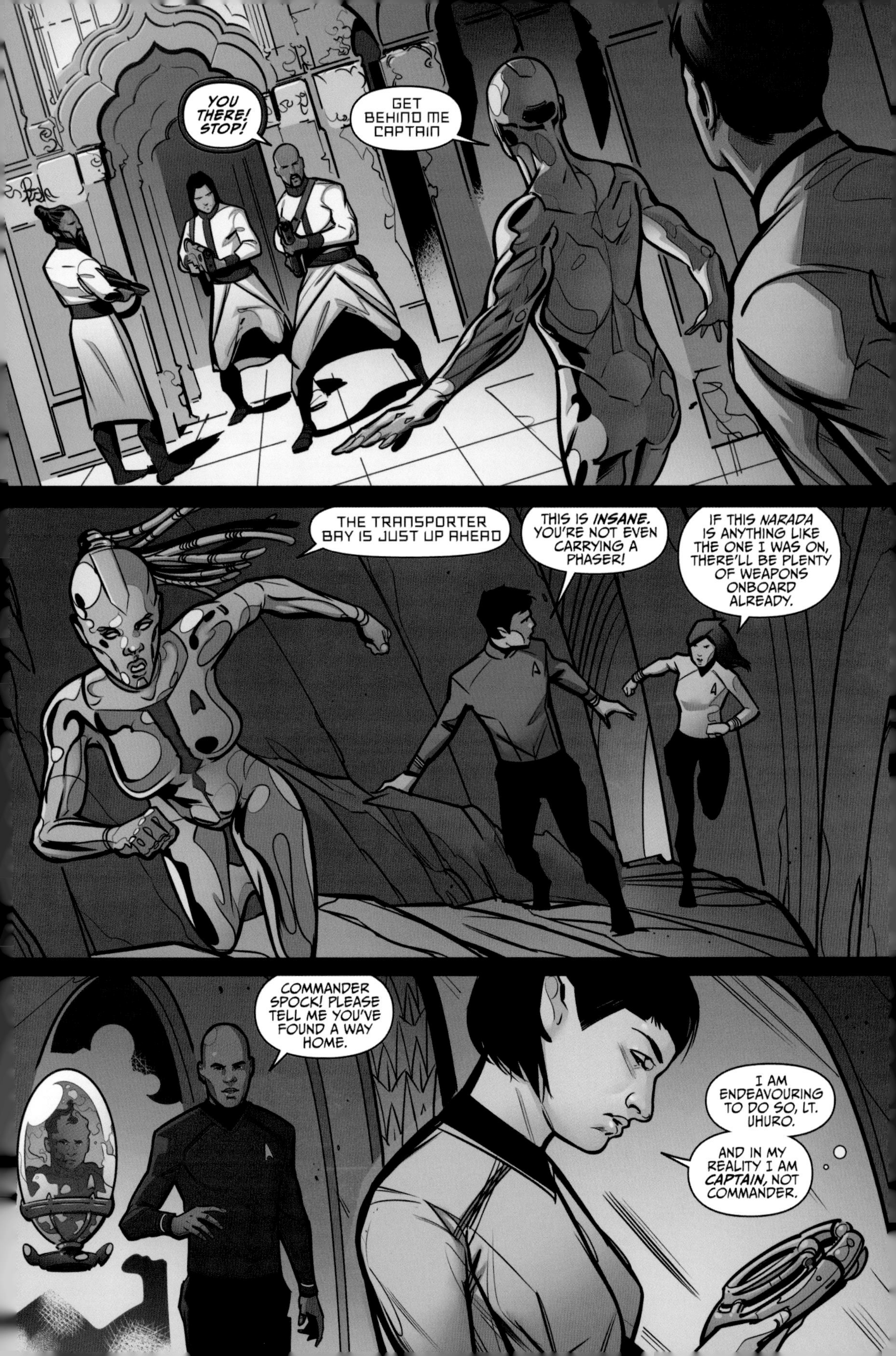

YOU THERE! STOP!
GET BEHIND ME CAPTAIN
THE TRANSPORTER BAY IS JUST UP AHEAD
THIS IS *INSANE.* YOU'RE NOT EVEN CARRYING A PHASER!
IF THIS *NARADA* IS ANYTHING LIKE THE ONE I WAS ON, THERE'LL BE PLENTY OF WEAPONS ONBOARD ALREADY.
COMMANDER SPOCK! PLEASE TELL ME YOU'VE FOUND A WAY HOME.
I AM ENDEAVOURING TO DO SO, LT. UHURO.
AND IN MY REALITY I AM *CAPTAIN,* NOT COMMANDER.

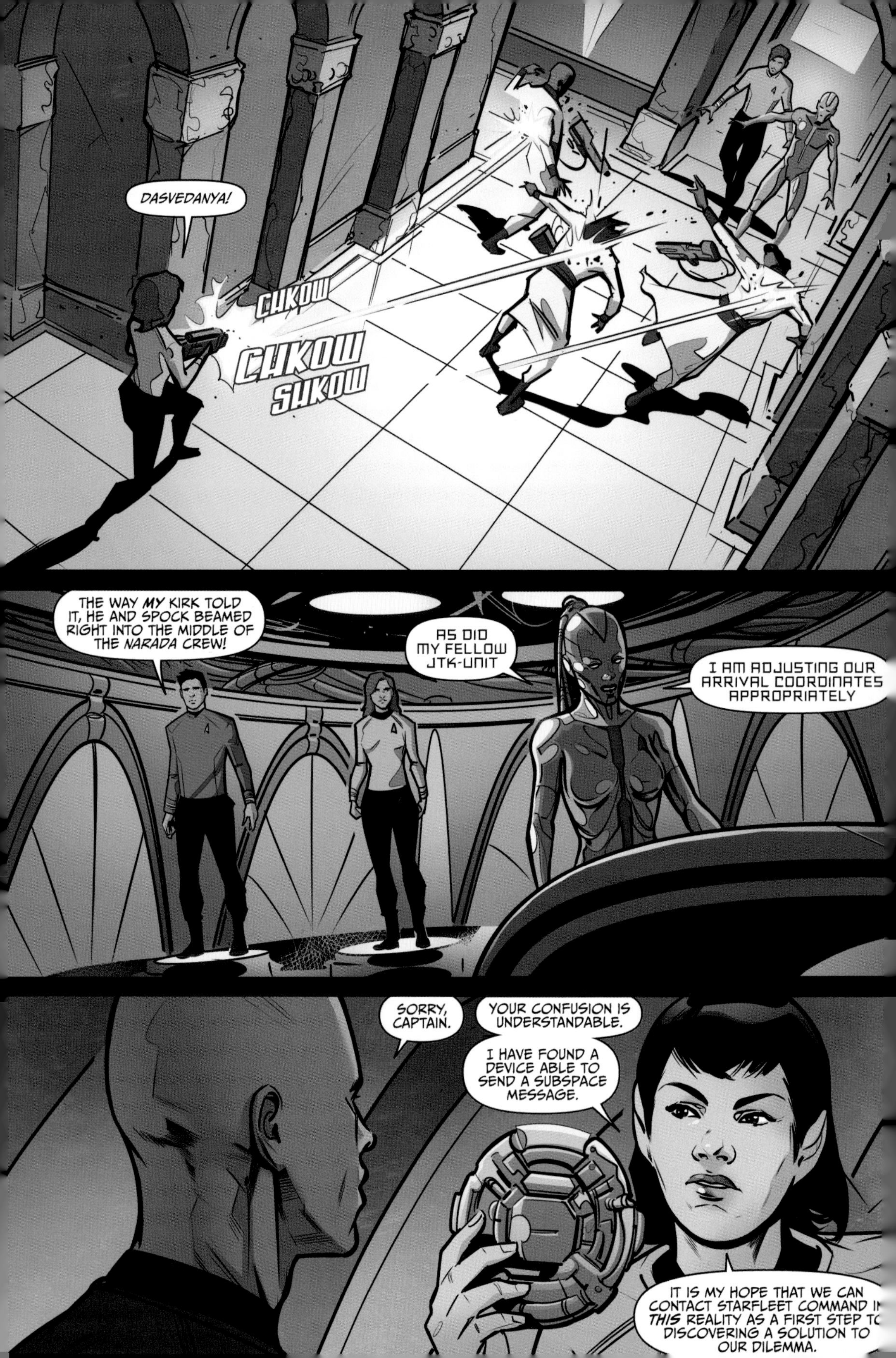
DASVEDANYA!
CHKOW
CHKOW
SHKOW
THE WAY *MY* KIRK TOLD IT, HE AND SPOCK BEAMED RIGHT INTO THE MIDDLE OF THE *NARADA* CREW!
AS DID MY FELLOW JTK-UNIT
I AM ADJUSTING OUR ARRIVAL COORDINATES APPROPRIATELY
SORRY, CAPTAIN.
YOUR CONFUSION IS UNDERSTANDABLE.
I HAVE FOUND A DEVICE ABLE TO SEND A SUBSPACE MESSAGE.
IT IS MY HOPE THAT WE CAN CONTACT STARFLEET COMMAND IN *THIS* REALITY AS A FIRST STEP TO DISCOVERING A SOLUTION TO OUR DILEMMA.

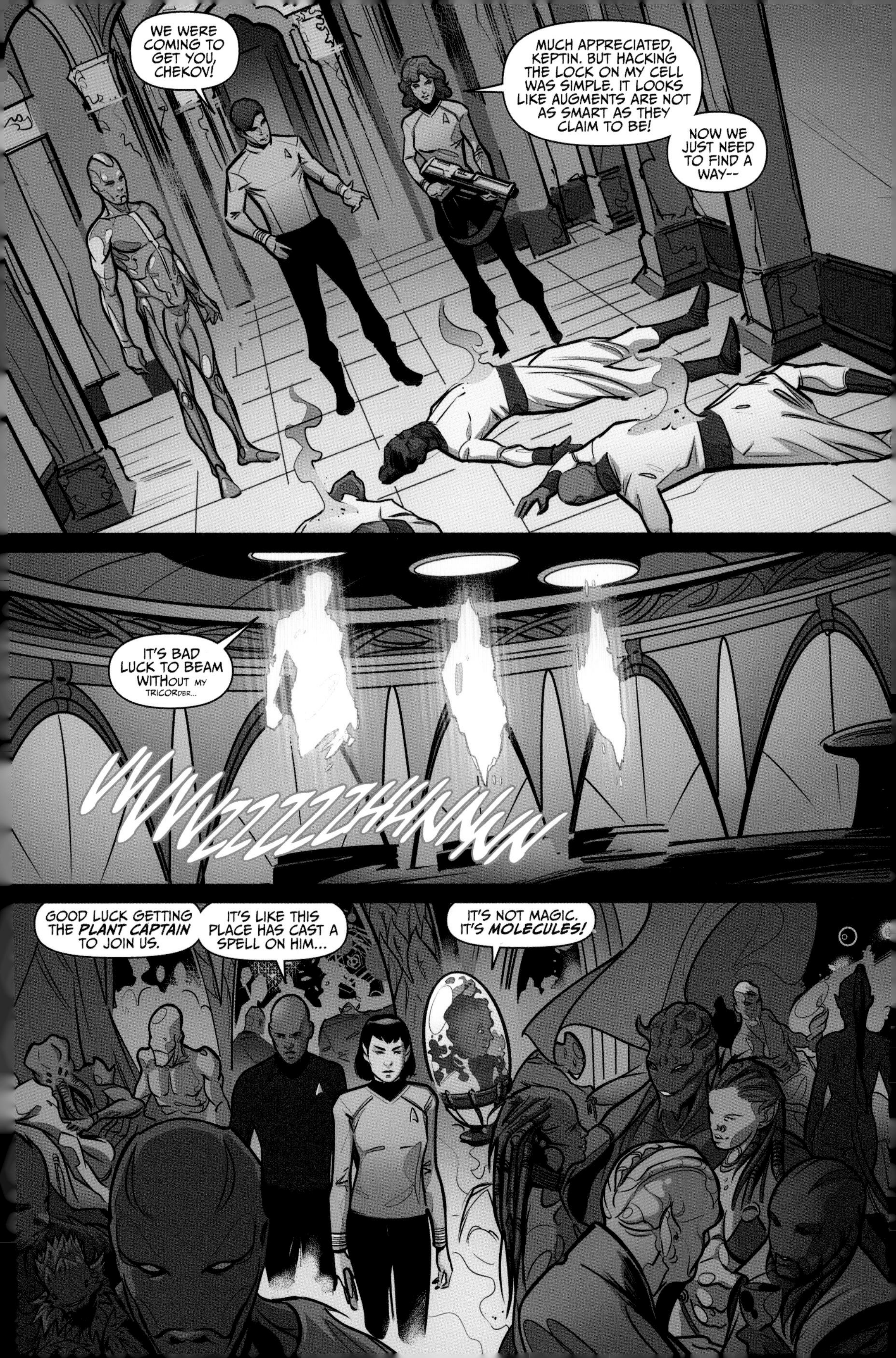
WE WERE COMING TO GET YOU, CHEKOV!
MUCH APPRECIATED, KEPTIN. BUT HACKING THE LOCK ON MY CELL WAS SIMPLE. IT LOOKS LIKE AUGMENTS ARE NOT AS SMART AS THEY CLAIM TO BE!
NOW WE JUST NEED TO FIND A WAY--
IT'S BAD LUCK TO BEAM WITHOUT MY TRICORDER...
VVVVVZZZZZHHNNNN
GOOD LUCK GETTING THE *PLANT CAPTAIN* TO JOIN US.
IT'S LIKE THIS PLACE HAS CAST A SPELL ON HIM...
IT'S NOT MAGIC. IT'S *MOLECULES!*

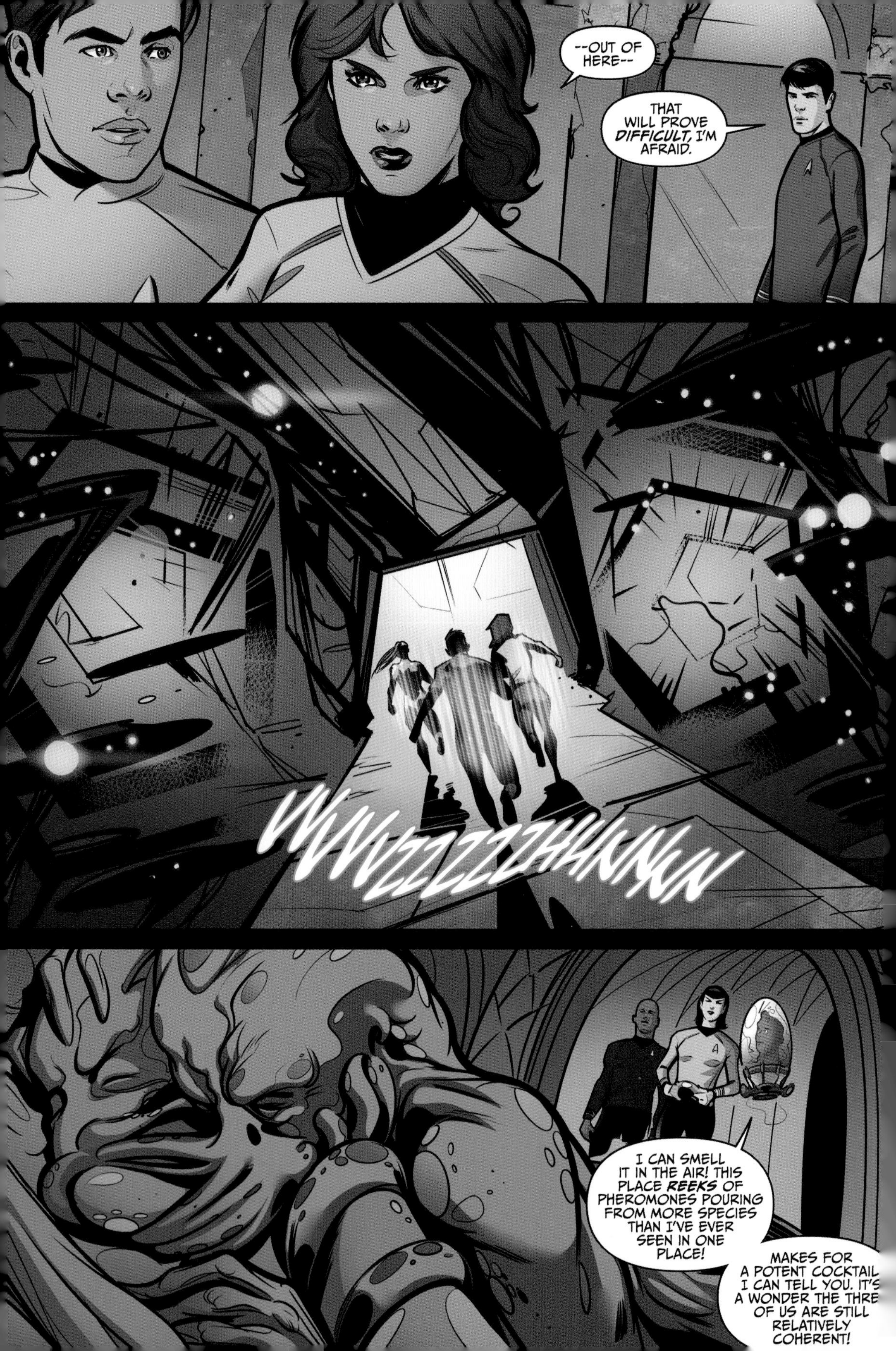
--OUT OF HERE--
THAT WILL PROVE DIFFICULT, I'M AFRAID.
VVVVVZZZZZHHHNNNN
I CAN SMELL IT IN THE AIR! THIS PLACE REEKS OF PHEROMONES POURING FROM MORE SPECIES THAN I'VE EVER SEEN IN ONE PLACE!
MAKES FOR A POTENT COCKTAIL I CAN TELL YOU. IT'S A WONDER THE THRE OF US ARE STILL RELATIVELY COHERENT!

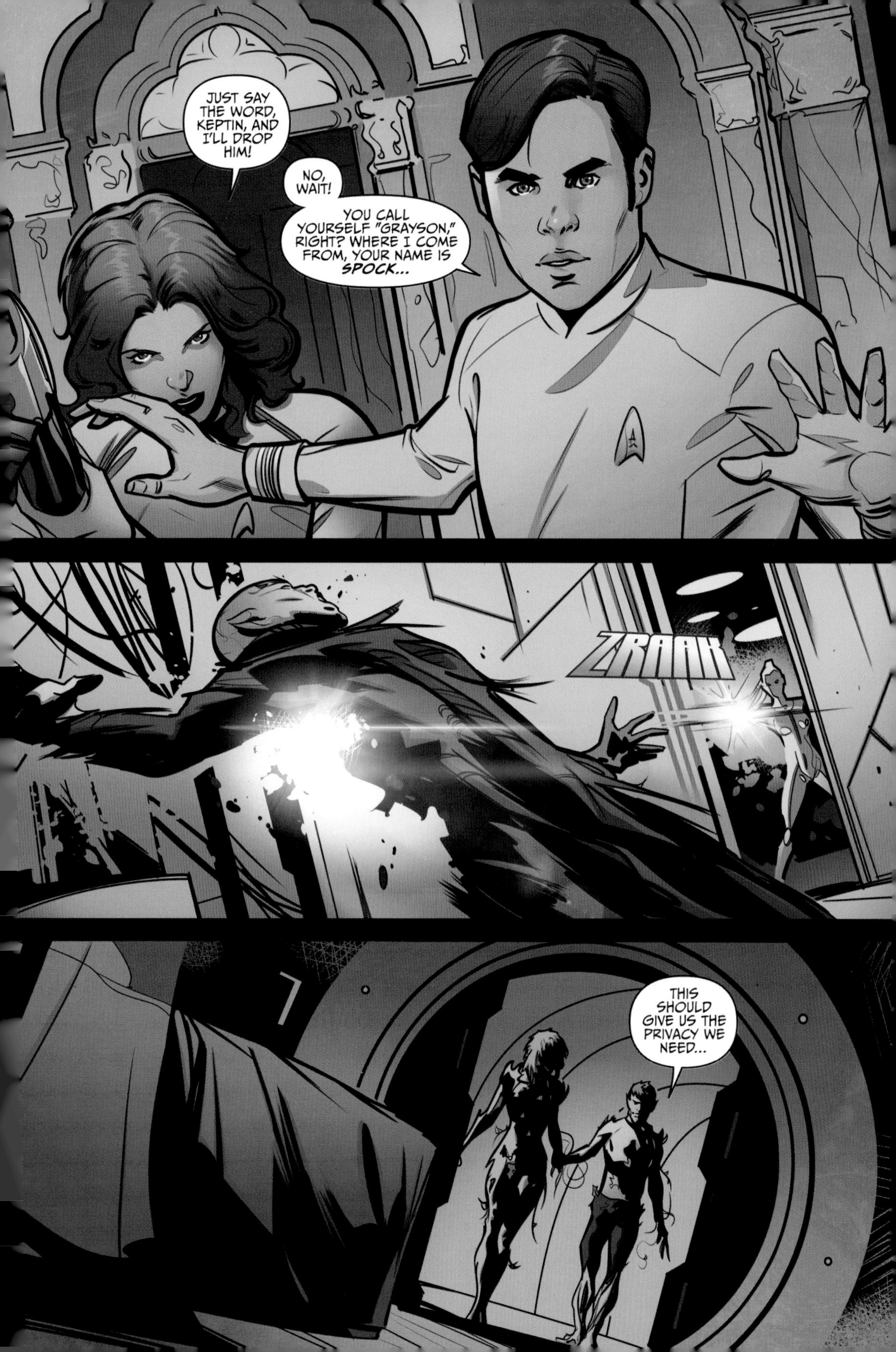
JUST SAY THE WORD, KEPTIN, AND I'LL DROP HIM!
NO, WAIT!
YOU CALL YOURSELF "GRAYSON," RIGHT? WHERE I COME FROM, YOUR NAME IS SPOCK...
ZRAAK
THIS SHOULD GIVE US THE PRIVACY WE NEED...

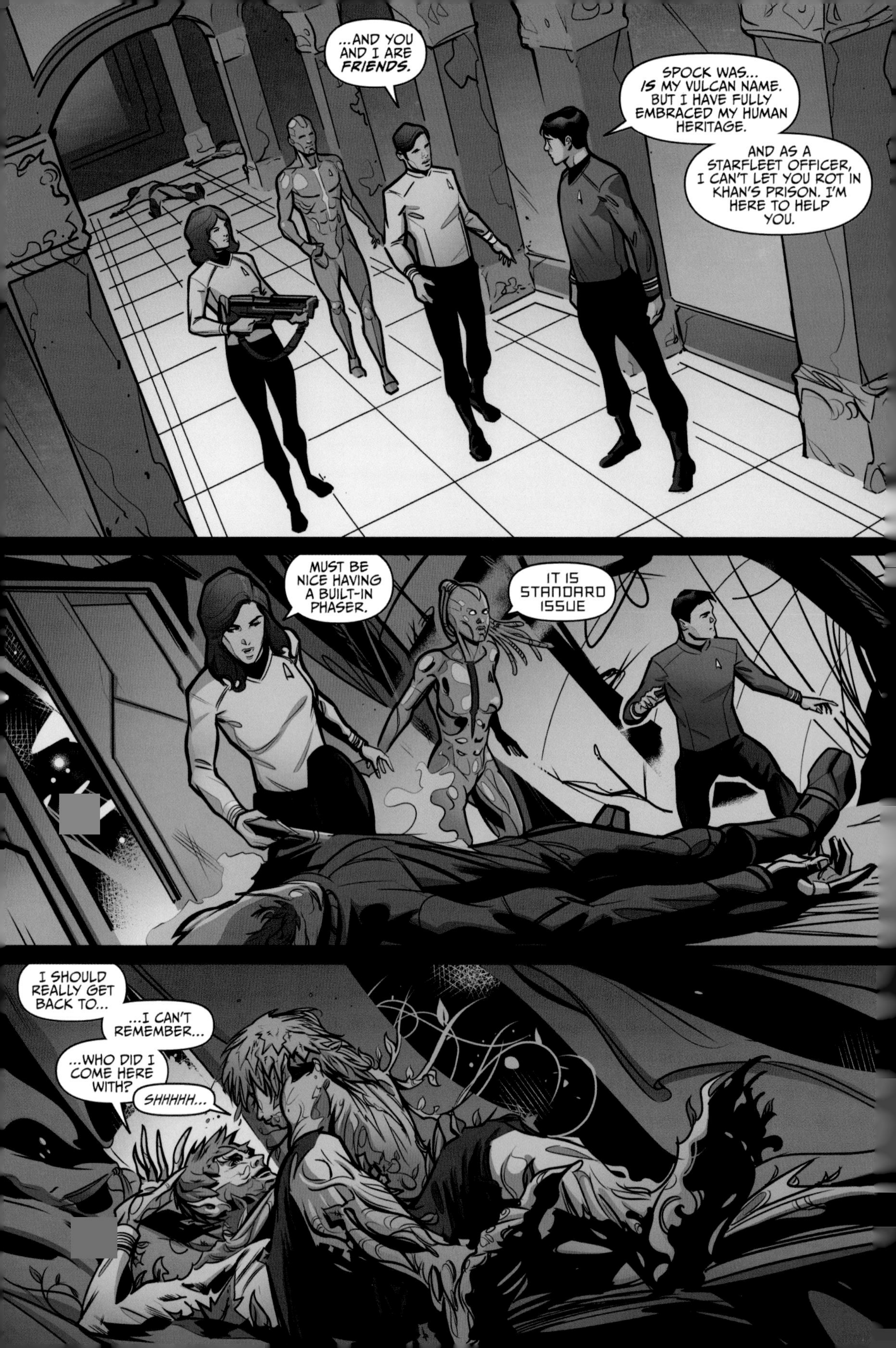

...AND YOU AND I ARE *FRIENDS.*
SPOCK WAS... *IS* MY VULCAN NAME. BUT I HAVE FULLY EMBRACED MY HUMAN HERITAGE.
AND AS A STARFLEET OFFICER, I CAN'T LET YOU ROT IN KHAN'S PRISON. I'M HERE TO HELP YOU.
MUST BE NICE HAVING A BUILT-IN PHASER.
IT IS STANDARD ISSUE
I SHOULD REALLY GET BACK TO...
...I CAN'T REMEMBER...
...WHO DID I COME HERE WITH?
SHHHHH...

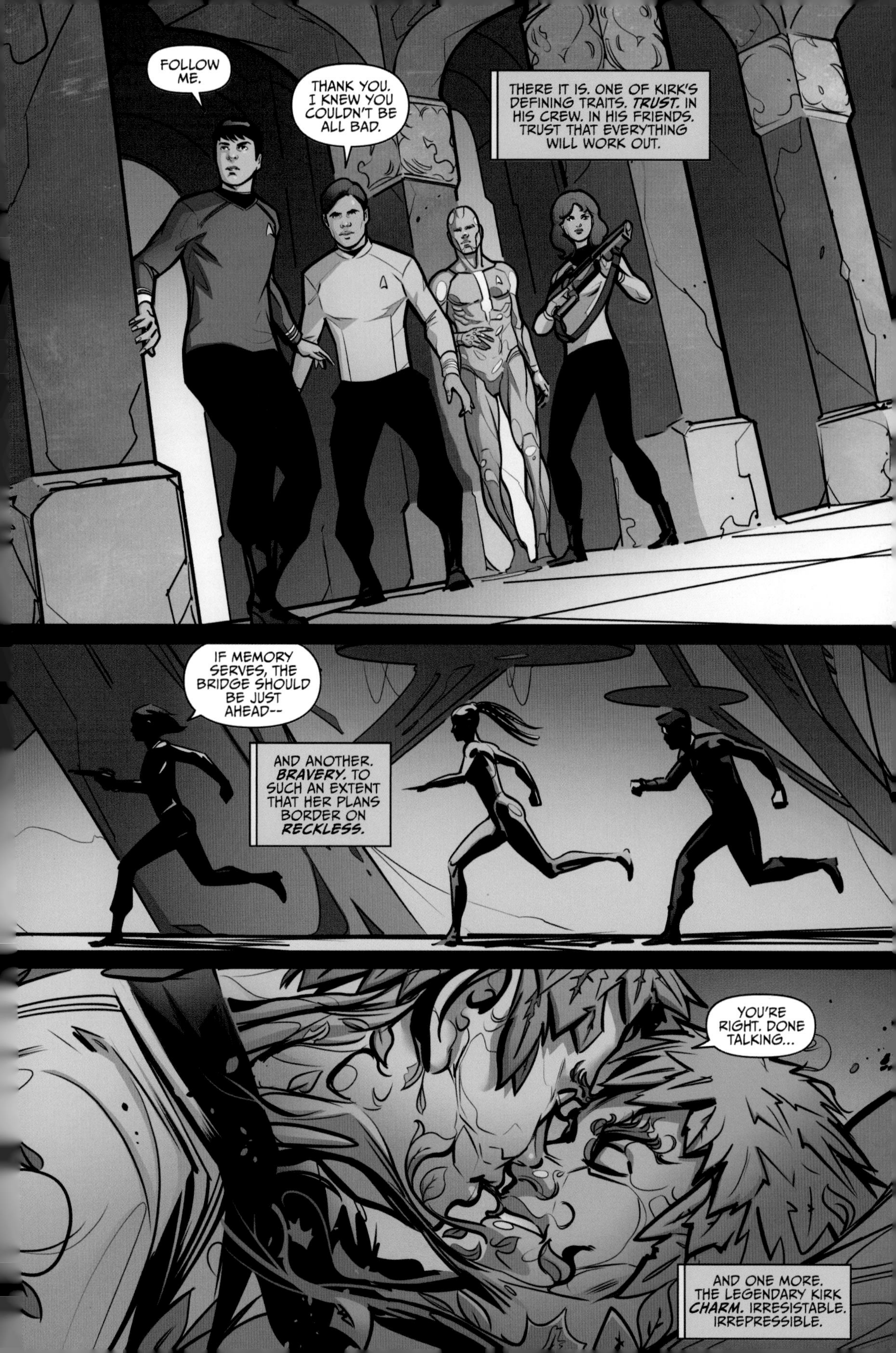
FOLLOW ME.
THANK YOU. I KNEW YOU COULDN'T BE ALL BAD.
THERE IT IS. ONE OF KIRK'S DEFINING TRAITS. TRUST. IN HIS CREW. IN HIS FRIENDS. TRUST THAT EVERYTHING WILL WORK OUT.
IF MEMORY SERVES, THE BRIDGE SHOULD BE JUST AHEAD--
AND ANOTHER. BRAVERY. TO SUCH AN EXTENT THAT HER PLANS BORDER ON RECKLESS.
YOU'RE RIGHT. DONE TALKING...
AND ONE MORE. THE LEGENDARY KIRK CHARM. IRRESISTABLE. IRREPRESSIBLE.

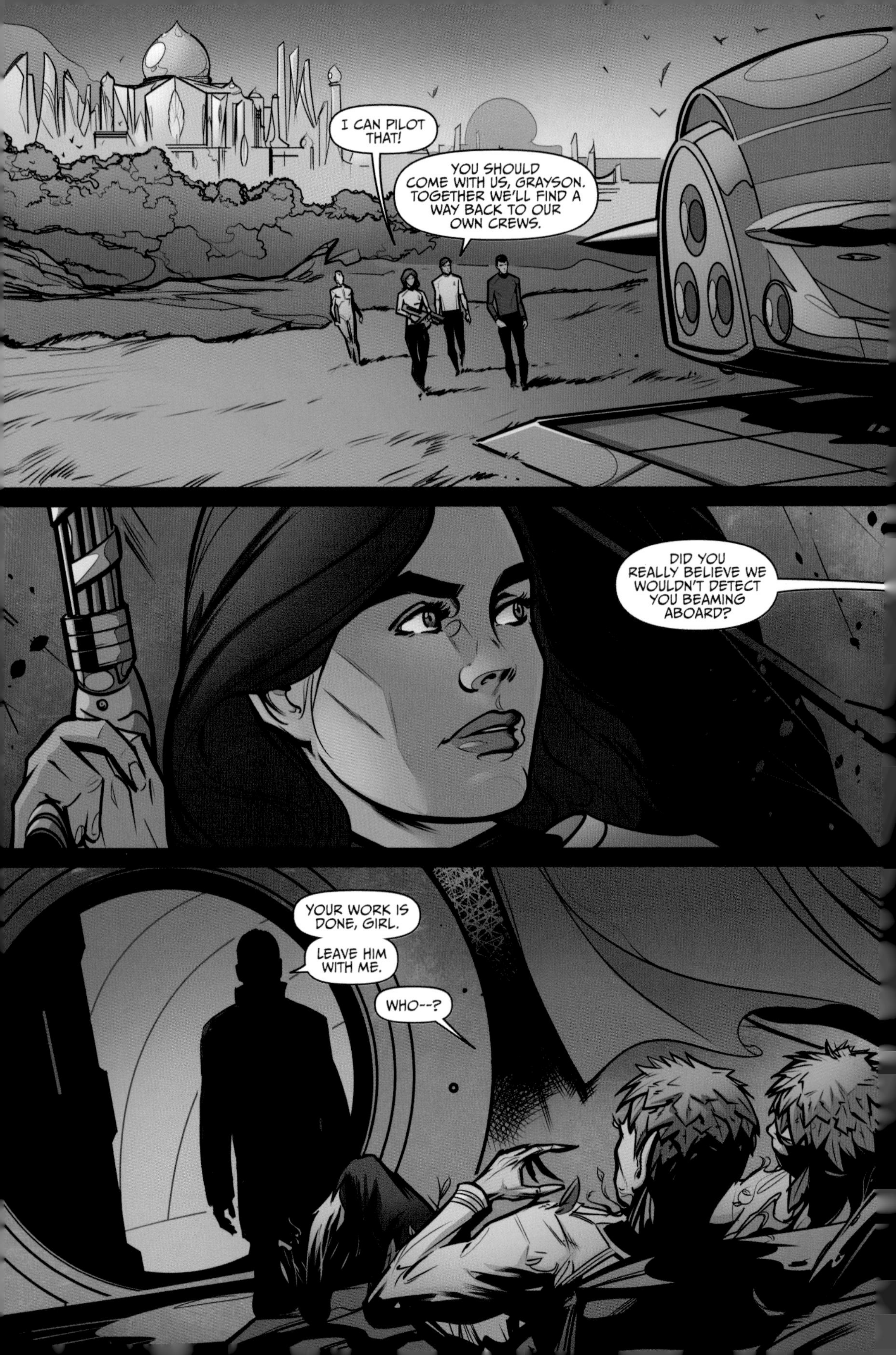
I CAN PILOT THAT!
YOU SHOULD COME WITH US, GRAYSON. TOGETHER WE'LL FIND A WAY BACK TO OUR OWN CREWS.
DID YOU REALLY BELIEVE WE WOULDN'T DETECT YOU BEAMING ABOARD?
YOUR WORK IS DONE, GIRL.
LEAVE HIM WITH ME.
WHO--?

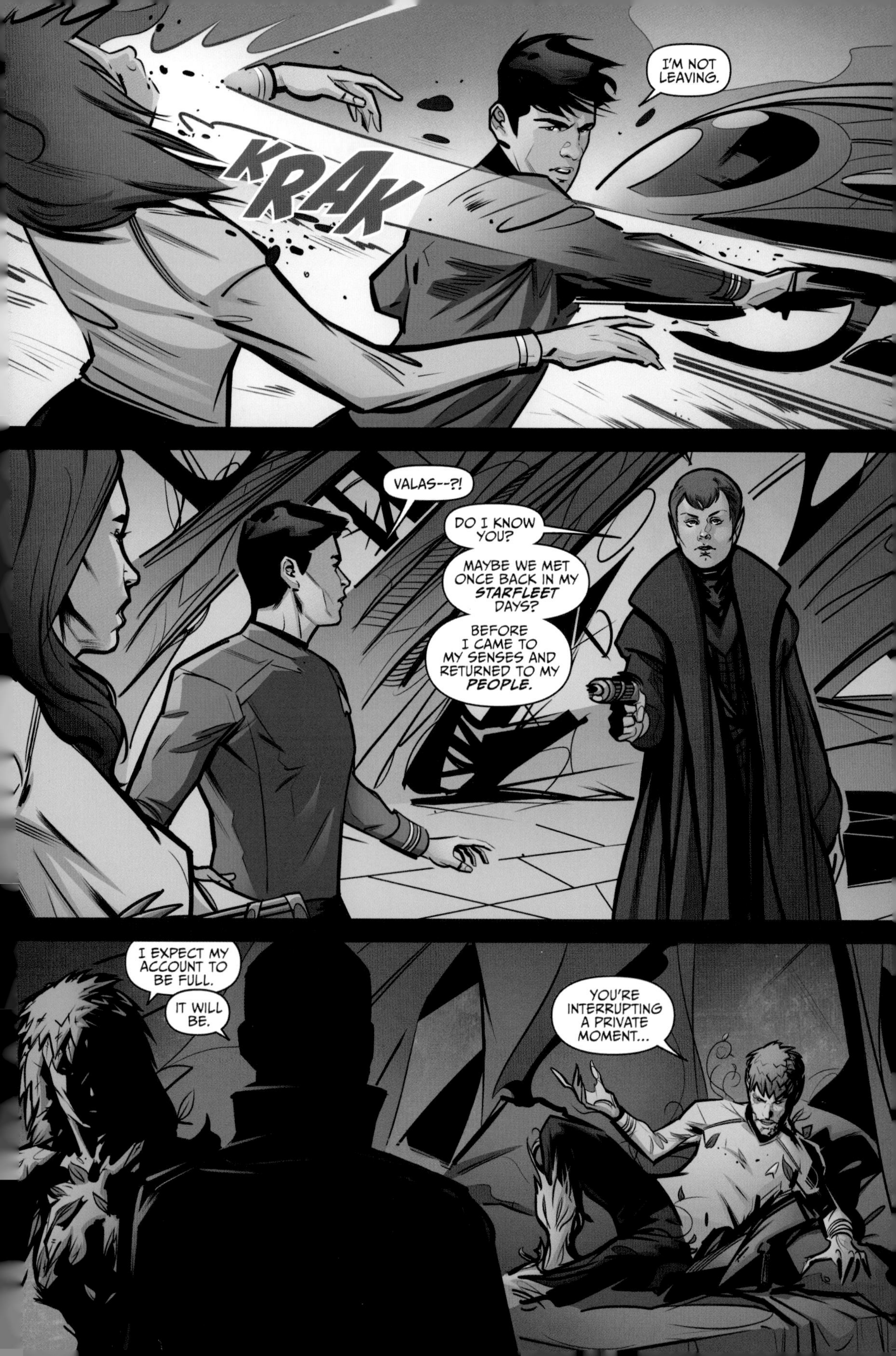
I'M NOT LEAVING.
KRAK
VALAS--?!
DO I KNOW YOU?
MAYBE WE MET ONCE BACK IN MY STARFLEET DAYS?
BEFORE I CAME TO MY SENSES AND RETURNED TO MY PEOPLE.
I EXPECT MY ACCOUNT TO BE FULL.
IT WILL BE.
YOU'RE INTERRUPTING A PRIVATE MOMENT...

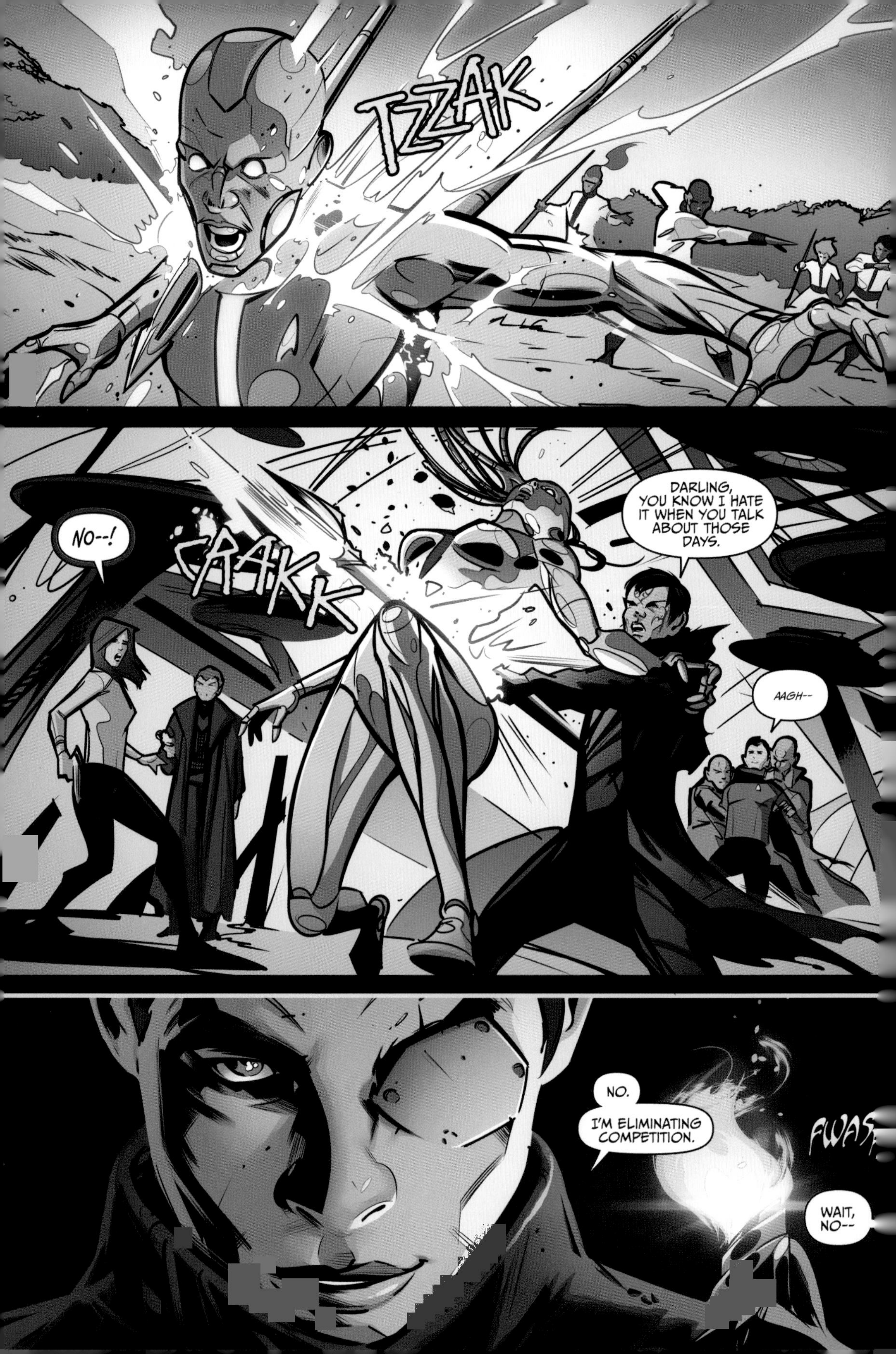
TZZAK
NO--!
CRAKK
DARLING, YOU KNOW I HATE IT WHEN YOU TALK ABOUT THOSE DAYS.
AAGH--
NO.
I'M ELIMINATING COMPETITION.
FWAS
WAIT, NO--

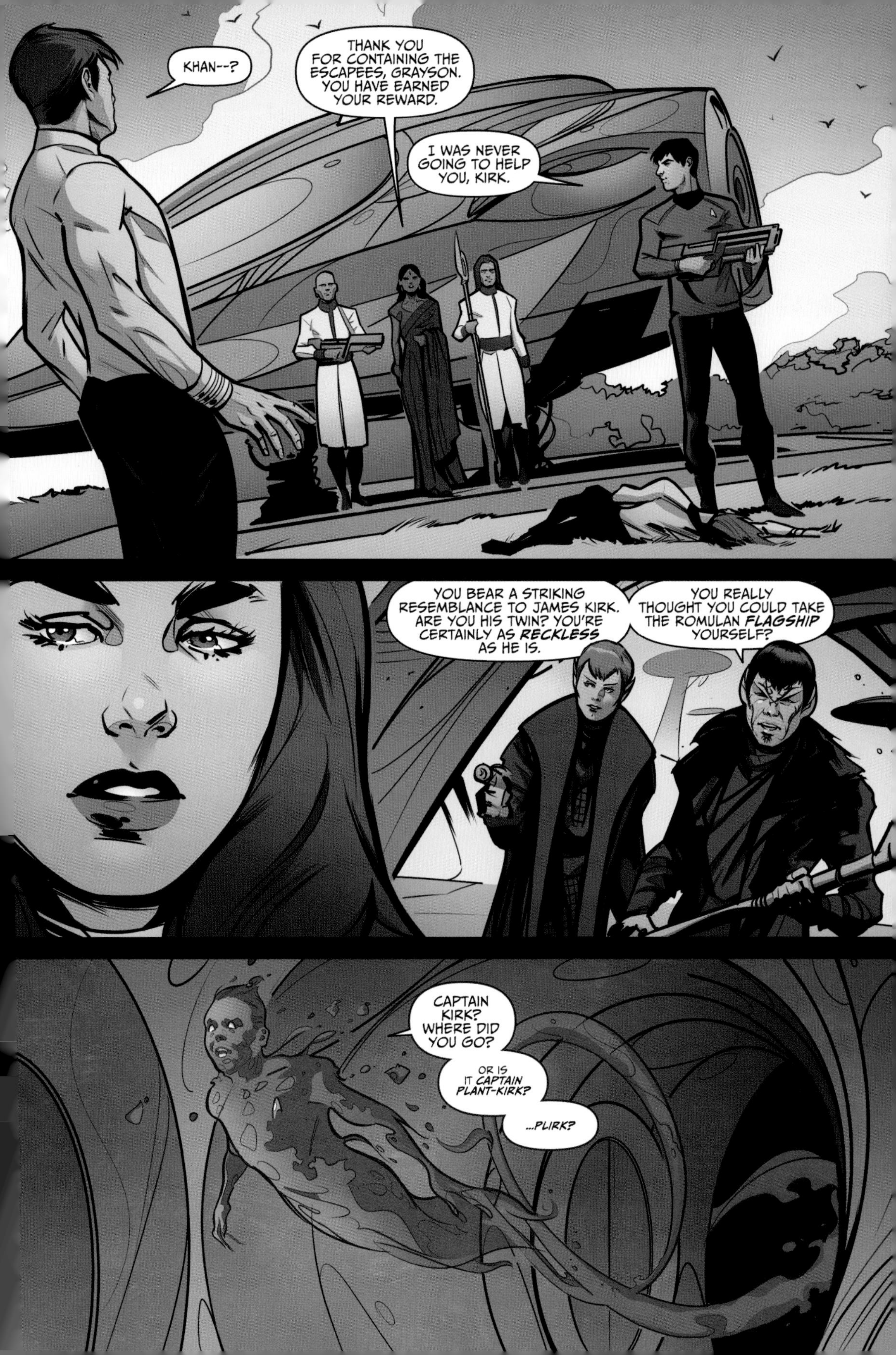
KHAN--?
THANK YOU FOR CONTAINING THE ESCAPEES, GRAYSON. YOU HAVE EARNED YOUR REWARD.
I WAS NEVER GOING TO HELP YOU, KIRK.
YOU BEAR A STRIKING RESEMBLANCE TO JAMES KIRK. ARE YOU HIS TWIN? YOU'RE CERTAINLY AS *RECKLESS* AS HE IS.
YOU REALLY THOUGHT YOU COULD TAKE THE ROMULAN *FLAGSHIP* YOURSELF?
CAPTAIN KIRK? WHERE DID YOU GO?
OR IS IT *CAPTAIN PLANT-KIRK?*
...PLIRK?

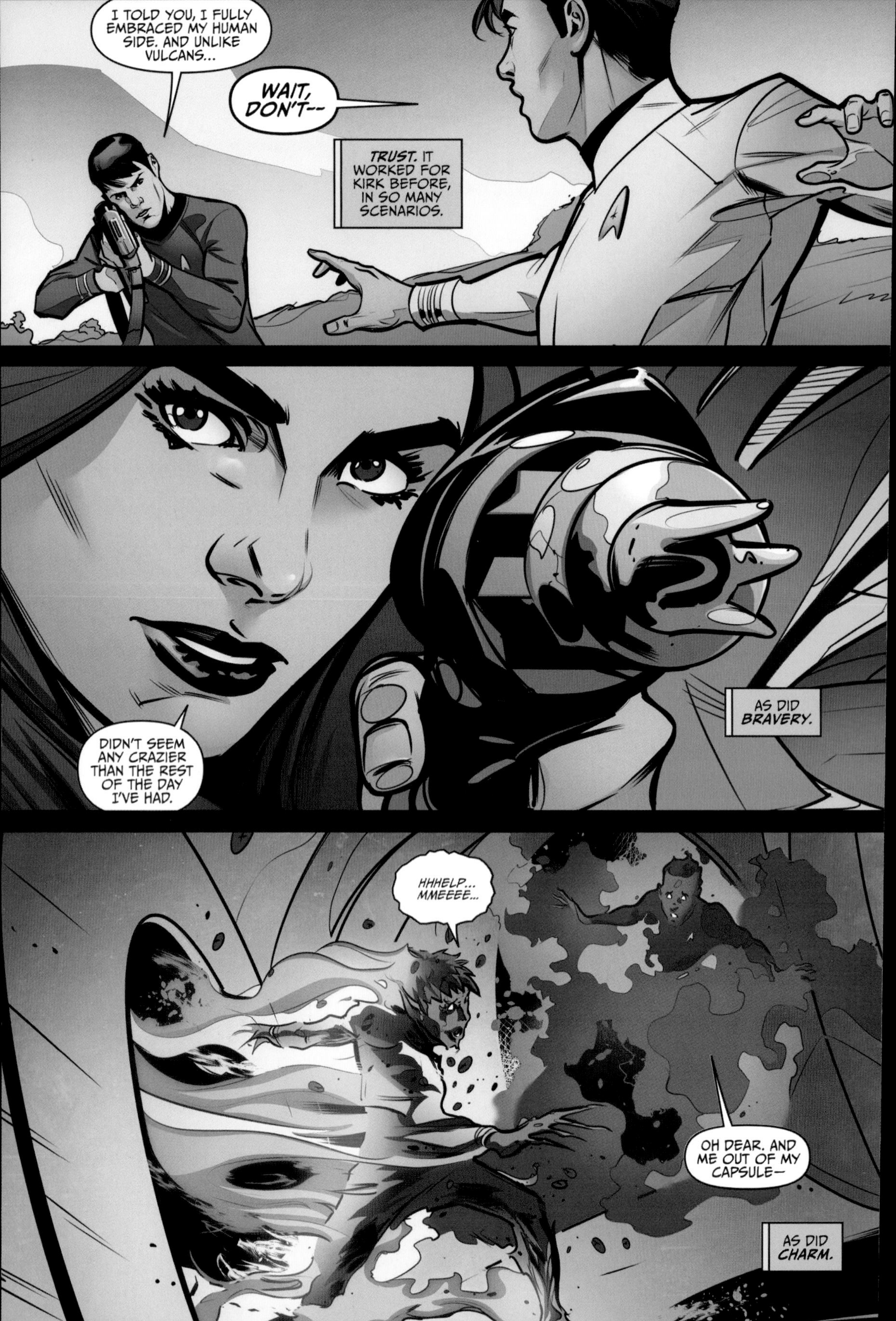

I TOLD YOU, I FULLY EMBRACED MY HUMAN SIDE. AND UNLIKE VULCANS...
WAIT, DON'T--
TRUST. IT WORKED FOR KIRK BEFORE, IN SO MANY SCENARIOS.
AS DID BRAVERY.
DIDN'T SEEM ANY CRAZIER THAN THE REST OF THE DAY I'VE HAD.
HHHELP... MMEEEE...
OH DEAR. AND ME OUT OF MY CAPSULE—
AS DID CHARM.

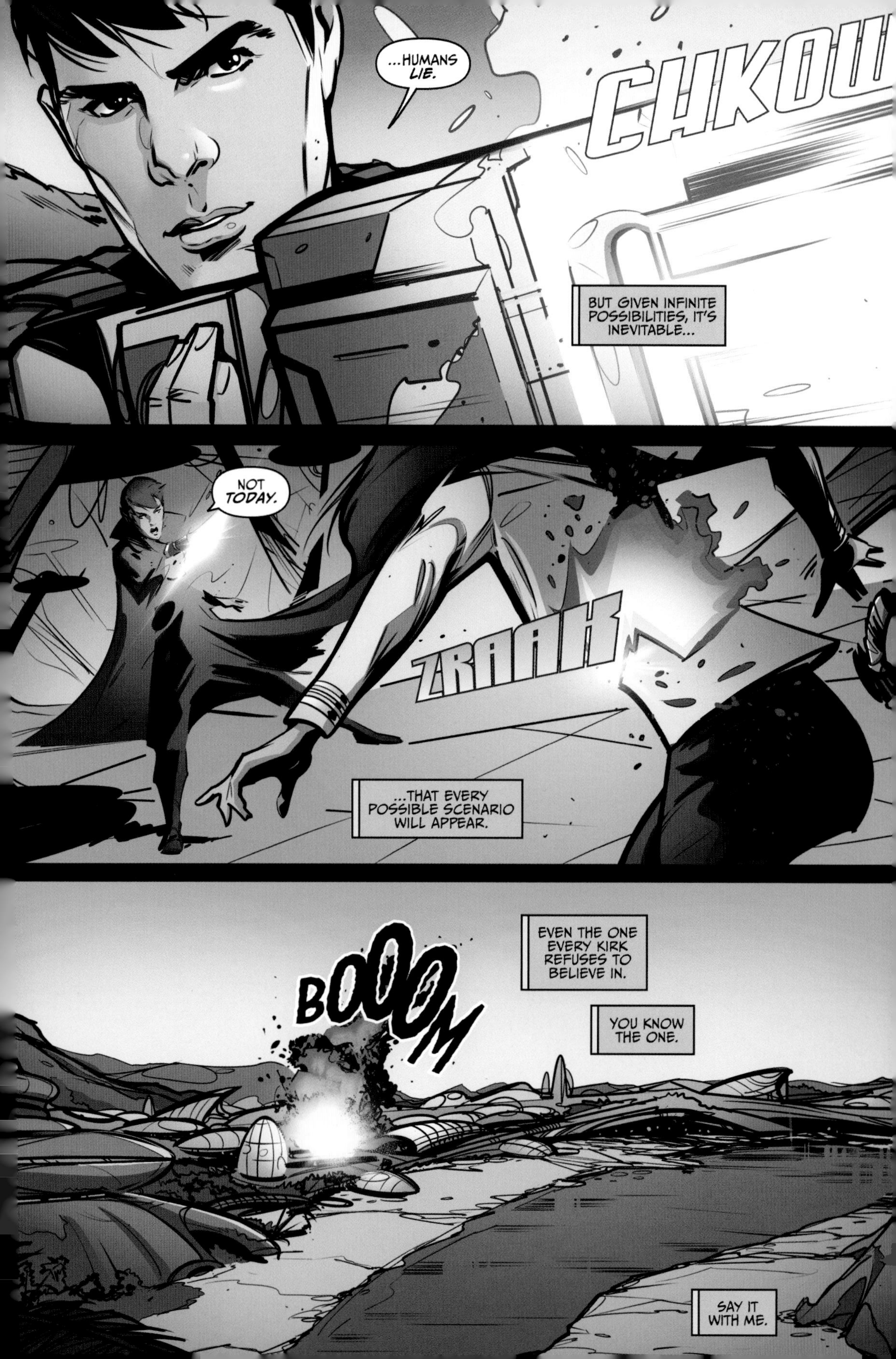

...HUMANS LIE.
CHKOW
BUT GIVEN INFINITE POSSIBILITIES, IT'S INEVITABLE...
NOT TODAY.
ZRAAK
...THAT EVERY POSSIBLE SCENARIO WILL APPEAR.
EVEN THE ONE EVERY KIRK REFUSES TO BELIEVE IN.
BOOOOM
YOU KNOW THE ONE.
SAY IT WITH ME.

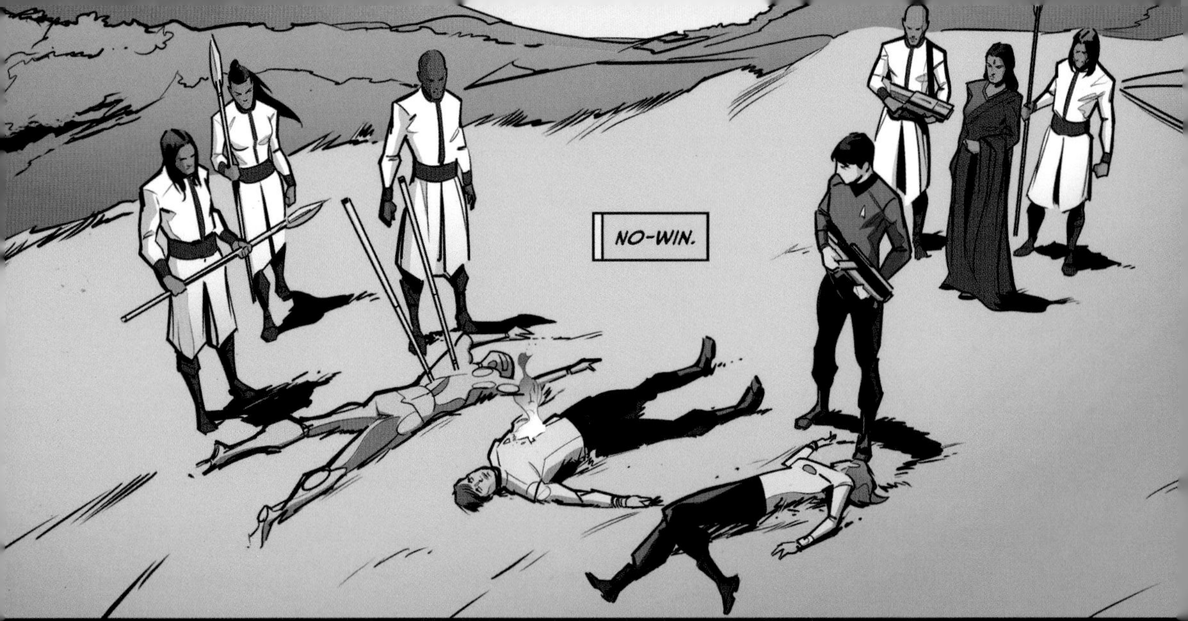
NO-WIN.

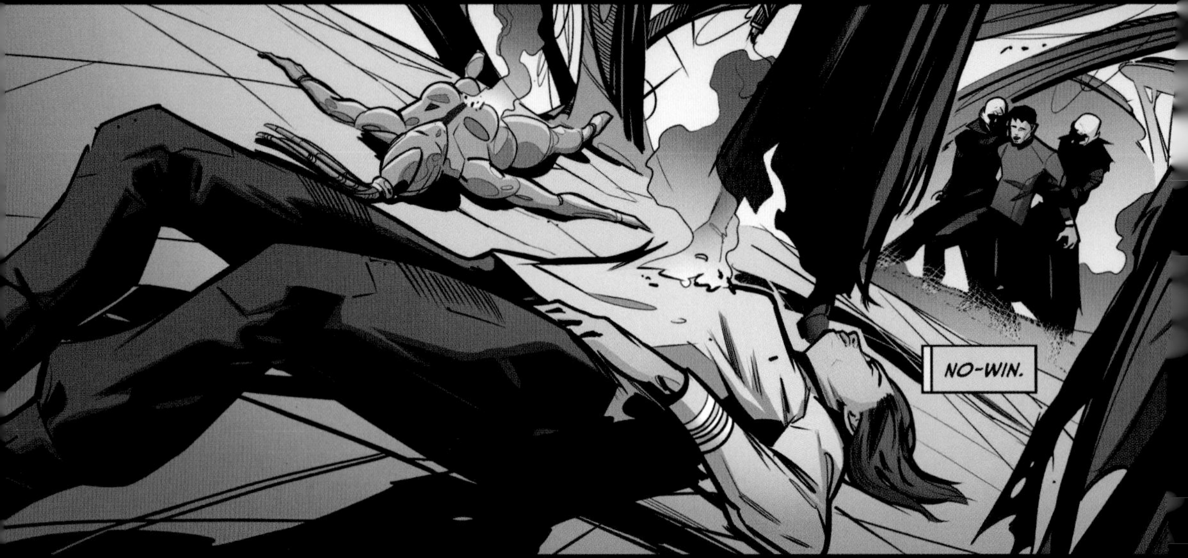
NO-WIN.

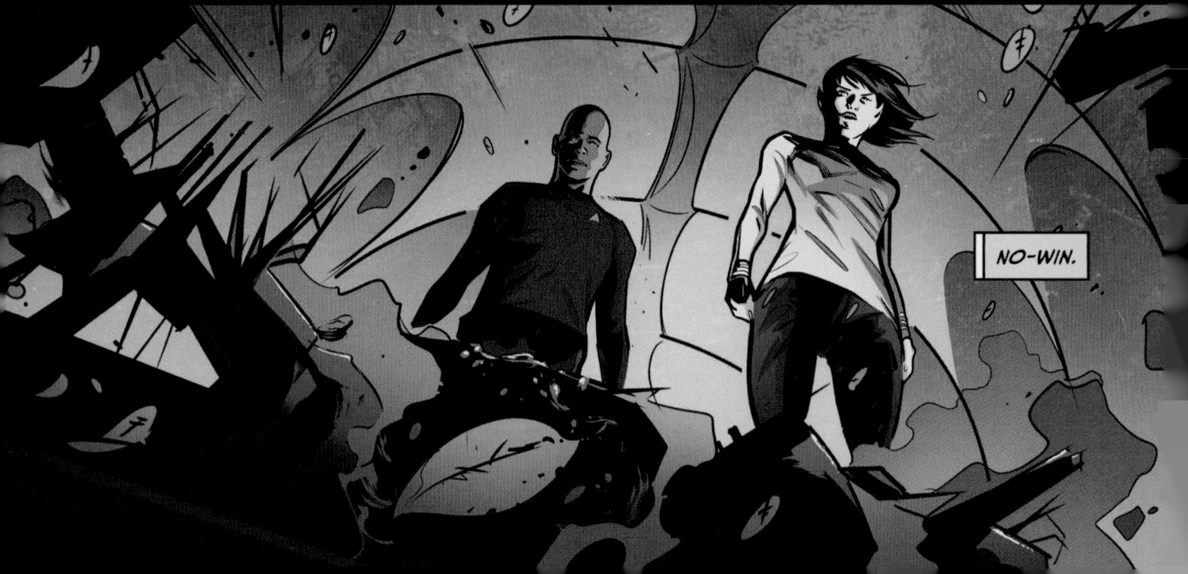
NO-WIN.

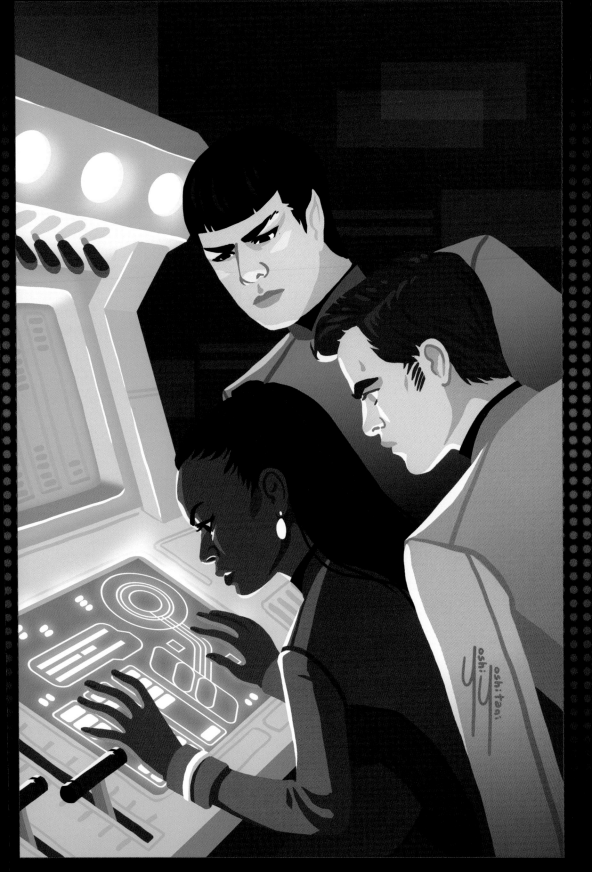

art by
Yoshi Yoshitani

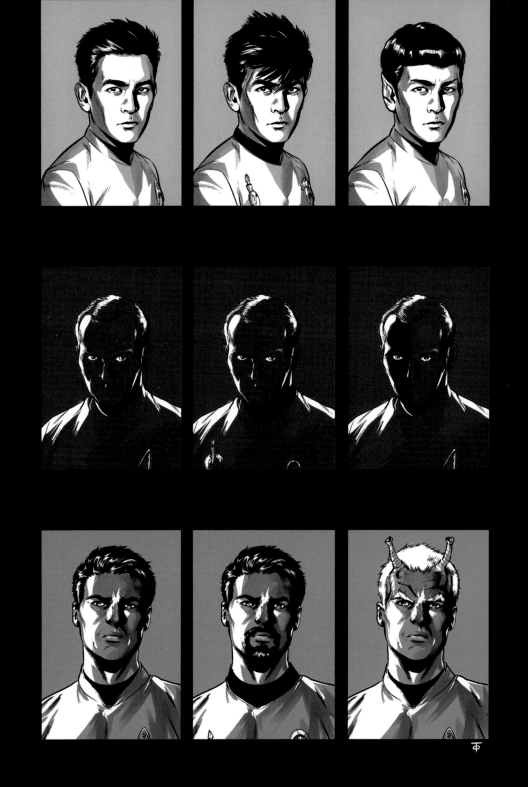

art by
Marcus To

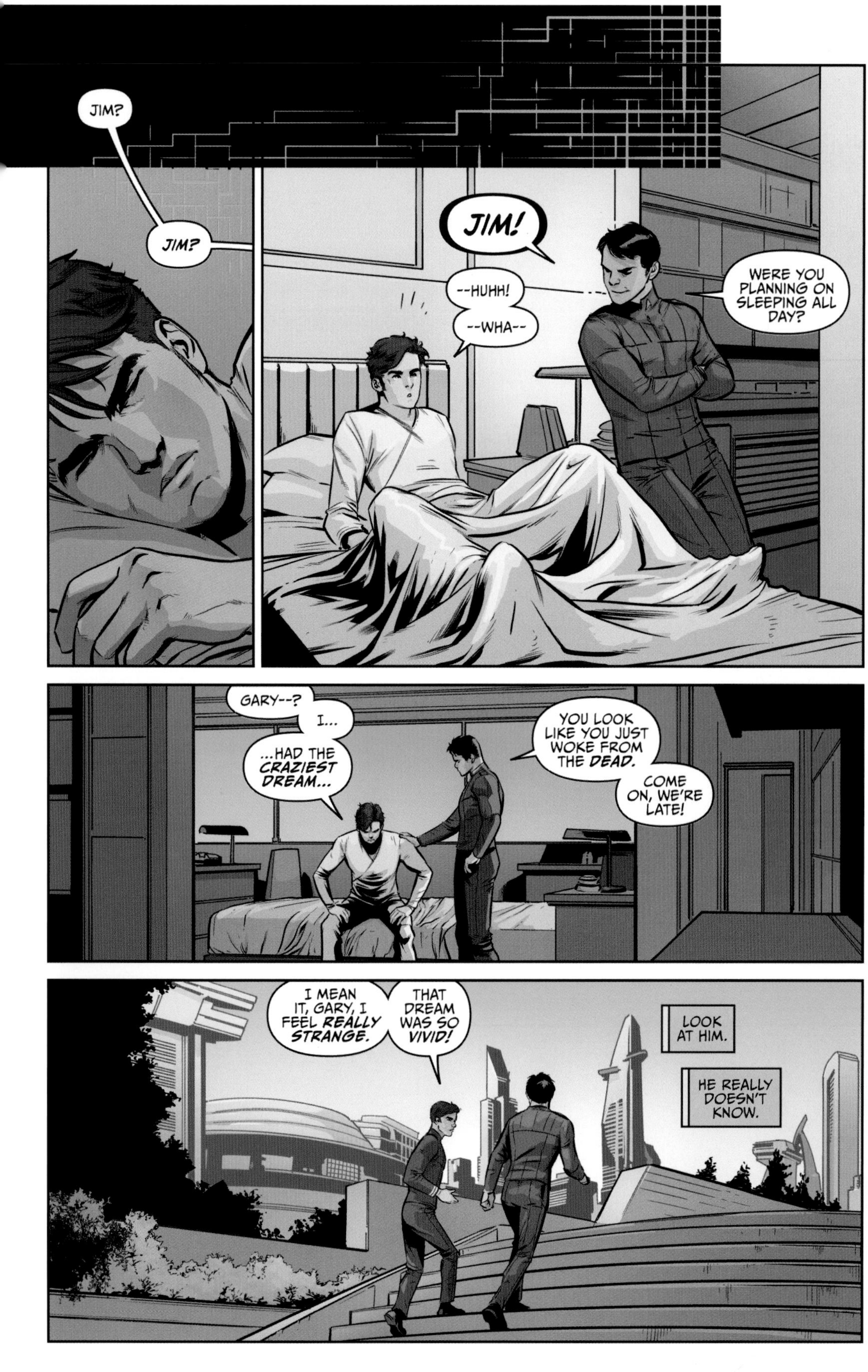
JIM?
JIM?
JIM!
--HUHH!
--WHA--
WERE YOU PLANNING ON SLEEPING ALL DAY?
GARY--?
I...
...HAD THE CRAZIEST DREAM...
YOU LOOK LIKE YOU JUST WOKE FROM THE DEAD.
COME ON, WE'RE LATE!
I MEAN IT, GARY, I FEEL REALLY STRANGE.
THAT DREAM WAS SO VIVID!
LOOK AT HIM.
HE REALLY DOESN'T KNOW.

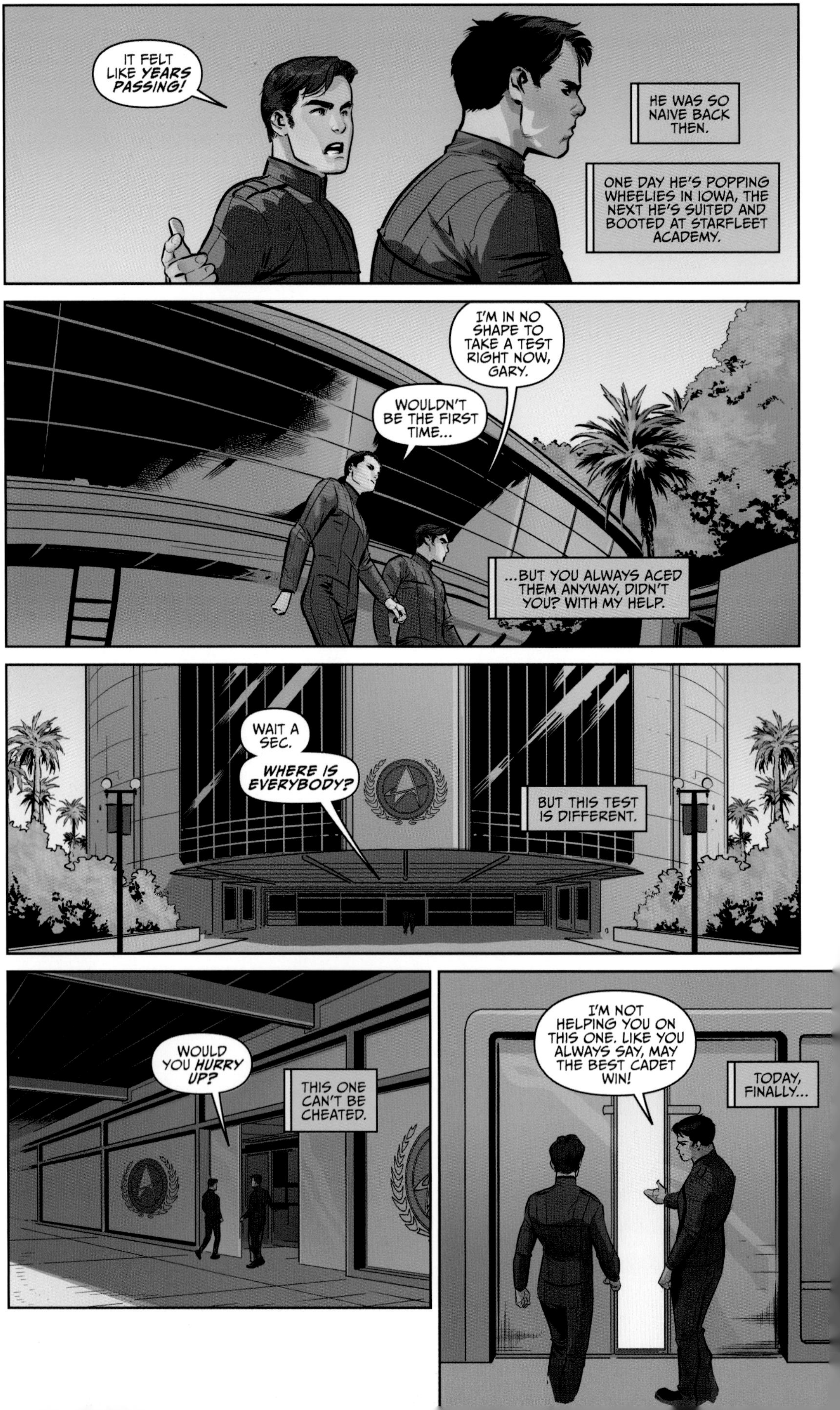
IT FELT LIKE YEARS PASSING!
HE WAS SO NAIVE BACK THEN.
ONE DAY HE'S POPPING WHEELIES IN IOWA, THE NEXT HE'S SUITED AND BOOTED AT STARFLEET ACADEMY.
I'M IN NO SHAPE TO TAKE A TEST RIGHT NOW, GARY.
WOULDN'T BE THE FIRST TIME...
...BUT YOU ALWAYS ACED THEM ANYWAY, DIDN'T YOU? WITH MY HELP.
WAIT A SEC.
WHERE IS EVERYBODY?
BUT THIS TEST IS DIFFERENT.
WOULD YOU HURRY UP?
THIS ONE CAN'T BE CHEATED.
I'M NOT HELPING YOU ON THIS ONE. LIKE YOU ALWAYS SAY, MAY THE BEST CADET WIN!
TODAY, FINALLY...

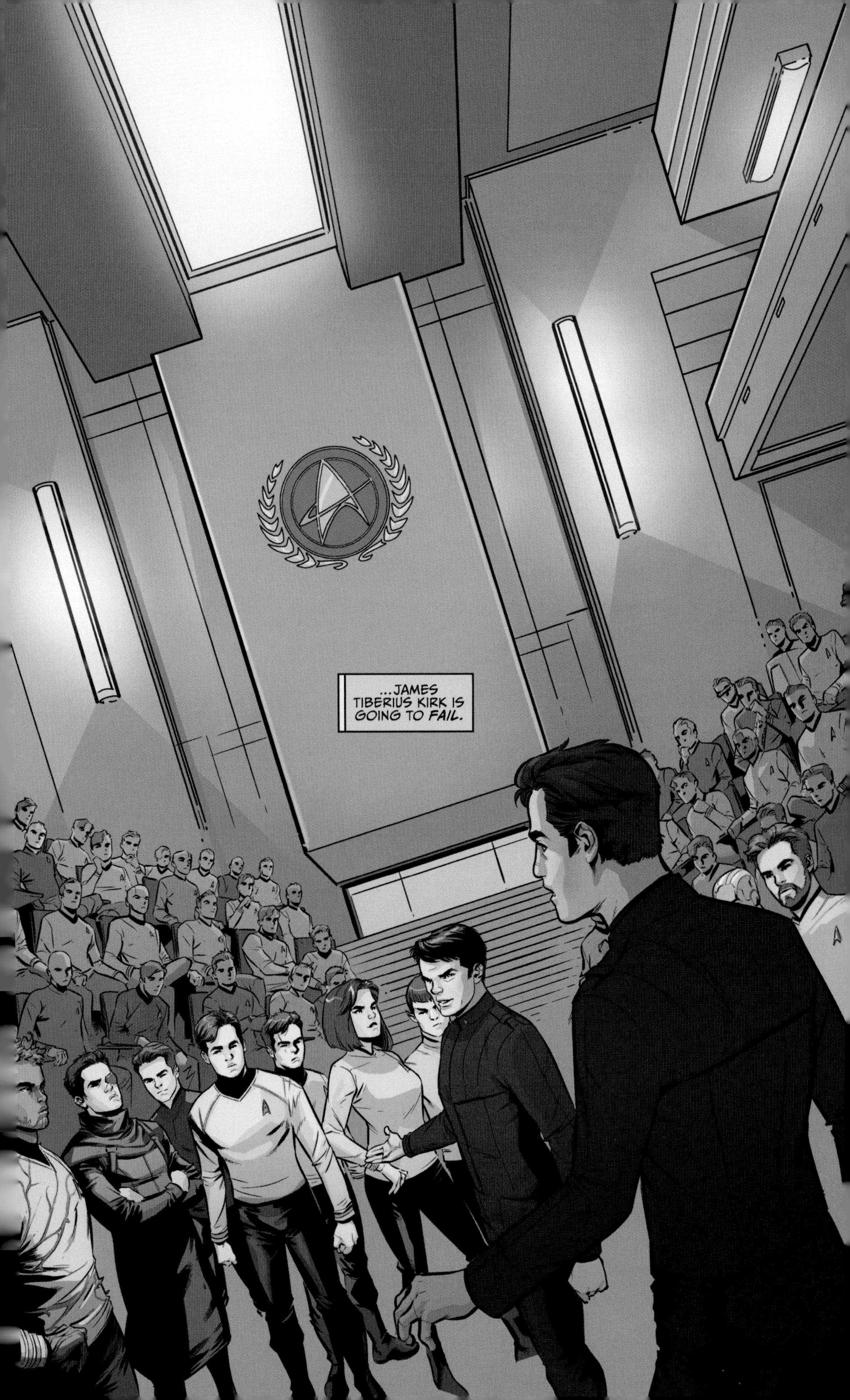
...JAMES TIBERIUS KIRK IS GOING TO *FAIL*.

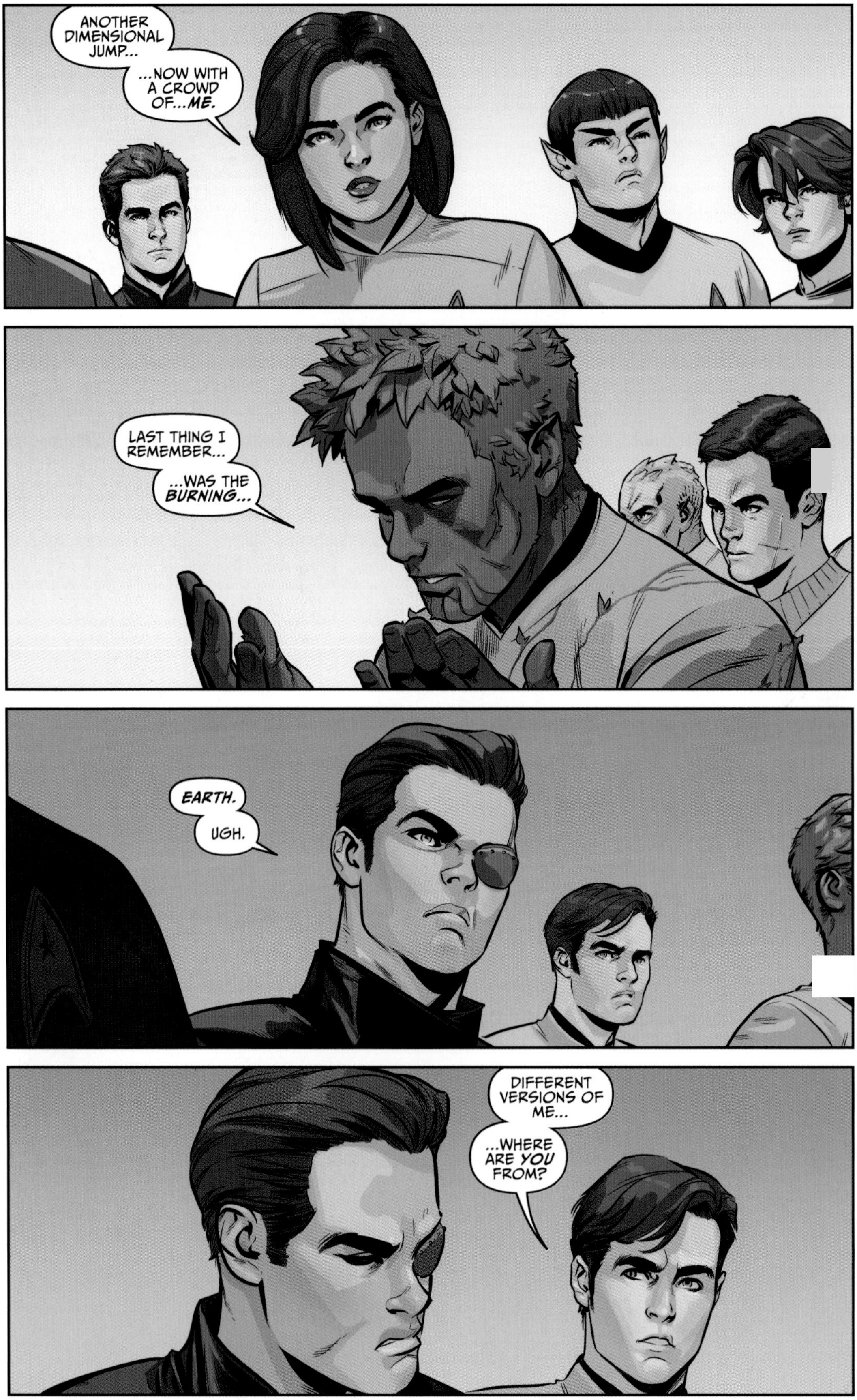
ANOTHER DIMENSIONAL JUMP...
...NOW WITH A CROWD OF...*ME.*
LAST THING I REMEMBER...
...WAS THE *BURNING...*
EARTH.
UGH.
DIFFERENT VERSIONS OF ME...
...WHERE ARE *YOU* FROM?

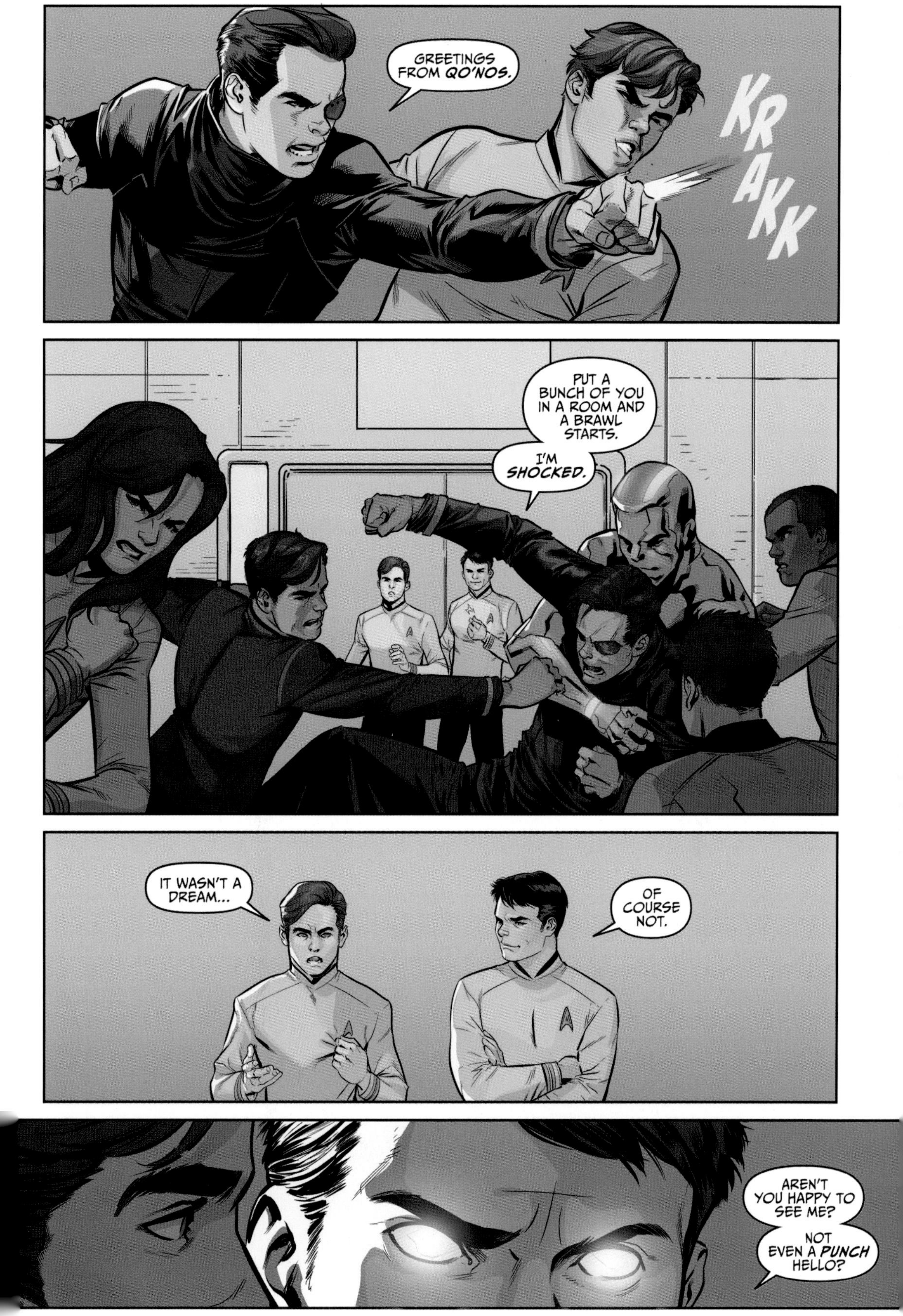
GREETINGS FROM QO'NOS.
KRAKK
PUT A BUNCH OF YOU IN A ROOM AND A BRAWL STARTS.
I'M SHOCKED.
IT WASN'T A DREAM...
OF COURSE NOT.
AREN'T YOU HAPPY TO SEE ME?
NOT EVEN A PUNCH HELLO?

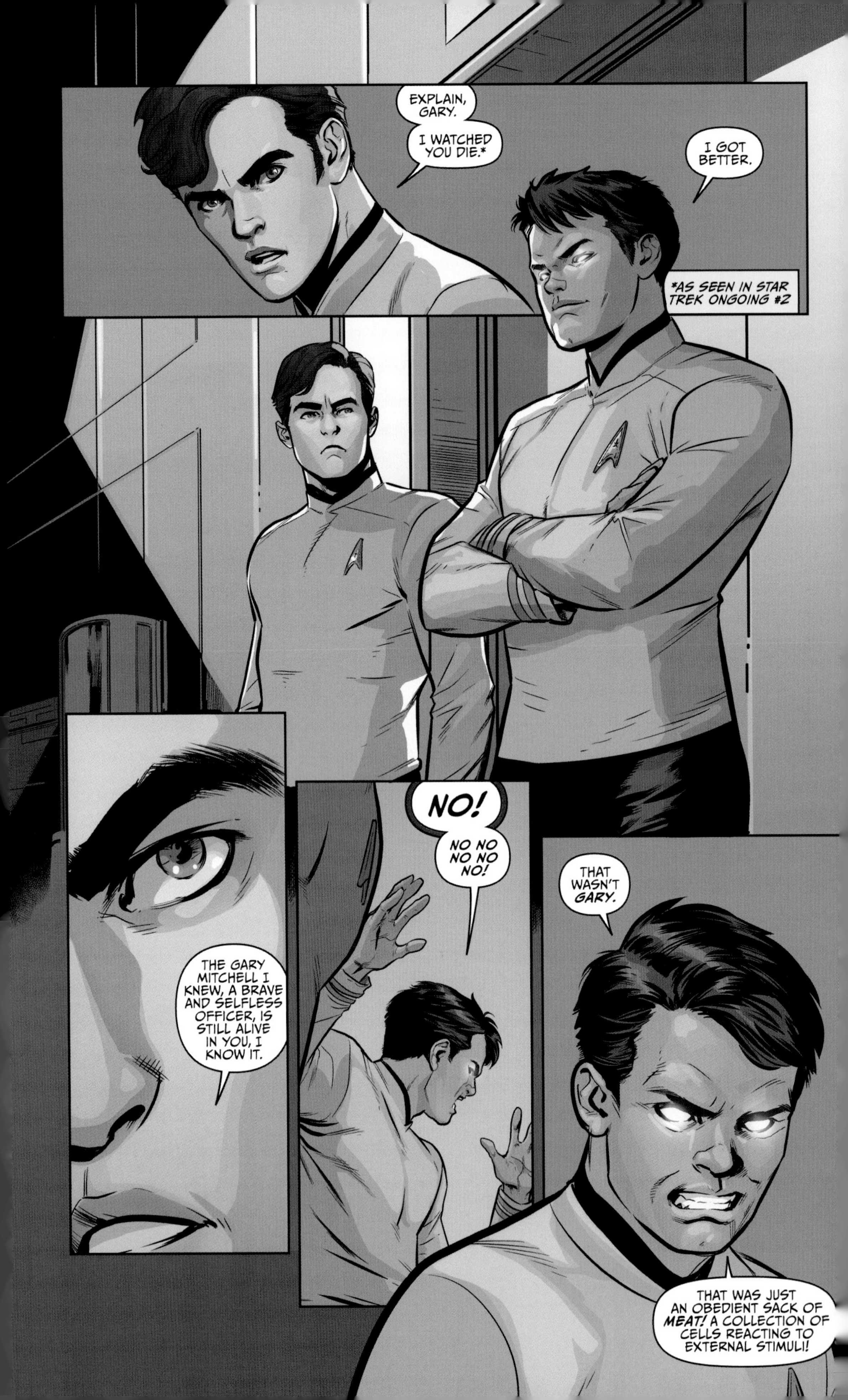
EXPLAIN, GARY.
I WATCHED YOU DIE.*
I GOT BETTER.
*AS SEEN IN STAR TREK ONGOING #2
THE GARY MITCHELL I KNEW, A BRAVE AND SELFLESS OFFICER, IS STILL ALIVE IN YOU, I KNOW IT.
NO!
NO NO NO NO NO!
THAT WASN'T GARY.
THAT WAS JUST AN OBEDIENT SACK OF MEAT! A COLLECTION OF CELLS REACTING TO EXTERNAL STIMULI!

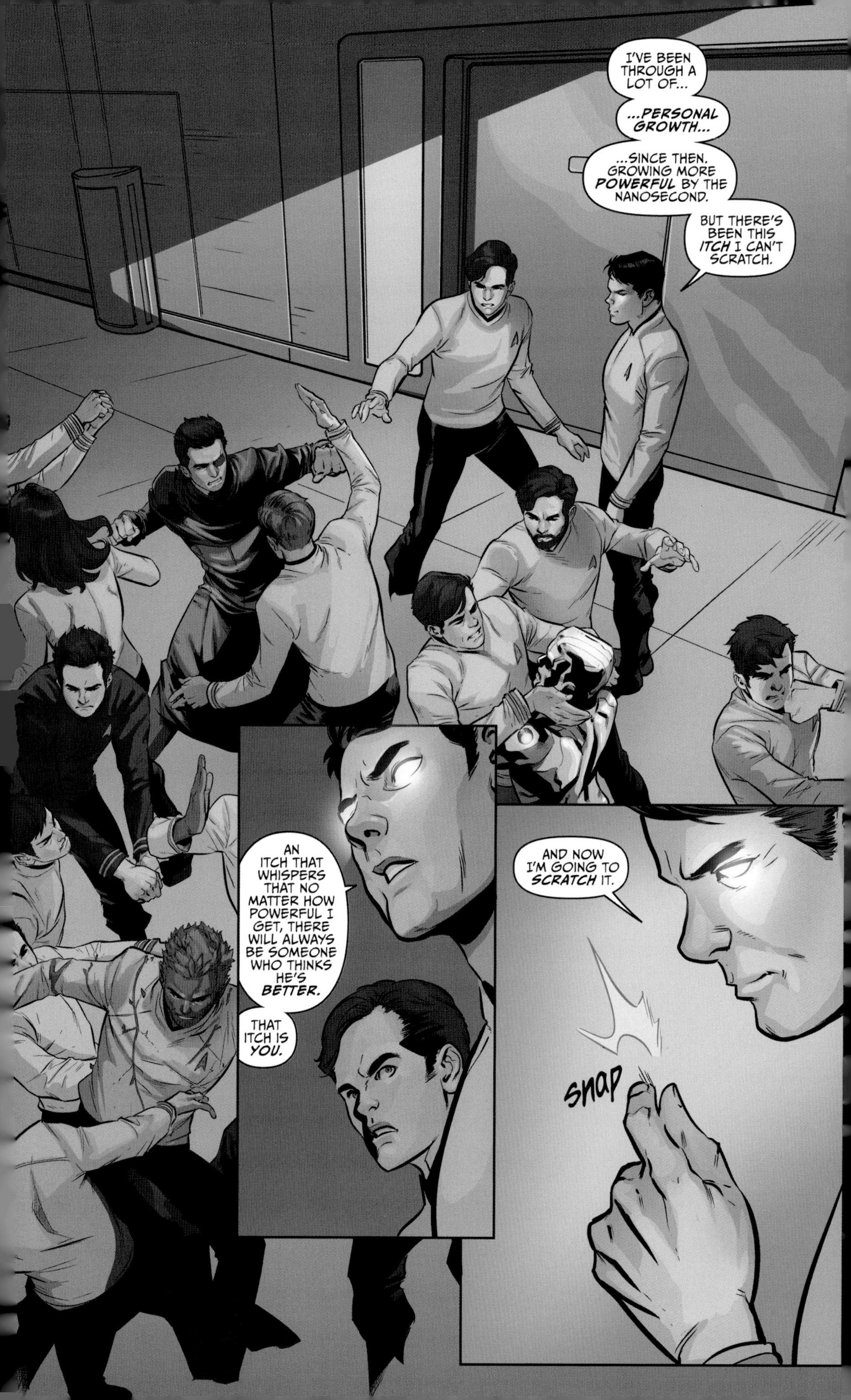
I'VE BEEN THROUGH A LOT OF...
...PERSONAL GROWTH...
...SINCE THEN. GROWING MORE POWERFUL BY THE NANOSECOND.
BUT THERE'S BEEN THIS ITCH I CAN'T SCRATCH.
AN ITCH THAT WHISPERS THAT NO MATTER HOW POWERFUL I GET, THERE WILL ALWAYS BE SOMEONE WHO THINKS HE'S BETTER.
THAT ITCH IS YOU.
AND NOW I'M GOING TO SCRATCH IT.
SNAP

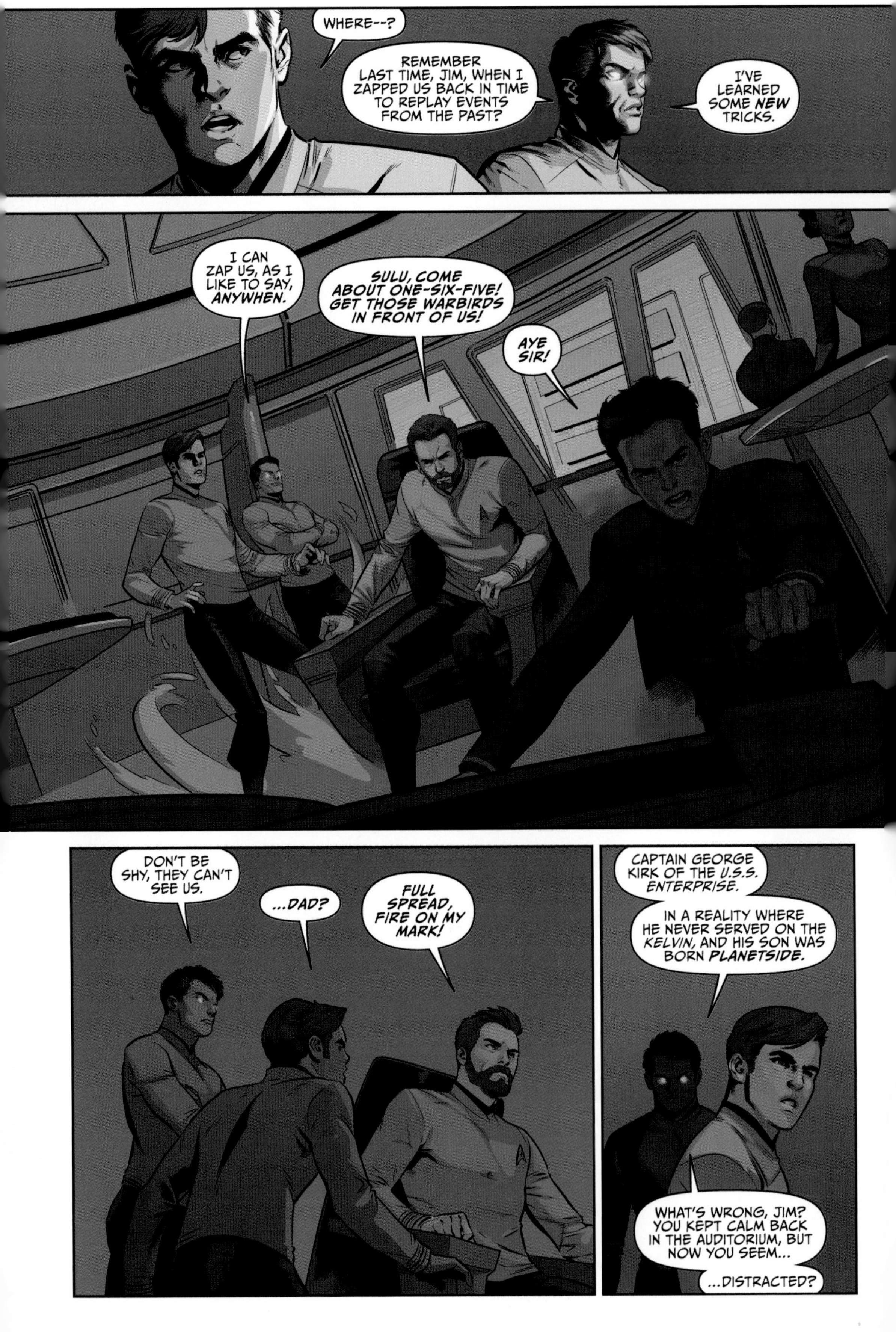
WHERE--?
REMEMBER LAST TIME, JIM, WHEN I ZAPPED US BACK IN TIME TO REPLAY EVENTS FROM THE PAST?
I'VE LEARNED SOME NEW TRICKS.
I CAN ZAP US, AS I LIKE TO SAY, ANYWHEN.
SULU, COME ABOUT ONE-SIX-FIVE! GET THOSE WARBIRDS IN FRONT OF US!
AYE SIR!
DON'T BE SHY, THEY CAN'T SEE US.
...DAD?
FULL SPREAD, FIRE ON MY MARK!
CAPTAIN GEORGE KIRK OF THE U.S.S. ENTERPRISE.
IN A REALITY WHERE HE NEVER SERVED ON THE KELVIN, AND HIS SON WAS BORN PLANETSIDE.
WHAT'S WRONG, JIM? YOU KEPT CALM BACK IN THE AUDITORIUM, BUT NOW YOU SEEM...
...DISTRACTED?

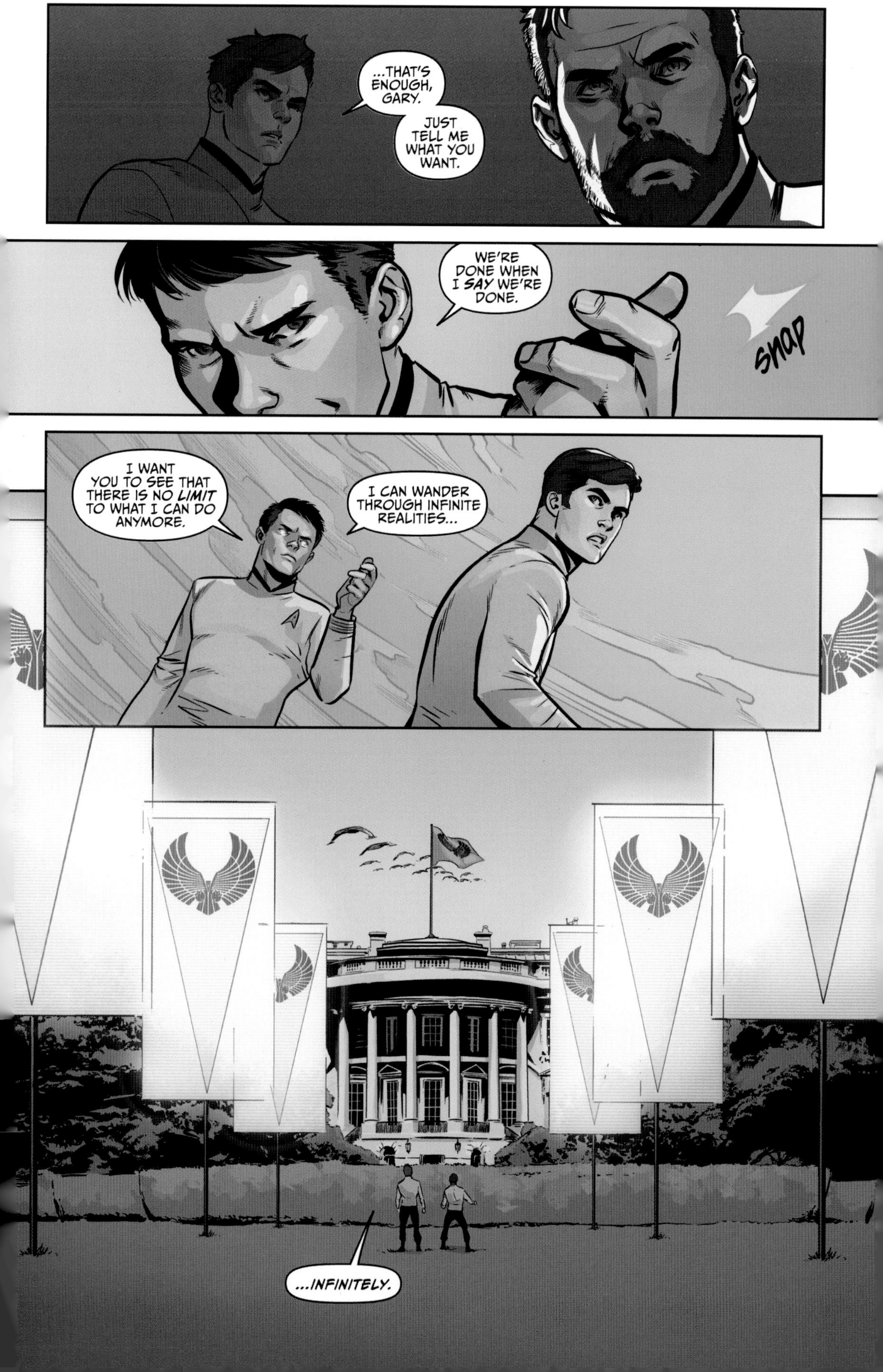
...THAT'S ENOUGH, GARY.
JUST TELL ME WHAT YOU WANT.
WE'RE DONE WHEN I SAY WE'RE DONE.
SNAP
I WANT YOU TO SEE THAT THERE IS NO LIMIT TO WHAT I CAN DO ANYMORE.
I CAN WANDER THROUGH INFINITE REALITIES...
...INFINITELY.

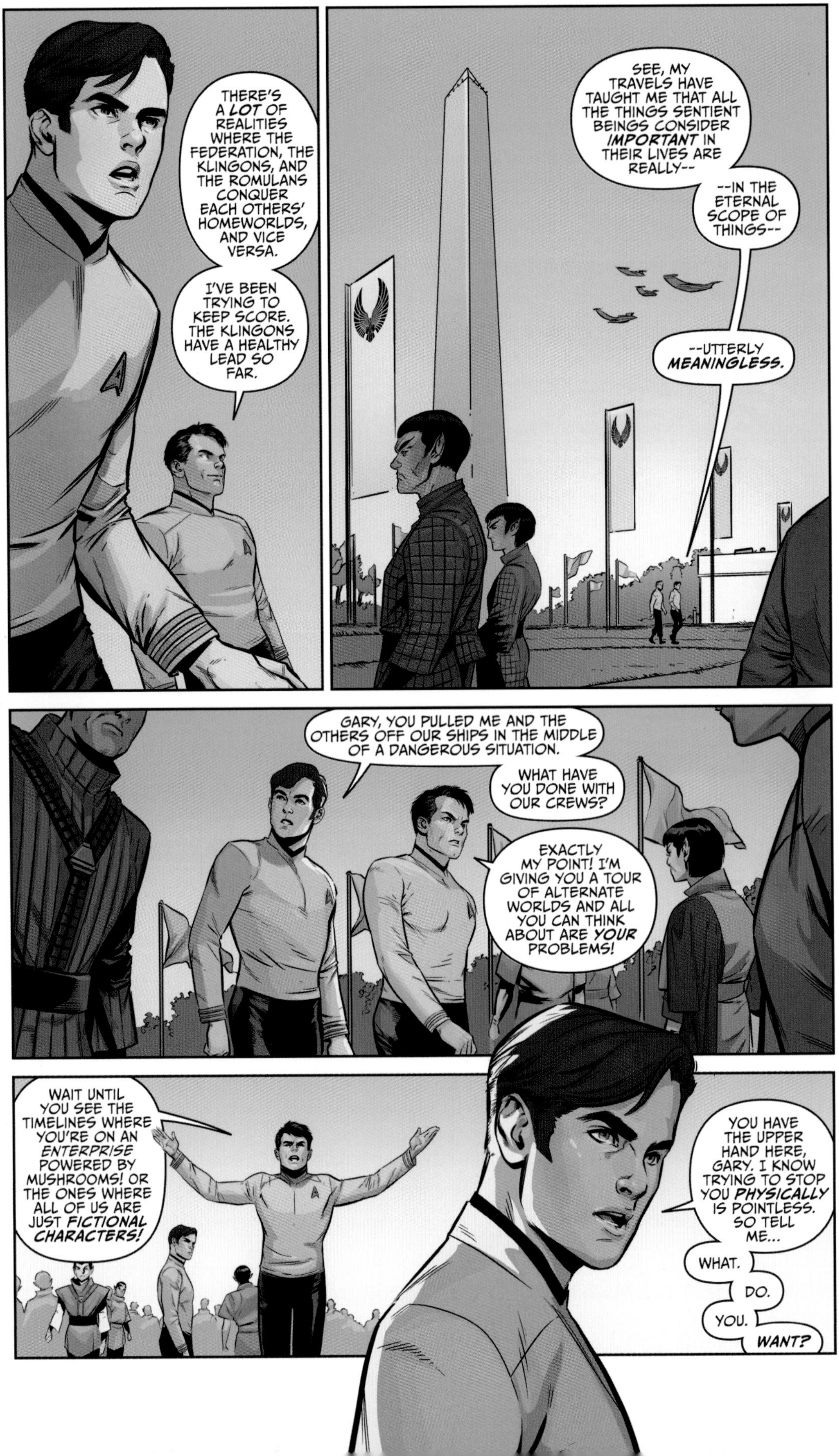

THERE'S A LOT OF REALITIES WHERE THE FEDERATION, THE KLINGONS, AND THE ROMULANS CONQUER EACH OTHERS' HOMEWORLDS, AND VICE VERSA.
I'VE BEEN TRYING TO KEEP SCORE. THE KLINGONS HAVE A HEALTHY LEAD SO FAR.
SEE, MY TRAVELS HAVE TAUGHT ME THAT ALL THE THINGS SENTIENT BEINGS CONSIDER IMPORTANT IN THEIR LIVES ARE REALLY--
--IN THE ETERNAL SCOPE OF THINGS--
--UTTERLY MEANINGLESS.
GARY, YOU PULLED ME AND THE OTHERS OFF OUR SHIPS IN THE MIDDLE OF A DANGEROUS SITUATION.
WHAT HAVE YOU DONE WITH OUR CREWS?
EXACTLY MY POINT! I'M GIVING YOU A TOUR OF ALTERNATE WORLDS AND ALL YOU CAN THINK ABOUT ARE YOUR PROBLEMS!
WAIT UNTIL YOU SEE THE TIMELINES WHERE YOU'RE ON AN ENTERPRISE POWERED BY MUSHROOMS! OR THE ONES WHERE ALL OF US ARE JUST FICTIONAL CHARACTERS!
YOU HAVE THE UPPER HAND HERE, GARY. I KNOW TRYING TO STOP YOU PHYSICALLY IS POINTLESS. SO TELL ME...
WHAT.
DO.
YOU.
WANT?

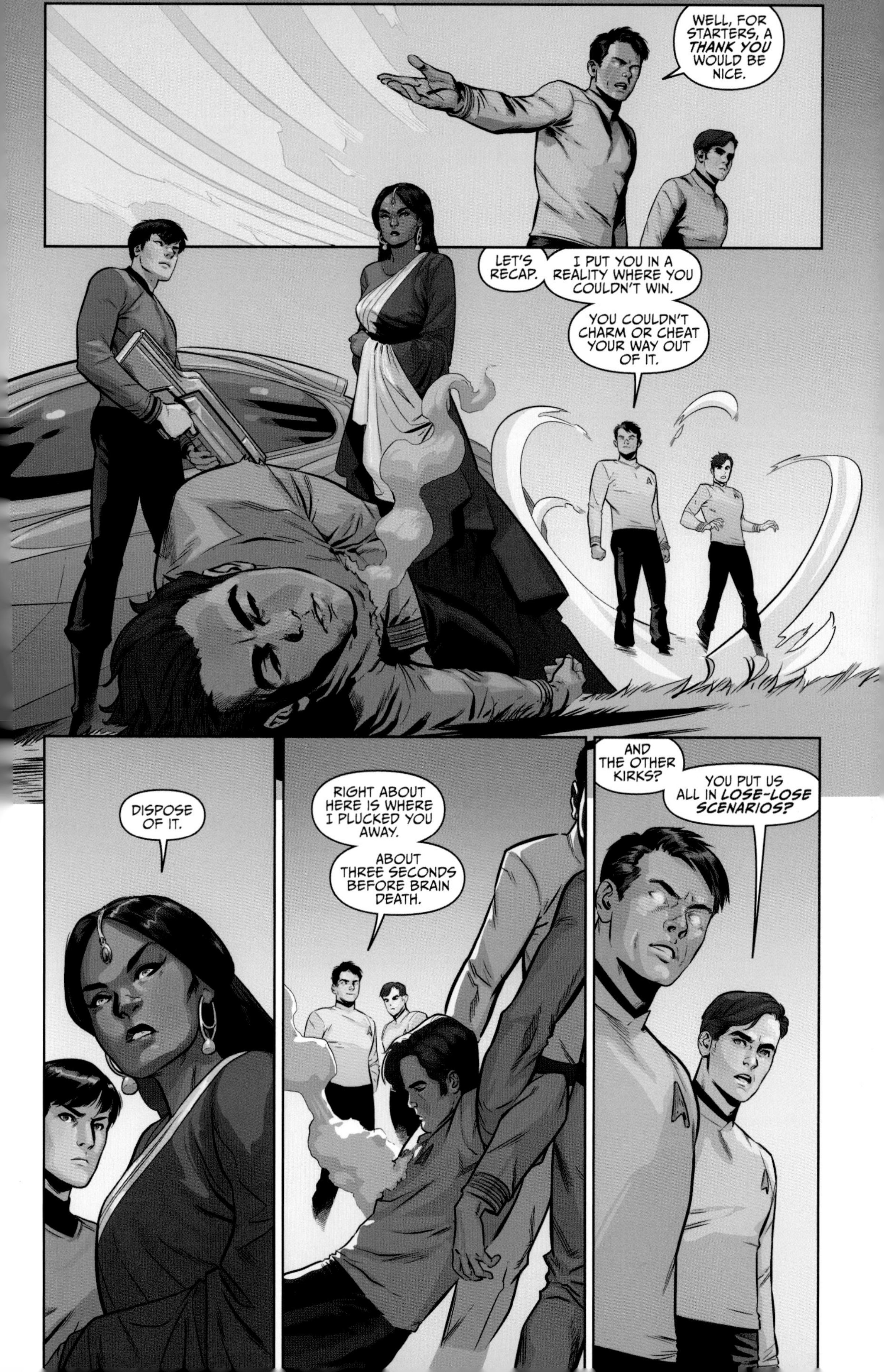

WELL, FOR STARTERS, A *THANK YOU* WOULD BE NICE.
LET'S RECAP.
I PUT YOU IN A REALITY WHERE YOU COULDN'T WIN.
YOU COULDN'T CHARM OR CHEAT YOUR WAY OUT OF IT.
DISPOSE OF IT.
RIGHT ABOUT HERE IS WHERE I PLUCKED YOU AWAY.
ABOUT THREE SECONDS BEFORE BRAIN DEATH.
AND THE OTHER KIRKS?
YOU PUT US ALL IN *LOSE-LOSE SCENARIOS?*

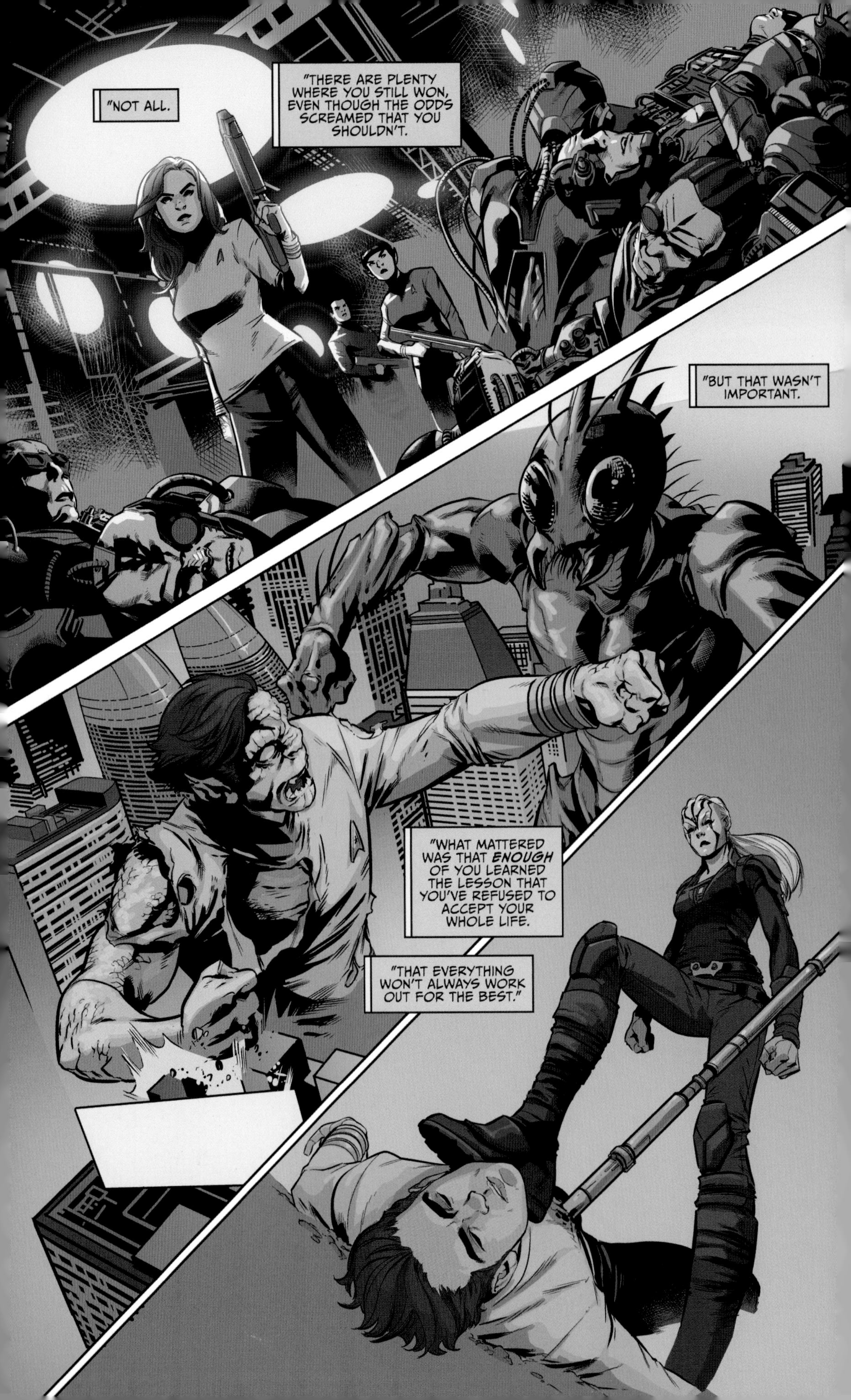
"NOT ALL.
"THERE ARE PLENTY WHERE YOU STILL WON, EVEN THOUGH THE ODDS SCREAMED THAT YOU SHOULDN'T.
"BUT THAT WASN'T IMPORTANT.
"WHAT MATTERED WAS THAT ENOUGH OF YOU LEARNED THE LESSON THAT YOU'VE REFUSED TO ACCEPT YOUR WHOLE LIFE.
"THAT EVERYTHING WON'T ALWAYS WORK OUT FOR THE BEST."

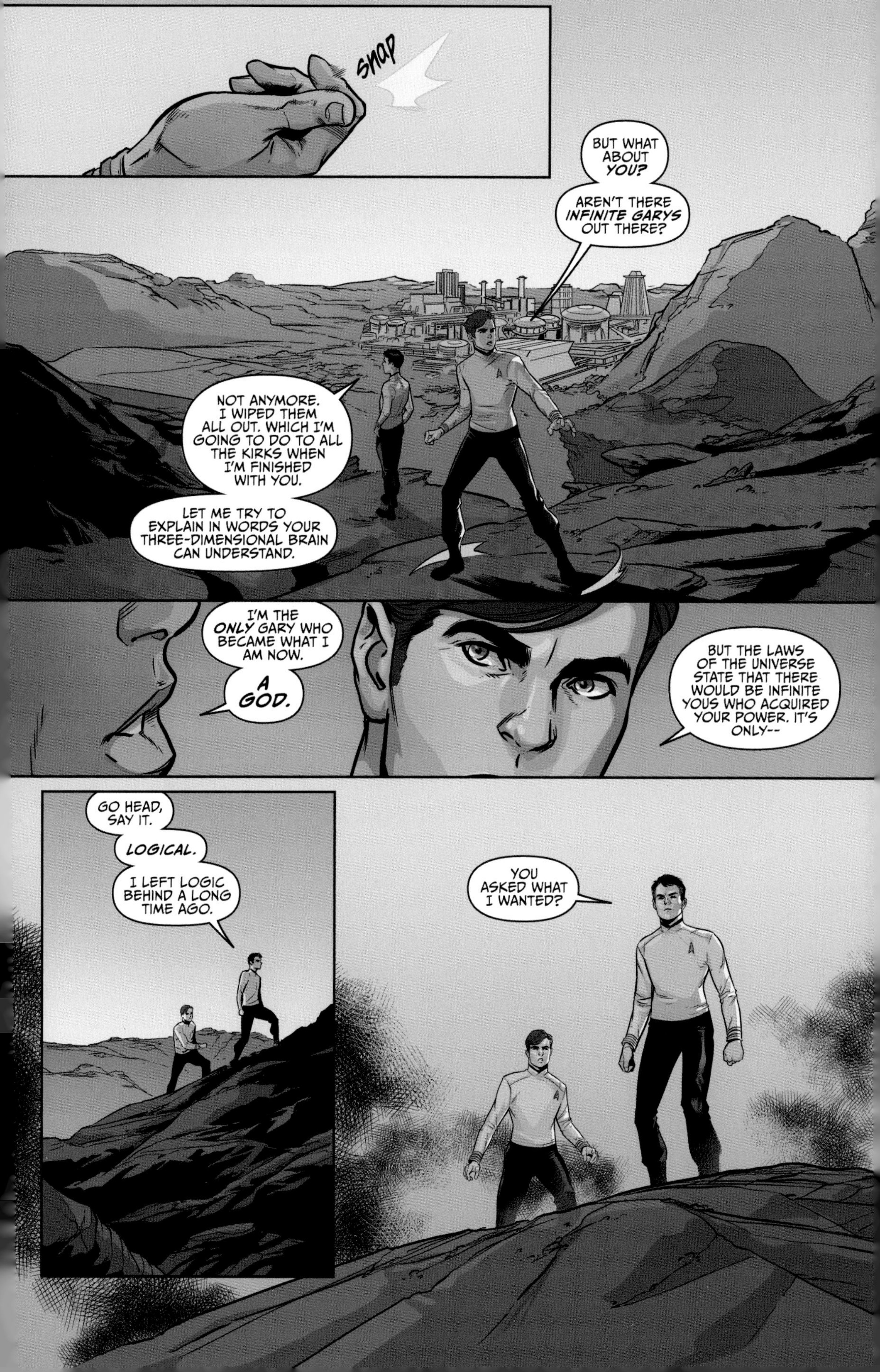
SNAP
BUT WHAT ABOUT YOU?
AREN'T THERE INFINITE GARYS OUT THERE?
NOT ANYMORE. I WIPED THEM ALL OUT. WHICH I'M GOING TO DO TO ALL THE KIRKS WHEN I'M FINISHED WITH YOU.
LET ME TRY TO EXPLAIN IN WORDS YOUR THREE-DIMENSIONAL BRAIN CAN UNDERSTAND.
I'M THE ONLY GARY WHO BECAME WHAT I AM NOW.
A GOD.
BUT THE LAWS OF THE UNIVERSE STATE THAT THERE WOULD BE INFINITE YOUS WHO ACQUIRED YOUR POWER. IT'S ONLY--
GO HEAD, SAY IT.
LOGICAL.
I LEFT LOGIC BEHIND A LONG TIME AGO.
YOU ASKED WHAT I WANTED?

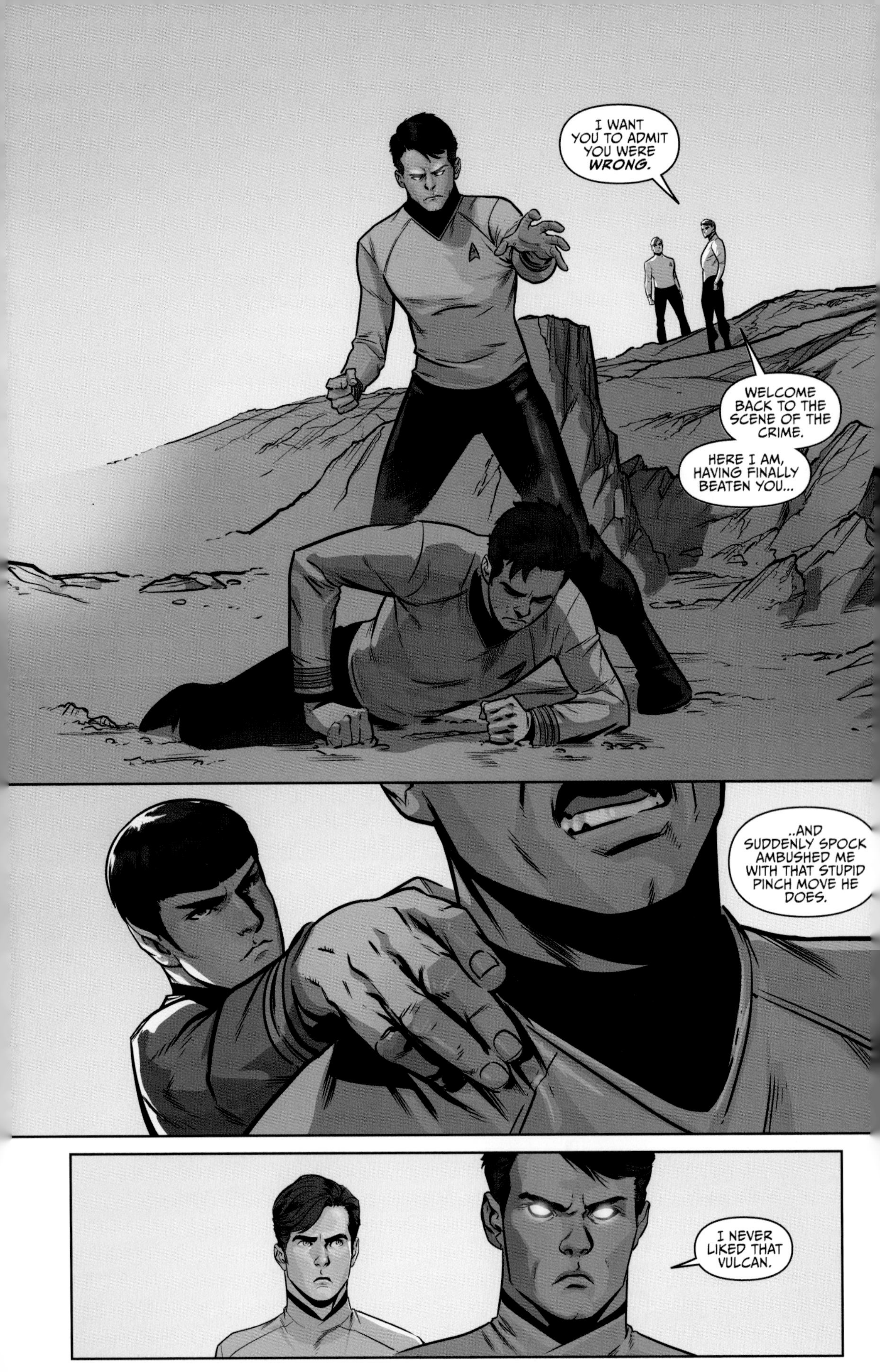
I WANT YOU TO ADMIT YOU WERE **WRONG.**
WELCOME BACK TO THE SCENE OF THE CRIME.
HERE I AM, HAVING FINALLY BEATEN YOU...
..AND SUDDENLY SPOCK AMBUSHED ME WITH THAT STUPID PINCH MOVE HE DOES.
I NEVER LIKED THAT VULCAN.

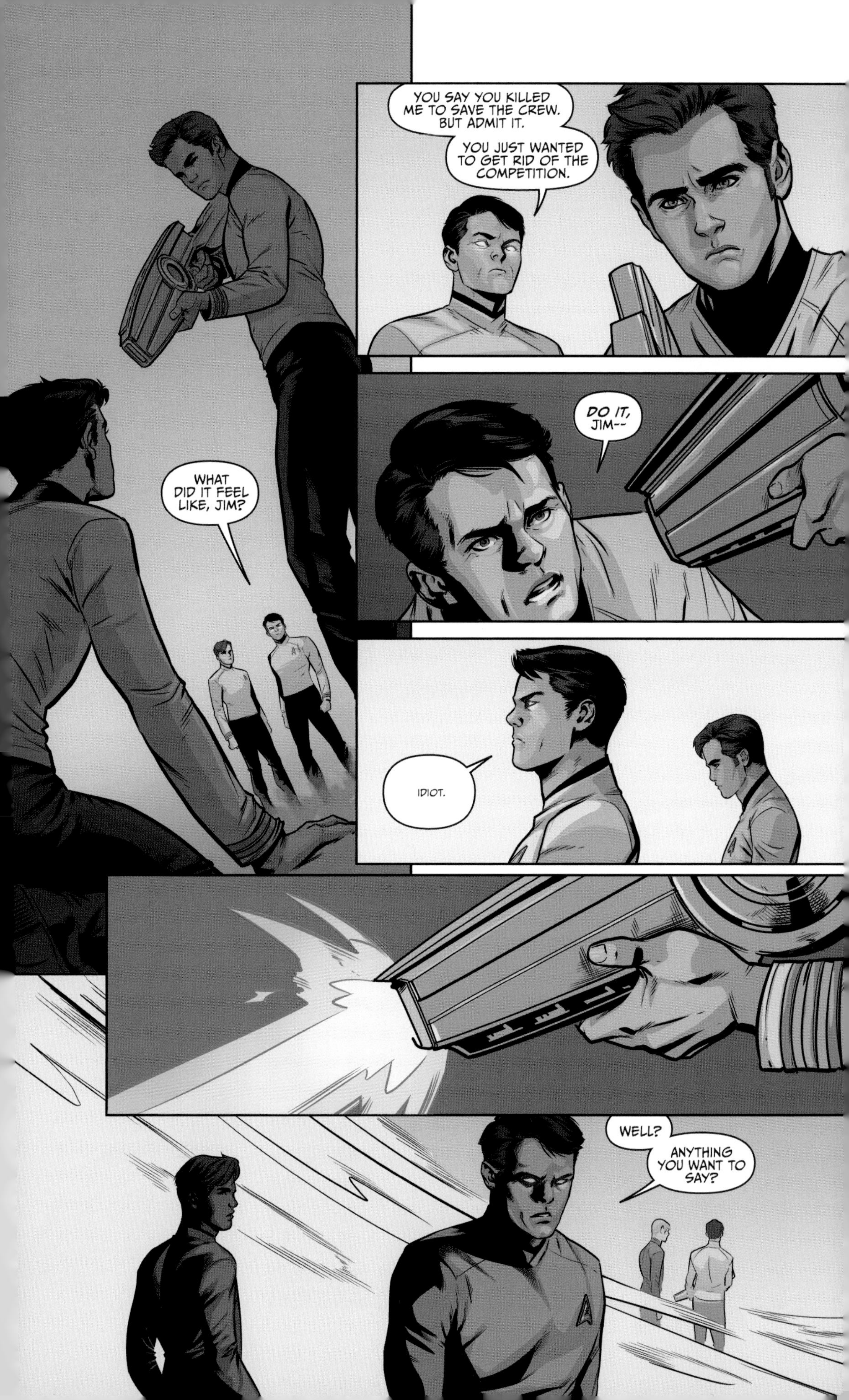
WHAT DID IT FEEL LIKE, JIM?
YOU SAY YOU KILLED ME TO SAVE THE CREW. BUT ADMIT IT.
YOU JUST WANTED TO GET RID OF THE COMPETITION.
DO IT, JIM--
IDIOT.
WELL?
ANYTHING YOU WANT TO SAY?

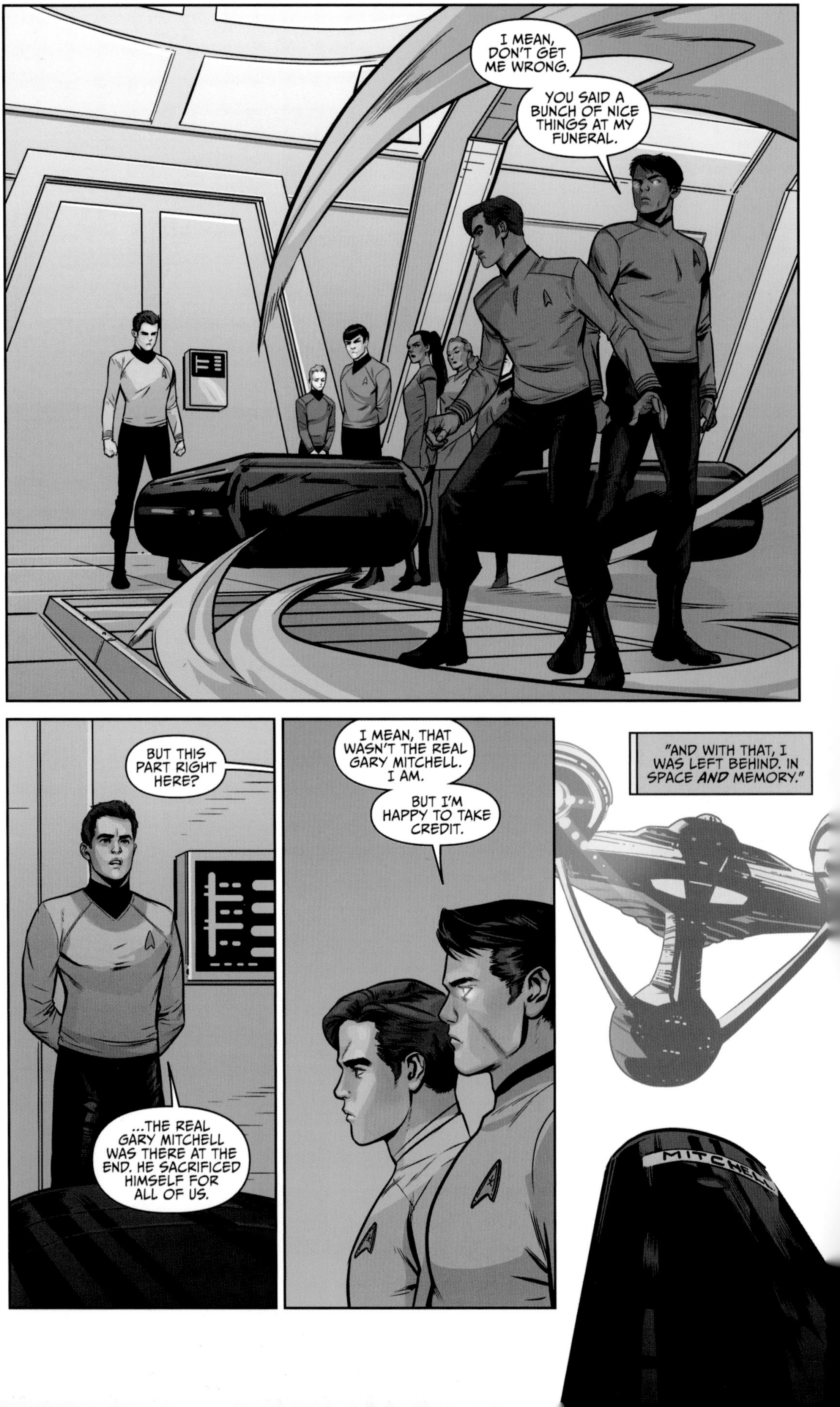
I MEAN, DON'T GET ME WRONG.
YOU SAID A BUNCH OF NICE THINGS AT MY FUNERAL.
BUT THIS PART RIGHT HERE?
...THE REAL GARY MITCHELL WAS THERE AT THE END. HE SACRIFICED HIMSELF FOR ALL OF US.
I MEAN, THAT WASN'T THE REAL GARY MITCHELL. I AM.
BUT I'M HAPPY TO TAKE CREDIT.
"AND WITH THAT, I WAS LEFT BEHIND. IN SPACE AND MEMORY."
MITCHELL

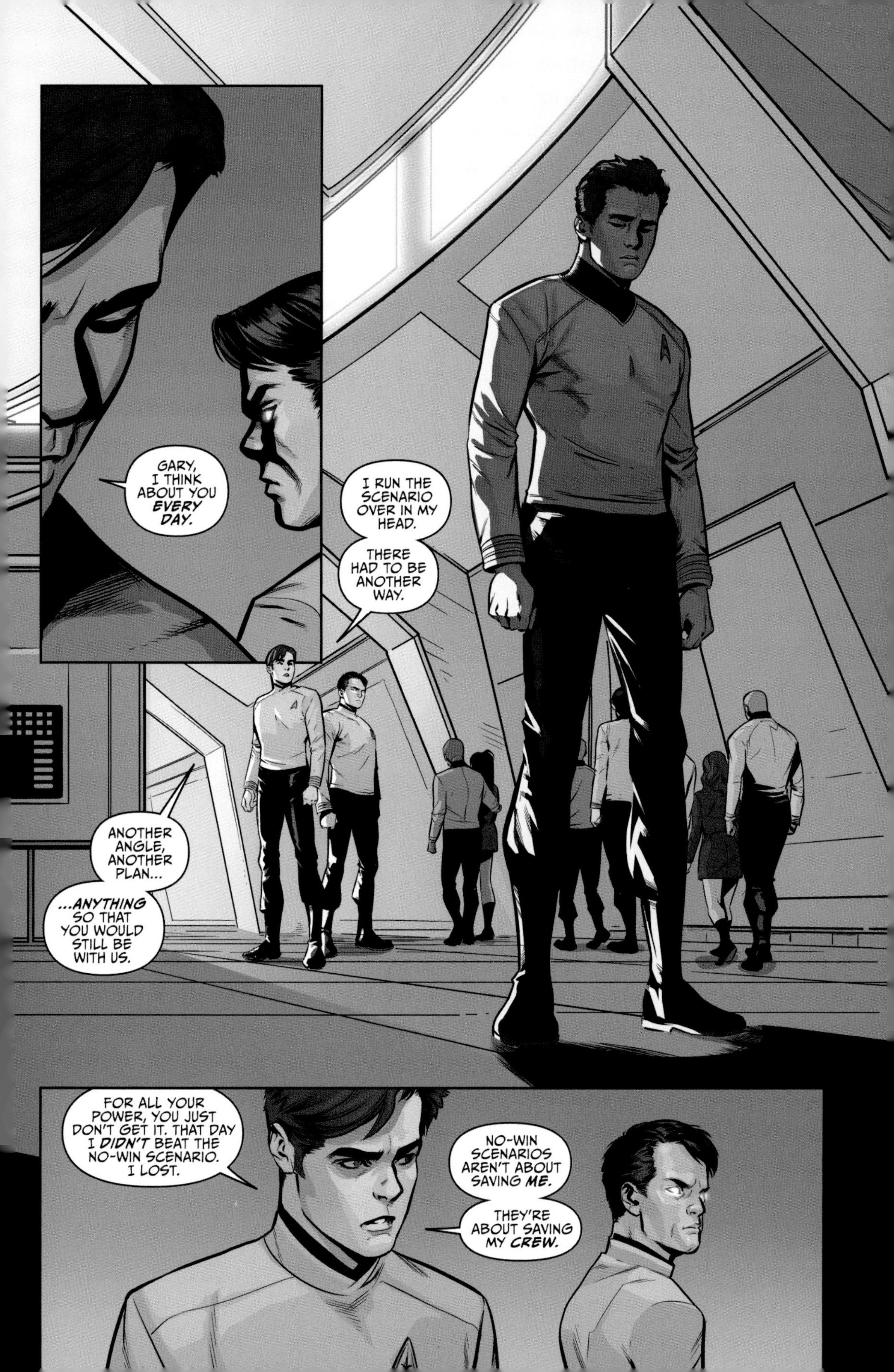
GARY, I THINK ABOUT YOU *EVERY DAY.*
I RUN THE SCENARIO OVER IN MY HEAD.
THERE HAD TO BE ANOTHER WAY.
ANOTHER ANGLE, ANOTHER PLAN...
...ANYTHING SO THAT YOU WOULD STILL BE WITH US.
FOR ALL YOUR POWER, YOU JUST DON'T GET IT. THAT DAY I *DIDN'T* BEAT THE NO-WIN SCENARIO. I LOST.
NO-WIN SCENARIOS AREN'T ABOUT SAVING *ME.*
THEY'RE ABOUT SAVING MY *CREW.*

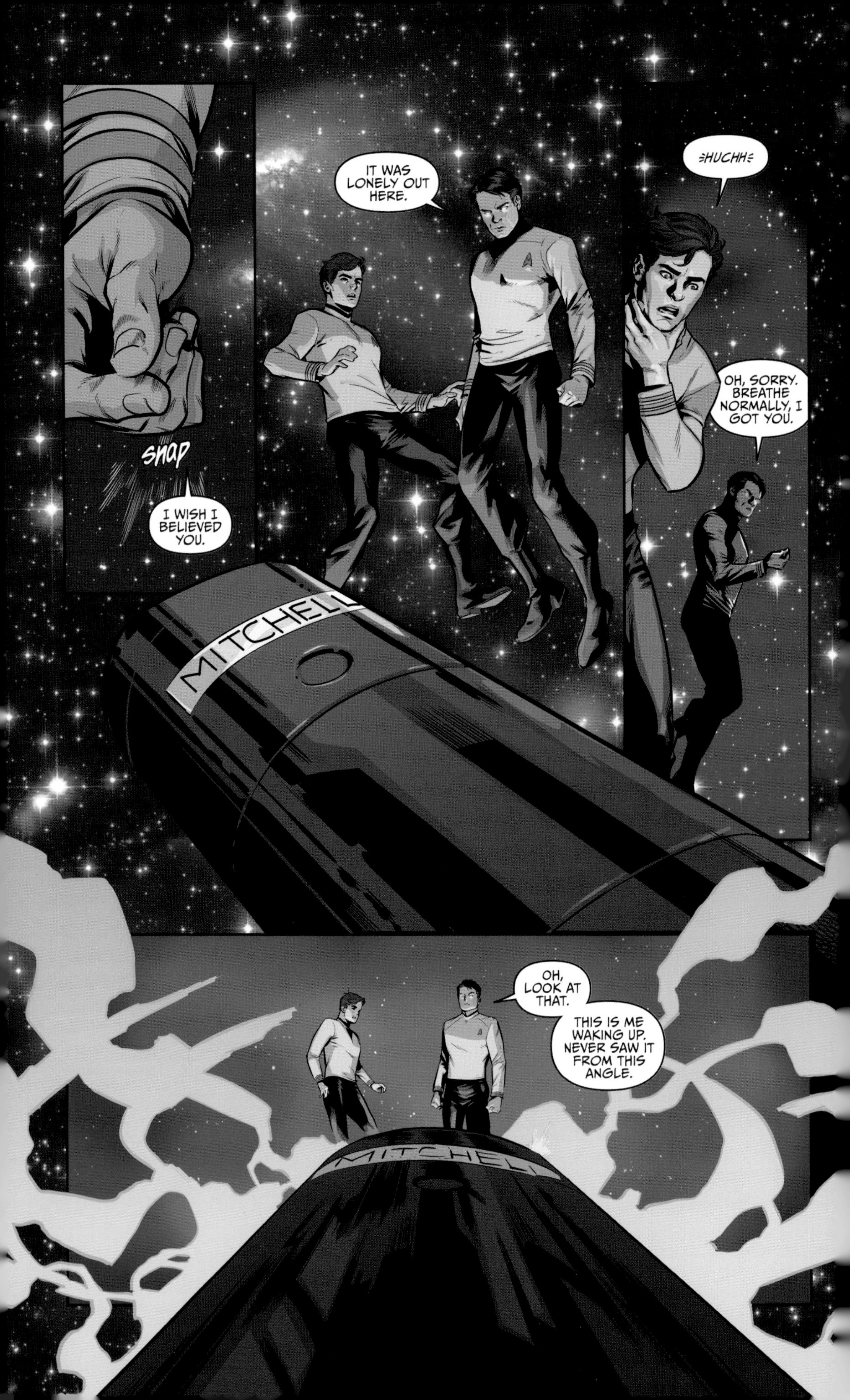

SNAP
I WISH I BELIEVED YOU.
IT WAS LONELY OUT HERE.
HUCHH
OH, SORRY. BREATHE NORMALLY, I GOT YOU.
MITCHELL
OH, LOOK AT THAT.
THIS IS ME WAKING UP. NEVER SAW IT FROM THIS ANGLE.
MITCHELL

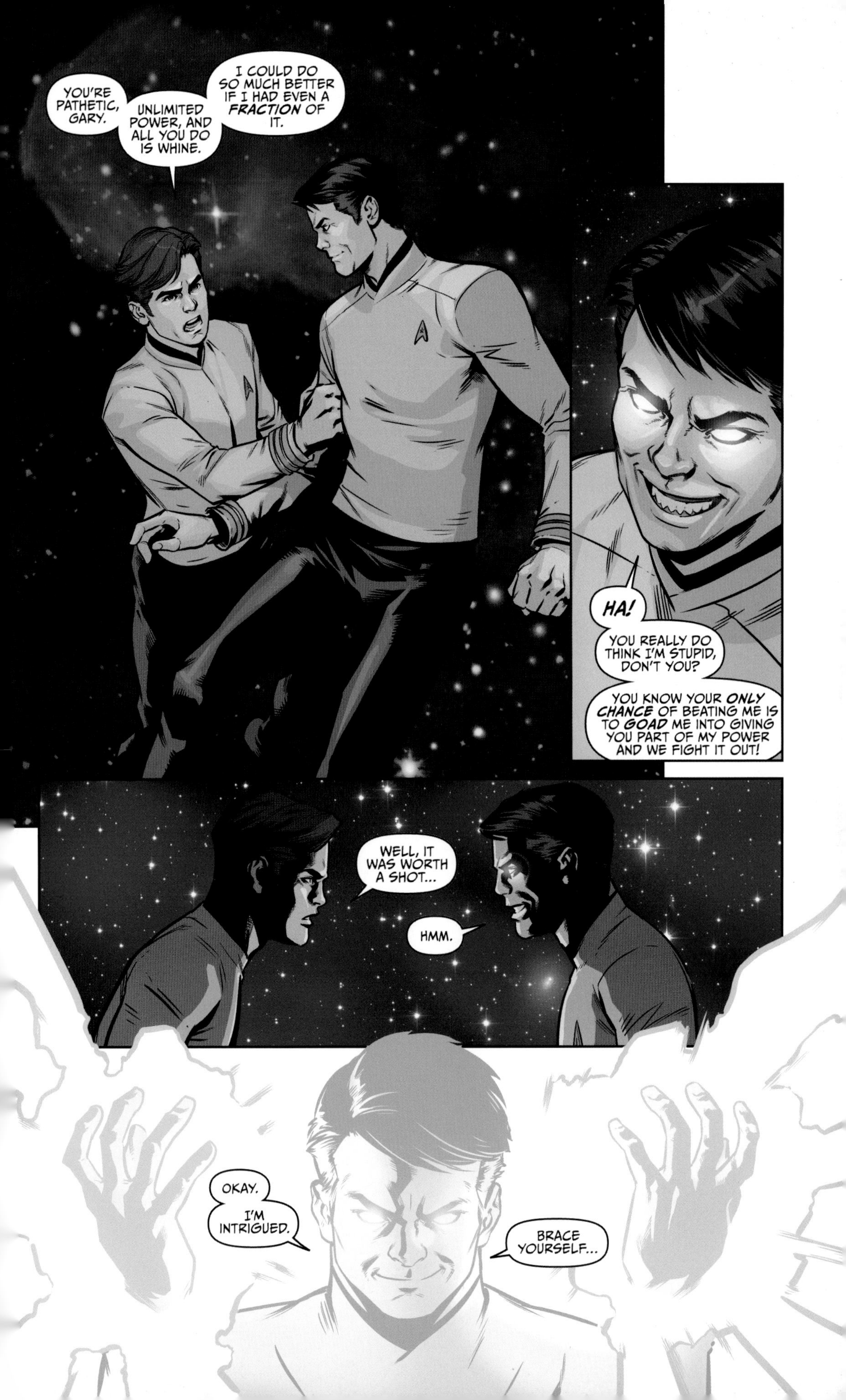
YOU'RE PATHETIC, GARY.
UNLIMITED POWER, AND ALL YOU DO IS WHINE.
I COULD DO SO MUCH BETTER IF I HAD EVEN A FRACTION OF IT.
HA!
YOU REALLY DO THINK I'M STUPID, DON'T YOU?
YOU KNOW YOUR ONLY CHANCE OF BEATING ME IS TO GOAD ME INTO GIVING YOU PART OF MY POWER AND WE FIGHT IT OUT!
WELL, IT WAS WORTH A SHOT...
HMM.
OKAY.
I'M INTRIGUED.
BRACE YOURSELF...

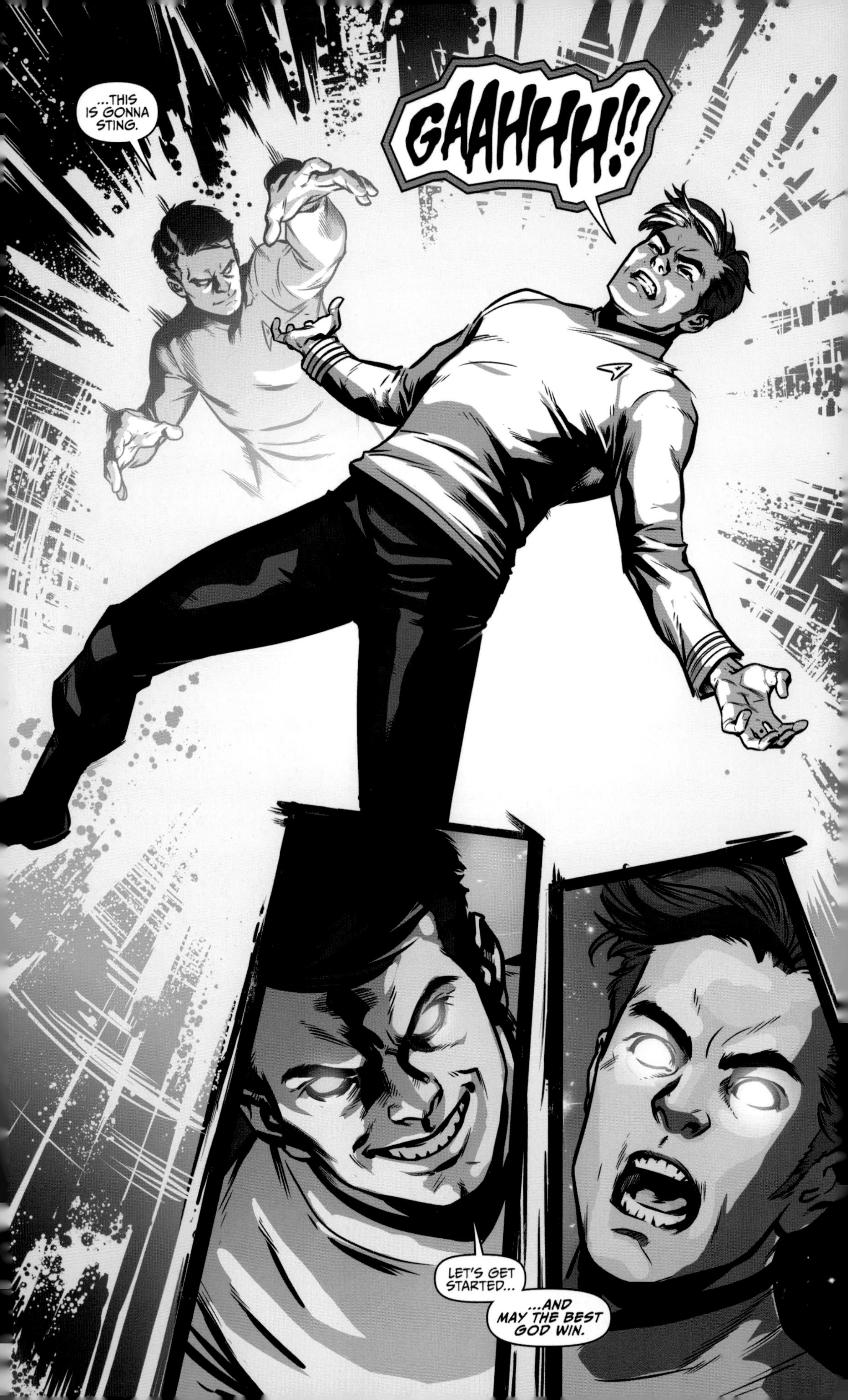
...THIS IS GONNA STING.
GAAHHH!!
LET'S GET STARTED...
...AND MAY THE BEST GOD WIN.

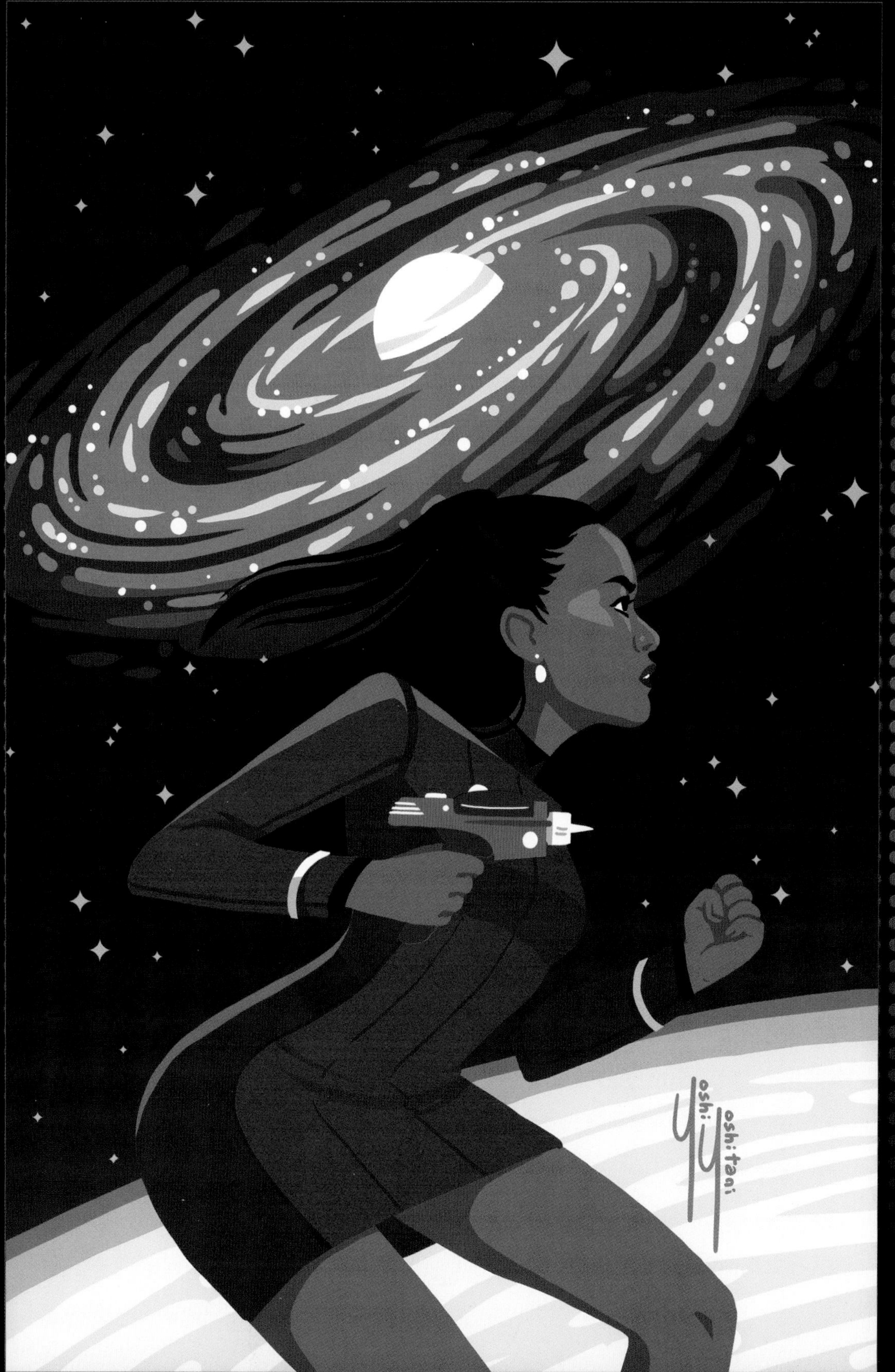
Yoshi Yoshitani

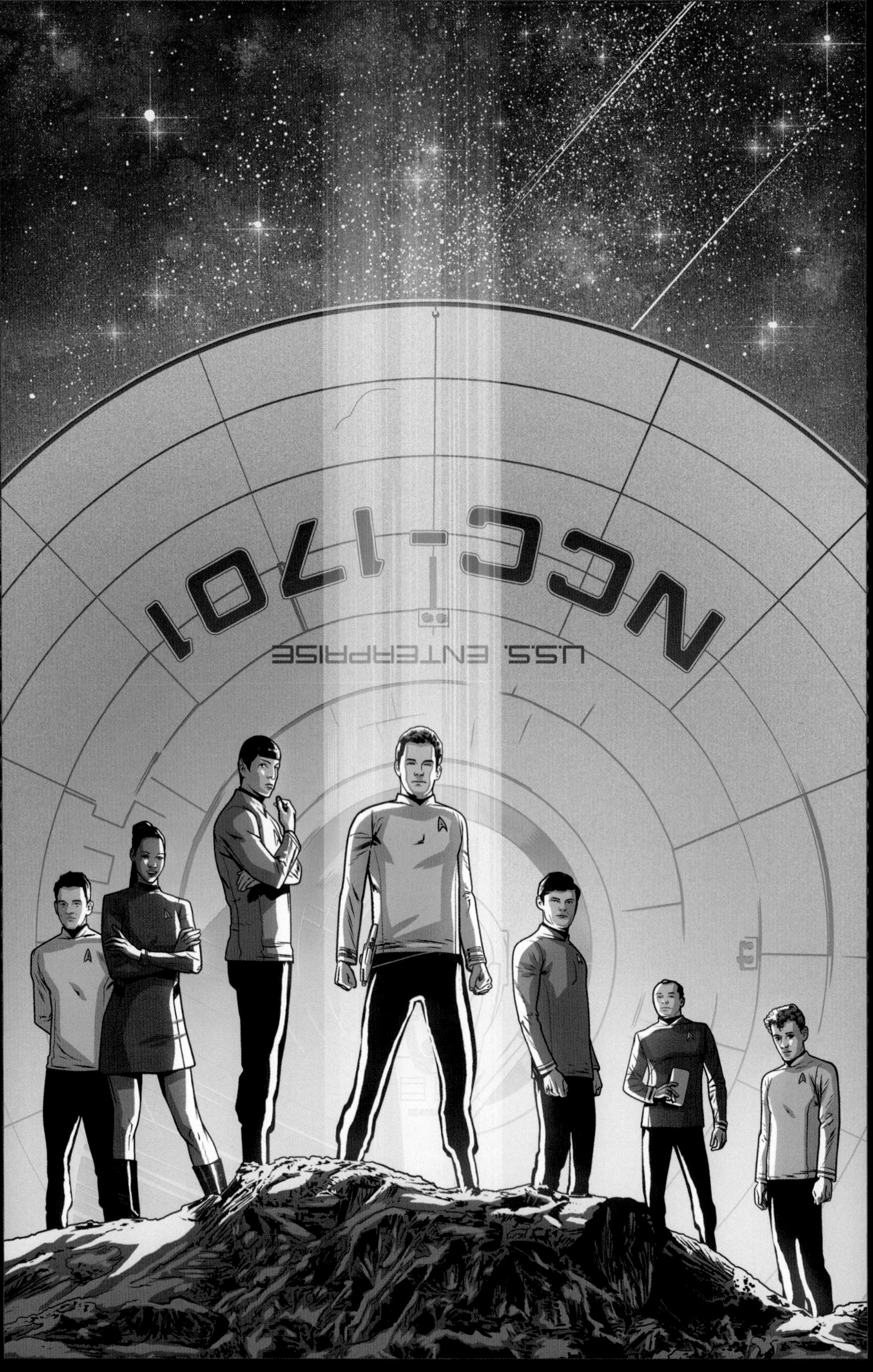
NCC-1701
U.S.S. ENTERPRISE

art by
Josh Hood

colors by
Jason Lewis

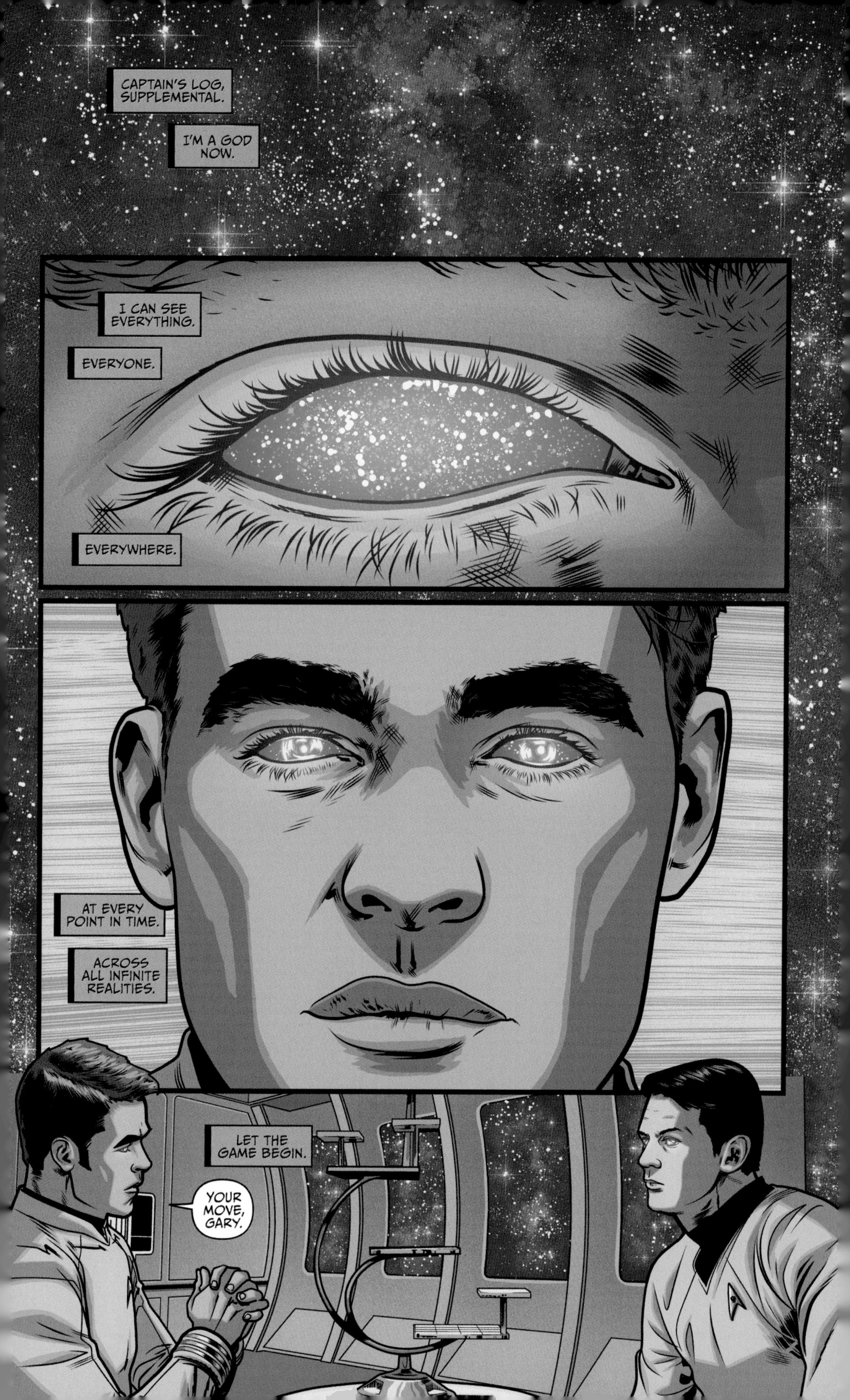
CAPTAIN'S LOG, SUPPLEMENTAL.
I'M A GOD NOW.
I CAN SEE EVERYTHING.
EVERYONE.
EVERYWHERE.
AT EVERY POINT IN TIME.
ACROSS ALL INFINITE REALITIES.
LET THE GAME BEGIN.
YOUR MOVE, GARY.

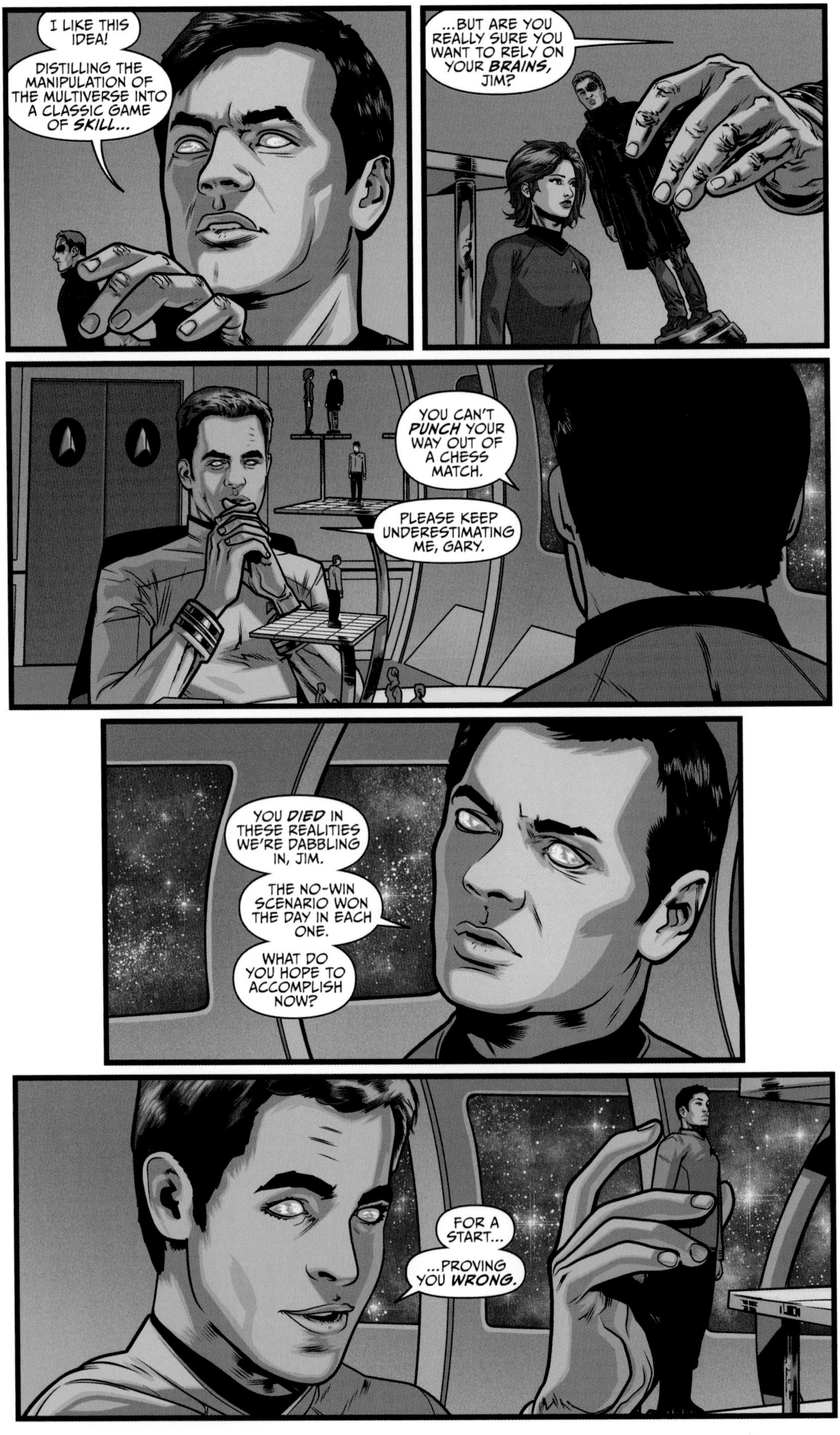
I LIKE THIS IDEA!
DISTILLING THE MANIPULATION OF THE MULTIVERSE INTO A CLASSIC GAME OF SKILL...
...BUT ARE YOU REALLY SURE YOU WANT TO RELY ON YOUR BRAINS, JIM?
YOU CAN'T PUNCH YOUR WAY OUT OF A CHESS MATCH.
PLEASE KEEP UNDERESTIMATING ME, GARY.
YOU DIED IN THESE REALITIES WE'RE DABBLING IN, JIM.
THE NO-WIN SCENARIO WON THE DAY IN EACH ONE.
WHAT DO YOU HOPE TO ACCOMPLISH NOW?
FOR A START...
...PROVING YOU WRONG.

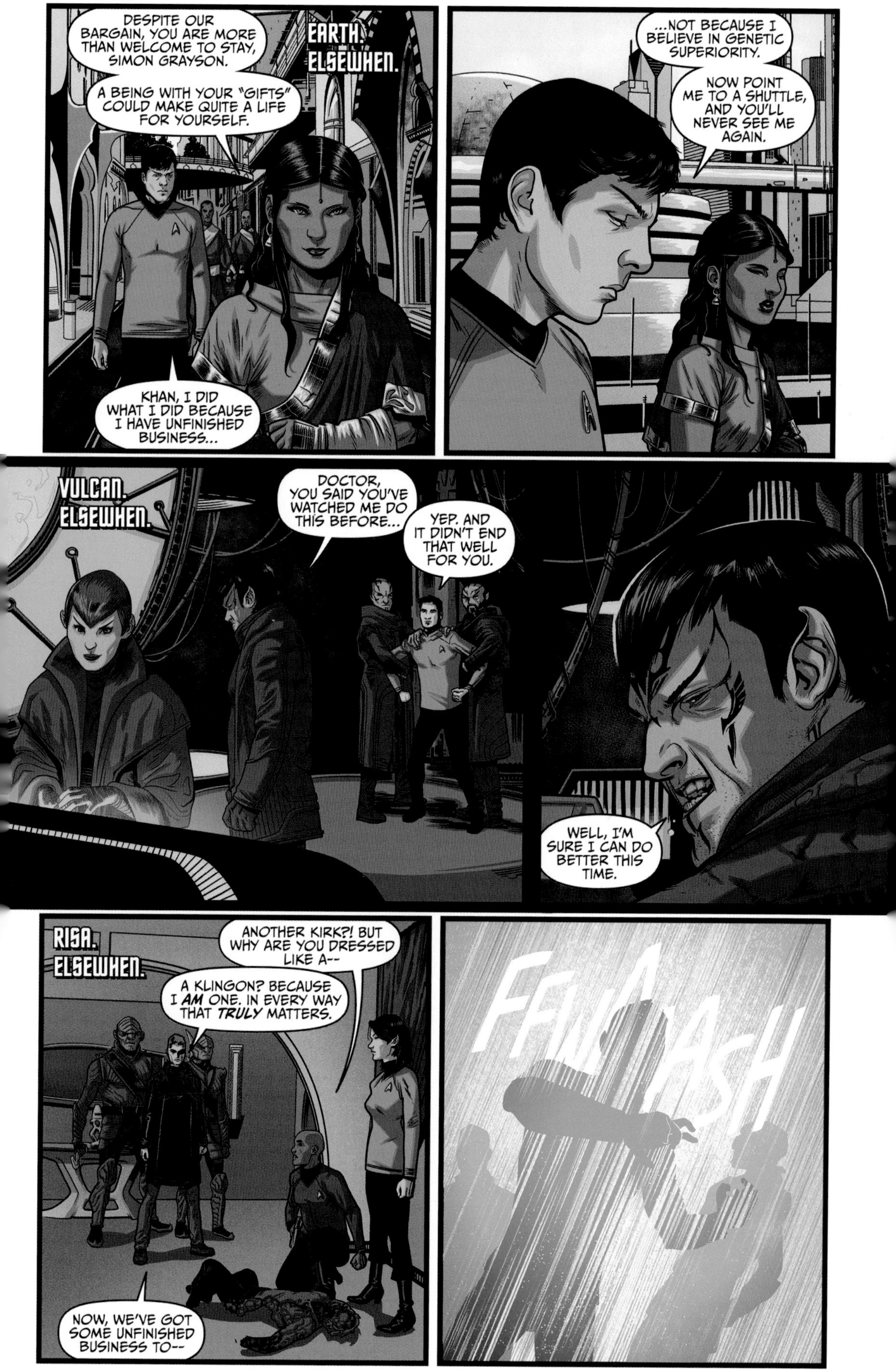

EARTH. ELSEWHEN.
DESPITE OUR BARGAIN, YOU ARE MORE THAN WELCOME TO STAY, SIMON GRAYSON.
A BEING WITH YOUR "GIFTS" COULD MAKE QUITE A LIFE FOR YOURSELF.
KHAN, I DID WHAT I DID BECAUSE I HAVE UNFINISHED BUSINESS...
...NOT BECAUSE I BELIEVE IN GENETIC SUPERIORITY.
NOW POINT ME TO A SHUTTLE, AND YOU'LL NEVER SEE ME AGAIN.
VULCAN. ELSEWHEN.
DOCTOR, YOU SAID YOU'VE WATCHED ME DO THIS BEFORE...
YEP. AND IT DIDN'T END THAT WELL FOR YOU.
WELL, I'M SURE I CAN DO BETTER THIS TIME.
RISA. ELSEWHEN.
ANOTHER KIRK?! BUT WHY ARE YOU DRESSED LIKE A--
A KLINGON? BECAUSE I **AM** ONE. IN EVERY WAY THAT **TRULY** MATTERS.
NOW, WE'VE GOT SOME UNFINISHED BUSINESS TO--
FFWAASH

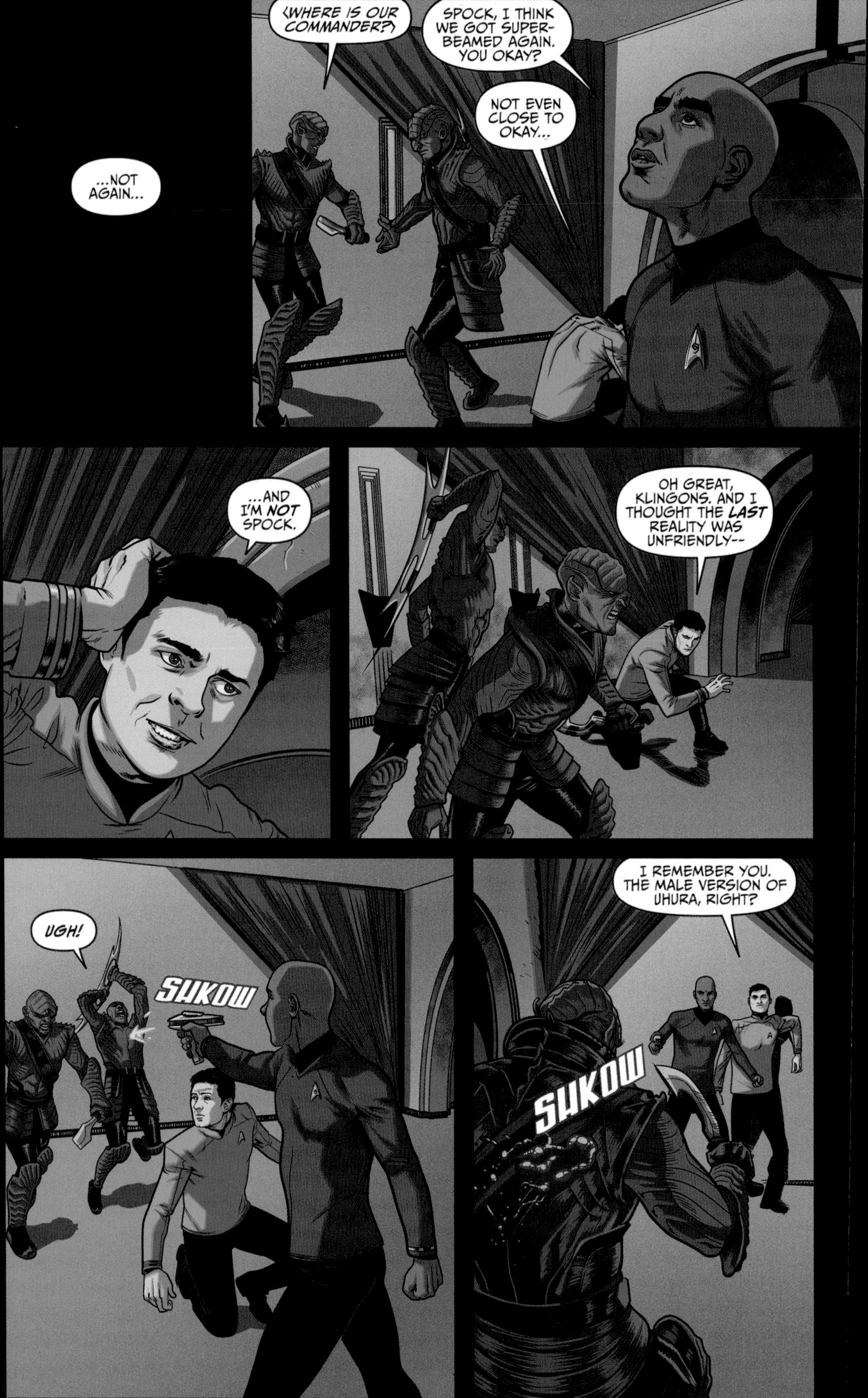
...NOT AGAIN...
‹WHERE IS OUR COMMANDER?›
SPOCK, I THINK WE GOT SUPER-BEAMED AGAIN. YOU OKAY?
NOT EVEN CLOSE TO OKAY...
...AND I'M NOT SPOCK.
OH GREAT, KLINGONS. AND I THOUGHT THE LAST REALITY WAS UNFRIENDLY--
UGH!
SHKOW
I REMEMBER YOU. THE MALE VERSION OF UHURA, RIGHT?
SHKOW

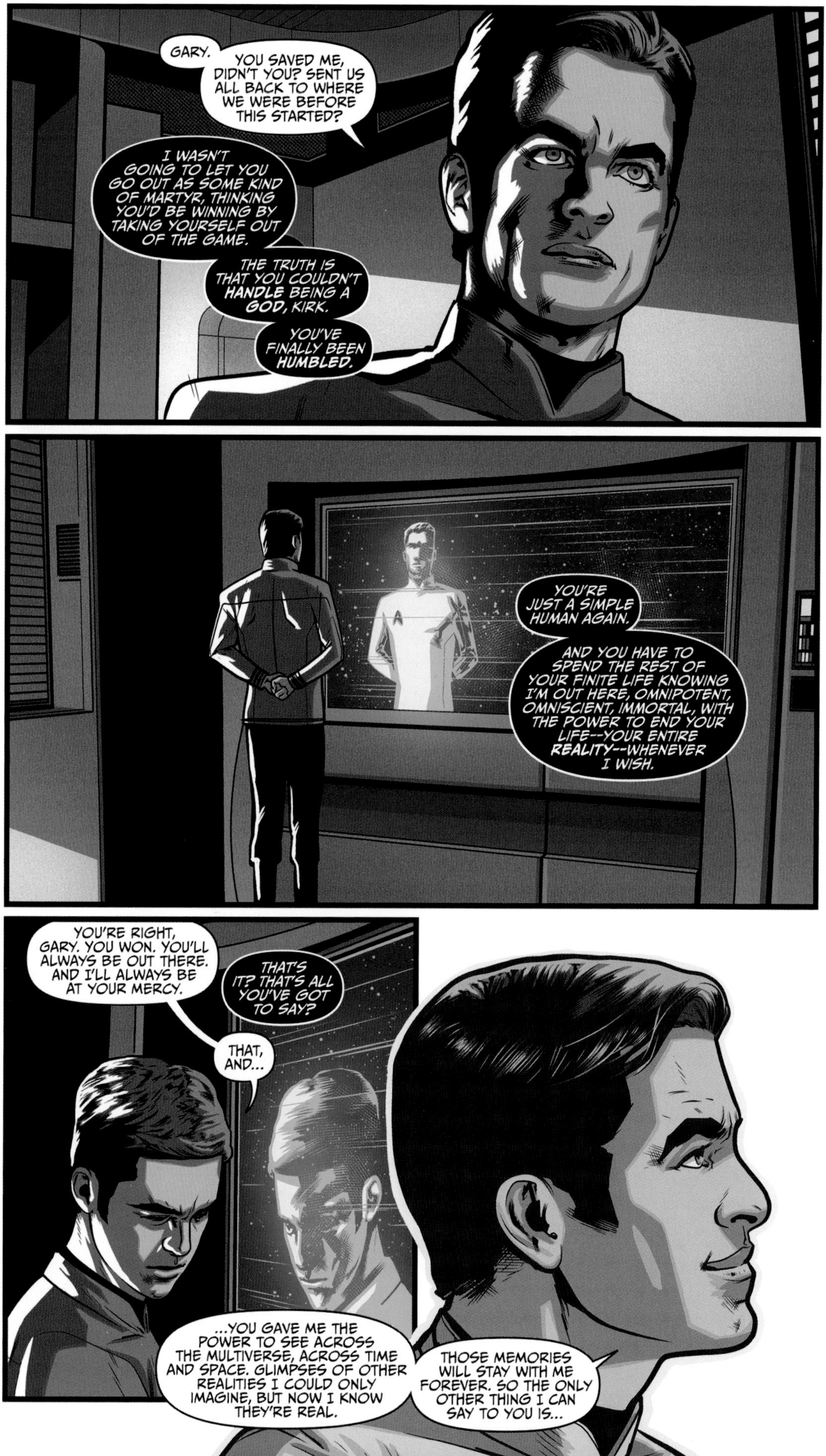
GARY.
YOU SAVED ME, DIDN'T YOU? SENT US ALL BACK TO WHERE WE WERE BEFORE THIS STARTED?
I WASN'T GOING TO LET YOU GO OUT AS SOME KIND OF MARTYR, THINKING YOU'D BE WINNING BY TAKING YOURSELF OUT OF THE GAME.
THE TRUTH IS THAT YOU COULDN'T HANDLE BEING A GOD, KIRK.
YOU'VE FINALLY BEEN HUMBLED.
YOU'RE JUST A SIMPLE HUMAN AGAIN.
AND YOU HAVE TO SPEND THE REST OF YOUR FINITE LIFE KNOWING I'M OUT HERE, OMNIPOTENT, OMNISCIENT, IMMORTAL, WITH THE POWER TO END YOUR LIFE--YOUR ENTIRE REALITY--WHENEVER I WISH.
YOU'RE RIGHT, GARY. YOU WON. YOU'LL ALWAYS BE OUT THERE. AND I'LL ALWAYS BE AT YOUR MERCY.
THAT'S IT? THAT'S ALL YOU'VE GOT TO SAY?
THAT, AND...
...YOU GAVE ME THE POWER TO SEE ACROSS THE MULTIVERSE, ACROSS TIME AND SPACE. GLIMPSES OF OTHER REALITIES I COULD ONLY IMAGINE, BUT NOW I KNOW THEY'RE REAL.
THOSE MEMORIES WILL STAY WITH ME FOREVER. SO THE ONLY OTHER THING I CAN SAY TO YOU IS...

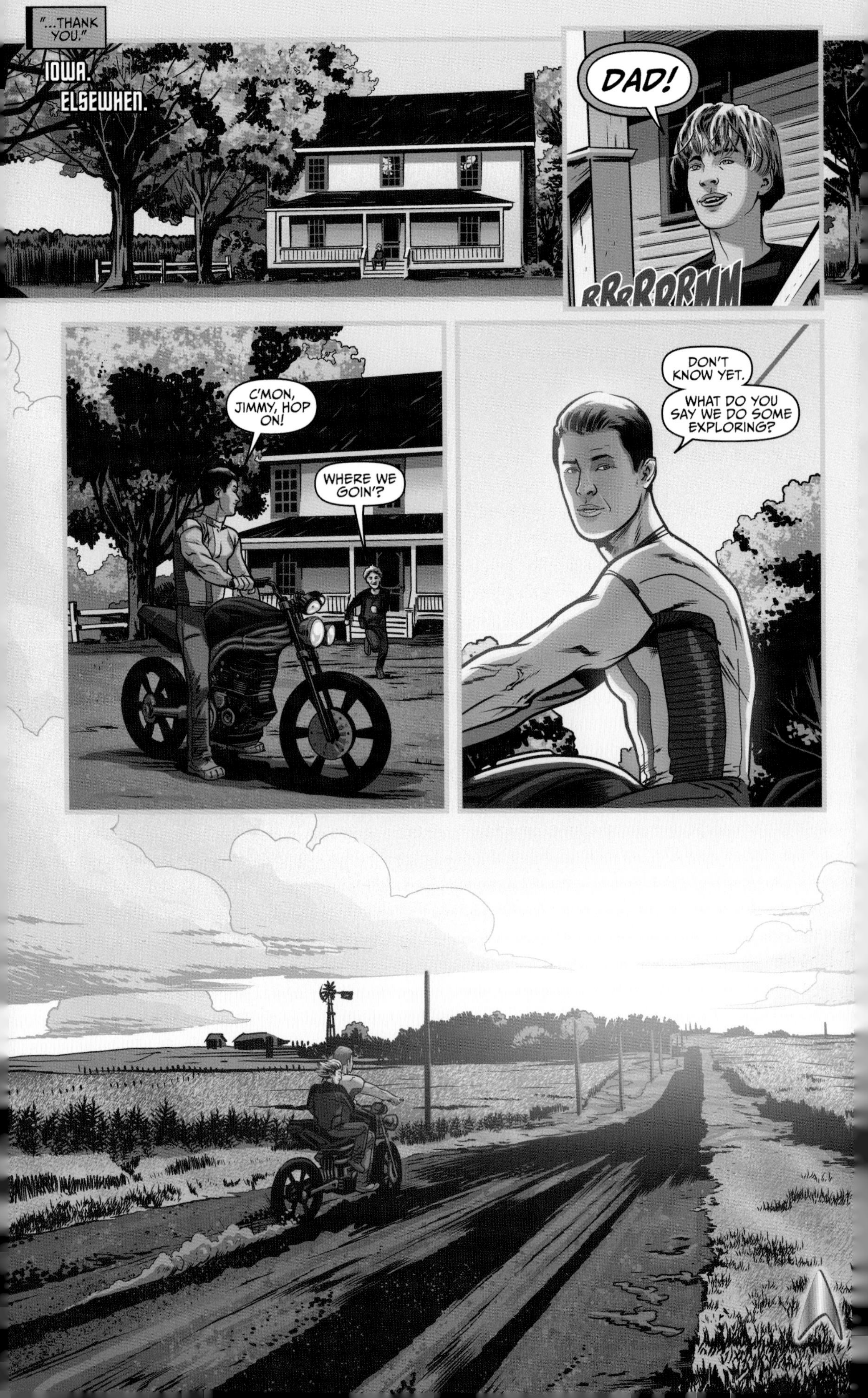

"...THANK YOU."
IOWA.
ELSEWHEN.
DAD!
BRRRRRRMM
C'MON, JIMMY, HOP ON!
WHERE WE GOIN'?
DON'T KNOW YET.
WHAT DO YOU SAY WE DO SOME EXPLORING?

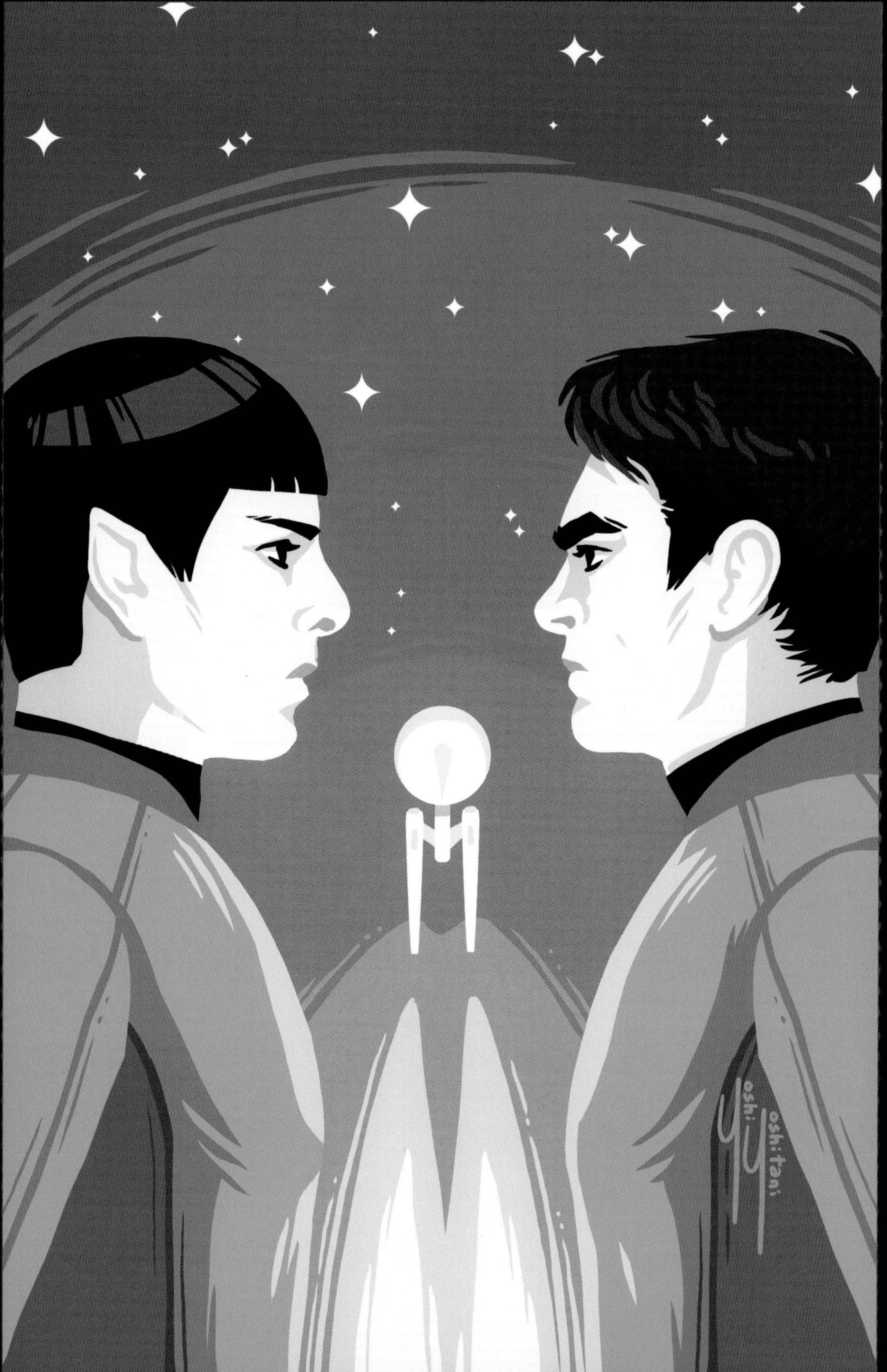

art by
Yoshi Yoshitani

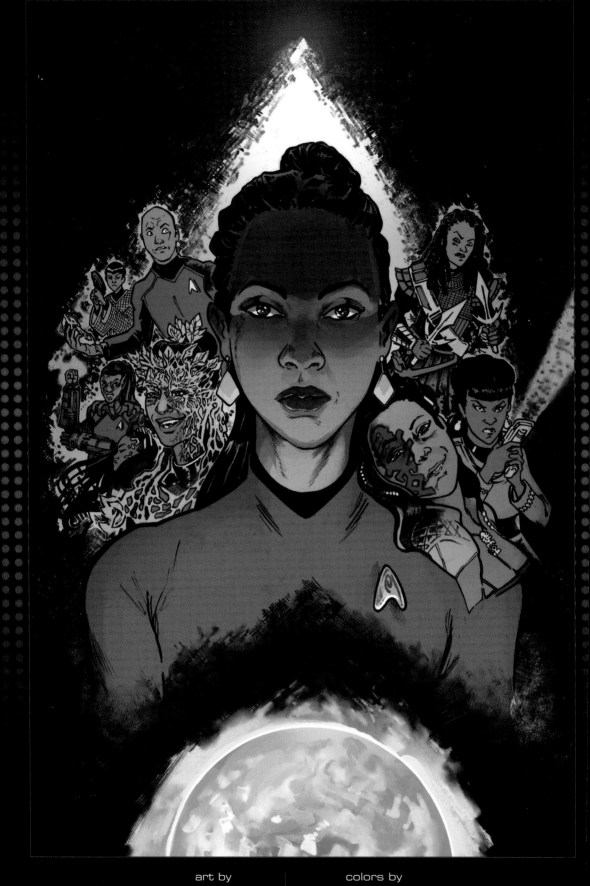

art by
Tana Ford

colors by
Triona Ferrell

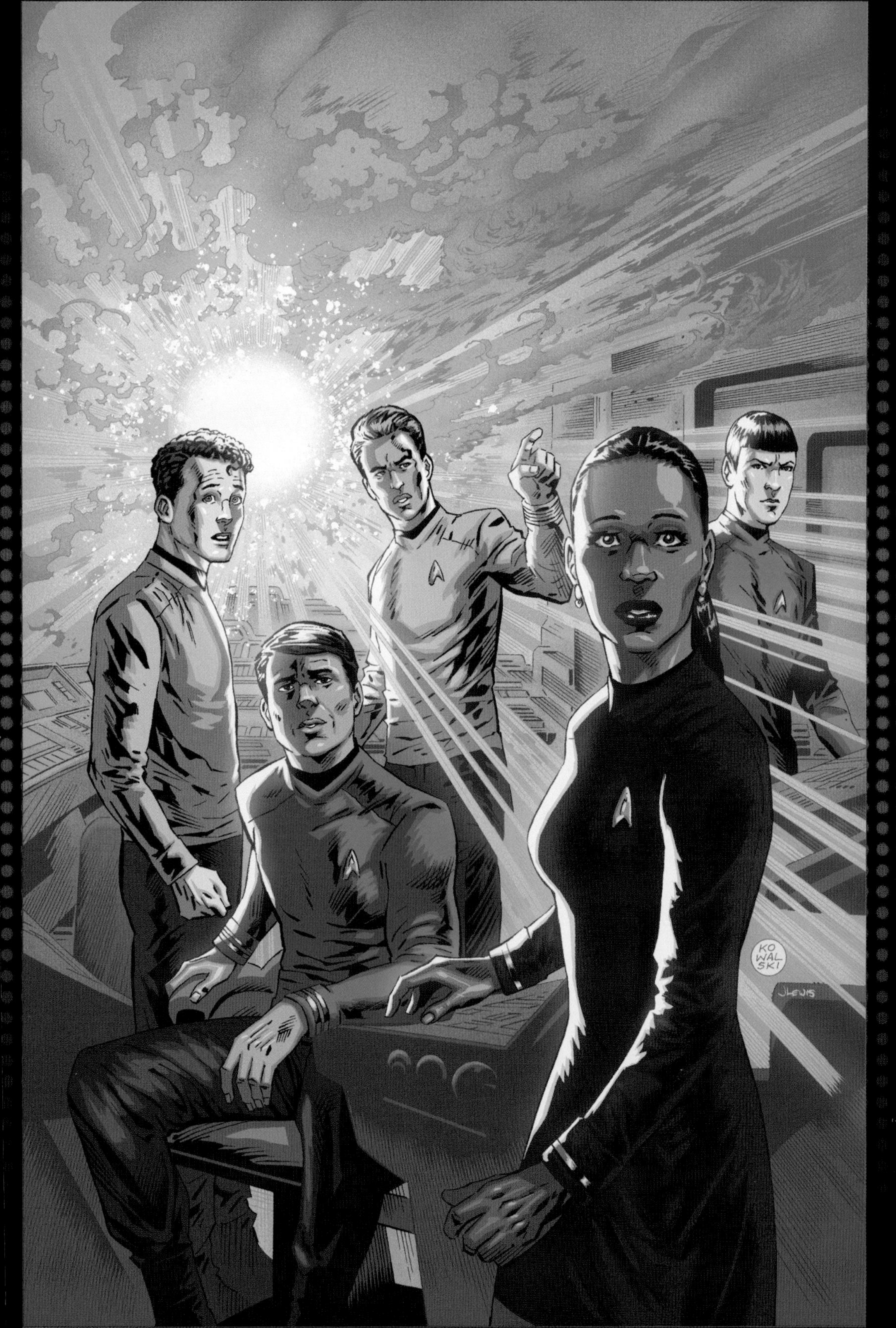
KO WAL SKI
JLEWIS

ARTIST ANGEL HERNANDEZ. PAGE / COVER X
TITLE STAR TREK. BOLDLY GO. ISSUE #15 MONTH / /

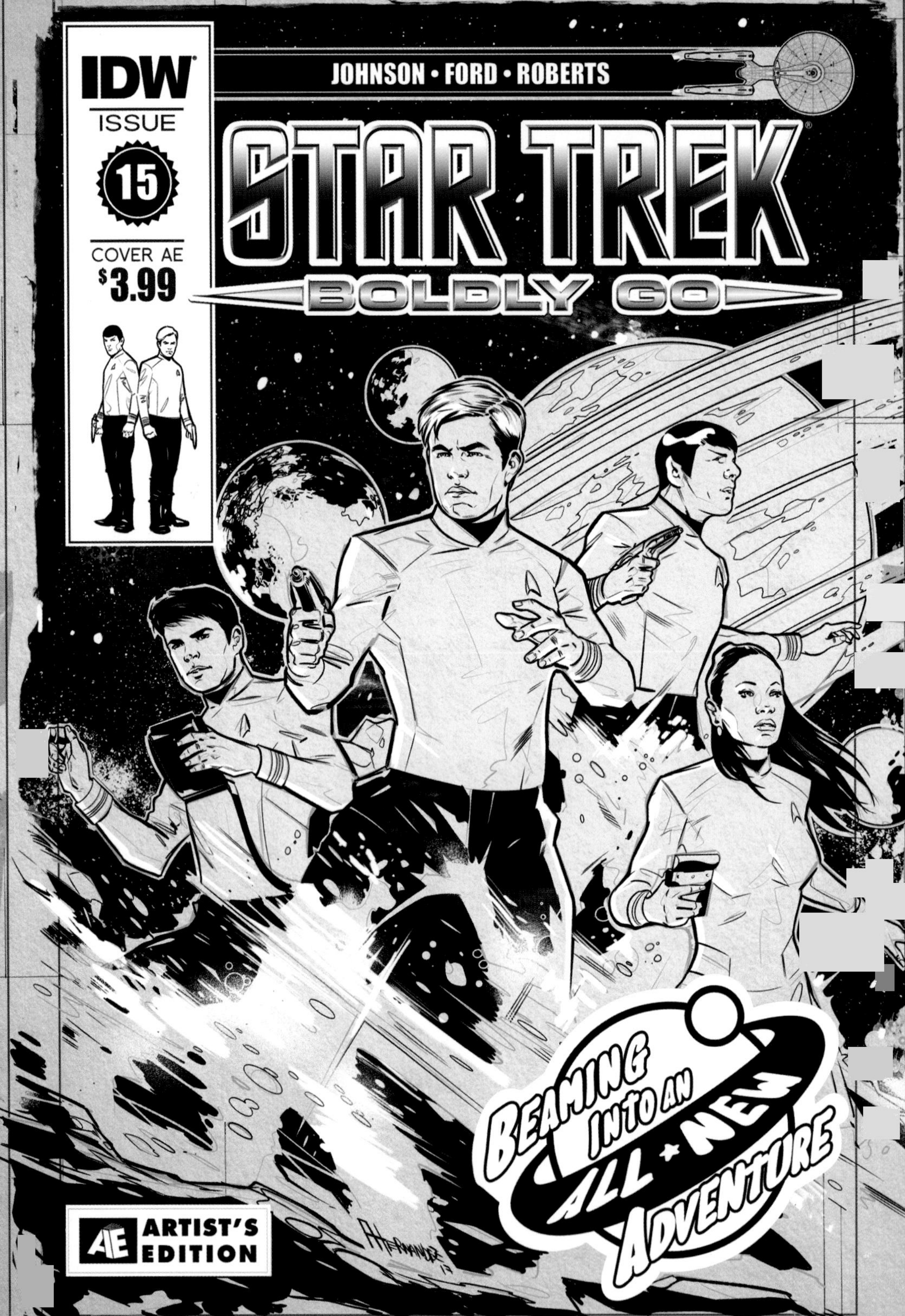
IDW
ISSUE
15
COVER AE
$3.99
JOHNSON • FORD • ROBERTS
STAR TREK
BOLDLY GO
BEAMING INTO AN ALL • NEW ADVENTURE
AE ARTIST'S EDITION

MAKE SURE NO IMPORTANT ARTWORK IS IN THE BLEED AREA, IT WILL BE CUT OFF!

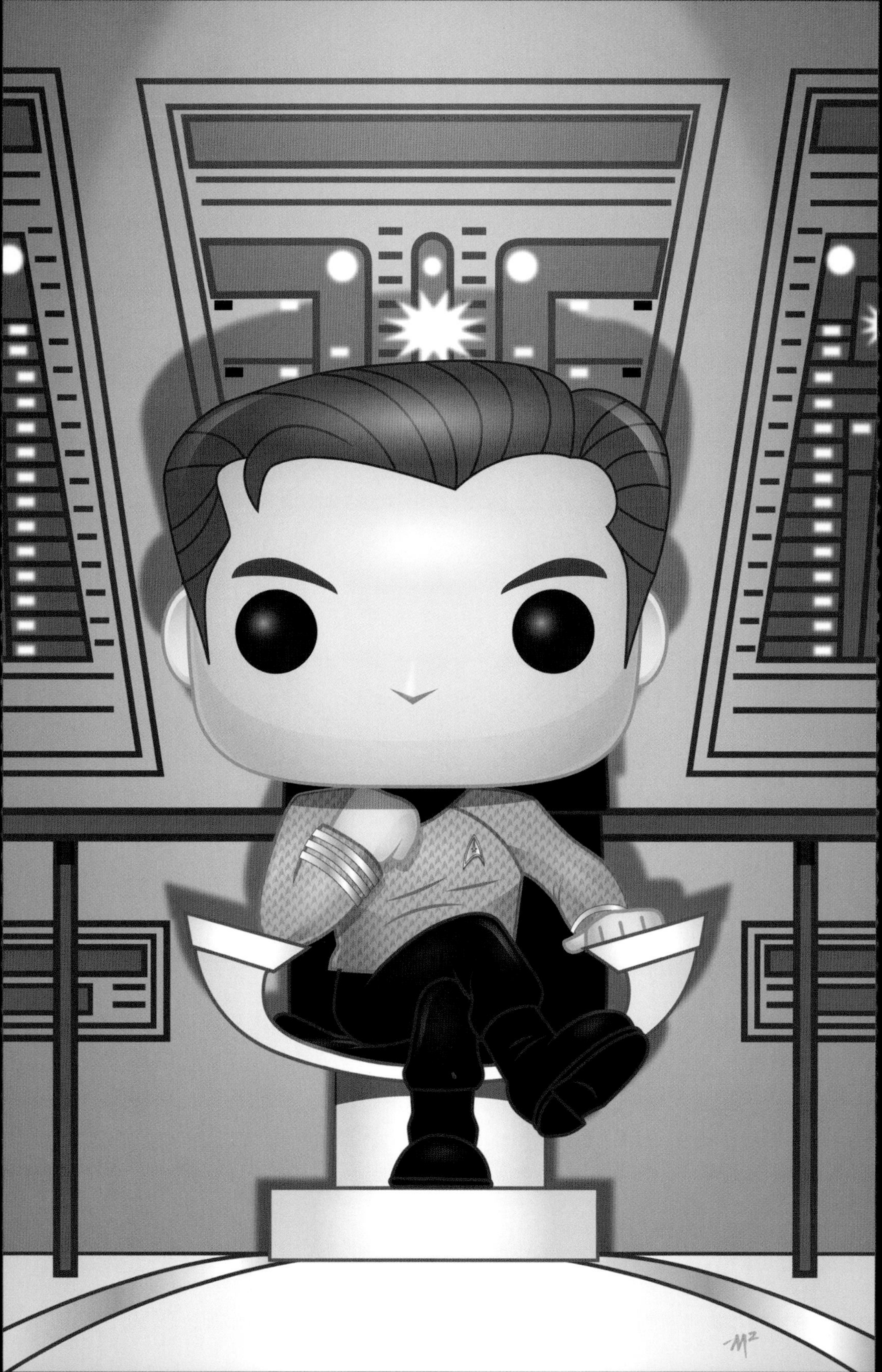

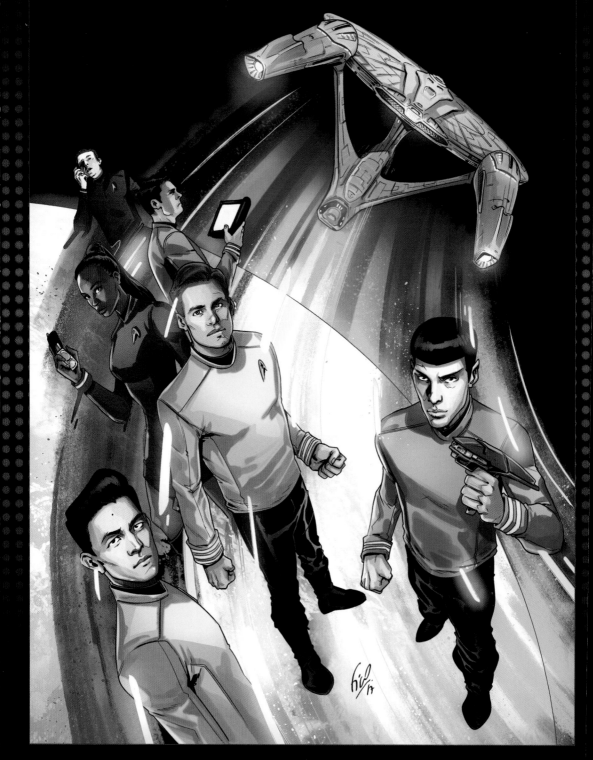

art by
Fico Ossio

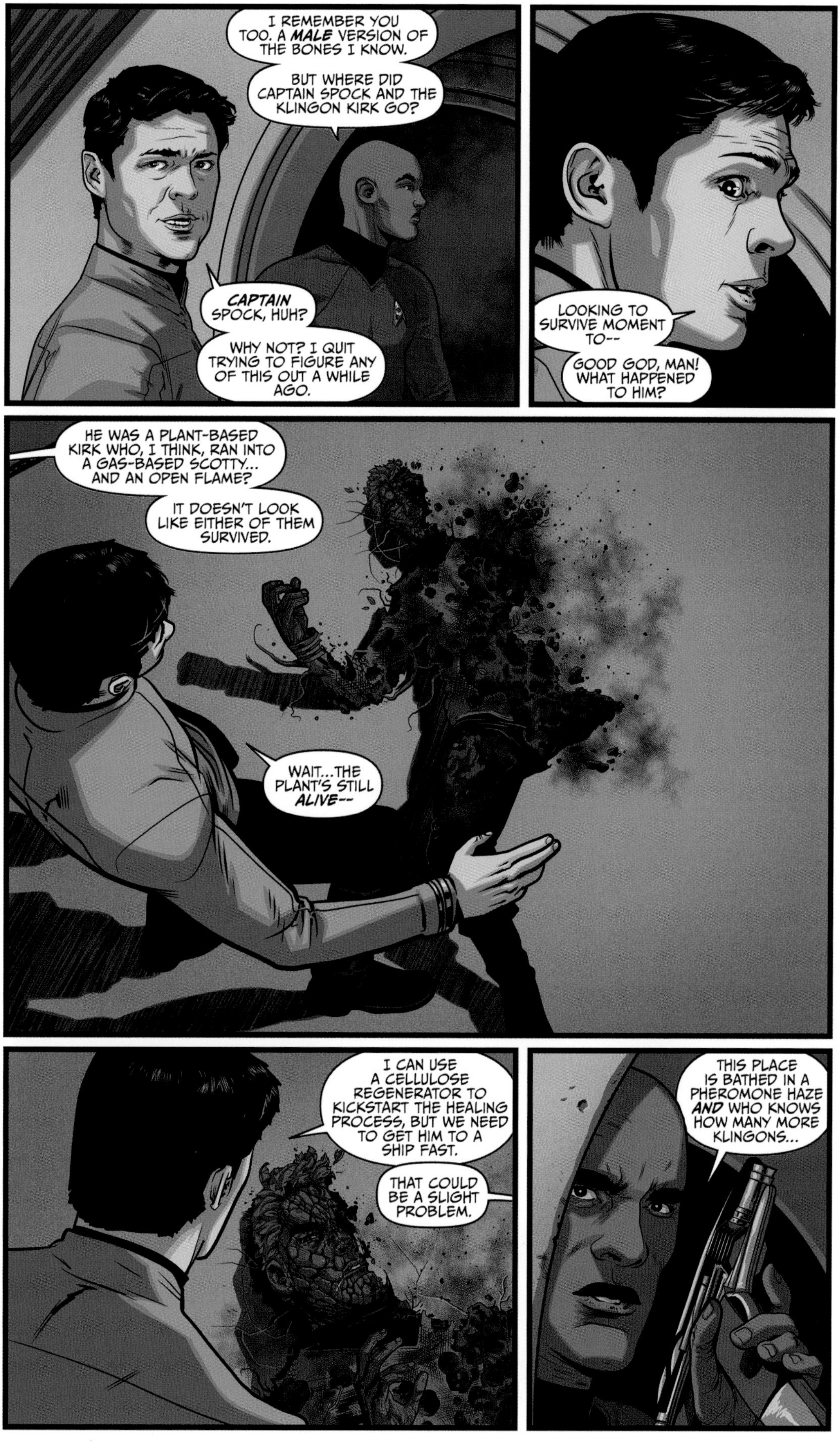
I REMEMBER YOU TOO. A MALE VERSION OF THE BONES I KNOW.
BUT WHERE DID CAPTAIN SPOCK AND THE KLINGON KIRK GO?
CAPTAIN SPOCK, HUH?
WHY NOT? I QUIT TRYING TO FIGURE ANY OF THIS OUT A WHILE AGO.
LOOKING TO SURVIVE MOMENT TO--
GOOD GOD, MAN! WHAT HAPPENED TO HIM?
HE WAS A PLANT-BASED KIRK WHO, I THINK, RAN INTO A GAS-BASED SCOTTY... AND AN OPEN FLAME?
IT DOESN'T LOOK LIKE EITHER OF THEM SURVIVED.
WAIT...THE PLANT'S STILL ALIVE--
I CAN USE A CELLULOSE REGENERATOR TO KICKSTART THE HEALING PROCESS, BUT WE NEED TO GET HIM TO A SHIP FAST.
THAT COULD BE A SLIGHT PROBLEM.
THIS PLACE IS BATHED IN A PHEROMONE HAZE AND WHO KNOWS HOW MANY MORE KLINGONS...

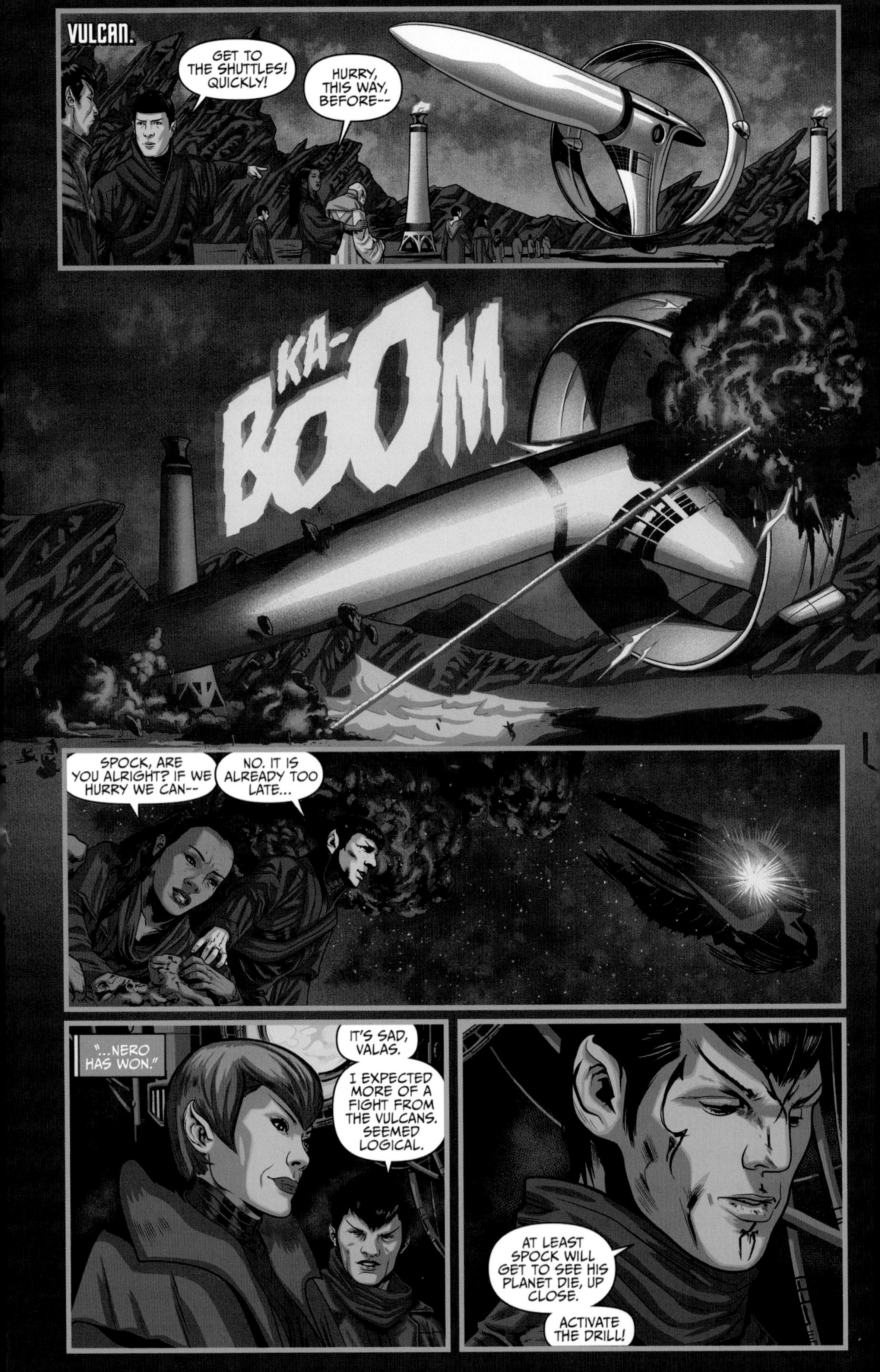
VULCAN.
GET TO THE SHUTTLES! QUICKLY!
HURRY, THIS WAY, BEFORE--
KA-BOOM
SPOCK, ARE YOU ALRIGHT? IF WE HURRY WE CAN--
NO. IT IS ALREADY TOO LATE...
"...NERO HAS WON."
IT'S SAD, VALAS.
I EXPECTED MORE OF A FIGHT FROM THE VULCANS. SEEMED LOGICAL.
AT LEAST SPOCK WILL GET TO SEE HIS PLANET DIE, UP CLOSE.
ACTIVATE THE DRILL!

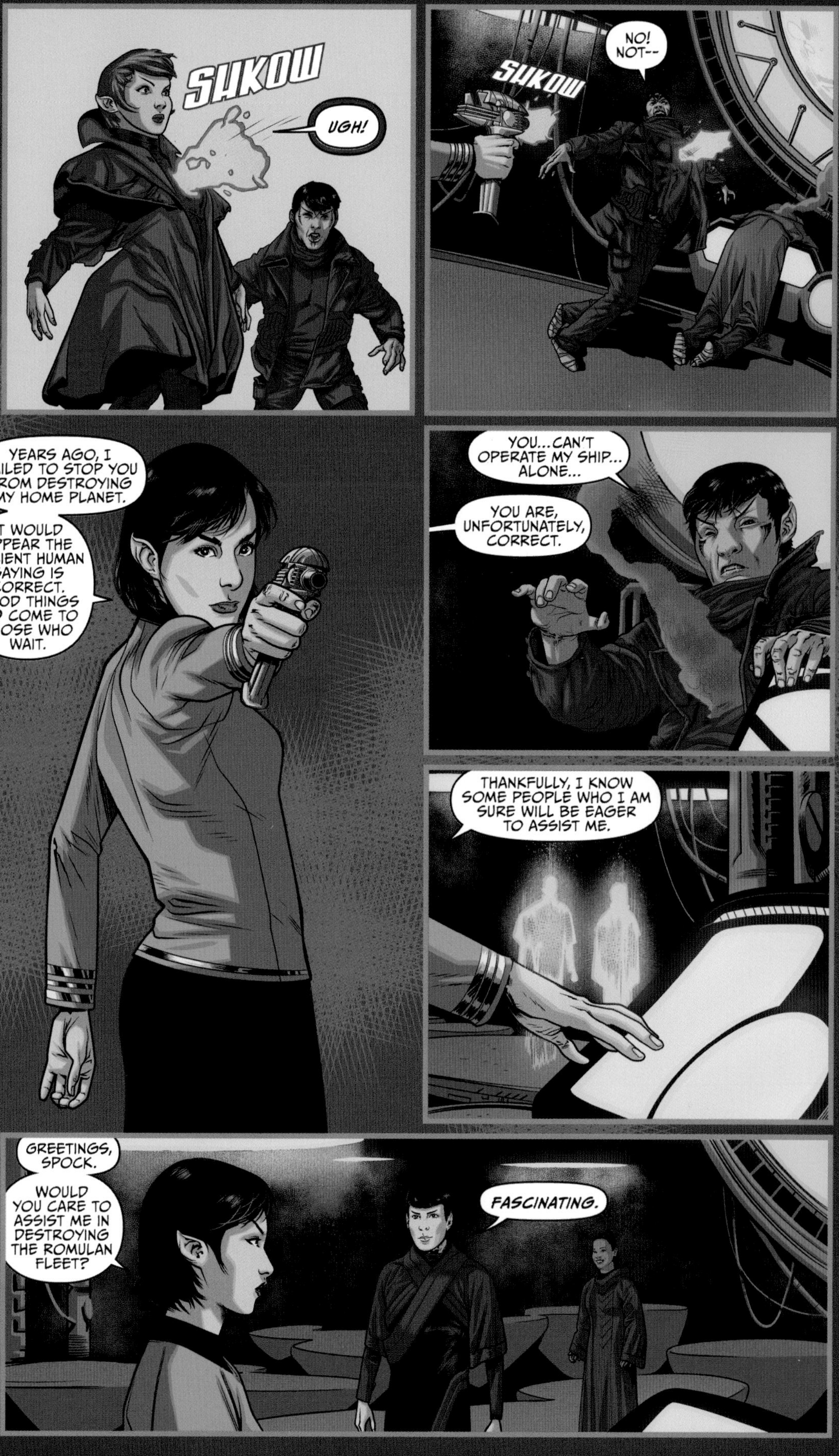
SHKOW
UGH!
SHKOW
NO! NOT--
YEARS AGO, I FAILED TO STOP YOU FROM DESTROYING MY HOME PLANET.
IT WOULD APPEAR THE ANCIENT HUMAN SAYING IS CORRECT. GOOD THINGS DO COME TO THOSE WHO WAIT.
YOU...CAN'T OPERATE MY SHIP... ALONE...
YOU ARE, UNFORTUNATELY, CORRECT.
THANKFULLY, I KNOW SOME PEOPLE WHO I AM SURE WILL BE EAGER TO ASSIST ME.
GREETINGS, SPOCK.
WOULD YOU CARE TO ASSIST ME IN DESTROYING THE ROMULAN FLEET?
FASCINATING.

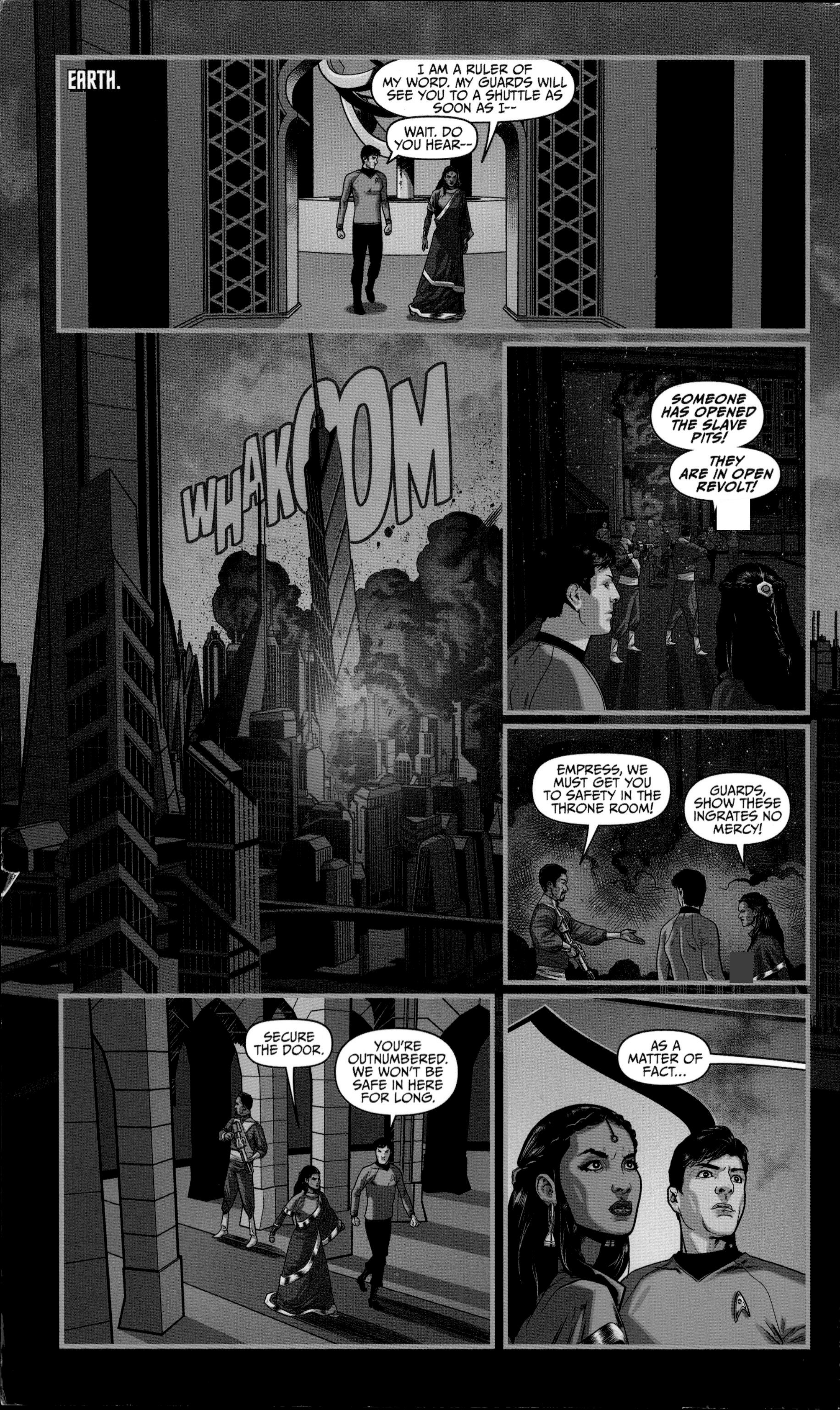
EARTH.
I AM A RULER OF MY WORD. MY GUARDS WILL SEE YOU TO A SHUTTLE AS SOON AS I--
WAIT. DO YOU HEAR--
WHAKOOM
SOMEONE HAS OPENED THE SLAVE PITS!
THEY ARE IN OPEN REVOLT!
EMPRESS, WE MUST GET YOU TO SAFETY IN THE THRONE ROOM!
GUARDS, SHOW THESE INGRATES NO MERCY!
SECURE THE DOOR.
YOU'RE OUTNUMBERED. WE WON'T BE SAFE IN HERE FOR LONG.
AS A MATTER OF FACT...

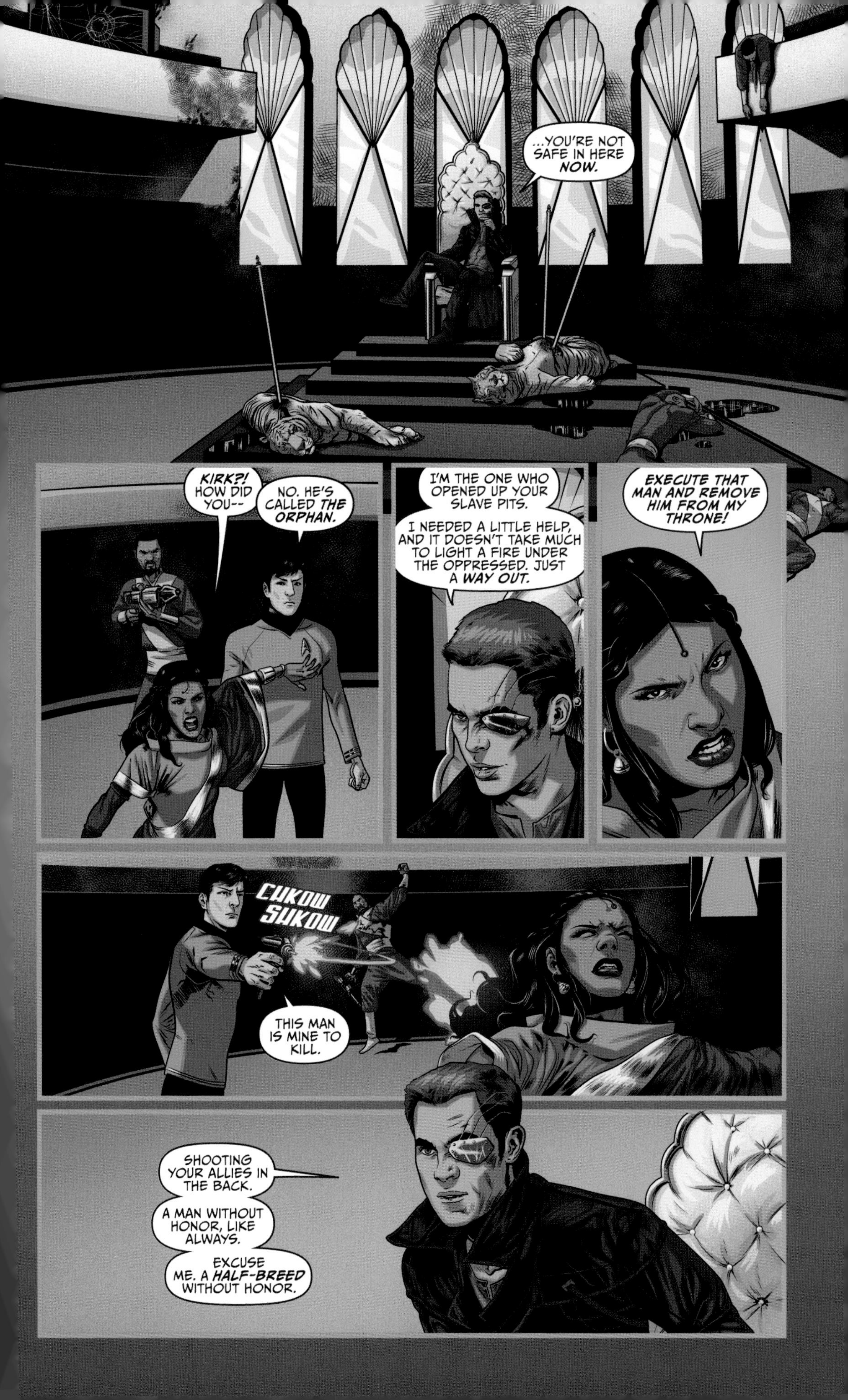
...YOU'RE NOT SAFE IN HERE *NOW.*
KIRK?! HOW DID YOU--
NO. HE'S CALLED *THE ORPHAN.*
I'M THE ONE WHO OPENED UP YOUR SLAVE PITS.
I NEEDED A LITTLE HELP, AND IT DOESN'T TAKE MUCH TO LIGHT A FIRE UNDER THE OPPRESSED. JUST A *WAY OUT.*
EXECUTE THAT MAN AND REMOVE HIM FROM MY THRONE!
CHKOW
SHKOW
THIS MAN IS MINE TO KILL.
SHOOTING YOUR ALLIES IN THE BACK.
A MAN WITHOUT HONOR, LIKE ALWAYS.
EXCUSE ME. A *HALF-BREED* WITHOUT HONOR.

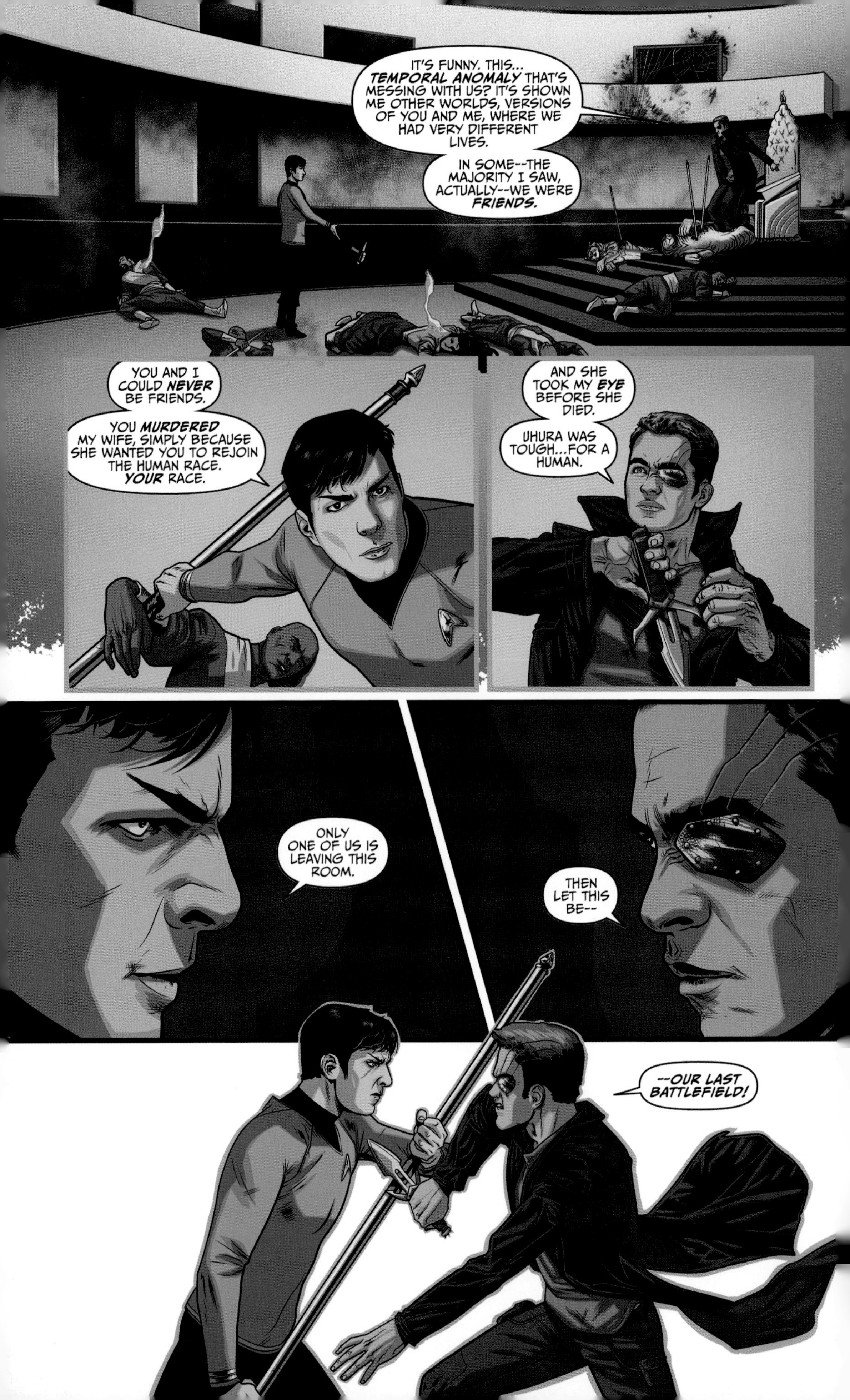
IT'S FUNNY. THIS... TEMPORAL ANOMALY THAT'S MESSING WITH US? IT'S SHOWN ME OTHER WORLDS, VERSIONS OF YOU AND ME, WHERE WE HAD VERY DIFFERENT LIVES.
IN SOME--THE MAJORITY I SAW, ACTUALLY--WE WERE FRIENDS.
YOU AND I COULD NEVER BE FRIENDS.
YOU MURDERED MY WIFE, SIMPLY BECAUSE SHE WANTED YOU TO REJOIN THE HUMAN RACE. YOUR RACE.
AND SHE TOOK MY EYE BEFORE SHE DIED.
UHURA WAS TOUGH...FOR A HUMAN.
ONLY ONE OF US IS LEAVING THIS ROOM.
THEN LET THIS BE--
--OUR LAST BATTLEFIELD!

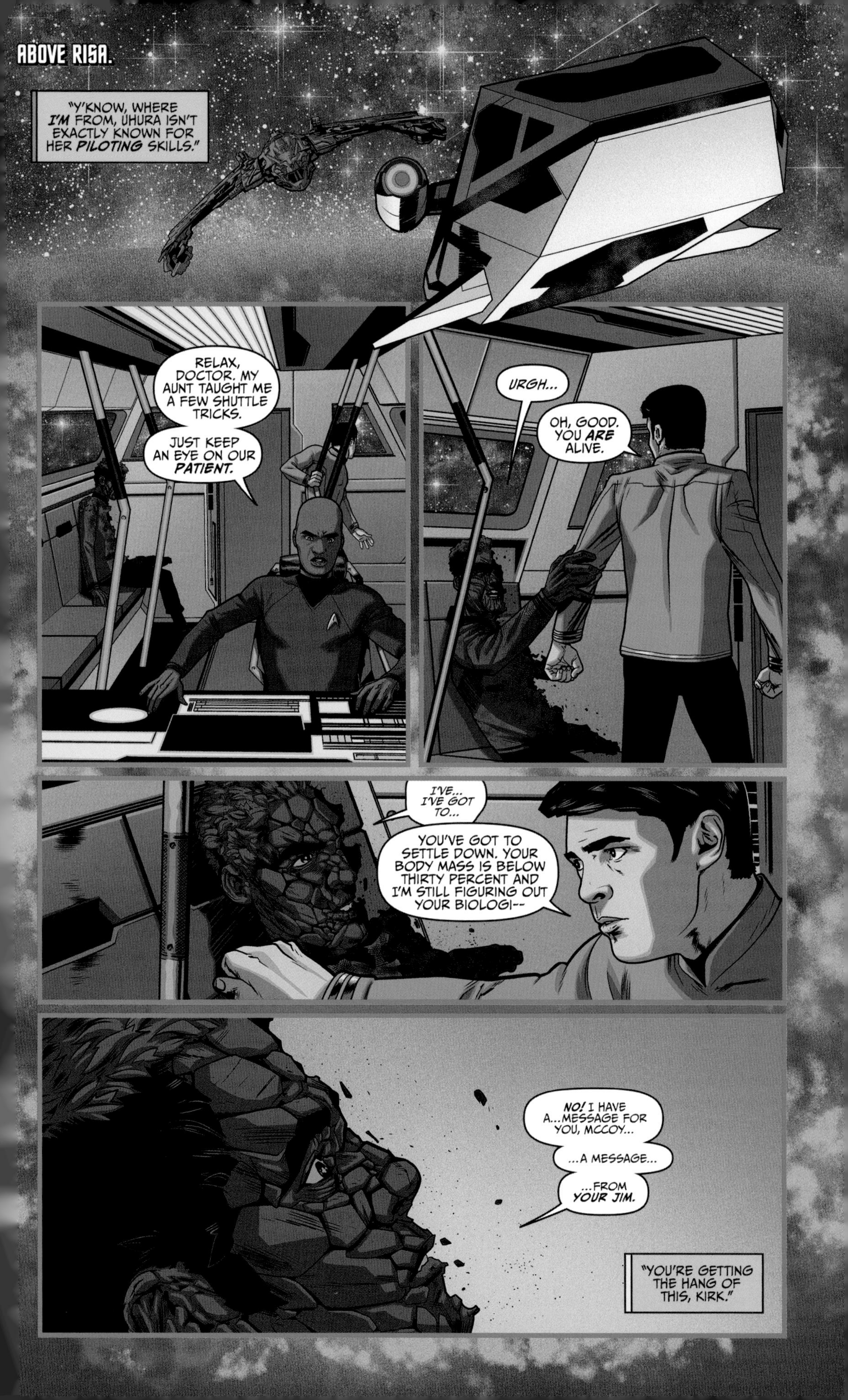
ABOVE RISA.
"Y'KNOW, WHERE I'M FROM, UHURA ISN'T EXACTLY KNOWN FOR HER PILOTING SKILLS."
RELAX, DOCTOR. MY AUNT TAUGHT ME A FEW SHUTTLE TRICKS.
JUST KEEP AN EYE ON OUR PATIENT.
URGH...
OH, GOOD. YOU ARE ALIVE.
I'VE... I'VE GOT TO...
YOU'VE GOT TO SETTLE DOWN. YOUR BODY MASS IS BELOW THIRTY PERCENT AND I'M STILL FIGURING OUT YOUR BIOLOGI--
NO! I HAVE A...MESSAGE FOR YOU, MCCOY...
...A MESSAGE...
...FROM YOUR JIM.
"YOU'RE GETTING THE HANG OF THIS, KIRK."

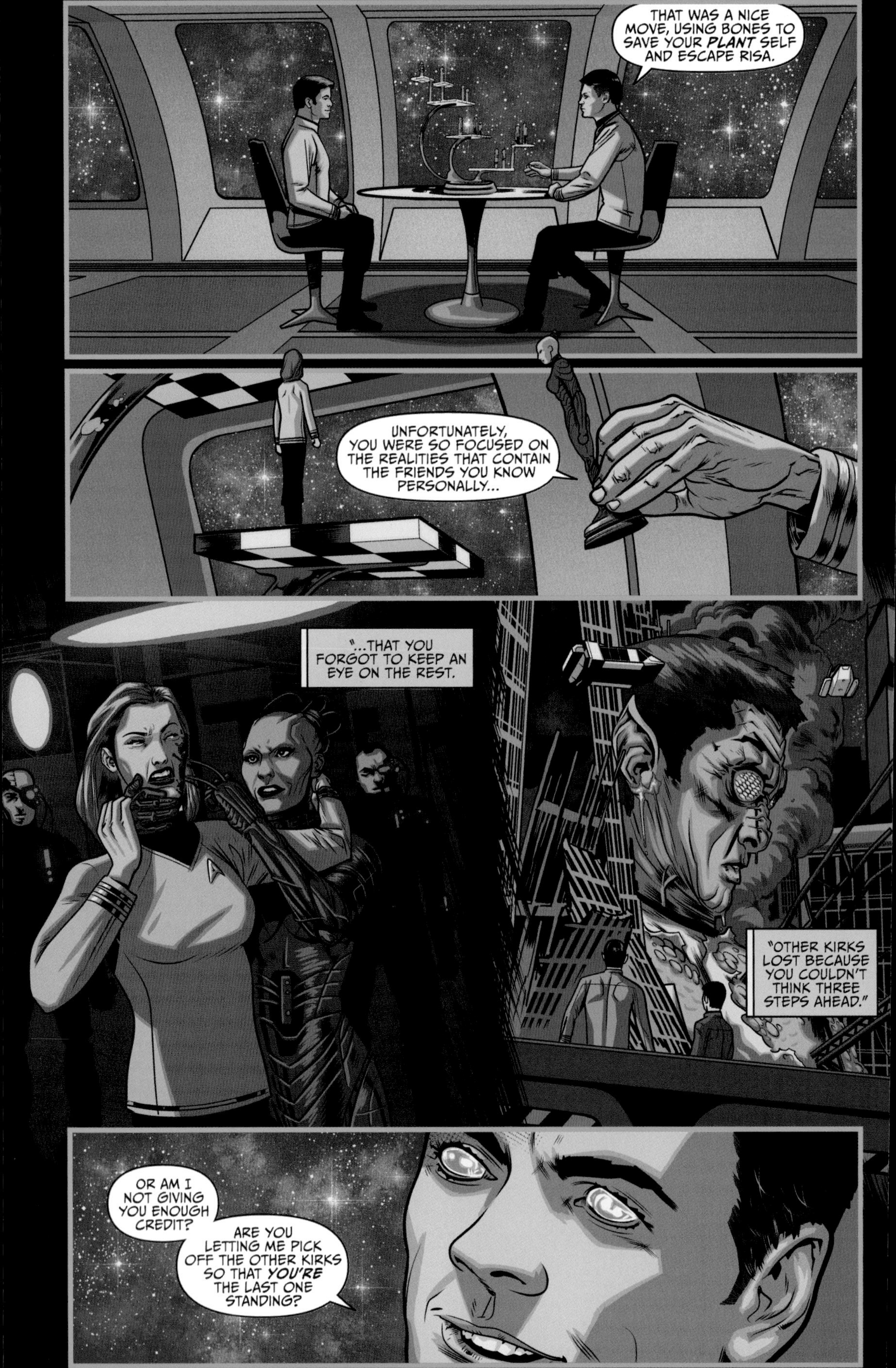
THAT WAS A NICE MOVE, USING BONES TO SAVE YOUR *PLANT* SELF AND ESCAPE RISA.
UNFORTUNATELY, YOU WERE SO FOCUSED ON THE REALITIES THAT CONTAIN THE FRIENDS YOU KNOW PERSONALLY...
"...THAT YOU FORGOT TO KEEP AN EYE ON THE REST.
"OTHER KIRKS LOST BECAUSE YOU COULDN'T THINK THREE STEPS AHEAD."
OR AM I NOT GIVING YOU ENOUGH CREDIT?
ARE YOU LETTING ME PICK OFF THE OTHER KIRKS SO THAT *YOU'RE* THE LAST ONE STANDING?

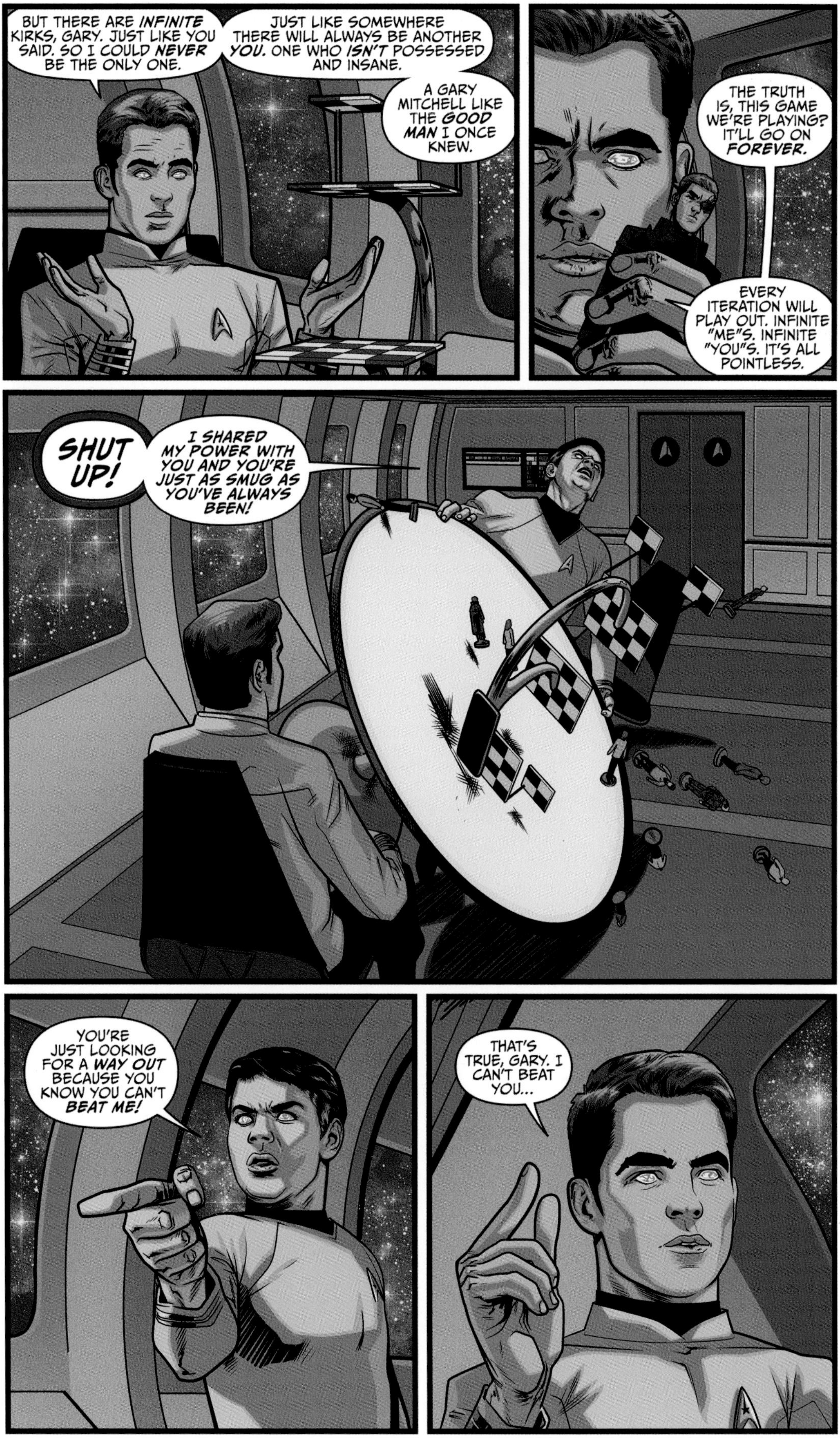
BUT THERE ARE INFINITE KIRKS, GARY. JUST LIKE YOU SAID. SO I COULD NEVER BE THE ONLY ONE.
JUST LIKE SOMEWHERE THERE WILL ALWAYS BE ANOTHER YOU. ONE WHO ISN'T POSSESSED AND INSANE.
A GARY MITCHELL LIKE THE GOOD MAN I ONCE KNEW.
THE TRUTH IS, THIS GAME WE'RE PLAYING? IT'LL GO ON FOREVER.
EVERY ITERATION WILL PLAY OUT. INFINITE "ME"S. INFINITE "YOU"S. IT'S ALL POINTLESS.
SHUT UP!
I SHARED MY POWER WITH YOU AND YOU'RE JUST AS SMUG AS YOU'VE ALWAYS BEEN!
YOU'RE JUST LOOKING FOR A WAY OUT BECAUSE YOU KNOW YOU CAN'T BEAT ME!
THAT'S TRUE, GARY. I CAN'T BEAT YOU...

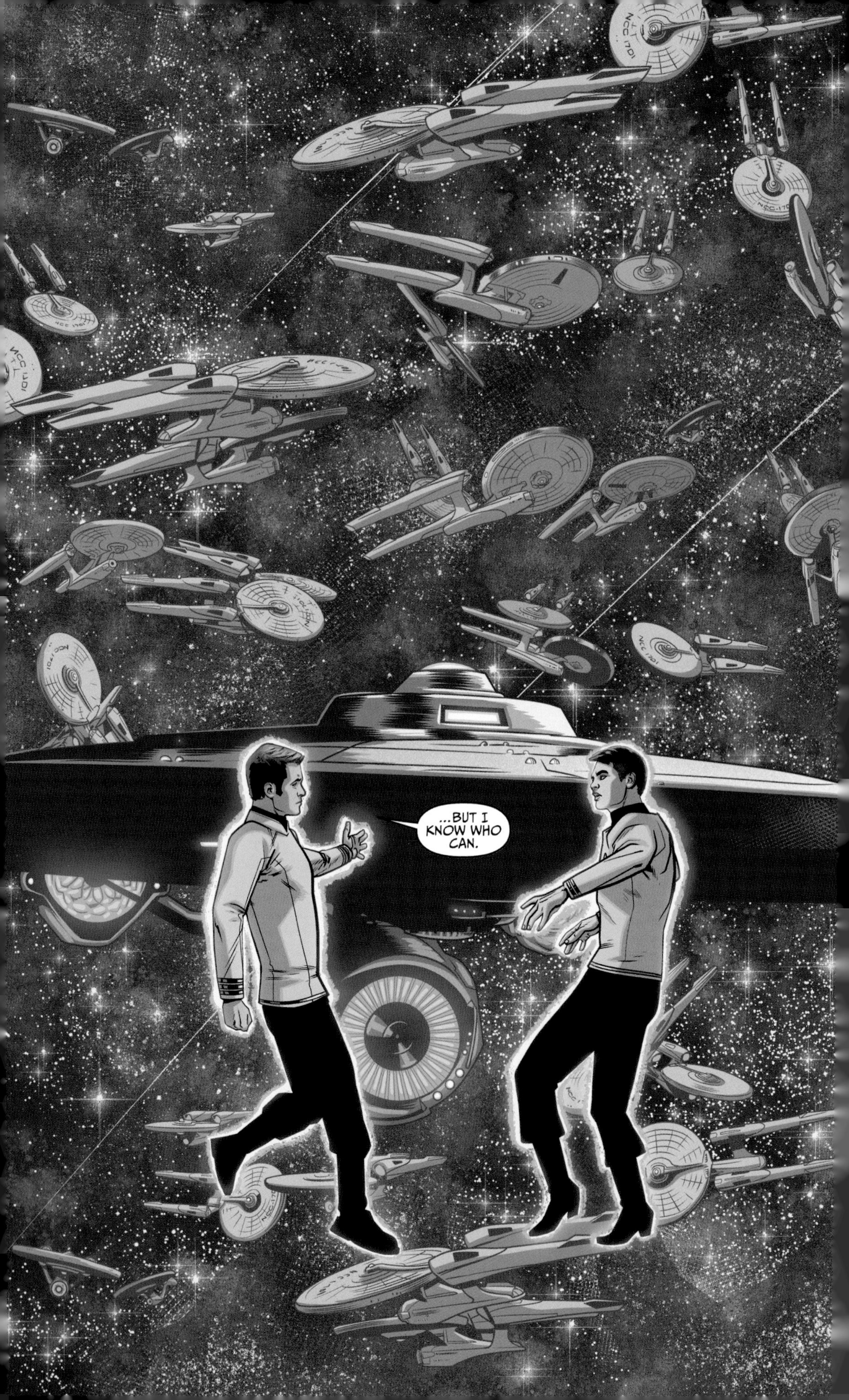
...BUT I KNOW WHO CAN.

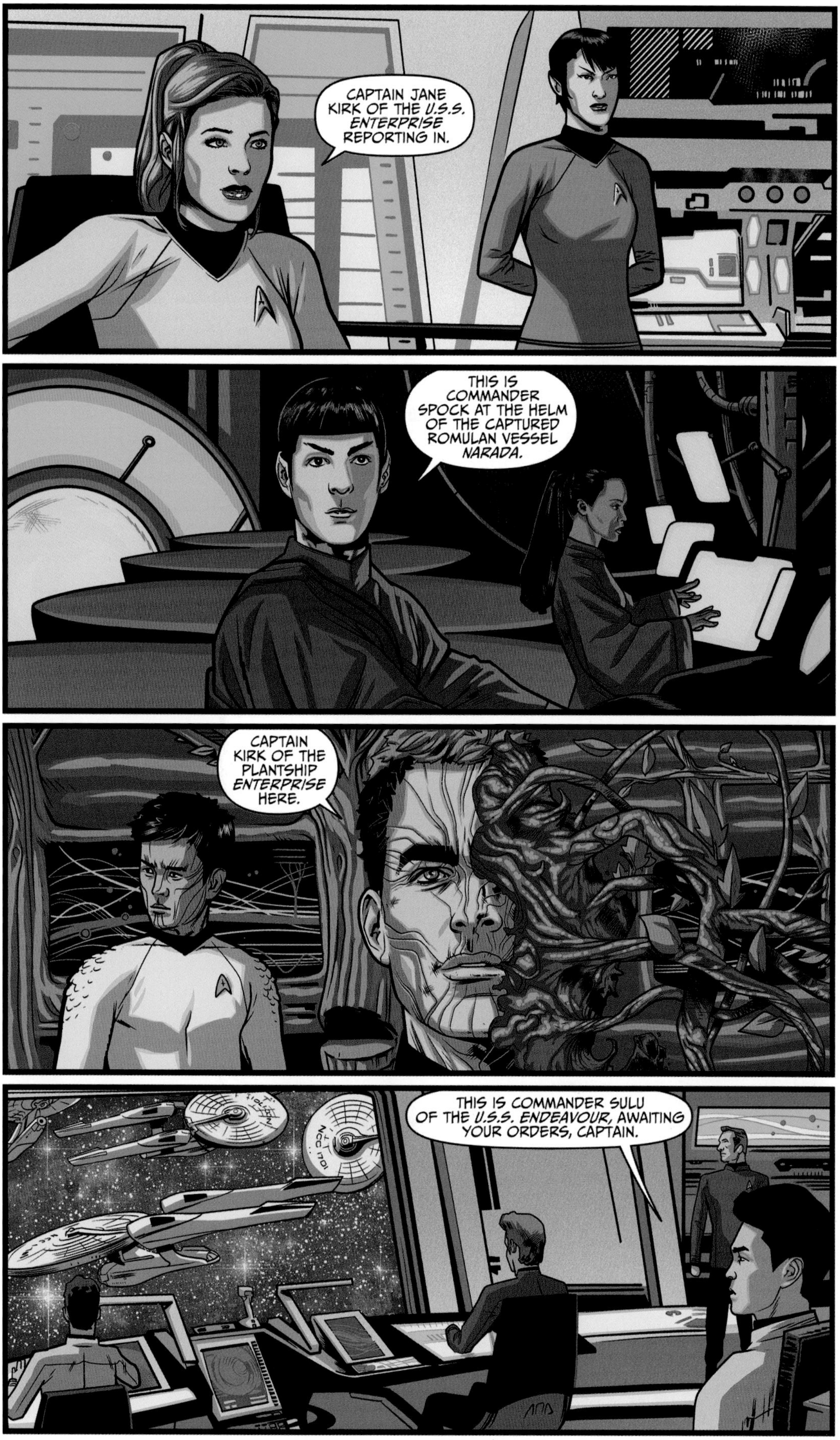
CAPTAIN JANE KIRK OF THE *U.S.S. ENTERPRISE* REPORTING IN.
THIS IS COMMANDER SPOCK AT THE HELM OF THE CAPTURED ROMULAN VESSEL *NARADA.*
CAPTAIN KIRK OF THE PLANTSHIP *ENTERPRISE* HERE.
THIS IS COMMANDER SULU OF THE *U.S.S. ENDEAVOUR,* AWAITING YOUR ORDERS, CAPTAIN.

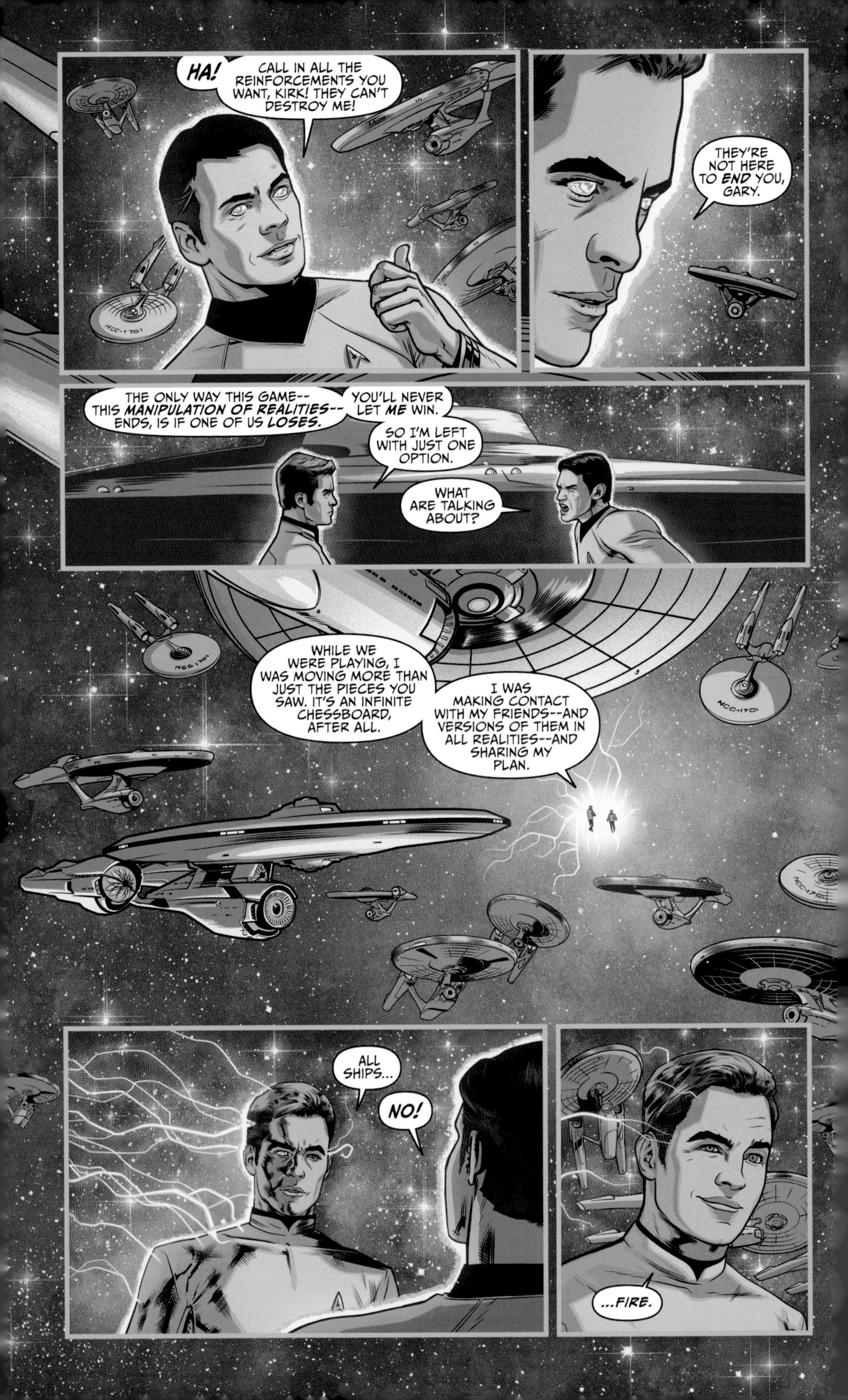
HA!
CALL IN ALL THE REINFORCEMENTS YOU WANT, KIRK! THEY CAN'T DESTROY ME!
NCC-1701
THEY'RE NOT HERE TO END YOU, GARY.
THE ONLY WAY THIS GAME-- THIS MANIPULATION OF REALITIES-- ENDS, IS IF ONE OF US LOSES.
YOU'LL NEVER LET ME WIN.
SO I'M LEFT WITH JUST ONE OPTION.
WHAT ARE TALKING ABOUT?
WHILE WE WERE PLAYING, I WAS MOVING MORE THAN JUST THE PIECES YOU SAW. IT'S AN INFINITE CHESSBOARD, AFTER ALL.
I WAS MAKING CONTACT WITH MY FRIENDS--AND VERSIONS OF THEM IN ALL REALITIES--AND SHARING MY PLAN.
NCC-1701
NCC-1701
ALL SHIPS...
NO!
...FIRE.

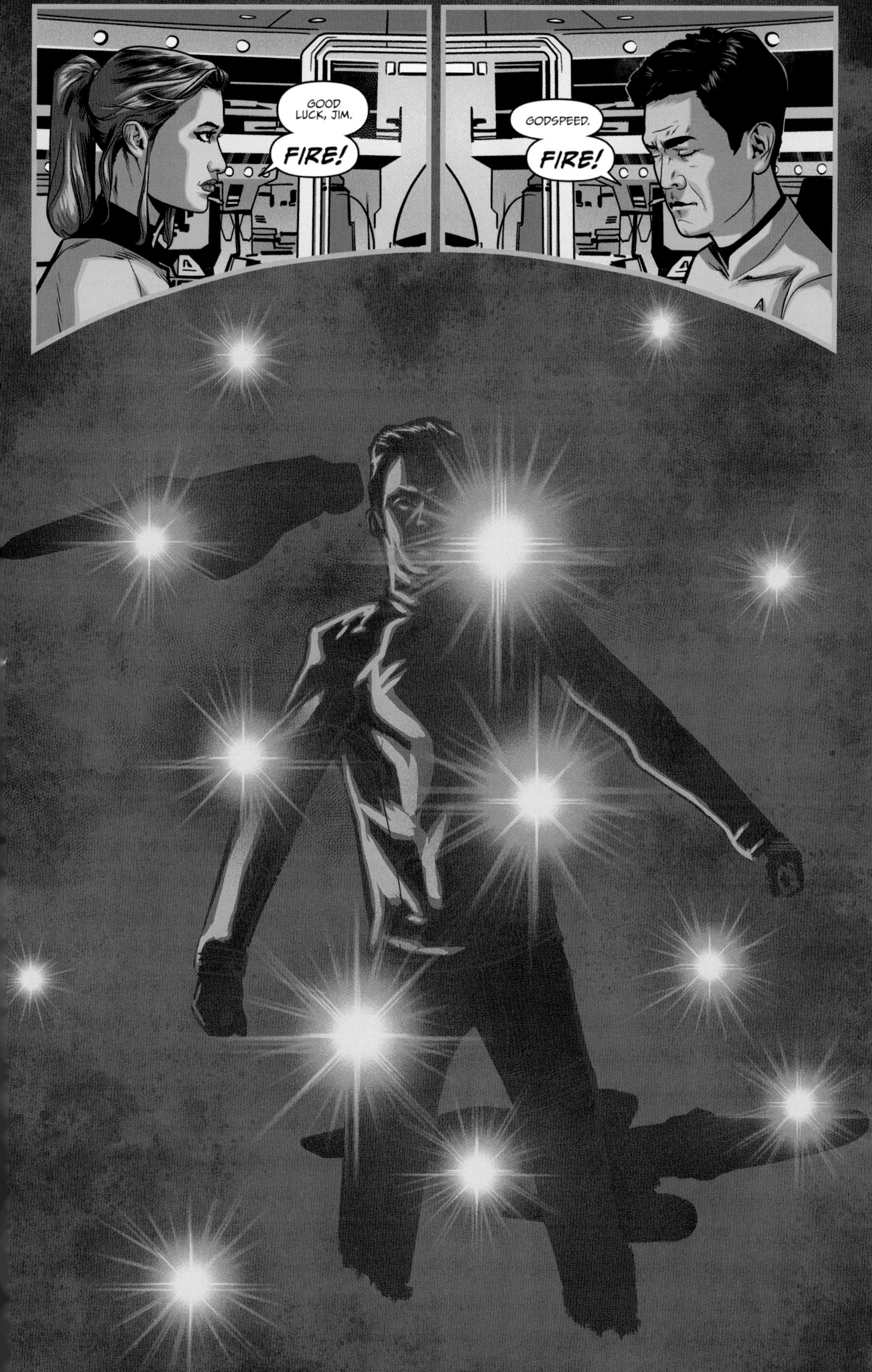
GOOD LUCK, JIM.
FIRE!
GODSPEED.
FIRE!

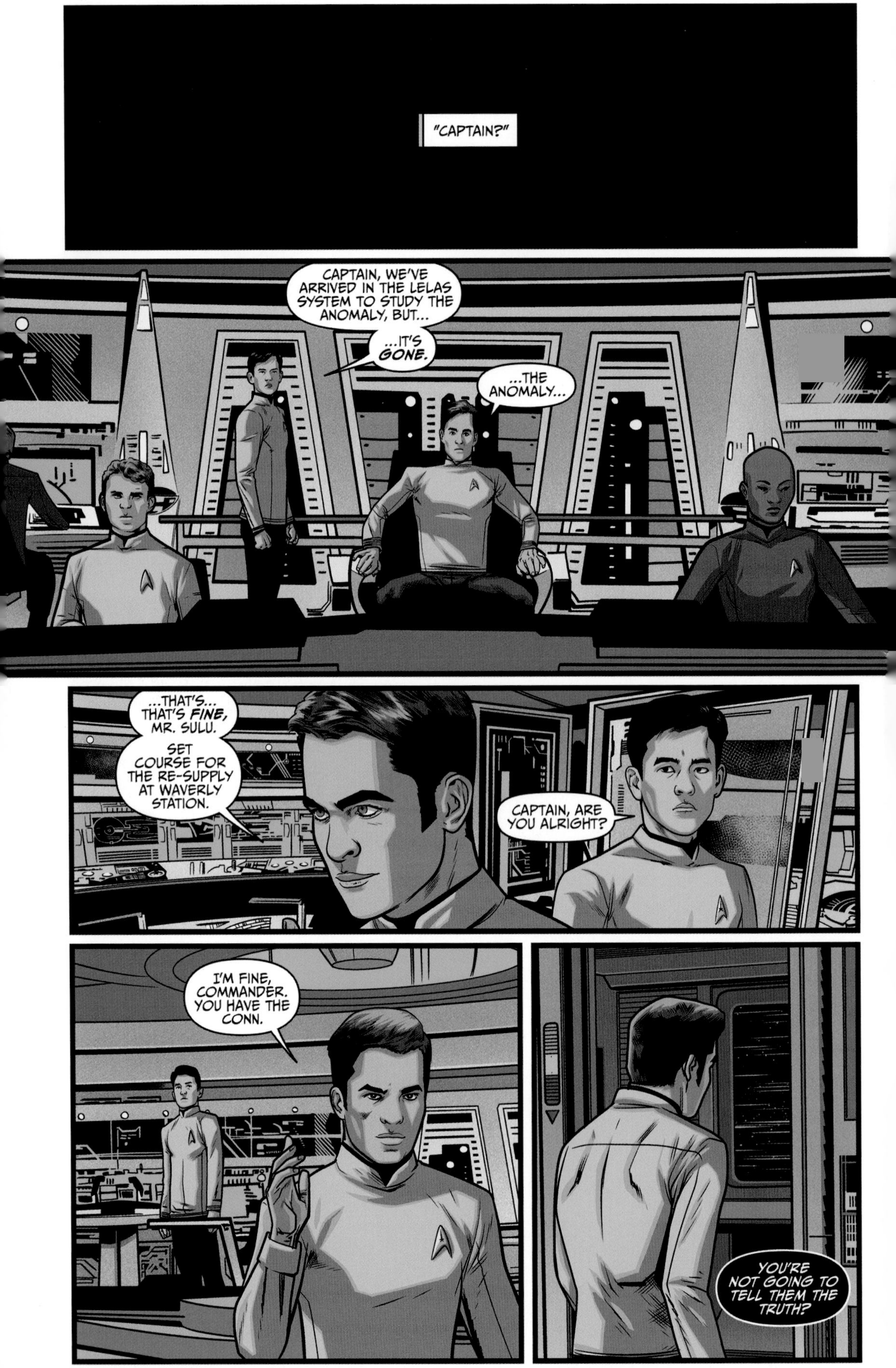
"CAPTAIN?"
CAPTAIN, WE'VE ARRIVED IN THE LELAS SYSTEM TO STUDY THE ANOMALY, BUT...
...IT'S GONE.
...THE ANOMALY...
...THAT'S... THAT'S FINE, MR. SULU.
SET COURSE FOR THE RE-SUPPLY AT WAVERLY STATION.
CAPTAIN, ARE YOU ALRIGHT?
I'M FINE, COMMANDER. YOU HAVE THE CONN.
YOU'RE NOT GOING TO TELL THEM THE TRUTH?

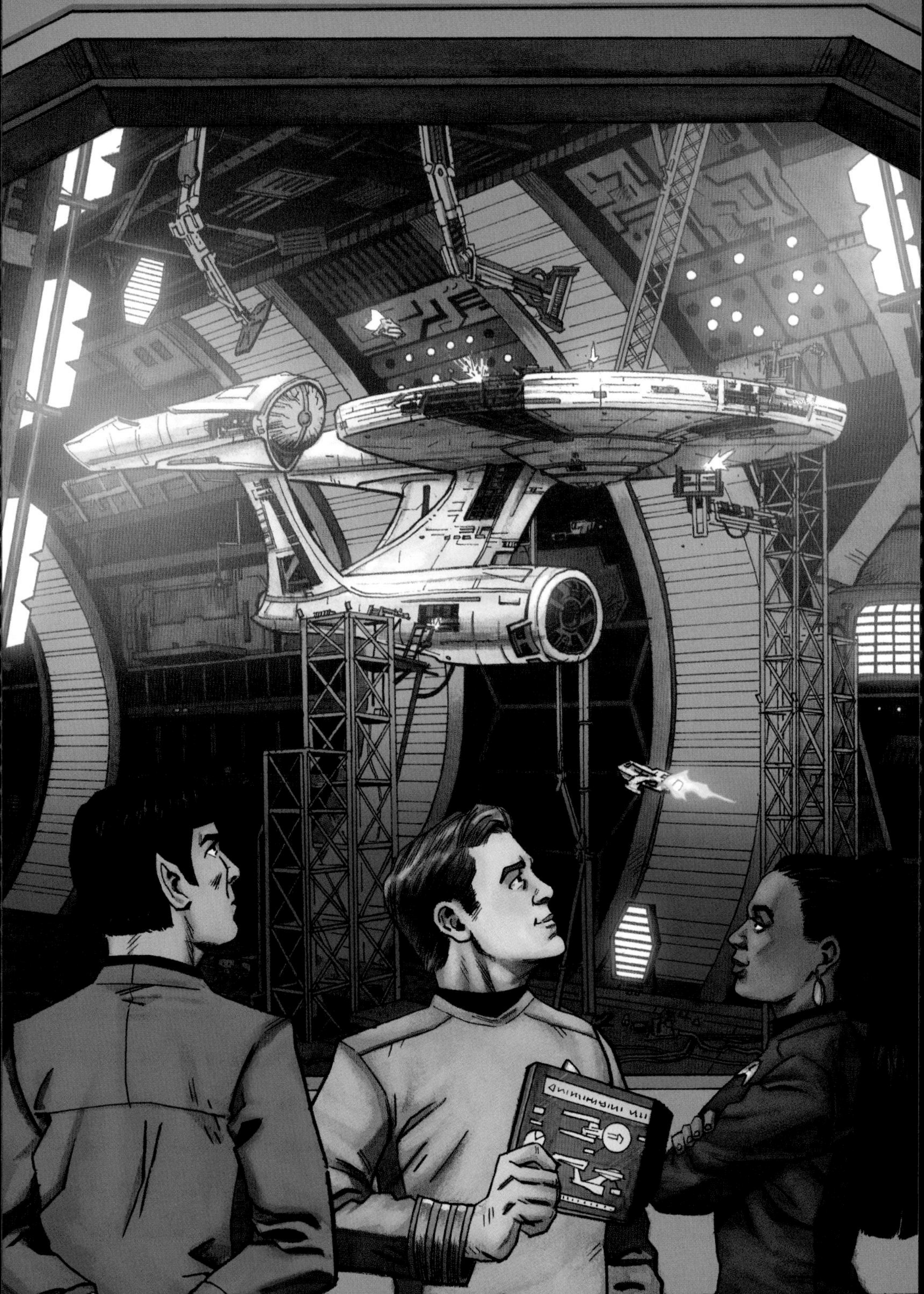

art by
Eoin Marron

colors by
Jordie Bellaire

inks by
Megan Levens

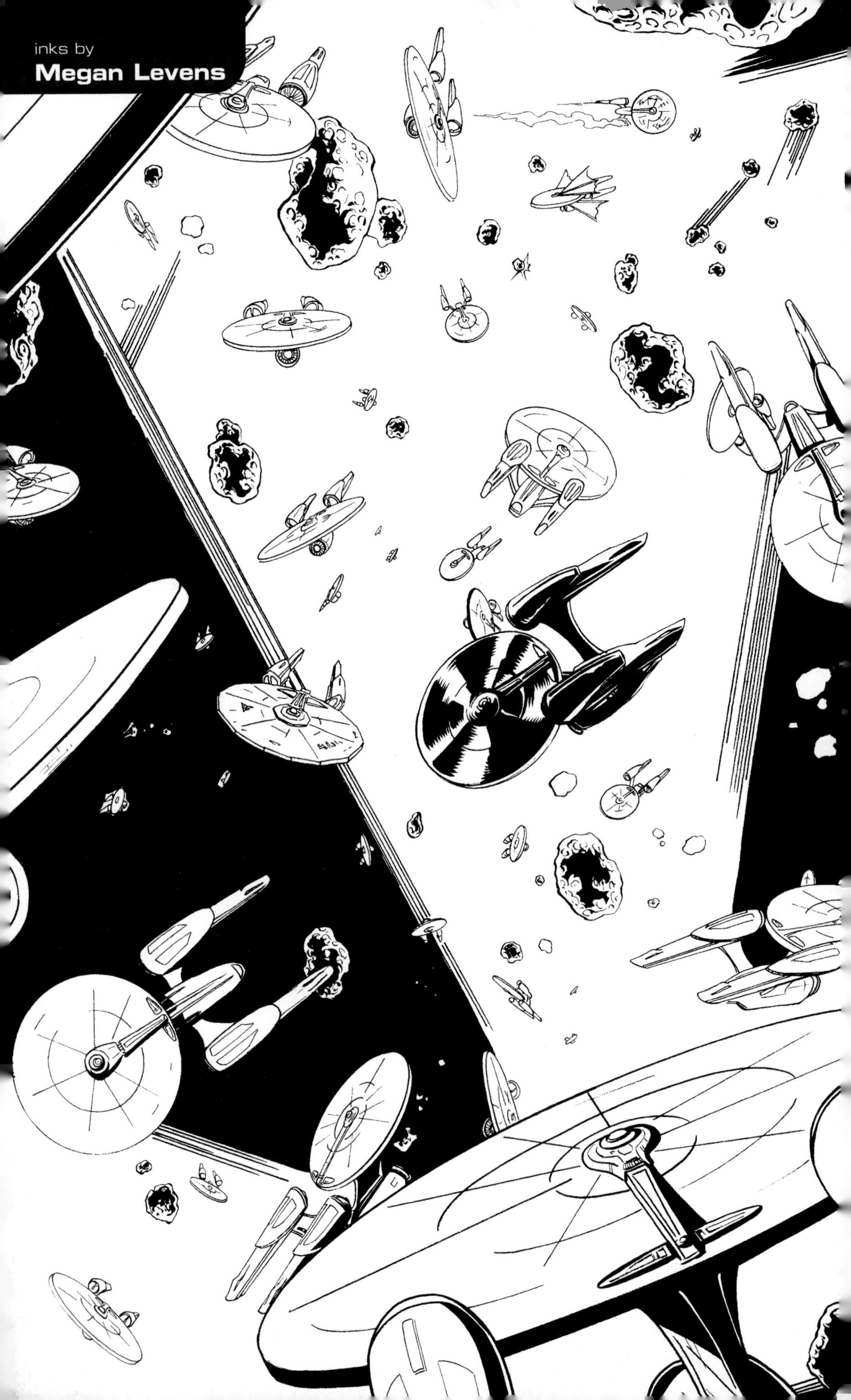

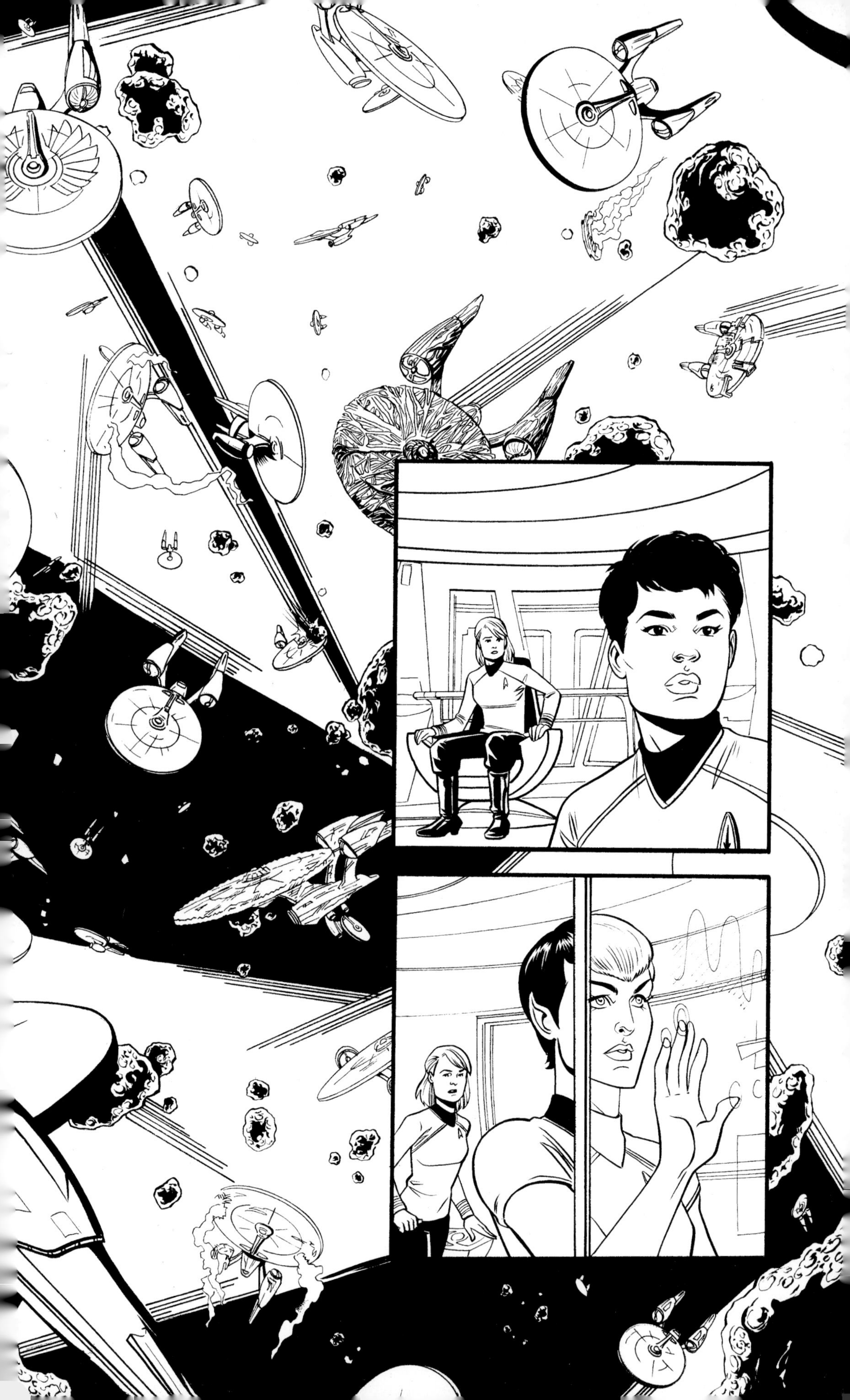

STAR TREK

BOLDLY GO

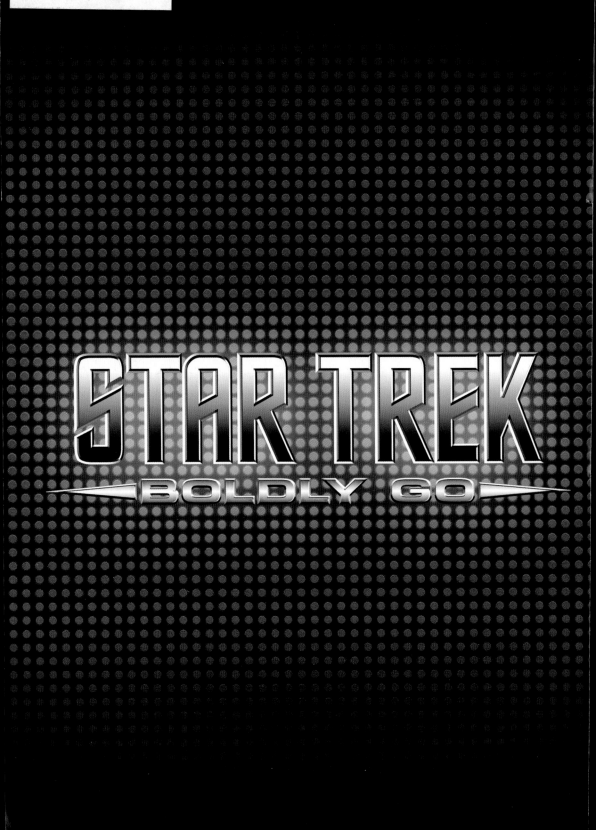